CHARLES THE BOLD

CHARLES THE BOLD

THE DOG YEARS

 *A Novel*

YVES
BEAUCHEMIN

TRANSLATED BY WAYNE GRADY

McCLELLAND & STEWART

Original title: Charles le téméraire

Copyright © 2004 by Éditions Fides
Published under arrangement with Éditions Fides, Montreal, Quebec, Canada
English translation copyright © 2006 by McClelland & Stewart Ltd.

Translated from the French by Wayne Grady
This translation comprises the first half of *Charles Le Téméraire: Un temps de chien.*

Hardcover edition published 2006
Trade paperback edition published 2007

Library and Archives Canada Cataloguing in Publication

Beauchemin, Yves, 1941–
[Charles le téméraire. English]
    Charles the Bold : the dog years : a novel / Yves Beauchemin ; translated by Wayne Grady.

Translation of Charles le téméraire.
"A Douglas Gibson book."
ISBN 978-0-7710-1147-4 (bound). – ISBN 978-0-7710-1148-1 (pbk.)

    I. Grady, Wayne   II. Title.   III. Title: Charles le téméraire. English.

PS8553.E172C5213 2006   c843.'54   C2006-901892-8

We acknowledge the financial support of the Government of Canada through the Book Publishing Industry Development Program and that of the Government of Ontario through the Ontario Media Development Corporation's Ontario Book Initiative. We further acknowledge the support of the Canada Council for the Arts and the Ontario Arts Council for our publishing program.

For their generous help and invaluable advice, the author would like to thank Antoine Del Busso, Georges Aubin, Lucille Beauchemin, Diane Martin, Viviane St-Onge, Michel Therrien, and the indefatigable Michel Gay

For its financial assistance, the author also wishes to thank La Société de développement des arts et de la culture de Longueuil

Typeset in Minion by M&S, Toronto
Printed and bound in Canada

A Douglas Gibson Book

This book is printed on acid-free paper that is 100% recycled, ancient-forest friendly (100% post-consumer recycled).

McClelland & Stewart Ltd.
75 Sherbourne Street
Toronto, Ontario
M5A 2P9
www.mcclelland.com

1 2 3 4 5   11 10 09 08 07

To Viviane

1

A lot of serious praying on his behalf had gone on by the time Charles finally poked his glistening head from between the thighs of his mother, who was bent double with pain. A light but steady rain was falling on the streets of Montreal, and buses wove along them loaded with half-soaked, half-awake passengers. Just down the street, on rue Ontario, waitresses in scuffed shoes replied kindly to the equally scuffed pleasantries of their customers. On the ground floor of the building across the street, a hardware-store owner was taking a shower, vigorously soaping his bulging belly while trying to recall where he'd put a stack of invoices. As usual, the Macdonald's cigarette company was busy filling the neighbourhood with the smell of tobacco smoke. Twenty metres straight down, in the dark bowels of the island of Montreal, a brand-new subway train was creeping along a tunnel that still smelled of fresh concrete; its driver, a serious, even formal man, held himself rigid between two inspectors in suits who were taking notes for the official inauguration, which was to take place in three days. The eleventh of October, 1966, was underway.

"Push, madame, push! It's almost over," cried the ambulance driver. He'd arrived fifteen minutes earlier, too late to be of much help in the birth.

He was tall and blond and a bit pudgy, an aficionado of sausages and beer, and he didn't like being hurried. When he had to move, though, he knew how to do it smartly and efficiently. With a curt nod to his partner standing at the other end of the rumpled bed, he grabbed Charles's head (the baby's name had been decided on for some time) and gently began to pull. The face appeared, then the shoulders, at which point the ambulance driver's eyes widened with surprise.

In the course of his dozen-year career as a paramedic he had assisted in a good many childbirths, some of them under unbelievable circumstances. But

1

the newborns had always come out looking pretty much the same – red in the face and scowling, as though furious at having been forced to leave the warm, dark bubble they'd been floating in for the past few months. But this one was different: his skin was pink and smooth, his facial features calm, apparently unfazed by the violent efforts being made to extract him. He seemed to have remained plunged in deep, delicious sleep. "He's dead," the driver thought with a shudder.

Hurriedly he removed the afterbirth, cut the umbilical cord, grabbed the infant by the feet, and gave him a few good whacks on the backside. Charles gave a sharp cry, which cleared a glob of mucus from his throat, then immediately calmed down again. While he was given a quick bath before being placed in the arms of his mother, who gazed on him adoringly with eyes half-crossed from exhaustion, he went back to sleep, the shadow of a smile on his lips. "Brain damage," the driver thought. He looked at his partner, who was busy drying the mother's face, and motioned towards the door with a questioning lift of his chin.

Seated in the kitchen with a full beer in front of him and two empties on the table, Wilfrid Thibodeau gazed at the rain-spattered window and stretched his legs. There were already nine butts in the pig-shaped ashtray at his elbow, and a tenth was dangling from his lips. He'd had the radio on low in an attempt to drown out his wife's screams; an announcer, his voice vibrating with sincerity, was describing the magnificent sale of household electrical appliances being held at all the Brault & Martineau stores, but no syllable of his panegyric reached the carpenter's ears, for his thoughts were as sullen and grey as the rain that was soaking the city. This premature birth had really screwed up his morning. Looking up, he saw one of the ambulance drivers standing in the kitchen doorway, smiling and motioning for him to get up.

"It's done, Mr. Thibodeau. A bouncing baby boy, chubby and content."

The other driver appeared behind the first, then came into the kitchen and shook the new father's hand.

When Alice saw her husband, she forgot the contractions that had so recently torn at her body, and a sweet but worried smile smoothed the creases in her face:

"Come and see him," she breathed, her voice softened by exhaustion. "He's so beautiful . . . a real little prince . . . Aren't you happy? It wasn't so bad, was it? Did you get hold of your boss?"

"Yeah, yeah, no problem," he replied, a bit ashamed of himself for feeling so annoyed. "Get some rest now," he added, trying to put more tenderness into his voice than he felt.

He cast a curious and somewhat startled glance at the tiny being, asleep and wrapped up in a towel in his wife's arms. Okay, then. That was that. She had what she wanted, a baby. As weak and vulnerable as he was, he'd be taking up all her attention from now on. He'd be the one running things around here. That's the way things worked. Wilfrid Thibodeau was the eldest in a family of six kids, and he knew all about the upheavals that came with the appearance of a new baby. He felt helpless, out of sorts and vaguely irritated, and floating over all these feelings was a wave of emotion that he had no idea what to do with.

Alice laid her hand on his arm:

"I'm sorry this all happened so suddenly, my poor Wilfrid. If I'd known it was coming so quickly, I'd have asked you to bring me to the hospital . . ."

He answered her by caressing her arm distractedly. The ambulance driver appeared again at the door:

"I called a doctor to come and take a look at you," he said, "just in case . . . You can't be too careful in situations like these. He said he'll be here in half an hour."

He took another look at the baby. "Jeez," he thought, "what a mug he has on him! He's not sleeping in that towel, *he's basking in it*! Not ten minutes old and already he's got the world by the short and curlies. If Jocelyn handed me a baby like that I'd kiss her feet! . . . Nevermind, nevermind," he chided himself. "You're getting all worked up over nothing, you idiot. It's all in your head."

■ ■ ■

But the ambulance driver was not mistaken. Charles Thibodeau was born with a natural gift for happiness. One week after his birth he was sleeping through the night, he hardly ever cried, and he suckled determinedly but without insistence, as though he sensed that he had to go easy on his mother. Nature spared him almost entirely from colic, indigestion, and diaper rash. When his milk teeth appeared, his swollen gums didn't seem to bother him at all; he chewed contentedly on the ends of his fingers, or on the little rubber lamb his mother gave him, or on anything else that came within reach, his

3

peaceful and joyful disposition hardly affected. When he slept, the house could fall down around his crib without waking him up. He was smiling at two months, then laughing in great bursts, at everything and nothing. Smiles sprang to his lips like dandelions on a spring lawn.

"He's always happy, this one!" exclaimed his grandmother, a tiny widow who, though only sixty-five, was already bent with age. She lived in the Gaspésie and came to visit her daughter once a year. "He'll be a good little boy. He'll make his wife happy and he'll get along well with his boss."

Where had his good disposition come from? Certainly not from his mother, who was pretty enough but timid, pale, and a bit on the scrawny side, forever struggling against fatigue (her job at the clothing factory exhausted her), and who had hardly told a joke in her life. An air of resigned melancholy hung over Alice; it was so subtle and had become so much a part of her that she mistook it for life itself. And yet he got it even less from his father, a short, taciturn man given to flashes of anger, for whom life was nothing but an endless series of chores and drudgery made occasionally tolerable by beer, televised hockey, and sex.

If Charles got his pleasant nature from anyone it must have been from a distant ancestor, someone to whom black thoughts never occurred, and who, at the end of a long and satisfying life, had died peacefully in the consoling knowledge that he had lived in the best of all possible worlds. Either that or at the moment of his conception a mysterious explosion had taken place somewhere in the galaxy, and he had somehow become the beneficiary of its influence . . .

So much so that at the age of one Charles was such a beautiful child, so chubby of cheek, so bubbling over with health, so content with his lot in life, that he made his pediatrician feel completely useless. These qualities were accompanied, moreover, by an inexhaustible supply of energy and a voracious curiosity. The apartment on rue Dufresne was for him a vast terrain of discovery that occupied his every waking minute. No corner, no matter how many doors or gates were in the way, was immune from his impetuous need to explore. Merely walking into the kitchen required his father or mother to exercise a certain degree of caution and a great deal of attention, since the floor would generally be strewn with pots, casserole dishes, platters, plates, utensils, and all sorts of other things (he had figured out how to open drawers and had even pulled one or two of them down on top of himself). When he went into

4

his parents' bedroom, it was to empty the drawers of the night tables and the dresser, crawl under the bed or pull off the sheets and blankets, which he liked to wrap himself up in. The bathroom towels were his carpets, he filled the toilet bowl with pots and pans, laundry detergent, and bars of soap, and one morning Wilfrid, forgetting to check the tub before getting in, stepped into a pool of shampoo that the grimacing Charles was in the process of eating.

Once or twice his enthusiasms nearly ended in tragedy. One afternoon in October his parents took him to Expo '67, which at the time was still sparkling with its final glory. Jumping up in Alice's arms to reach a bunch of balloons that were bouncing in front of him, he nearly fell from the top of the monorail. His mother just managed to grab him by one foot and hold him as he dangled over the side, screaming in terror.

"There's no bloody end to it!" his father cried out in despair. "What're we going to do when he's fifteen?"

For his second birthday Alice made a vanilla cake with chocolate icing, placed two candles in it, set it on the table and invited the neighbours and their three children to come over for dessert after dinner. They arrived at the appointed time, and Wilfrid showed them into the living room. Alice, making coffee in the kitchen with her back to the table, heard a spongy sound followed by a sort of sigh that made her turn around. Charles had tugged at the tablecloth, and the cake and its plate had fallen on his head, which was now unrecognizable as a head except for the tip of Charles's nose poking out through a mound of cake and chocolate.

"Oh my God, Charles, what have you done?"

Wilfrid came into the kitchen and uttered a cry of rage. He managed to control himself while his wife, with her neighbour's help, made a pitiful attempt to wipe her son's face. But as soon as she had finished he grabbed Charles by his waist and began slapping him with the palm of his hand as though the child's backside were a drum. Charles pursed his lips, puckered his brows, let out a tiny moan, but he did·not cry. When his clothes had been changed and he was put back on his feet, he took refuge in a corner, sitting with his back against the wall, and gave his father a look that Alice would never, ever forget. Two minutes later his good nature had returned and he was playing happily with a pile of blocks in his bedroom.

"I'm going to do something about that kid, you just see if I don't," Wilfrid said to his neighbour while the two women worked at the table trying to

5

salvage some of the cake for the other children, who were whining. It was clear he would go to any length to instill a little discipline in the child's head.

Two days later Charles terrified his mother. Coming home from work, she stopped to pick him up at the babysitter's and was getting ready to carry him up the stairs in his stroller (they lived on the second floor) when she suddenly remembered she needed something at the grocer's and that she didn't have any money with her.

"Wait here one second, Charles, Maman will be back in a minute."

And she ran up to the apartment. Fifteen seconds later she was back at the top of the stairs, where she let out a piercing shriek. Charles, bent forward with his arms outstretched, had his head stuck (or so it seemed to Alice) in the jaws of an enormous German shepherd. Her shriek frightened the animal, and it ran off.

"Oh my God, did that dog hurt you, my precious?"

But apparently it had not. On the contrary, Charles's cheek, shiny with dog slobber, suggested strongly that he had been holding the dog affectionately and that the dog had been returning his affection. Charles screwed up his face and waved his arms, wildly upset that the dog was no longer there.

■ ■ ■

Charles attracted hugs and smiles from neighbours, even from strangers, but he also attracted dogs. In incredible numbers. He had only to appear in the street and every dog in the neighbourhood would come running. Like humans, they seemed to go bananas over his chubby face with its cheerful, sparkling eyes, over his impetuous, cascading laughter, even over his awkward grapplings, which often left tufts of hair between his fingers. Taking Charles for a walk was a complicated and somewhat tiring affair for Alice, who was not fond of dogs. Had that damned German shepherd, which had not been seen since, spread the word around in canine circles? Did dogs possess some kind of communications network that could get them massed together on the sidewalk in an instant? No one in the neighbourhood had ever seen anything like it before.

The hardware-store owner who lived across the street, and whose name was Fernand Fafard, used to come across to see the "dog king" playing in his yard: he'd ruffle the boy's hair, pinch his cheeks, tickle the point of his chin;

6

in short display all the marks of affection that strangers bestow on children who have captured their hearts. He was in his mid-thirties, tall and burly, with a large mouth and a big voice. He was sort of puffy, especially around the waist, and he was already losing his hair, but his face was open and friendly.

"They like you, those pooches, eh, kid?" he'd say. "You have a way with them, kind of a magic touch."

Then, turning to Alice, who always listened to him with a nervous smile:

"A tiger would crawl under a door to please that kid, Madame Thibodeau. It's a gift he's got. A rare gift! You should encourage it."

It was a strange and often amusing state of affairs, but it had its downside: when it was time for Charles to go indoors and leave his four-legged friends behind, his parents had to suffer twenty long minutes of kicking and screaming. It was absolute torture, like having a wisdom tooth pulled.

"Maybe we should get him a dog," Alice suggested to her husband one night.

"What would we do with a dog?" Wilfrid replied. "You work all day, I work all day: a dog'd go nuts cooped up in the apartment by itself. And bored dogs always take it out on their owners. We'd come home and find it shitting on the carpet or chewing the leg off the table. No way, no dog for us."

And the thin little man with cheeks framed by two vertical creases that made him look austere and bitter rolled his dark eyes and wagged his thick, work-scarred fingers.

2

C harles had just turned three when his mother became pregnant for the second time. He was still as rambunctious as ever, extremely clever for his age, with a huge capacity for making friends and an equally marked propensity for dropping them whenever, in his opinion, he had been treated unfairly.

On weekdays, on her way to work, Alice would drop him off at a neighbour's on rue Lalonde, a woman named Catherine who had turned her basement into a daycare and, with the help of a young woman named Mélanie, looked after a dozen children. Charles loved going there and quickly made a conquest of both women, who found him adorable and exasperating. He would throw himself into games with enthusiasm and imagination that could suddenly turn into terrible fits of anger when things didn't go his way; hugs and punches succeeded one another with a sometimes dizzying swiftness. With an excess of generosity he would happily share half his lunch with a friend, but woe betide any poor playmate who pinched one of his carrot sticks or a handful of raisins!

His unstable character caused him to perfect the art of asking forgiveness. He understood instinctively that what he needed first and foremost was charm.

"Mélanie," he would murmur to the daycare helper, his eyes lowered after a particularly explosive episode, "are you still mad at me? I'll be good from now on, I promise . . ."

And with a calculatedly woebegone expression on his face, he would sidle up to her and wrap himself around her leg.

"Oh, Charlie," Mélanie would say, smiling despite herself, "it really would be good if you controlled yourself a bit more . . ."

But when she saw his tearful look (and detected the slyness underlying it) she would break out laughing, pinch his cheeks, and kiss the tip of his nose:

"You little manipulator," she would say. "That's what you are, you know, a manipulator. I pity the poor woman who falls in love with you, you charmer, you."

■ ■ ■

Another thing Charles learned to develop was his power of persuasion. Alice would get him to the daycare every morning around seven o'clock. It was only two blocks from their house, and every day they were escorted by a canine delegation that had been waiting for them at the bottom of the apartment stairs from the first glimmers of dawn. The delegation consisted of anywhere from a dozen to fifteen representatives, all of them brimming with exuberant joy at being reunited with their long-lost friend and benefactor, from whom they had been separated for such an interminably long night. Their number would diminish somewhat if it was pouring rain or intensely cold, or if there was a heavy snowstorm, but there were never fewer than five of them, and while they walked the two blocks to the daycare Charles would feed his companions crusts of bread or other leftovers from the table that he had kept overnight in a plastic bag. His mother fought off the more insistent among them as best she could, sometimes getting runs in her stockings for her pains. She asked him many times not to feed the dogs, but Charles silenced her objections with an argument that was as irrefutable as it was simple. It was broken down into three major points:

1. If they weren't going to let him have a dog in the house, they had to at least allow him to play with dogs in the street.

2. The bread crusts and table scraps would just go into the garbage, which didn't need them; why not give them to the poor dogs, who were always so hungry?

3. If Alice were a dog, wouldn't she want him to play with her?

■ ■ ■

One morning in November, Alice and her son were making their way with difficulty to the daycare, assailed by gusts of heavy, wet snow; the huge flakes pelted their eyes and blew into the sleeves and collars of their coats, where they oozed and spread like tiny glaciers. The storm had buried the city under a thick, melting layer of slush, and tramping through it was like stepping into buckets of guts. In spite of it, Charles was busily feeding the few courageous dogs that had ventured out into this opening act of winter when he suddenly saw a new face in the pack. It was a small dog, thin and yellowish, with huge, protruding eyes, limping painfully along with the others, jostled by this one, snarled at by that, trying without success to snap up a crust but keeping at it just the same, despite his desperate condition.

Charles stopped and, pushing away the other animals, knelt down by the yellow dog and opened the plastic bag. The dog barely had time to grab a morsel of food before Alice grabbed her son by the shoulder and dragged him quickly towards the daycare.

"Maman!" Charles began crying. "He'll die if I don't give him some food! Look how sick he is!"

"This is no time to be feeding dogs! What are you trying to do, catch pneumonia? Will you listen to me, now? You'll just have to stop giving scraps to the dogs altogether if you can't show me you can be reasonable about it!"

His face glistening with tears and melted snow, Charles moved reluctantly on, pulled by his mother but turning back to look at the yellow dog, which was trying its best to follow, wagging its rear end and falling further and further behind.

Before going inside, Charles had time to see his little protégé push itself through the half-open gate into the daycare's small play area.

"You drive me crazy sometimes, you really do," Alice sighed as she took off his heavy, wet coat amid the confusion of the other arriving children.

Then she kissed him hurriedly and left, since the factory did not tolerate its employees being late.

As soon as she was gone Charles found a chair and dragged it over to a window, climbed up, and looked outside. Dogs came and went in the play area, sniffing the ground and casting envious looks up at Charles, who was safe and warm indoors. The little yellow dog was sitting apart from the others, near the seesaw, looking sadly up at the window, shaken every now and then by a violent shudder, his bedraggled coat white with snow. The other dogs appeared to be avoiding it, as though they already knew the terrible fate in store for it.

"Poor little thing," thought Charles. "It's going to die for sure."

"What are you doing over there, Charles?" asked Mélanie, enmeshed in a whirlwind of arms, legs, boots, and snowsuits.

"I'm looking at my dog," the boy replied, his voice quavering.

"Your dog? What dog? Is there only one out there today?"

"No, there are lots of them."

"Well, which one are you looking at?"

"I'm looking at my yellow dog," he said, sounding sadder and sadder.

"What's wrong with your yellow dog?"

"He's going to die."

"Who's going to die?" asked a small, hairy boy with a bare right foot and a boot in his left hand. He ran to the chair and tried to climb up, but Charles pushed him off.

"Be careful, children, careful!" Mélanie said, coming over. "Be nice, you two." She bent down and looked through the window:

"You may be right," she said. "He doesn't look too happy, does he?"

Charles looked her straight in the eye:

"We have to let him in, Mélanie," he said. "When he gets warmed up, he'll be better."

"Yeah," said Marcel, who had succeeded in climbing up on the chair. "He'll be much better, that's for sure. It's too cold out there."

And nodding his head in approval he placed his hand on Charles's shoulder to indicate a united moral appeal.

"Sorry, kids, no can do. It's against the rules."

"What are rules?" asked Marcel.

"Rules are what tell us what we can and can't do in the daycare."

"Do the rules say we can't help a sick dog who is dying from the cold outside?" asked Charles.

"No, the rules say we can't let any animals in the daycare because they might have diseases that would hurt the children."

"Phooey! I kiss dogs all the time, all the time, all the time, and I never get sick. The rules are stupid."

"Maybe," Mélanie said, a little embarrassed. "But we have to follow them anyway."

Bright red spots appeared on Charles's cheeks, always a bad sign, his eyes crinkled, his mouth tightened, and a tremor ran up his arms.

"I want the yellow dog to come in and get warm, Mélanie," he said in a low, trembling voice. "If you won't let him come inside, I'm not moving from this spot."

11

And he clung stubbornly to the back of the chair.

"Come on, Charles, be reasonable," Mélanie pleaded, in a voice that betrayed her guilty conscience.

"If you don't let him in, I'm not moving from this spot," Charles repeated through clenched teeth.

"Me too," chimed in Marcel, although with much less conviction.

Mélanie had to leave then because other children had arrived and a kerfuffle had broken out at the back of the room.

Charles kept looking through the window into the play area. The dog pack had disappeared, but the yellow dog was still shivering beside the seesaw, its caved-in body now all but buried in a snowbank.

Suddenly Charles jumped down from the chair, crossed to the vestibule, and ran out into the yard. A few seconds later he came back in carrying the dog, which lay listlessly in his arms, head hanging heavily down, eyes half closed, paws dripping, and body wracked with violent fits of shivering.

Through the door, which was slightly ajar, heavy snowflakes slowly spiralled into the room and landed on the floor, where they instantly became puddles of water.

Mélanie planted herself in front of Charles, a boot in each hand; anger showed on her face and from her half-opened mouth and trembling lips came the dry, pinched voice that she very rarely used and which the children feared more than anything; Charles burst into tears:

"Mélanie," he cried, tears running down his cheeks, "please, Mélanie, let him come in. He'll die if we leave him out there!"

Four young girls came up and stood beside Charles and they, too, began to cry.

Mélanie, stymied for a second, glanced uncertainly at the dog. She seemed almost about to give in when the animal, shaken suddenly by a violent spasm, opened its mouth and a long stream of greenish liquid shot out and splashed onto the floor.

"No, out of the question!" she said, grabbing the dog from Charles. "This dog is sick and it's staying outside!"

She opened the door and deposited the dog on the step.

Charles climbed back up onto the chair, wrapped his arms and legs through the bars and rungs like an octopus, and closed his eyes, determined not to move again until his protégé was saved.

Mélanie left the room and returned with a roll of paper towel and began wiping up the mess on the floor; the children watched for a moment, then little mocking smiles appeared on their lips and they began slowly circling the chair, teasing and poking at Charles who, much to their surprise, made no response.

"Come on, children," Mélanie said, taking two of them by the hand. "Let's leave Mr. Sulks in peace."

A few minutes later she looked back into the room to see how Charles was doing. His hands were still gripping the chairback. He hadn't moved a hair. But his eyes were open and he was staring furiously through the window.

Half an hour went by. Then Catherine appeared. She was a woman in her thirties, with plump arms and impressive thighs that bulged out the material of her black trousers. Her expression was pleasant and full of energy. When she stood before Charles a gentle shiver passed through his body and he blinked, but he continued staring through the window in silence.

"What's the problem, Charles? Mélanie tells me you've got a case of the sulks."

"I'm not sulking."

"What are you doing, then?"

"I'm sad."

"What are you sad about?"

"I'm sad because I want to help a sick dog and Mélanie won't let me."

"Where is it, this dog?"

"Outside. Where he's dying of cold."

Catherine glanced out the window and a small frown settled into the corners of her mouth.

"I can't let it inside, Charlie my boy," she said. "It's against the rules. It could bring in all kinds of diseases."

"The man who made up that rule is stupid," Charles muttered, unmoved. "He never had a dog, or else he hates dogs. When a person is sick you don't leave him outside to freeze to death. It's the same with a dog."

He looked at Catherine and saw that he had scored a hit. He got to his knees on the chair, his eyes bright and pleading, his lips trembling, his hands pressed together:

"Please, Catherine, let him come in . . . Put him in a cardboard box and keep him in your office until he gets warm. He's too sick to move anywhere,

13

I know he is. No one will see and I won't tell anyone, I promise. Will you, Catherine? You will, won't you?"

Catherine placed her hands on her thighs and slowly nodded her head, trying to think of some way out.

"I don't have a box, Charles."

"Yes, you do! I saw one yesterday. It came with the stuff for the kitchen."

Catherine, feeling more and more trapped, dug her fingernails into her pantlegs, filling the silence with quiet scratching sounds.

"All right, you win. My God, you're a stubborn little mule. Go ask Mélanie for the box, and I'll try to find some rags to put around him. But not a word to anyone, do you understand?"

Charles came back joyfully with the box, and Catherine lined the bottom of it with rags. Then he raced for the door, but she grabbed him by the arm:

"No, you don't! I'll get the dog."

When she opened the door, a fresh flurry of snowflakes zigzagged their way into the room. The dog was huddled on the doorstep, its head drawn back into its shoulders, its muzzle between its paws, desperately trying to preserve as much body heat as it had left. Catherine lifted it up and carried it inside, kicking the door shut with her heel.

Charles, mute with joy, jumped up and down and clapped his hands together.

The few seconds during which it was suspended in the air in Catherine's hands was a terrifying experience for the little yellow dog. Its vision, blurred by melting snow, had suddenly become clear and fixed automatically on a small crack in a kickplate a foot or so away. The crack had then suddenly zoomed in towards him crazily, enveloped him in an impenetrable darkness, then returned just as suddenly to its former size and place as though nothing had happened; the dog had then understood within its soul that it was going to die very soon and that nothing was going to save it from its fate. A terrible sadness spread through its chest, as though someone had pierced it with a long needle; it gave a terror-stricken groan and began to struggle. Charles threw himself towards it, tore it from Catherine's hands, and held it against his body, where the animal curled up into a trembling ball.

"Don't be afraid, little puppy, we're going to take care of you."

He held it away from him and looked deeply into its eyes.

"We're going to take care of you, I said. Stop shaking, okay?"

The dog gave another groan, but soon it was placed in the cardboard box on a bed of rags, and someone picked up the box and carried it to a place where the voices of children were little more than a distant murmur. It stretched its legs straight out and began sniffing at the rags. Slowly its hair dried, and the exhausting shivering that was killing it began to subside.

The little dog died just before noon. Charles, faithful to his promise despite an almost uncontrollable urge to know what was happening, did not go into the office once all morning. When Catherine came to tell him that the little yellow dog was dead, he asked to see it one more time. Curled up into a ball on its side, its forepaws stretched out and stiff, it was staring up at the ceiling with a haggard eye, its jaws slightly parted. A small child began whining in the next room, and Charles had the horrible impression that it was the dog that was making the pitiful noise, reproaching him for having failed to save its life.

He began to sob:

"I wanted to help him, but I didn't do it fast enough . . . He was outside too long . . . I was too late . . . Now he'll never be my friend, never, *never!*"

Catherine caressed his hair and then, to help lessen his grief, suggested that they bury the dog in the yard, under the old cherry tree. That way he'd still be with Charles, sort of. Charles thought that was a good idea. During rest time, he helped Catherine dig a hole in the still-soft earth. But once the box was placed in the bottom of the hole he ran back into the daycare as fast as he could; he couldn't stand the sight of shovelfuls of dirt landing loudly on his poor friend.

Days passed and he recovered his good spirits. But from time to time, during the day's activities, he would leave the others and go over to the foot of the old cherry tree and stand there for several minutes, his hands behind his back, looking down at the ground with a thoughtful expression on his face.

3

On June 4, 1970, Alice Thibodeau gave birth to a baby girl, whom they named Madeleine. Charles thought she was very red and extremely ugly. Her screams made the glasses in the kitchen cupboard rattle, and she suffered from a condition that had a long, complicated name. Her wails followed Charles everywhere, piercing his eardrums. No matter how many doors he closed or how loud he turned up the television, the voice was always there; it filled the apartment like a hand filled a mitten. Only in the bathroom – which was at the other end of the apartment from the baby's room and filled with street noises that came in through its partially open window – could Charles find any relief from it, and could even at times forget it was there. But the room was tiny. He could barely spread his arms in it. After five minutes he wouldn't be able to stand it any more, and would have to come out.

And so he took to spending his time between coming home from daycare and supper in the small, paved yard behind the building their apartment was in. Most of it was taken up by an enormous truck. It was separated from the neighbouring yard by a high, chain-link fence through which he could see two enormous green plastic garbage pails, which sometimes smelled so awful he had to stay away from the fence.

Often three or four dogs would be waiting for him in the alley, tails wagging furiously as Charles opened the gate to let them into the yard. The gate was hard to open – the first time it took him more than ten minutes. He always had bread crusts for them in his pockets. And he passed the time by teaching them things. He climbed on the back of the biggest dog and rode it like a horse. He let the others chase him under the truck. Sometimes Alvaro, the Portuguese boy who lived across the alley, came over to play with him. When that happened he had to put the dogs back in the alley because Alvaro didn't

16

like them very much and was mean to them; one day a mongrel collie with long, dirty hair, who was usually very friendly, bit the boy's cheek. The wound wasn't deep, but from then on Charles made sure the dogs were out of the yard before the boy came over.

Whenever Charles and Alvaro got together their heads bubbled with ideas. The truck became a tramp steamer, a locomotive, a space ship, a mountain that had to be climbed, or a jeep that was bouncing across dangerous territory. They could hang on to the side-mirrors, climb into the box, or, when they were certain no one was watching from one of the windows, walk carefully across the roof of the cab and down onto the hood. Unfortunately the truck's doors were always locked. Sometimes they would lose their footing and slide down onto the asphalt, but luckily they never hurt themselves.

Alvaro was usually fun to be with and full of energy, but there were times, right in the middle of a game, when he would suddenly stop, and a strange look would come over him. His dark face would turn almost brown; he would seem annoyed at something, not want to continue with what they were doing, and return to his own yard without a word.

Sooner or later Charles would have to go in, too; the door to the second-floor balcony would open and his father, or sometimes Alice, though less often, would come out and call him in for supper. Then he would have to face his new sister, who hadn't seemed to have found anything better to do than scream at the top of her lungs. They would eat supper without talking, a sad and mournful meal, often cooked by Wilfrid since Alice was still weak from childbirth and spent whole days in bed with the baby. They usually just had soup and sandwiches or hot dogs, or sometimes a meat pie bought from the grocer's and served with canned vegetables.

Alice, wrapped in her inevitable bathrobe, little Madeleine pressed against her, picked at her food and sighed. Hunched over his plate with a sullen, defeated expression, Wilfrid ate noisily, with jerking movements, one hand stroking the inside of his thigh. It was a tic that Charles had always noticed in his father, and though it intrigued him mightily, he'd never dared ask his father about it. His mother also intrigued him. Why was she always so tired? Her face had changed so much since the baby was born; it was thinner and paler, her skin seemed to have hardened and turned shiny in some bizarre and unpleasant way. Small blue veins had appeared on her cheeks and throat and on the backs of her hands. Do all babies make their mothers so sick? Why have them, then? Maybe mothers don't have any choice? Maybe they have to have babies in order to be real grown-ups? Maybe the police force people to have babies?

One night around eight o'clock, Charles had just put himself to bed with Simon, his faithful teddy bear. Alice had come to tuck him in and had even told him a bedtime story, as she used to before. For once the baby wasn't screeching. Peace reigned in the apartment; he could hear the rumble of the refrigerator, the creaking of the floorboards, and, through the wall, the sound of the neighbour talking to her sister-in-law on the phone, as she did all day long.

Charles closed his eyes and stretched his legs under the blankets, holding Simon close. It was a delicious feeling. He began to think about the little yellow dog, but not sadly this time, more as if the dog were still alive and he would find it waiting for him at the daycare tomorrow. Then his thoughts split in two and he began thinking about being in an airplane. He was way up in the sky, flying with the yellow dog, who looked down on the tops of the houses and barked loudly.

Then suddenly he opened his eyes and realized that he wasn't hearing a dog barking; it was a baby crying. Madeleine had woken up and was scream-ing again.

"Another trip to Emergency?" his father was shouting at the other end of the apartment. "I've had it up to here, goddamnit! This'll be the second time this week. How'm I supposed to pay for it?"

There was a low murmur in response.

Charles, furious at having been awakened from his dream, jumped out of bed and stomped in bare feet down the hall to his parents' bedroom without knowing what he was going to do. As soon as he passed through their door the baby stopped crying, the little hypocrite! He saw his mother lying in bed with the baby in her arms, and his father, leaning against the windowsill, staring down at them with a fearsome expression on his face. Charles looked at the baby, its own face red and contorted, its thin arms ending in fingers that looked like little pink worms; he felt a deep hatred for it rise up, and he gave into it, even though he knew it was something ugly:

"Maman," he said, approaching the bed with a syrupy smile on his lips, and not taking his eyes off his sister, "Mommy, can I hurt her, just a little bit?"

His father straightened in surprise and smiled. Charles was speechless with amazement. It was the first time in his life he could remember his father smiling at him.

■ ■ ■

The next day little Madeleine was taken to Sainte-Justine Hospital, where she died a week later. On the day of the funeral Charles stayed at the daycare and didn't feel particularly sad. After all, he told himself, if all she was ever going to do was scream all day and all night, she was better off dead.

That was how he'd explained it to the dogs on his way to the daycare that morning (he'd been making the trip on his own for a few months). And the dogs, although they were obviously more interested in the bread crumbs and chunks of meat he gave them, seemed to agree, which was some comfort to him.

When he got home that night, the baby's crib, the changing table, the little mobile of multicoloured stars that Charles had liked, everything that would have reminded him of his little sister, had disappeared. Her room was completely empty.

He ate supper alone with his father. Alice wasn't hungry and wanted to lie down. Wilfrid had ordered a pizza all-dressed (Charles's favourite) and was attentive and even at times affectionate toward his son, which made Charles a bit nervous. He didn't scold Charles for stuffing his face when he asked for a third slice, nor did he seem to notice when Charles accidentally let out a huge burp after guzzling a whole can of Pepsi.

The house was calm and quiet. It seemed too big all of a sudden, and somehow cold. Charles wondered if he might have ended up liking his little sister after all, despite all her screaming.

"Are you sad?" Wilfrid asked him, slowly wiping his fingers on the table-cloth.

"Yes, I am," Charles replied.

Then, in a brave rush of honesty, he added: "But not as sad as Mommy, that's for sure!"

■ ■ ■

Within a week, Charles's friends at the daycare, his daily walks back and forth with the dogs, and playing in the paved backyard with Alvaro (he played a lot with Alvaro now) had more or less resumed their former place in the boy's consciousness, and his good spirits had returned. The only thing that reminded him that he'd had a little sister who got sick was his mother's health. Alice didn't go back to work at the garment factory on Boulevard Saint-Laurent. Instead she spent all day in the apartment, always in her dressing gown, as though she were still looking after the baby. When she did leave the house, it was only to go to the doctor's, which she did at least once a week.

One evening, listening to his parents talk during supper, Charles discovered that his mother was suffering from the same illness that had killed Madeleine. But he didn't worry too much about it, because Alice had just received her plastic card. A few days earlier, she'd announced that the government was going to give everyone a marvellous card that would let them go see a doctor whenever they wanted to, and it wouldn't cost them a penny!

So, Charles told himself, his mother would surely go to the best doctor in the world and get better, because she was a grown-up and grown-ups are much stronger than babies.

Charles's father didn't see things that way. He became more and more sullen and irritable, and yelled if Charles made the slightest sound in the house, which meant he either had to stay put in front of the television set or else go outside even when he didn't want to. If not he'd get a clip on the back of the head, which was happening more and more often! He was learning by now to hide his tears, and even to quickly think about something else whenever he got one. That way it didn't seem to hurt so much.

Now his father drank beer not only before supper but also after, sometimes three or four bottles, sometimes more. He often fell asleep in front of the television early in the evening. Then Charles could pretty much do what he liked, since his mother, exhausted from her day, always went to bed as soon as the dishes were done; still, he tried to behave himself as much as possible so as not to upset her.

Then one night, without telling anyone, Wilfrid didn't come home for supper. He came home late at night, making a lot of noise and waking Charles up. Alice cried. After ten minutes the apartment was quiet again, and the next morning no one mentioned the incident. Charles knew better than to ask questions. He sensed that something had changed in his life, but he couldn't imagine what it was all about.

A few days later Wilfrid skipped supper again. This time he came home even later, sober, apparently, but in a vile temper, spoiling for a fight. His parents' bedroom door banged open. Charles, hugging Simon and holding his legs so stiff his feet felt like ice, listened to his father's shouting; he felt as though his heart had swollen up to twice its size and was crushing his lungs. The shouts came through the wall: ". . . always sick! . . . This is no way to live! . . . I'm fed up to here with it! . . . Leave me alone! . . . I don't have to explain myself to you or anyone else! . . ."

That night Charles had a nightmare. A little boy he didn't know had had his hand cut off beside the truck in the backyard. An axe lay at his feet, covered in blood, the still-quivering hand on the ground beside it. Who could have done such a horrible thing? The boy was shaking his stump and yelling, and blood was flying everywhere. Charles woke up crying. It was early in the morning. Alice came into his room and sat on his bed, rubbing his back. A thin, grey light filtered in through the drawn blind, diluting the darkness in the room.

He thought about his nightmare all morning. He had no idea what it meant. When he came home at the end of the day, he refused to go out into the backyard to play by the truck, despite repeated calls from Alvaro. From time to time during the evening, he cast a suspicious glance at his bed. Could nightmares be hiding in the mattress, or under the blankets?

By now Wilfrid was missing supper two or three times a week and not coming home until the morning, when he showed up to shower and change his clothes. But at least there was no more fighting. Alice buttoned her lip, averted her eyes, and kept to herself. She continued to waste away to nothing. Her movements became more and more shaky and uncertain. Coming into the living room one evening, Charles looked at her watching television. She was sitting on the sofa, the bluish-white light from the TV screen illuminating her face. It looked hard and angry, like one of those masks you get at Hallowe'en that are supposed to scare you and make you laugh at the same time. Suddenly everything became clear to him. He went up to her and took her hands in his, something he never did:

"You should go see a different doctor, Mama," he said, "because the one you're seeing now doesn't seem to be very good."

She rubbed the back of his neck; he didn't like the way her fingers felt so cold.

"My poor little Charlie," she said, "the doctors are doing everything they can, don't worry. No one could do anything more."

"Then you're going to get better, right, Mama? It's just that it's taking longer than you thought."

That night it took him longer to fall asleep than usual. He sat Simon on his chest and wiggled his toes as he thought about things. What sickness could his mother have? When he asked her, she just shook her head and gave him a sad smile, the way adults do with children when they don't want to answer their questions. Then she said, "I'm just tired, my darling. Just very, very tired."

She was lying, of course. He remembered the conversation at dinner, when he'd learned that she had the same sickness that Madeleine had had. How could a baby die from being tired? Babies were brand new! Maybe if his father was nicer to her, spent more of his time in the apartment like he used to, then she'd get better faster?

He clutched his teddy bear and whispered to it:

"Simon, Simon . . . please tell me how to make her get better. Please!"

■ ■ ■

At daycare, Charles almost never thought about his mother. To see the way he laughed, ran about, shouted, invented games only to change the rules to suit himself, asked for a second helping at snack time at the top of his lungs, mercilessly teased the other children, then wrapped himself around Mélanie begging her forgiveness, no one would ever have suspected that his mother was about to die. Like most people with strong natures, Charles was able to compartmentalize the various aspects of his life in order to focus his energies and survive. He never once referred to the drama that was taking place at home; a single step down that path would have plunged him into despair. It was no doubt his instinct for survival that led him to adopt such an attitude, and far from distancing him from his mother, it somehow brought him closer to her, allowing him to behave just as Alice would have wanted. When Mélanie expressed her surprise one day that his mother was no longer bringing him to the daycare, he simply looked away and said, "She's busy these days." The sadness in his voice gave him away, however, and Mélanie understood that all was not well in the Thibodeau household. She didn't dare ask him too many questions. Several days later Catherine asked a neighbouring parent to walk home with Charles in the evenings, since his father never came to pick him up.

■ ■ ■

Returning home from daycare one evening, Charles heard a strange voice coming from the kitchen, but his surprise lasted only a few seconds; he soon recognized the voice of one of their neighbours:

"Ah, here's our brave little boy!" cried Lucie Fafard, the wife of the hardware-store owner. "How're you doing, dear? My goodness, look at the rosy red cheeks on him! I'll bet you'll make pretty short work of my chicken pot pie, won't you?"

But her cheerfulness sounded false and displeasing to Charles. Without saying a word he went over to his mother, who was sitting at the table in her usual housecoat, and pressed himself against her.

"What's the matter? Well, you don't know me that well, I guess," the woman went on, picking up a paring knife and beginning to peel some potatoes. "We've only talked two or three times, haven't we? But we see each other in the street all the time, don't we, Charles?"

"He's a bit shy," Alice said, smiling weakly. "He'll get over it, you'll see. He likes having people around."

"He's like me, then, poor little tyke. Pretty soon we'll be getting on like a house on fire, won't we? Would you do me a favour? Take this bag of potatoes and put it in the cupboard for me."

After listening to the two women talking for a while, Charles found out that Madame Fafard had run into his mother in the street that afternoon and suggested she come up every night and prepare their dinner, just until Alice got back on her feet. But from the way she was acting, a bit too jolly, a bit too forced, the boy guessed that his mother was not going to get her health back, that one day she would be taken to the hospital like his little sister, who had died there.

The air suddenly whooshed out of his lungs, and he clung to his mother's arm so tightly she gave a small cry:

"What's got into you, my pet? You're hurting me!"

23

At which point Charles dashed off into his room and shut the door. Simon was lying on the pillow. He winked when he saw Charles to let him know it would be good to spend some time together.

"Simon!" Charles cried joyfully.

He threw himself on the bed and his fears soon vanished. Taking his bear in his arms, he pushed a chair over to the window and climbed up on it; M. Victoire, their landlord, had his head stuck under the hood of his taxi, trying to fix it again. M. Victoire's skin was very dark, and every time he saw Charles he said, "Hey there, Charlie boy!" and began to laugh. Of all the men that Charles had met, M. Victoire had the nicest voice.

All Charles could see of him was his legs and the small of his back and they weren't moving, as though M. Victoire were asleep, or maybe dead. But then a loud, sharp, metallic noise came from under the hood and, to Charles's great relief, M. Victoire shouted: "Holy Jumpin' Jeepers!"

Charles laughed and jumped down from the chair. Placing Simon on the floor beside him, he began building a tall tower with his blocks. He had just finished it when there was a quiet tapping on his door.

"Dinner's on the table, Charles." It was Madame Fafard.

Charles made a face, then turned his head away when the door opened.

"You must be starving, you poor thing. It's almost six-thirty."

"No, I'm not," Charles said, giving her an unfriendly look.

But he got up and followed her into the kitchen. The whole apartment was filled with the delicious smell of chicken pot pie. As though sensing that her presence made Charles uncomfortable, Madame Fafard went home as soon as she'd placed the meal on the table. Charles ate hungrily, although Alice barely touched her food. She asked him how his day at the daycare had been. Then she gave him a second helping of pie and went to bed; he finished it in front of the black-and-white TV that was on the counter beside the sink, the one his father never allowed them to watch during mealtimes because he said it annoyed him too much.

■ ■ ■

One Saturday afternoon, while he was colouring on the living-room floor with Alvaro, two men came into the apartment with a stretcher to take his mother away. She had had a very bad night. Before leaving, she called him

24

into her room and hugged him for a long time, crying, kissing him again and again on his cheek and his forehead, making him promise to be good, to take his bath every night and to eat all his dinner. He nodded without saying anything, feeling a huge emptiness opening up inside him. Standing beside the bed, his face dejected, his eyes red and swollen, blinking from exhaustion, Wilfrid watched them and rubbed his chin with his hand. He went out with his wife and the two ambulance drivers, and Lucie Fafard came over to look after Charles until his father returned.

Charles went back into the living room, where Alvaro was waiting for him and started colouring again as though nothing had happened. This time, however, his friend's fooling around, drawing horns on the figures in the colouring book, adding extra arms and antennas in the silliest places, didn't make him laugh. He was trying to keep the picture of his mother alive in his head, but it was as though her face were evaporating away, leaving nothing behind but a sort of cold, grey dust and an unbearable sadness.

■ ■ ■

From then on, Charles's life was different in every possible way. At the end of each day, instead of going straight home after leaving daycare, he went to wait for his father in a restaurant called Chez Robert, on rue Ontario, not far from the apartment. Signs in the restaurant announced that it specialized in Canadian Cuisine, had Daily Specials and a Take-Out Menu, and that the place was Fully Licensed. Robert himself had long ago taken off with an English osteopath who walked with a slight limp but was otherwise not bad-looking, leaving his wife the business and debts amounting to three times more than the restaurant was worth. Rosalie Guindon had taken it in stride; she moved in with the cook, who by a strange coincidence was named Roberto and was three times the man her ex-husband had been, and the two of them had worked hard for five years paying off the debts and getting the restaurant back on its feet. It was now a profitable business. Wilfrid knew the owner well and, after a few months, became friendly with one of the waitresses, Sylvie Langlois. She was a fine-looking woman of thirty-eight with a definite fondness for beer.

Charles would be at the restaurant every day at five-thirty, seated in a booth with a glass of milk (courtesy of Rosalie), and watching television or listening to the conversations of the other customers, who consisted of a wide variety of really interesting types. Monsieur Morin was a long-time regular, a retired bachelor who came in every night at a quarter to six on the dot, ordered the soup of the day, a half club sandwich (no fries), and a bowl of rice pudding (he didn't like to eat much in the evenings). Then he would play a few hands of solitaire, all the while teasing Rosalie about her weight, always finding new ways to draw attention to it, with Rosalie for her part always finding new ways to shut him up. Both of them enjoyed the exchange immensely. Monsieur Victoire came in most days for his "end-of-the-day beer," giving Charles a big smile and sometimes ruffling his hair, then settling in to his torrid, clownish courtship with the waitresses, especially the blushing Liette, who was only eighteen and frightened easily, to the great enjoyment of the customers. Charles didn't understand much of what was said, but he laughed along with everyone else, mostly at Monsieur Victoire and his antics. But some nights he was quiet, as though he had retreated into himself, slouched in the booth, looking sad and vaguely annoyed at everything.

When it wasn't too busy in the restaurant, Rosalie would come over and pick him up and sit him on her knee:

"You're thinking about your mother, aren't you, poor little fella. It's tough for a kid your age to go through something like that. But everything will be all right in the end, you wait and see. Everything always works out for the best, one way or another."

Sometimes Sylvie came over, too, but she never picked him up and put him on her knee. She just smiled at him for a few moments, her eyes blinking against the smoke from her cigarette.

If Wilfrid was late getting there, it was understood between him and Rosalie that Charles would be given his supper. Charles quickly learned that if he wanted to fit in at Chez Robert, he would have to be not only well behaved but also pleasant and useful; he would also have to be generous with compliments about the meals he was served. When he finished eating, he would go around to the tables collecting ashtrays and emptying them in the trash. Rosalie was amused and impressed, and began calling him "Tom Thumb, my little waiter."

One night Wilfrid phoned the restaurant to say he had an emergency at work and wouldn't be able to get there until ten o'clock, and he asked Sylvie if she could take his son back to the apartment (he had given Charles his own key that very morning), make sure he brushed his teeth, and put him to bed. Rosalie was vehemently against this idea, and she and Roberto talked about it in the kitchen. Charles didn't know Roberto that well, because he was always either busy in the kitchen or else standing at the back door getting some fresh air. So he didn't know that he had captured Roberto's heart as well. After a long discussion it was decided that Charles would sleep in the restaurant until his father arrived. And rather than risk the restaurant's reputation by having someone asleep in one of the booths, Roberto decided to put him under the counter. All he had to do was move a few cases of pop and three huge tins of mustard; Rosalie ran to her house to get a comforter for a mattress, and a blanket and pillow. Charles stretched out under the counter near the cash register, studying the comings and goings of countless nylon-clad legs, as happy as a seal swimming in a school of fish.

■ ■ ■

The next week Charles spent the better part of two nights under the counter. Rosalie began grumbling about it under her breath, since both nights coincided with Sylvie's nights off.

"He must think we're a couple of idiots," she said to her partner. "And Sylvie, too!"

"Maybe, Rosie, but he pays up," replied the pragmatic Roberto. "Last week he gave us five dollars for three junior dinners. Can't complain about that."

"I can complain if I want to. It's a question of principles. That's no way to bring up a kid. I was at the cash a little while back and I heard this sniff coming from under the counter. I bent down and the poor little thing was crying. Not loud, mind you, trying his best not to disturb us. You know who he was thinking about as well as I do. No one's told him yet, but he knows his mother's on her way to her grave. No more mother, and now his father's hardly around. Some future, I'd say."

Roberto waved his greasy hand (he'd been kneading the pizza dough):

"And *I'd* say djou're making a mountain outta a molehill, Rosie."

"What do you mean? Thibodeau needs that kid like he needs a hole in the head. Oh, he's not a bad sort, I'll give him that, but he'd sell his son or give him away without a moment's hesitation, just like that, good riddance! In half an hour he'd've forgotten he ever had a son. He doesn't have a father's instinct,

27

that's what I'm saying. I've known a few men in my time, Roberto, and they don't all have your sweetness of heart, you big softie. How many men do you know who'd let themselves be fleeced by their girlfriends like you do?"

"Hey, we agreed not to talk about that."

"Sorry."

Roberto's eyes had flashed with anger, then quickly softened:

"Life ain't so easy for him, Rosie. His wife dying, a four-year-old kid to look after, his own family keeping outta sight, his mother-in-law too far away to be any good to him, and on top of that he has to make a living like everyone else!"

"You forgot to mention Sylvie," Rosalie said tersely as she went back to the cash. "He's banging her while his wife's fighting for her life."

Roberto gave a tired sigh and went back to his pizza dough. Women, he thought. Whenever you want to make sure you've been misunderstood, all you have to do is ask them! Poor Wilfrid, he didn't ask to be in his shoes . . . Having a sick wife for a few months don't turn a guy into a saint, you know. The body has needs, goddamnit! Rosalie's criticisms had brought out his penchant for male bonding.

Still, two hours later, when he was sitting at the counter in the almost empty restaurant, sipping a beer and thinking about the carpenter, he was definitely annoyed when he suddenly felt a hand on his shoulder:

"Hey, there, Roberto!" Wilfrid said in that rejuvenated, triumphant voice that always comes, even to a tired man, after an hour or two in bed with a woman. "How's business? My boy didn't get under your feet, did he? Here," he added, slipping a ten-dollar bill into Roberto's shirt pocket. "For taking such good care of him these past coupla weeks."

"No, no, no, that's much too much," Roberto protested, keeping the money, his previous estimate of the carpenter having swiftly returned.

"It's worth that and much more," Wilfrid replied, stooping under the counter.

Charles was so sound asleep that his father had to carry him home in his arms. He took off the boy's shoes and put him to bed fully clothed, careful not to wake him.

After work he'd gone to the hospital to visit Alice, and the look she had given him when he left had stayed with him as though printed on his forehead. The idea of spending another evening alone in the apartment with his son had filled him with despair. So he'd called Sylvie. She'd invited him up to her place, they'd had a few beers, and before long they'd ended up in bed as usual. And all the while the look Alice had given him continued to haunt him. He'd tried his hardest to play the energetic, passionate young lover, but Sylvie wasn't deceived:

"You aren't really here with me tonight, are you, my pet. Maybe you should have spent the evening somewhere else."

And he hadn't known what to say.

"Good God," he said now, looking down at his son, lost in sleep, one arm draped over the side of the bed and his hand half-open, "what am I going to do with you from now on?"

And for a long while he sat in a chair tipped back beside the rumbling refrigerator, smoking one cigarette after another, trying without success to come up with an answer to his question.

4

Charles was zigzagging around the playground, arms outstretched, chasing his friend Freddy like a fighter plane closing in on an enemy aircraft, when Mélanie appeared at the door.

"Your father's here," she called. "He wants to talk to you."

He walked towards the daycare, dragging his feet through the dead leaves that were beginning to litter the ground. Why do they always do this whenever I'm having fun? Having fun was hard enough these days.

Wilfrid Thibodeau was waiting for him in the vestibule. Charles looked at him in astonishment. His father seemed to have aged incredibly since that morning. How had he gotten so old so quickly? His forehead was wrinkled, his cheeks had sunk in, his skin was the colour of old cardboard that had been lying in the street, and his eyes, his eyes . . . you could hardly see them! They were half-closed, hidden behind red and swollen eyelids.

"Mommy wants to see you," he said in a low voice. And then turning towards the door he motioned Charles to follow him.

The car sped through the nearly deserted streets. Sitting next to his father in Alice's seat, Charles found the rumbling of the motor vaguely disturbing. Minutes passed. Wilfrid looked directly ahead, silent and impassive. They turned a corner onto a busier street and were forced to slow down. A huge, red-and-white tanker truck, the kind that delivered furnace oil, was blocking their passage. It kept stopping and emitting loud sighs, which made Wilfrid Thibodeau keep his foot on the brakes.

"Mommy isn't doing very well, Charles," he said suddenly, his voice soft and higher-pitched than usual. Charles barely recognized it. He didn't like the sound of it. To fill the silence that followed, and to prevent his father from saying anything else, he reached out and pressed the button that turned on the radio.

The music was suddenly interrupted by a special news bulletin. A man announced in serious, solemn tones that a group of terrorists calling themselves the Quebec Liberation Front had just kidnapped a British diplomat somewhere in Montreal. The police were making inquiries. The prime minister of Canada and the premier of Quebec would be issuing statements later in the day.

"What's a diplomat, Papa?"

"What? Oh, it's a man who works for one country in another country."

"And British? What's that?"

"The English. Not the English who live here, the English in England."

Charles sat back in his seat, satisfied. He imagined three cowboys with red polka-dotted bandanas pulled up over their faces and carrying huge six-guns, making off with a man wearing over-sized glasses and a red tie, his face showing no emotion even though tears were welling up in his eyes.

"Goddamned criminals," his father grumbled between clenched teeth. "I hope they squash the sons of bitches like bugs."

The music came back on and Charles returned to his imaginary scene, in which one of the criminals was pulling the diplomat along by his tie. But the Englishman was pulling back, his face turning as red as a ketchup bottle. Suddenly the car stopped in a parking lot, and Charles got out and followed his father. They went up one steep street and turned onto another, much bigger street, this one flanked by an enormous park with trees that had already lost half their leaves. On the right was Nôtre-Dame Hospital, where they were helping his mother get better.

When they entered the hospital's foyer, a violent commotion started up in Charles's head. The criminals and the diplomat vanished as though carried off by a blast of wind and were replaced by a vision of his mother: Alice, thin and pale, lying still on her bed, eyes closed and barely breathing. He felt pain and fear take over his entire body. It took an enormous effort to keep walking behind his father, who was moving quickly towards the elevators. If it were up to him, he would have waited quietly in the foyer, huddled against a wall.

Wilfrid pushed softly on the half-opened door and, taking his son by the hand, entered a darkened room that was bathed in a bluish light. In the bed nearest the door, an old woman was making a strange clacking sound with her teeth as she breathed from a tube taped under her nose. Charles went past without looking at her and stopped at the second bed.

There another woman was sleeping. She looked very thin, with her arms lying at her sides. Wilfrid pulled a chair close to this bed, picked Charles up and sat him on the chair so he could have a better view of the woman. Charles vaguely recognized his mother's hair, but the rest of her was completely changed. Could this really be his mother? Maybe they'd gone into the wrong room, and Alice was waiting for them somewhere else, smiling. He looked at her in a daze. With her lined face, her thin, shiny nose with its flared nostrils, and her bony, pointed chin she looked almost threatening to him. He didn't know what to do or think about this. He turned and looked at his father.

"We'll wait for her to wake up," Wilfrid murmured with a sad smile.

Gradually a strange impression took hold of Charles's mind. He imagined that the bluish shadow filling the darkened room like smoke was coming from his sleeping mother's face, that the shadow would spread throughout the hospital, then envelop the city and eventually the whole world, shutting all the light out of their lives forever. His eyes filled with tears and he began to shake.

"Mama," he said quietly, "Mama, wake up . . ."

Suddenly Alice opened her eyes and looked at him. A languid smile, still thickened by sleep, appeared on her lips, and she slowly lifted one of her arms. Charles jumped out of his chair and, kneeling on the bed, leaned over his mother and put his arms around her neck.

"Careful, you'll smother her," Wilfrid said, reaching to pull the child away.

"Leave him," Alice said with surprising force. "It's been so long since I've seen him. My poor little boy," she murmured tenderly in his ear. He sniffed and nuzzled against her face like a young animal that has returned numbed with terror from a long, lonely voyage. They stayed entwined in an exchange of sighs and incomprehensible monosyllables while the carpenter, his hand suspended in mid-air, watched them with a kind of intimidated amazement. Mother and son remained immobile for several minutes, until suddenly the young woman's body relaxed, and her arms fell listlessly back onto the bed. Charles sensed that he was making it hard for her to breathe, and so he half sat up. His father picked him up gently and sat him back on the chair. Alice had closed her eyes, and a calm expression was momentarily softening the terrible gauntness of her face.

"You're going to get better, Mama," Charles declared with a happy assurance. "But you have to eat more: you're much too thin!"

Alice nodded weakly and smiled, keeping her eyelids closed. At last she had seen her son again. Life had granted her her final wish and now had no more to offer; from now on, all her strength would be devoted to hollowing out a blessed emptiness inside her in which she could bury her suffering.

■ ■ ■

Her funeral was held on the twentieth of October, 1970, at Saint-Eusèbe-de-Vercil Church, on rue Fullum. The few mourners were spread out in the cavernous though somewhat shabby nave, through which wafted the faint odour of incense, dust, and mildew: her family, one or two co-workers from the garment factory, and half a dozen neighbours, including the hardware-store owner Fafard and his wife, Lucie. The priest stood at the railing, a little to the left of the ultramodern altar that had been placed in front of the old altar with its golden, sculpted figures, that was forgotten now at the end of the chancel. Charles, who was seated a few metres away between his father and his grandmother, watched, wide-eyed, as the priest gave the funeral oration. He was a squat, thickset man, with a grave face and slow gestures; specially rich blood must keep his stomach round, Charles thought, and its weight could be heard in his unctuous, sonorous voice.

"Alice," the voice began, heavy with solemnity and sadness, reminding the mourners of the reason for their being there: "Alice, this servant of God, this faithful wife and loving mother, this tireless worker who served as a model employee to those who worked at her side, this Alice is no longer with us. Alice, my dear brethren, my cherished sisters, has gone to Heaven to prepare a place for her husband, her son, and for all her loved ones . . . God in his infinite mercy, has taken her to be among His chosen children . . ."

Charles looked up in amazement at his father and then at his grandmother, as though to say: "Why does he call her Alice? He never met her in his life!"

And his thoughts returned to the convoy of soldiers he'd been seeing for the past few days in the streets of the city.

■ ■ ■

The day after Alice's death, Wilfrid had stayed home to look after the funeral arrangements. After consulting the Yellow Pages, he'd called several funeral homes, looking for the best price, horrified each time by the figures he was

33

quoted. Finally he found one that gave him a package that seemed slightly less outrageous. Not that he had much choice: a husband has to give his dead wife a proper burial. Charles, sitting across from him, listened without understanding much more than that the whole business was infinitely distressing and terribly expensive.

"Let's go," his father said.

Wilfrid sat him in the car, and they headed towards rue Darling, where the funeral director was waiting for him to sign the contract and discuss the final details of the ceremony. They had turned east on Ontario but were stopped almost immediately by a barricade that was blocking the road. Soldiers with rifles slung over their shoulders were asking all drivers for identification. A long line of trucks, their boxes covered with khaki canvas and their engines idling, gave off the pungent odour of diesel fuel. There were soldiers everywhere, running around in clumsy confusion, rifles clattering, dashing into stores and private residences, stomping up and down stairs, staring hard at pedestrians, cracking jokes amongst themselves, and guffawing loudly. A heavy, continuous throbbing came from the sky, and when they looked up, they saw helicopters appear above the rooftops, hover for a few seconds like gigantic insects, making a deafening racket, then disappear quickly to put on the same show somewhere else.

Montreal had been besieged by the Canadian Army.

Charles, on his knees in his seat, turned his head in every direction, his eyes wide as saucers.

"What are all these soldiers doing, Papa?"

"They're looking for criminals."

"What criminals?"

"Criminals," he spat, then added: "You're too young to understand."

When they returned to the house, Wilfrid turned on the radio and sat in the kitchen with a worried look, listening to a series of special bulletins that kept interrupting the regular programming. From time to time Charles came out of his room, where he was playing by himself, and stood at the kitchen door, keeping quiet, watching, not daring to ask questions.

That evening they had gone to Chez Robert for dinner, Wilfrid not being in the mood to cook. A strange atmosphere pervaded the place. Everyone spoke in low, serious tones, keeping an eye on the television, as though they all had a stake in the events being depicted. Rosalie had the thoughtful, vaguely disgruntled look she wore on the rare occasions when she went to mass.

She came over and sat beside Charles, ruffling his hair.

"Poor Monsieur Laporte," she sighed. "I hope they don't hurt him. As if being a minister isn't hard enough!"

"You think it's hard?" laughed a young man wearing a black shirt, who lived a few blocks away and had acquired a certain prestige in the neighbourhood because he went to university. "Oodles of cash, limousines at your beck and call night and day, playing golf with all the fat cats . . . Ha! Laporte's nothing but an exploiter. They say he hangs out with the mob."

The looks that were turned his way were so fierce and reproachful that the young man sank his head into his shoulders and didn't say another word.

When they'd returned to the apartment later that night, Wilfrid sent Charles to bed and went into his own bedroom. He stood for a while looking at Alice's clothes hanging in the closet, then opened a drawer and examined some photographs. Shrugging his shoulders, he went into the kitchen to get a beer, then sat in the living room in front of the TV; there'd been an announcement earlier that the prime minister, Pierre Elliott Trudeau, was going to make a statement to the people.

Curled up under his blankets, Charles tried to go to sleep, but the events of the day swirled in his head and filled him with misgiving. He tried singing himself to sleep, with Simon on his chest, but after a while he got out of bed and quietly made his way to the living room, attracted by the murmuring sound of the television.

On the screen he could see a man with not much hair and a thin face with bright red cheeks, sitting at a table with papers in front of him. With an icy stare, his face white as though too heavily made up, he looked like a dead man recently risen from the grave. In a nasal, firm voice he was justifying the extreme measures the government had just taken:

". . . Tomorrow the victim could be the manager of a bank, or a farmer, or a child. It could even be a member of your family . . ." .

Wilfrid turned and saw his son standing immobile, listening. The seriousness of the events had changed the carpenter. Instead of yelling, "What are you doing there, you? Get back into bed this instant!", he simply said: "Can't sleep?" Then he added: "It's the prime minister . . . the head of Canada."

Charles remained in the doorway for a few minutes, then went back to bed. Wilfrid drank two more beers, occasionally muttering vague imprecations at the Quebec Liberation Front, then was overcome by fatigue. Before falling asleep, however, he checked each window and made sure both doors to the apartment were locked. His son heard him and the unusual precautions frightened him.

Charles awoke in the middle of the night with a start; there was a loud beating above the house, incredibly powerful, making the windows of his room vibrate. Helicopters! Had the criminals decided to kidnap a child? And could that child be him? The sound moved away quickly, but he couldn't go back to sleep. He was filled with a kind of terrified exaltation that made him glad they were gone, yet left him wishing they would come back.

These curious events had an extraordinary effect on Charles; Alice's death lost all sense of reality in his mind. He knew he would never see his mother again, that she had gone somewhere to join his little sister, she of the terrible voice, and would not be coming back, but the dark cloud that had taken over the city, the serious and strained faces of the grown-ups, the whispered conversations, the continuous barrage of special newscasts on the radio and TV, to which everyone listened eagerly despite their unceasing repetition, had somehow served to numb his childish sorrow.

■ ■ ■

The priest returned to his position behind the altar; he raised his hands above his head, pronounced the ritual words, and everyone went down on their knees. Charles preferred to remain standing, because he could see better that way. But his mind soon began to wander; he wiggled about, scratched his behind, picked up a small, black book that was on a shelf in front of his chest, opened it, then closed it again. Behind him, Lucie Fafard leaned toward her husband and whispered:

"Poor thing . . . I really wonder what's going to happen to him now . . . I'll bet a dollar to a doughnut his father doesn't pay any more attention to him than he would to an old boot!"

The hardware-store owner thought he detected an obscure longing in her tone; he gave his right shoulder a brusque shrug, as though a flea had just bitten him, which in him was a sign that he was annoyed. His wife noticed it and looked at him, alarmed. "I know where this is going," he said to her in his head. "You want to take him in. Out of the question! With two kids already and a business to run I've got enough on my plate, and so do you. Why the hell do you have to go around solving everyone else's problems for them?"

The service ended. The priest walked up the central aisle sprinkling holy water on the coffin as the pallbearers rolled it slowly towards the exit, followed by the family and friends, most of whom were coughing, exchanging suitable looks, tugging at their ties, straightening the folds in their dresses; then the doors opened wide, and that was when there occurred the event that made the strongest impression of the day on Charles.

The small group of mourners were scattered about the forecourt when they heard a loud rumbling coming from the right, from the direction of rue Fullum; everyone stopped and looked, and all conversations abruptly halted. The rumbling continued and increased, punctuated by backfirings and blasts of horns. Suddenly a long line of trucks crammed with soldiers appeared at the corner of the street; an arm was raised through the window of the leading truck, there was the crackling sound of walkie-talkies and fragmented voices, and the line stopped with a great squealing of brakes; soldiers jumped out of the trucks, weapons in hand, and regrouped on the sidewalk. A man in a black helmet, his shoulders flashing red braid, took several steps towards the stairway leading up to the church, at the top of which the mourners stood transfixed, watching the scene unfold below them. Then the man turned his back, shouted an order in English, and the soldiers fell into tight formation, two deep, heels clicked, arms shouldered, facing the church. The lack of precision in their movements caused a long, low clatter. The trucks were turned off. Silent faces appeared in every window on the street, doors were opened by the curious, others came out onto their balconies. The usual racket that filled the neighbourhood gave way to silence, pierced only by the distant sounds of the city, a weak and confused rumbling punctuated now and then by sharp squeals, low growls, lingering frayed voices.

Lined up in front of the church, the soldiers remained motionless, waiting for the command from their captain, who seemed content to stand staring at them with his hands behind his back.

"What are they doing here?" asked a woman in a low voice behind Charles. "Are they going to arrest someone?"

Charles turned to look at his father, who, looking straight ahead, cleared his throat and put his hand on his son's shoulder. Far from being reassured by this, Charles broke out in a sweat and his calves began to twitch.

Suddenly there was a shuffle of movement to their left, the sound of muffled protestation, and then Fernand Fafard charged forward, his face scarlet, and began descending the stone steps in the direction of the officer:

"Get the hell out of here!" he shouted in a voice strangled with anger. "Let us bury our dead in peace!"

A tremor ran through the line of soldiers, and the small group in the fore-court also stirred.

"Fernand! Get back up here!" called a woman's voice.

"He's flipped his lid!"

"Monsieur Fafard! They'll arrest you! Come back!"

The hardware-store owner seemed already to have regretted his outburst; he hesitated a second, but then his pride forced him to continue advancing on the officer. The latter turned towards him and fixed him with a wither-ing stare, which seemed an extension of his fine, black moustache.

"Go away!" Fafard shouted, although with somewhat less assurance. "You're upsetting everyone here. We haven't done anything. Go away!"

Calmly turning his head towards his men, the officer gave a brief order and Charles, his hands covering his mouth, saw two soldiers detach them-selves from the formation, grab the hardware-store owner, and force him into the back of one of the trucks. Everyone in the forecourt shouted "No!" and began running down the stairs in confusion.

■ ■ ■

Fernand Fafard was released two days later. Some higher-up decided that a show of military strength at a funeral was tactless and in bad taste, and the officer in charge had been reprimanded; he weathered his disgrace at the Four Seasons Hotel with a prostitute and a bottle of dry gin; his binge further impaired his judgment so that he cracked his head on the corner of a table and vomited prodigiously for two straight hours; six months later he developed an abdom-inal hernia and an extremely uncomfortable fistula in his anus.

The hardware-store owner's denouement was more complex; some con-sidered him a hero, others thought he'd been a fool, although the latter were clearly in the minority. The *Montréal-Matin* published an article about him, complete with a photograph in which the "simple shopkeeper" was praised for "having plenty of pluck" and for knowing "how to instill proper respect for the solemnities of a funeral." In the weeks following his arrest, business at the store improved by fifteen per cent, and even after that it settled down to around a steady six, which prompted the simple shopkeeper to declare to his wife and children and anyone else who happened to be listening that "it pays to stand up for what's right, and to hell with pussies!"

But the incident at the church had burned a black hole in Charles's memory: he was never able to recall his mother's burial. Alice's coffin disappeared into the earth and into oblivion; similarly, the child's sorrow suffocated and became lost, stealthily disappearing into a filigree of holes that would eventually result in a painful collapse.

For the moment, however, his attention and energy were completely taken up by the need to adapt to his new life.

Wilfrid set about putting his things in order with a great deal of determination. First off, to save money he decided that Charles would go to daycare only on Mondays and Fridays. The rest of the week he would play near the restaurant, under Sylvie's lacklustre eye. Two or three times a day she would glance out the window or the rear door to see if the boy was still in the vicinity and keeping out of trouble. Not that she worried if he wasn't visible, even for long periods of time; it hardly interfered with her work, although it would drive Rosalie and even Roberto crazy. They stuck their noses outside regularly to make sure Charles had not been run over by a truck or snatched by a child molester or dragged off by the pack of dogs from the little park on rue Coupal, where anything could happen and often did, or at least to make sure he wasn't setting fire to a stack of old newspapers in their garbage bin. But most of the time he could be found in the Fafard's yard on Dufresne, playing with Henri, the Fafard's little boy, with whom he had formed a close friendship after Alvaro had so suddenly moved away.

```
┌─────────┐
│         │
│    5    │
│         │
└─────────┘
```

W as it the (relative) solitude of widowerhood that became intolerable for Wilfrid? Did the ache of loneliness mercifully reduce the pain of losing his wife? Whatever it was, barely three months after Alice's death, Sylvie Langlois and all her belongings moved into the carpenter's apartment. Not that that made any difference to Charles's eating habits; since Sylvie worked four nights a week at Chez Robert, the boy continued to take most of his meals there.

His life at home, however, underwent a sea change. Sylvie didn't exactly show open hostility towards him, but neither did she display any particular affection. She decided, for example, to turn his bedroom into a "television room," and moved Charles in the room once occupied by his sister Madeleine, which was much smaller and harboured no fond memories for the child. What was more, because she wanted "to take better advantage of our nights off," she convinced Wilfrid to send Charles off to bed the minute he swallowed his last mouthful of dinner. Charles had grown used to having things a certain way, and now everything was turned on its head. He resisted it at first, but in the end he bowed to the new regime, even though it often took him a long time to get to sleep. Curled up with Simon, staring up at the ceiling, he listened to the shouts of children playing in the street, tried to make out the television programs he could just hear coming from his old room, which the dividing wall transmitted to him with a benevolent indifference; sometimes he was distracted by the strange sighs and groans interspersed with sharp cries and laughter that came from his father's bedroom (he could not bring himself to call it anything else).

Sylvie also decided that he needed to change his socks and underwear only every two days, because, as she said, "she had better things to do with her life than spend it bent over a washing machine."

On the other hand, she got up every morning and fixed Charles a good meal (which Wilfrid could not, since he left the house very early to go to work). She considered it a tenet of healthy eating that the day could not properly begin without a well-filled stomach, and she would have considered it a mark of shame if Charles ate his breakfasts at the restaurant – although it would have seemed quite natural to Charles, since he took all his other meals there.

Sometimes she could be surprisingly generous. One afternoon, for example, Mademoiselle Galipeau, the local hairdresser, came into the restaurant with a haggard look on her face. Taking a stool at the counter, she ordered a hot chocolate in a trembling voice, and after three sips broke down and poured out her heart to the entire restaurant: Mittens, her beloved cat, with whom she had shared her life for going on fourteen years, had died two days before in the most atrocious agony, having swallowed a length of nylon thread that literally sliced through her intestines. She cursed the veterinarian who hadn't found the cause of her suffering until after she was dead! Monsieur Victoire, who owned the building the Thibodeaus's apartment was in, said something mildly consoling, and instantly regretted it, for Mademoiselle Galipeau burst into the most wretched sobs, crying with her face in her hands like a little girl; the death of a child could not have been more painful to her. Sylvie stood behind the counter watching her for a moment, somewhat taken aback, then leaned over and began patting the woman on the shoulder.

"Take her home," said Rosalie, her eyes moistening as she twisted the corner of her apron.

"But I haven't paid for my chocolate," protested the hairdresser as Sylvie led her towards the door.

"I'll take care of it, Mademoiselle Galipeau," Sylvie told her, "it's no trouble, don't even think about it."

In her apartment, the old woman insisted on making Sylvie a cup of tea, then launched into a long list of Mittens's virtues, which could only have been appreciated by those who were extremely close to her, since she was also shy and very particular. Sylvie listened, smiling, nodding her head and patting the woman's hands. Two days later, after a diligent search, she found Mademoiselle Galipeau another cat, "gentle, quiet and fixed," although it took her a week to convince the hairdresser to take the animal into her home; Mademoiselle Galipeau felt she was betraying the memory of her poor Mittens.

"It's never good to have a hole in your life," Sylvie told her. "That's where the sorrow gets in. Look at this poor little thing, look at the way he looks at you. He's asking you to love him!"

A few days later, however, when she saw that the hairdresser was in a better frame of mind, the interest and friendship she had shown towards the woman seemed to vanish. She hardly acknowledged Mademoiselle Galipeau when the woman greeted her in the street, as though her thoughts were elsewhere now; the page had turned, Sylvie had moved on.

She was a secretive, self-absorbed woman, a good worker but unsociable, generous at times but rarely to the same person twice, as though her generosity, so easily exhausted, required the stimulant of novelty to set it going again. She seemed to find contentment only in front of the television, glass of beer in hand – and perhaps also in the arms of the grumpy carpenter who, in bed, became her charming, gentle knight.

Charles benefited from a few days of grace in her eyes, but after that he was just another kid, like all the others, which to her meant deadly boring, a necessary adjunct to the man who made love to her every night and saved her a considerable amount of money by letting her live in his apartment.

The relationship that established itself between the boy and the woman was a curious one. Neither was particularly fond of the other, but neither seemed to resent the other's presence, either. As though by common accord, although nothing was ever said, they managed to limit their social contacts to the bare essentials, and to carefully avoid any open skirmishes: they each instinctively understood that mutual indifference and polite neutrality were their only hopes for rendering their lives together tolerable, if not pleasant. Wilfrid was often surprised by Charles's attitude towards his partner:

"He has the makings of a diplomat, that little guy," he said to Sylvie one day. "Do you notice how he never gets under your feet? Whenever you ask him to do something he always does it right away and never makes a fuss. But he makes sure you ask him as little as possible. He's no fool, that's for sure."

"I'd do the same if I were in his shoes," Sylvie replied, unperturbed, exhaling a long plume of smoke.

■ ■ ■

And so two years passed. At the beginning of the winter of 1972, Wilfrid became unemployed. But he did not let himself become idle. He went to see Monsieur Victoire and got permission to make himself a little workshop in the basement of the apartment building. The next week he passed a circular around the neighbourhood, announcing his availability for doing home repairs and odd jobs. But he rarely had any clients, and so he soon took to spending most of his afternoons in the Amis du Sport, a bar a little south of the neighbourhood, on Iberville. Sitting at a table with a few of the bar's regulars, he would erect pyramids of empty draft glasses under the owner's unamused eye, and make his way home in the early evenings with a slur in his speech and his clothes stinking of cigarette smoke.

During this time, when he wasn't at daycare, Charles played at his friends' houses or in the street with his rowdy pack of dogs, or else ran errands for Rosalie, who paid him with cookies or french fries and pretty much gave him the run of the kitchen, where he would collect leftovers and other goodies for his long-tongued friends.

An unfortunate incident almost put an end to the poor beasts' gastronomical privileges. Charles had just opened the back door of the kitchen to fill his plastic bag with juicy bits of past-due and slightly smelly meat when an ash-blond mongrel spaniel with one small and one large ear dashed between his legs, shot across the room like a meteor, and, nearly knocking down a waitress who was carrying in a trayful of dirty dishes, burst into the dining room; running his intrepid eye over the guests, he picked out Monsieur Bissonnette – a travelling salesman who was always dressed to the nines – and made off with a pork chop from his plate, spattering his trousers with gravy and mashed potatoes as he went.

When the mess was cleaned up as much as possible, Roberto went up to Charles and pointed his monumental index finger at the boy's nose:

"It's a good thing for you I have a gentle nature, my lad, and for now we'll leave it at that. But if this happens *once more*, those dogs of yours will be living on snow and crushed gravel. Do I make myself clear?"

"Yes, Roberto," Charles replied with a contrite expression that would have moved an anvil to pity.

■ ■ ■

Since his birthday fell in October, Charles couldn't start school until the following year, and he was greatly offended by this injustice, since it condemned him to playing with little kids among whom he felt his prodigious maturity was entirely wasted. He dreamed about his admittance into the mysteries of school life; the snatches of conversation he overheard in the street between those privileged few who were born before October 1966, their silent disdain if by chance they deigned to look his way, instilled in him the sense that school was a different kind of life, one almost as exhilarating as that of adults, but also a bit disturbing, since it apparently required one to give oneself over to extremely complicated activities and to submit to formidable competition.

That winter a change came over his behaviour. A sort of seriousness appeared in him at times. He remained an active and happy child, still easygoing, but he would isolate himself from his playmates on occasion, sit in a corner not speaking, his mind elsewhere, or else he would leave the room altogether and go into his bedroom, where he would spend hours slumped in front of the television, his eyes unfocused, his chest heaving deep sighs, a thousand miles from whatever was going on on the screen, and groaning to be left alone whenever Wilfrid or Sylvie urged him to go outside to get some fresh air. One night the waitress found him lying fully clothed on his bed, his head buried in his arms. Thinking he was asleep, she touched his shoulder to wake him for dinner; his body stiffened, he began breathing loudly and he refused to move. His father finally had to come and drag him forcibly to the table, where he picked at his food and sulked during the entire meal. Such moods became more and more commonplace, and one day Sylvie complained about them to her boss.

"But, my poor girl," said Rosalie, "it's his mother's death coming back to haunt him."

"Oh, come on! He was only four when she died!"

"So? When you're four you have all your heart even if you don't have all your reason. I was three and a half when I lost my grandfather, who lived with us after the Spanish 'flu took his wife. Well, my mother said I had nightmares for three months. And why do you think? Because I loved him, he was my Grampa, he took me everywhere with him, spoiled me rotten, always buying me sweets and ice cream – his death hit me harder than anything else I've ever been through, including my father's and mother's, and I always got along well with both of them. Sure I was only three and a half when he died,

44

but I can still see him in my mind's eye, my Grampa Odilon; I see myself sitting on his lap, him telling me stories while he smokes his pipe, or teasing me, or me sitting on the counter in the dairy bar while he orders me an ice-cream cone. I can even hear his voice . . . So Charles, you know . . ."

But Sylvie was unconvinced. "It's been *two years* since Alice died," she said, shaking her head. "I don't care who . . ."

"No, you listen to me: he's suffering from a delayed reaction."

She leaned closer after taking a look around the restaurant to make sure no one else could hear her:

"If you want my opinion," she said, keeping her voice low, "it was the October Crisis that did it. It disrupted that boy's grieving. Trucks full of soldiers interrupting the funeral . . . Think about it! And Monsieur Fafard being arrested in front of his eyes! Not to mention the atmosphere that poisoned everything at the time. Don't you remember? Everyone was on pins and needles, myself included, it would take nothing to put us in a sweat, suspicions hitting us left and right all the time. I remember shutting the restaurant one night at nine o'clock because my knees were shaking so hard I couldn't stand up at the cash. No need to look farther than that, my dear: that child is finally going through his period of mourning."

"Well, all I can say is, I hope he gets over it soon," the waitress replied, looking away.

And she went off to attend to a customer.

■ ■ ■

That afternoon, Wilfrid and his drinking buddies built such a huge pyramid of glasses on their table in front of the television that a silence fell over the room; everyone stopped what they were doing to watch. Then, in his excitement (and no doubt also in his cups), Pierrot jumped out of his chair to call the owner over to admire the masterpiece. Unfortunately, his knee caught the edge of the table and the whole thing came down in a cascade of broken glass loud enough to scare a deaf elephant. That brought the owner, who was furious, and who handed them a bill for $37.85, payable on the spot.

Still, it was with a light step that the carpenter left the bar and made his way home at six o'clock; though short of breath, his mind a little fuzzy, his cheeks pleasantly warm despite the dry wind that was riffling the puddles in the street, he could already imagine the smell of the dinner Sylvie was making for him (she got off at four o'clock that day and had promised him a stuffed chicken). Life wasn't that bad, he told himself, all things considered; work would start up again in the spring, he still had a small cushion in his bank account, he'd made some good friends down at the Amis du Sport, his health was okay, and on top of it all there was Sylvie.

He entered the building and began climbing the stairs to his apartment; the walls wobbled a bit, but his legs were still strong. Suddenly he stopped and rubbed his eyes; someone was shouting in the apartment. Then he heard a streak of swearing, made all but unintelligible by anger. He recognized Sylvie's voice, and then another voice even higher-pitched, which could only be that of his son.

"All right, all right, all right," he grumbled. "What the hell's going on!"

He hurried up the stairs, tripped on one of the steps, nearly flattened his nose and hurt his hand trying to grab the railing. A dark anger began to replace the good mood he'd come in with.

He opened the door, and Charles's strident voice jabbed at his ears like a fistful of needles.

"Go away! You're not my mother! I don't want you here! I hate you!"

Then a door slammed and all was quiet.

Wilfrid stumbled down the hallway, bouncing off the walls a few times, and went into the kitchen.

"So, you decided to come home!" Sylvie shot at him.

Sitting on a chair, her face red and puffed (for the first time, he thought she looked ugly), her hair in disarray, she was holding a dishtowel to her shin; a thin trickle of blood was running down her nylon stocking.

"What the hell's going on?" he said again, menacingly.

"What's going on," she said, raising her head, "is that you haven't taught your son how to behave! He calls me, I go into his room, and suddenly Bam! no warning, he throws a metal truck at my leg. Christ! It feels like it's broken, the little bastard!"

"Liar!" shouted Charles, coming into the room, his face streaked with tears and beside himself with fury. "I threw the truck at you because you tore up the birthday card my mother gave me. It's the only one I had left!"

"How was I supposed to know you were keeping it? It was lying on the floor!"

"You knew!" cried the boy, his voice choked by sobs. "And it wasn't lying on the floor. It was in my dresser. You're a liar!"

Sylvie gave the carpenter a look that clearly stated: "There, you see how he treats me? You choose: it's either him or me."

Wilfrid felt something like a roar of flame building inside him; the tip of the flame was burning his head, trying desperately to get out of his body, which began to tremble. He leapt on Charles, seizing him by the shoulders and throwing him against the wall. Then, grabbing him again, he began hitting him across the back and on his head. He beat him with such violence that Sylvie let out a cry and rushed at him: "Stop it! You're going to kill him! Have you gone crazy or something?"

When he didn't let up, she began pulling savagely at his hair; he suddenly lost his balance and fell onto the floor. Charles lay at his feet, his eyes half shut, not moving.

The carpenter stood up slowly, let out a belch, rubbed his face with his hand, and then looked around as though trying to figure out where he was.

"Put him to bed," he muttered.

Then he went into the bathroom, where Sylvie could hear him throwing up.

■ ■ ■

Charles stayed in bed for two days. He ate nothing, hardly drank a thing, spoke even less. He didn't seem to be in any pain, just wrapped in a cloak of silence that could have been caused by rage or despair. While undressing him, Sylvie had discovered huge bruises on his back and a red, swollen blotch on his left side. During the night she'd considered moving out of the house in order not to get further involved in anything so sordid and dangerous, but in the morning the rising sun had dispelled her anxiety, as it is said to have done so often for so many.

Wilfrid stayed away from the Amis du Sport for a week. The whole time Charles was in bed he hardly left the apartment, tormented by fear and remorse. He paced from room to room, hands in his pockets, mouth twisted into a scowl, unable to stop sucking his teeth in short, convulsive movements until his mouth became as dry as a piece of cardboard. Every so often he would go down into the basement intending to do some odd job just to get

47

his mind off things, but before long he'd be back upstairs, sneaking a look into his son's bedroom, where Charles was either asleep or pretending to be. He didn't dare call a doctor or take the child to the hospital for fear of the questions they'd ask, or afraid that Charles would tell the truth. He sensed that Charles was entirely capable of it.

On the third day Charles got out of bed early in the morning, dressed and made his way quietly into the kitchen. From his father's bedroom came a duet of snores that sounded comical in the silence of the apartment; Sylvie's were small and plaintive, almost musical, whereas his father's were loud and cavernous, as though they came from somewhere deep beneath the surface of the Earth. Charles poured himself a big bowl of cereal, added milk and tablespoons of brown sugar, and ate it hungrily. Then he put on his coat and went outside. Rue Dufresne was deserted and quiet, bathed in a fragile, shimmering light, a mixture of blues and mauves that seemed to be timidly trying to remove the darkness of the night. It had been snowing for two days but now the weather had turned mild; the street and the sidewalks were cleared, but the trucks had not yet come to take away the huge piles of snow that lined each side of the traffic lane. In front of him, Charles saw a slight, inviting depression in the snow. He turned and fell backwards into it and found himself sitting in a kind of soft chair that wrapped itself tenderly about him; he heaved a deep sigh and felt a sense of sweet sadness slowly spread through him.

His back barely hurt at all any more, and ever since the previous evening, when through partly opened eyes he'd seen his father's remorseful face, he also felt released from the fear that had gripped him.

In fact the fear had been transferred from him to his father. It was the only form of revenge that was open to Charles for the moment, and he would have taken some comfort from it if exhaustion hadn't erased all feeling from his mind. He didn't even have the strength to hate, had barely enough to slowly breathe in the fresh outside air and feel the warmth of his clothes and savour the pleasure of being alone. He closed his eyes. Behind him a car passed, the sound of its tires muffled by snow, then down at the corner the door to Chez Robert opened, and for a moment he could hear the chords of a guitar.

He remembered the first time he'd heard anyone playing that instrument. It had been a long time ago, when he was three. Before Alice became sick. They'd been hurrying down rue Ontario; the sun was baking the city. His mother held him by the hand and he'd noticed that her own hand was burning and moist, sending waves of heat down her arm and into his body and causing beads of sweat to break out on his forehead. He wanted to let go of her to cool off for a minute, but he wasn't allowed to. That was the rule: when he was with her in the street, he had to hold her hand because of cars and child snatchers . . .

They passed a store whose window was filled with musical instruments, all of them shining in the sun; the door to the store was wide open, and there was a man inside leaning against the counter playing a guitar. The music was so beautiful that Charles had asked his mother if they could go inside so he could listen to it. Alice agreed, though she'd been in a hurry, and they'd stood in front of the guitarist not saying a word. The man smiled at them and nodded, and then they had left, returned to their brisk walk down the sidewalk, Alice's hand still burning and sending all that heat into Charles's arm. But almost immediately his mother had decided that they needed something to cool them off. They stopped at a dairy bar; beside a low wall someone had placed a few wooden picnic tables, their fresh paint sparkling under a huge umbrella. They took their places, drank a large glass of water, and shared a chocolate ice-cream cone. He ate his half in large bites because the heat was making the ice-cream run down his hand, and all the time he was eating he could hear the man playing the guitar. It had made him feel very good. He told his mother that, and she had laughed and kissed his cheek.

It was one of the happiest memories of his life.

The door to Chez Robert opened again, and more notes from the guitar came out. He was humming them in his head when a sudden violent jolt to his chest knocked the dreams out of his head; the yellow spaniel with the different-sized ears had jumped on him and was frantically licking his face. He gently pushed it off and wiped his cheeks, then fell on the animal and held it in his arms and started to sob:

"You remember Alice, don't you, boy?" he said. "You remember when you used to come and walk with us to the daycare? She was pretty nice, my mother, wasn't she? I loved her a lot . . . But anyway now she's dead and I won't see her ever again . . . Not ever . . ."

The dog, as though sensing the gravity of the moment, waited patiently for Charles to let it go, though it never stopped wagging its tail.

6

That day Charles said he was going back to the daycare, and then left without saying anything more. Wilfrid stayed in the kitchen for a long time, sipping beer and anxiously watching the telephone. He was terrified that it would ring and it would be a social worker or – who knew – the police, asking embarrassing questions and saying they were coming to speak to him. But the day passed without incident.

His son came home at four o'clock. He seemed calm and even relatively happy; he sat in front of the TV, as he usually did when he came home from daycare, then went into his room and stayed there until dinner was ready. He ate a good meal, answered questions about his day, although briefly, without volunteering anything on his own, and avoiding even glancing up at his father. "Getting back to normal," Wilfrid told himself. "Just have to give it time. Mostly I've got to learn to control myself; I could end up in the slammer if I go on behaving like that! Can you see yourself in prison, you idiot? Just try getting work after that!"

Fear gave way to remorse, and then to a desire to make things up somehow to his son. Not that he thought such a thing was possible. How do you reconcile yourself with someone you've never really felt close to before, nor he to you? Still, habit alone didn't account for the vague feelings he had for Charles; there was a kind of fatherly love there, basic and crude though it was, never having found much nourishment to make it grow, yet yearning feebly for expression without quite achieving it.

"You could spoil the kid a bit, you know," Sylvie said to him one day. "It would solve a lot of problems. Spoil a kid rotten and he'll be a pain in the ass, but spoil him a little bit and he'll love you for it. After all, you've got another

50

dozen years or so before he leaves home, so you might as well make it as easy on yourself as you can . . ."

For a while Wilfrid tried hard to get on the good side of his son. At night when he came home he sometimes brought him a chocolate bar. One afternoon he took him to the movies to see *The Tall Blond Man with One Black Shoe*. But his efforts were without much success. Charles thanked him politely but remained cool and reserved, hardly spoke to him at all, and arranged to spend as much time outside the apartment as he could.

Then one night the carpenter had a brainstorm. Winter was drawing to a close; the previous week a businessman had hired him to do some repairs to a bowling alley; he'd been working at it from early morning until late at night, since the lanes were scheduled to reopen shortly. On the day of his inspiration, however, he left work at seven because of an equipment breakdown. He'd just come up from the Frontenac metro station, his mind dwelling comfortably on an evening spent with a case of beer in front of the television, when he saw his son on the sidewalk ahead of him, hopping about with a little friend surrounded by a half-dozen dogs. His face lit up, he gave his thigh a loud slap and hastened his step, smiling broadly.

"Hi there, son!" he called when he was about ten paces away.

"Hi, Papa," Charles replied, surprised by his father's tone. His face, which a moment before had been happy and animated, took on a pained, almost sullen expression; he went back to his game, but his heart no longer seemed to be in it.

Wilfrid remained standing next to the boys, who soon stopped playing, intimidated by his presence; a small, black, short-haired dog ran between the carpenter's legs, while another, a sort of bulldog, began sniffing at his lunch pail.

"Where do all these dogs come from?" Wilfrid asked, pushing the animal off. "I don't know anyone around here who has a dog."

"I don't know," Charles said, keeping his eyes down. He put his arms around the bulldog's neck and pulled it away from his father.

"That one there," said Charles's friend Henri, pointing to the black dog, "he lives over on rue Poupart, and the big one who's chewing his paw, he lives on Coupal. The others we don't know about . . ."

"You don't?"

"No, we don't know," said Henri, encouraged by the carpenter's interest. "Maybe they got lost, or maybe someone threw them out. It's possible . . . That one, though," he added, indicating the yellow spaniel with the different-sized ears, sitting before them as though following their conversation, "he for sure doesn't have a home, because he's been spending his nights in an old garage that nobody uses any more, over near our house; last month my father went out and took him a piece of insulation so he'd have something warm to sleep on."

"I'm surprised the pound hasn't picked him up by now," the carpenter said. "Don't you let him in the house sometimes?"

"Not very often. When he comes inside, my mother sneezes and her eyes start to run."

Charles had let go of the bulldog, which was now busy snuffling at a pop can by the curb, and was sitting jauntily astride the spaniel. The dog turned its head from time to time to lick the boy's hand.

"Would you like to keep him?" Wilfrid asked his son.

Charles's eyes widened and he almost choked. Had he heard correctly? Had his father, who had declared a hundred times that a dog wasn't worth the scraps from their table, and who rolled his eyes every time he saw Charles with his band of four-footed friends, really just asked him if he wanted to take the spaniel home?

The carpenter laughed at the expression of disbelief on his son's face:

"What's the matter, eh? Cat got your tongue? I asked you a question."

"Do you mean . . . you mean I can keep him at our place?"

"That's what I said."

A huge smile spread over the boy's face, and his eyes shone so brightly that they looked as though they were filling up with tears.

"Oh, yes! I'd like that very much, Papa . . . That would be the best present I've ever had in my life!"

"Well, then, bring him along," replied Wilfrid.

And under the dumbfounded gaze of Henri, who also knew of the carpenter's aversion to the canine race, Wilfrid continued on his way home while Charles, kneeling before the spaniel, explained to it the profound change of fortune that had just taken place in the dog's life.

Hearing the news, Sylvie let out a sigh deep enough to blow down the house, but the carpenter told her dryly that he was merely following the advice that she herself had given him.

"You wanted me to spoil him, didn't you? Well, I'm spoiling him. Do you know of anything that would make him *any* happier?"

"No. On the other hand, I don't know of anything that will make you less happy. I give it a week, and you'll be wanting to nail the bloody beast to a wall!"

"We'll take it one day at a time, my dear," was all he replied, in a philosophical calm.

. Ten minutes later Charles came in dragging the spaniel. Uncertain of what was happening and wanting to learn as much about its new surroundings as possible, the animal had carefully sniffed every step leading up to the apartment, then submitted the mat in the vestibule to an even more scrupulous analysis, and was now moving slowly down the hallway, its nose still to the floor.

"Ah, here you are at last," Wilfrid said. "I wondered what had happened to you."

"He's getting to know his new home, Papa," Charles replied. He was in such a state of bliss that his face had taken on a positively angelic expression.

They came into the kitchen. As though realizing that all this sniffing could be getting on someone's nerves, the spaniel wisely decided to postpone studying the floor and curled up in the corner.

Sylvie, who was sitting at the table drinking a beer, looked at the dog for a moment and then ground her cigarette out in the ashtray: "It's just a pup, for Chrissakes. Male or female?"

"Male," Charles said without hesitation. "He's a good dog."

She got up and went over to look at it more closely.

"Strange," she said. "He's got one ear smaller than the other. He must have lost part of it in a fight or something."

She bent down a little closer.

"And he stinks."

"He can be washed," Wilfrid said. "That's what running water's for."

Charles looked up at his father gratefully.

"Has it got a name?" Sylvie asked.

"I just call him the spaniel," said Charles. "That's what I was calling him until . . ."

The carpenter, eager to make up with his partner, put a hand on Sylvie's arm: "Any suggestions?" he asked her.

"Boff! How should I know?" Sylvie said, shrugging her shoulders and returning to her beer.

"Boff!" cried Charles, overjoyed. "That's a great name for him. We'll call him Boff."

He ran over to the dog, drowning it in a tidal wave of hugs and kisses that brought a smile even to Sylvie's bored face.

"From now on you're my Boff, do you understand? The only Boff in the whole world, the most beautiful dog of all dogs. I'm going to take good care of you always, you'll never be cold or hungry again, you'll have a roof over your head every night, this one, right here, 1970 rue Dufresne, remember that address. But you must be a good dog, eh? You mustn't ever break anything or tear anything up, and no barking at anything or disturbing people, or else you'll be in big trouble, understand?"

Boff wagged his tail lightly, making what he could of Charles's welcoming torrent of words; then he ran his tongue two or three times along Charles's face to let him know that he accepted the conditions the boy had laid out, whatever they were.

"Okay, that's all well and good," Sylvie intervened. "But he still stinks, that Boff of yours."

They took the dog into the bathroom and, despite its vigorous protests, placed it in the tub and gave it a full bath – using brush, soap, shampoo, and even some of Wilfrid's aftershave (Charles thought it would be a good way to cover up some of Boff's lingering odours). After the first bath, the water was almost black; after the second it was a dark brown; finally it turned a light blond, the colour of apple juice, and the tub blocked when they drained it; Wilfrid, armed with a toilet plunger, had to expend energy equal to at least two bottles of beer to unplug it. Meanwhile the dog, having submitted to a rubbing from Charles that nearly tore its hair out by the roots, decided instead to shake itself dry, thereby showering the walls, floor, and occupants of the room with water.

All during dinner the animal sat quietly in front of the refrigerator, despite its obvious interest in the hamburger patties on his hosts' plates, which it betrayed by flaring its nostrils; it no doubt knew instinctively that a crucial stage in its life as a dog had just begun, and that its behaviour over the next few hours would determine its entire future.

"He'll sleep in the kitchen," Wilfrid decided later that evening, and he placed an old blanket, folded in four, against the wall beside the fridge. "There you go, lie down!" he said.

Boff obeyed, lying with its muzzle between its paws, letting out a deep sigh and looking up at the carpenter as if to say: "Is there anything else I can do for you?"

But when Wilfrid got up during the night to empty his bladder, he saw that the dog had left its blanket; it had gone to find Charles and was curled up at the boy's feet, fast asleep.

"Back in the kitchen with you, go on!" grumbled Wilfrid, grabbing the dog by the scruff of the neck.

The dog crouched pitifully on its blanket. But in the morning it was back on Charles's bed.

"You stubborn son of a bitch!" Wilfrid shouted. "Get the hell out of here!"

Sylvie appeared in the door, yawning. "What's it to you if the dog wants to sleep with your son?" she said. "Lots of dogs do it and no one's died yet."

"I'm the boss around here, and it'll do what I tell it to do. If I want it to sleep in the kitchen then, goddamnit, it's going to sleep in the kitchen."

"You're not the dog's boss," Sylvie said, nodding towards Charles, who was sitting on his bed, legs dangling over the side, watching his father nervously. "He is. Who do you think's been feeding him all these years?"

"He doesn't wake me up, Papa," the boy said. "I didn't even know he was in the bed with me. And he's really clean. Now that we've given him a bath, he's as clean as we are."

After a brief discussion, the carpenter was forced to beat a retreat. But he did so with an ill grace, harbouring a secret wish for revenge.

■ ■ ■

As Wilfrid had hoped, the arrival of Boff lightened the atmosphere a bit, and Charles began to show some of his former spirit. His attitude towards Sylvie changed, too. Ever since their big fight the boy had hardly spoken to her, not so much out of sulkiness as from fear, since the terrible memory he retained of that incident filled him with dread that it would happen again; by limiting his contact with the waitress, he lessened the risk of another beating.

However, at some point over the next few days he overheard a conversation between his father and Sylvie that made him realize that it had been she who had urged Wilfrid to get closer to his son; it was to her that, deep down, he owed Boff; she was the one who had defended the dog the morning after its arrival in the apartment. Charles could begin to think of her at times as an ally, if a somewhat unreliable one: the timid teaspoons of friendship that he began to offer her were tempered with large dollops of caution. As for his father, he had now learned once and for all that, happy or sad, strict or generous, Wilfrid was a man he had to be wary of, especially when he'd been drinking.

Boff must have come to the same conclusion, after his own fashion. He behaved properly and quietly when the two adults were around, and was even friendly with them at times, but it was only to Charles that he gave his love. He followed the boy around as though his young master held the strings of his destiny in his hands; when Charles left him alone to play with his friends, he curled up on the boy's bed and waited for him, or else lay in the backyard under the balcony, the picture of dejection, having apparently renounced his years of vagabondage.

And so the months passed. Although he didn't know it, a huge trial was in store for Boff.

7

In September 1973, Charles began attending Saint-Anselme Elementary
School, on rue Rouen, along with Henri Fafard and dozens of other children from the neighbourhood. They went, gnawed by both fear and curiosity,
strapped into their backpacks and torn between their desire to act like *big kids*
and wishing they could be babies again in their mothers' arms.

Once he was over his fright (although it took a few days), Charles realized
that his teacher, a tall, thin woman with enormous, dark-brown, horn-rimmed
glasses, was not the terrible ogress she had first appeared to be, and – his second
realization, equally pleasant – that learning how to print *a*'s and *b*'s and *i*'s and
o's was well within his intellectual capabilities, and could even be fun. It took
him a little longer to appreciate another advantage of going to school: there,
unlike at home, he was perfectly safe.

Ginette Laramée's diction may have been a tad high and mighty, and she
definitely had mannerisms that grated on the more sensitive souls in her
charge, but after twenty-five years of navigating through the turbulent seas
of primary education she had not completely lost her unsatisfied instincts
for maternal affection; she was an aging spinster who would have liked to have
had children of her own, but consoled herself for her unfulfilled dreams and
solitary life by pouring her energies into her profession, as a lover of horses
pours himself into training; her love, if she was to be fulfilled by it, had therefore to be productive. A child who was a slow learner weighed on her heart,
and the sight of a pretty face, if it were to give her real pleasure, needed to be
accompanied by scholastic accomplishment. Each child received a small gift
from her on his or her birthday. She handed out unexpected hugs and kisses
freely; they were given exuberantly, and if they were a bit bony and awkward
they still never failed to bring a smile. No mother ever followed the course

of an illness, be it ever so slight, with more anxious attention. And in her presence all stutterers, squinters, and bearers of birthmarks or other natural disfigurements were assured of protection from the mocking remarks of their cruel classmates.

Over the years, the more difficult cases seemed to come her way; she wasn't always successful with them, in which case you had to watch out for her moods. But most often the snake charmers, the bottom-feeders, and the little piranha-fish, all those who liked to sow chaos in their wakes, ended up behaving themselves like everyone else, because her classroom was conducted at a fast, precise clip that demanded and received attention and held any unruliness in total check. She had therefore earned a reputation as a kind of pedagogical magician. Her minimum requirements for getting through a day were as follows:

1. Ten cups of tea (a kettle and hot plate were kept in a permanent state of readiness in a corner of the classroom, and it was highly recommended not to go near them);

2. A half-hour walk in the fresh air every day at noon, in fair weather or foul.

Mademoiselle Laramée was quick to notice how things were with Charles and conceived for him a strong and somewhat demanding affection, one that was something of a burden for the boy. With her encouragement, however, he began to show great progress. While his fellow pupils were still struggling with *ba, be, bi, bo, bu*, he was working on *bat, bed, big, bog*, and *bug*, looking ahead to *ball, bell, bill*, and *bull*, and even inching towards *call* and *cocoa*. While the others were snapping their pencil leads trying to twist the numerals 5 and 8 into shapes resembling pieces of tortured metal, Charles was already working on the fundamentals of addition.

"God put a good head on your shoulders," Mademoiselle Laramée would tell him in a low voice, leaning over his desk. "You must thank Him and work hard to fill it up."

Two or three other pupils provided him with a certain amount of competition, but generally it was Charles who came out ahead. Henri knocked himself out trying to keep up, but was always a lesson or two behind his friend.

Such circumstances could easily lead to jealousy, but not in this case. Ginette Laramée, pedagogical magician that she was, took great care to spread her praise and encouragement around the classroom as equitably as possible, so that at the end of the day each pupil was pleased with his or her own efforts, which made it almost impossible to be jealous of Charles's.

After several weeks of school, Charles's soul underwent a delicious expansion. Far removed from the stifling, vaguely menacing atmosphere that prevailed at home, for a few hours a day he became once again the happy, high-spirited little boy he'd been when Alice was alive. His successes filled him with a sense of satisfaction that was as new as it was uplifting, although he quickly learned that in order for them to be accepted he would have to be modest about them – braggarts attracted only mockery and punches – and not only modest but also generous and useful, sometimes even flattering. He had to avoid being called a sissy; a certain roughness in his manner went a long way towards giving him a kind of cachet. It was also important to keep a healthy distance between himself and the teacher at all costs – he was always careful to keep his back to her – so as to avoid being labelled her pet, a disgrace from which it seemed no one ever recovered.

Because of that, and also because he could never contain the extraordinary pleasure he felt at being in school, he became the class clown. Even in that he was more or less successful; grimaces and contortions when Mademoiselle Laramée's back was turned, animal impersonations, pretended idiocy or deafness, and so on. Such goings-on required a great deal of skill, since Ginette Laramée had a sharp eye and a low tolerance for lapses in discipline. Sometimes, however, he made even her laugh, which made his indiscretions all the sweeter.

One day, however, he stepped over the line, and the teacher, furious, shook him by one ear until it turned bright red, and tears came to his eyes.

"You will stay in after school," she told him. "You and I need to talk."

To save face he managed to give a little smirk of defiance, but inside he was shaking so badly he could hardly focus on what was left of the lesson.

"If you continue to act up in class," she warned him when the last pupil had left for the day, "I'm going to have to tell your mother."

"I don't have a mother, Mademoiselle," he said.

"You don't?"

"She died. Three years ago."

"You poor child," she murmured.

Charles looked up at her, surprised by her tone. There was pity in it, but also a sort of judgment (or so it seemed to him), as though she'd just discovered he was lame or had wet his pants.

She chided him a bit for his conduct, but gently, without conviction, as though the worst punishment he could receive had already been inflicted on him. Then she let him go.

He left the school with head bowed, dragging his feet, overcome by dark thoughts. Once again, Alice's death had come back to haunt him. Why did she have to leave him like this, he asked himself angrily. Caught between a father who didn't love him and a woman who couldn't care less if he were dead or alive? He was nothing but an orphan, a sort of walking disaster, who would never amount to anything because there was no one to help him along.

When he got home, the apartment was empty. Sylvie was at the restaurant, where he would go later for dinner, and his father wouldn't be home until later that night. But the happy, frenetic barking that came from the backyard told him that Boff was waiting for him.

He ran outside and let the dog off his leash, and Boff jumped on him and licked him with all eighteen paws and twenty-eight tongues, exhilarated by the greatest happiness he had ever known. He had spent hours in solitude, beset by dark wings whirling above his head that had made him despair of ever again seeing his cherished master. Despite the hunger that was gnawing at his stomach, Charles decided not to go to the restaurant, where Rosalie would have set aside a glass of milk and two Vachon cakes for him; he didn't want to see anyone, least of all Sylvie. Instead, he made himself a peanut-butter sandwich, part of which he gave to the dog.

"Come on, Boff," he called, running down the hallway, "let's go outside and see what's up."

There were no children in the street; Henri must have been doing his homework early so he could have the evening to himself, but Charles wasn't in the mood to see him anyway. He wandered aimlessly about the neighbourhood, closely followed by Boff, who sniffed at everything with great interest. Eventually he found himself in front of his old daycare. The play area was empty, but he could hear children's voices inside. He thought of going in to say hello to Mélanie, but he didn't: she would probably find such a visit strange, and anyway he didn't know what he would say to her.

He quietly opened the gate and, staying close to the wall, turned towards the play area, most of which was behind the building. Suddenly he understood why his steps had brought him to this place.

"Come here, Boff," he murmured, turning towards the dog. "I want to show you something."

Looking around to make sure no one was watching, he quickly moved towards the old cherry tree. A small shed in which various play accessories were stored shielded him from view from the building. With Boff watching closely, he knelt down and gently stroked the ground between two large roots that ran along the surface.

"Do you remember that little yellow dog I wanted to save a long time ago, when it was snowing? He was tired and sick and he couldn't stop shaking because he was soaking wet. It was the first time I'd seen him. He was so sad-looking. He died shortly after that. I was very sad and I asked if we could bury him here, just under where my hand is. He's right there, close to us. We can stay here for a while with him. Do you want to, Boff?"

Charles sat down between the roots and crossed his legs; Boff quickly came over and licked his cheek, then lay down beside him, his tail thumping quietly against the ground in a regular rhythm.

Suddenly Charles sensed a strange presence nearby, and a delicious feeling of peace came over him. He looked around and saw nothing out of the ordinary, but he knew that something was keeping him company, an invisible friend who had been waiting for him for a long time, and he knew it was the little yellow dog even though he had hardly known it, and despite the fact that its life had ended so soon after being brought in from the cold. But he realized, with a quiet sort of joy, that death had not completely separated them. He sat with his eyes half closed, Boff's warm body pressed against his leg, Boff himself going to sleep, his muzzle flat on the ground, the breath coming through his nostrils ruffling a few dry blades of grass in front of him.

"My little yellow dog," Charles murmured after a moment, "I'll come back to visit you often, I promise. Maybe you can tell me where Mama is?"

■ ■ ■

Charles wasn't the only one to suffer from bouts of sadness. Boff was subject to them as well. He had worries of his own, in a doggy sort of way. When his previous cruel and uncaring owners had abandoned him, they'd left him out in the cold, without food, alone and vulnerable to all the dangers that went with a nomadic, unprotected life. But although they didn't know it, they had also given him a magnificent gift: his freedom. For a year he had lived a life of pain and misery, dirty, reduced to skin and bones, obsessed with finding food, the target of a myriad bites and kicks, cars lunging at him from out of nowhere, well-intentioned idiots chasing him in order to bring him to the pound (they even caught him once, but he made a miraculous get-away). But still, despite all that, he had had his liberty. The only rules he had to follow were those of caution. As long as he was careful he could go where he wanted and do what he liked. Since coming to live with Charles, however, it was a whole new ball game.

Nothing would ever make him leave Charles, who was the love of his life, the sole source of all his joy. Three squares a day and a warm place to sleep weren't bad, either, not to mention the little metal tag around his neck that seemed to change the way people behaved towards him. But living in an apartment with only a small fenced-in yard behind it, after having known the freedom of wide open spaces, could make a day seem long! And on top of that he had to get used to other people's schedules: for several weeks now Charles had been leaving him alone for hours while he went to that school of his, where no dog could follow. He'd tried it one morning, slipping out of the apartment when the door was partly open. All he'd got for his trouble was a sharp word from Charles and a clip on the head from Sylvie, who was furious at having to run down the street after him in her housecoat and slippers with the whole neighbourhood watching. When she caught up with him, she almost bumped into Monsieur Morin, an old regular at Chez Robert, who took two steps back, eyes widening, hands on his hips, nose in the air, and lips curled in disgust, as though to say: "Aha, taken to working the streets, now, have we?"

"I'll get you for this," she'd hissed to the dog, dragging him up the stairs by the collar.

On the landing she gave him such a sharp whack that he'd bitten his own tongue, then she shut him up in the kitchen; five minutes later, when she'd finished getting ready for work, she left to go to the restaurant.

■ ■ ■

Boff circled the room, still in a foul mood. Someone had left a loaf of bread on the table in its plastic bag. He jumped up on a chair, pulled the bread off the table onto the floor, then shook it out of its bag and ate the whole thing. After that he felt heavy and uncomfortable, so he lay down on his blanket beside the refrigerator and had a long nap. When he woke up, he felt much perkier, but his honour was still outraged at the treatment he had received. Looking around, he sought a new outlet for his vengeance.

There was a washer and dryer at the rear of the kitchen, beside the back door. The dryer door was wide open, and inside he could see a pile of clothing. Boff got up, put his head through the opening and brought out three pairs of boxer shorts, seven socks, two face cloths and a towel, each of which he meticulously tore to shreds; the only thing he left untouched was a sweater belonging to Charles.

He was thirsty after his labours, so he drank some water from his bowl. Then he spied a magazine that had been left on the counter. With his paw he flicked it onto the floor and chewed it, slowly, reducing it to a pulp; he enjoyed the taste of coated paper and was sorry that there were no other magazines lying around. He thought of taking another nap, but the anger that his imprisonment stirred up in him continued to grind away at his molars. When Sylvie, taking advantage of a mid-afternoon lull, ran back to the apartment to change her stained blouse, he had attacked the bottom of the door that gave out onto the backyard and nearly chewed his way through it.

Despite Charles's worst fears, Wilfrid did not ban the dog from the house, nor did he talk of beating him; all things considered, he took it fairly calmly. He contented himself with grabbing the animal by both ears and staring into its eyes, muttering nasty threats, but that was all.

It was Wilfrid's pride that made him hold back his anger – after all, he was the one who had let the dog into the house in the first place. He also wanted to lay Sylvie's pessimistic predictions to rest. Charles would have liked to think it was also partly out of love for him, too, that his father must have sensed that the boy would never have got over the dog's loss.

From that day on, however, whenever no one was home, Boff was confined to the small backyard, attached to a chain, the chain to the clothesline. The hardware-store owner Fafard very generously gave them an old doghouse that had been gathering dust in the back of his garage. Charles was given the task of putting the dog on the chain the first time. He made Boff sit down in front of the doghouse, attached the chain to his collar, and explained to him carefully that there could be no barking or else their days together were numbered.

63

Boff listened, gently wagging his tail, then shook his head vigorously and sneezed twice, which Charles interpreted as a sign of agreement.

After barking for a few minutes anyway (to save face), Boff decided it was time to chew on the corner of his house. But he soon stopped, no doubt thinking that if he totally destroyed it, it would be held against him. After a few days he had become philosophical about his lot. However, word of his new situation spread quickly among the other dogs in the neighbourhood. Since the far end of the yard was enclosed by a dilapidated fence that was full of holes, it was easy for the smallest dogs to squeeze under a half-nailed board in order to visit him, which Boff appreciated greatly; these marks of friendship, however, were small recompense for the absence of his young master. Weekends and the hour when Charles returned from school were for him times of the wildest happiness.

Although Charles didn't realize it at the time, the incident in the kitchen was the beginning of a long, hard-fought battle between Boff and Wilfrid, a conflict that would have memorable consequences for the boy's future.

■ ■ ■

Charles gobbled up school as though it were a bar of milk chocolate. One November morning, with a cup of tea in one hand and a cookie in the other, Mademoiselle Laramée declared to her colleagues in the staff room that Charles was the best student in her class, the best student she had had in a long time, and that with a bit of luck and a lot of guidance he could "go far."

"His only problem," she said a little worriedly, "is that the rest of the class isn't moving ahead fast enough for him. He could easily become bored. But I try to keep him busy."

From then on, whenever Charles was seen in the school corridors, he was favoured by well-wishing smiles from all the teachers, and even the occasional affectionate pat on the head or shoulder. He felt a great deal of respect coming his way, and even began to consider himself as someone important enough to deserve it. He took care to hide these attentions from the other pupils, since despite his efforts to be accommodating and good company with his friends, he sometimes saw the glint of jealousy in their eyes.

One afternoon after school, when Charles and Henri had gone to see the huge Frontenac Towers construction project on rue Bercy, Fats Dubé, who was famous in the class for his ability to fart on demand, as well as for his total uselessness at anything else, came up to Charles with a smirk, after exchanging significant glances with two of his friends.

"Hey, Thibodeau," he said, "what did you get in dictation this morning?"

"Nine out of ten," Charles replied, then ill-advisedly added: "I came first."

"Oh, wow," said Fats Dubé's two companions, mockingly. "Aren't you the cat's ass!"

Henri, who sensed something ominous in the air, gave Charles a discreet poke in the ribs to let him know it was time to leave. But Fats Dubé planted himself in front of Charles.

"You know why he's so smart?" Fats asked, looking Charles straight in the eye with a sardonic smile. "It's because he's a queer. Queers always do good in school. Don't they, Thibodeau?"

Charles had only a vague idea of what he had just been called might mean, but he knew it was something outrageous, and his face tightened with anger.

"What have I done to you, you big tub of lard? Why don't you go home and let your mother change your diapers?"

Fats threw himself on Charles, and the two of them rolled around on the sidewalk. His two friends charged Henri at the same time; one of them soon fell back, holding his stomach with both hands (Henri was known for his wicked kick); the other, alarmed, beat a hasty retreat, but when he saw a broken tree branch on the ground, he picked it up and returned to the fray.

"Aha, so you want to fight dirty, eh!" cried Henri, who loved a good battle.

He charged the boy with a wild cry; the branch struck him on the shoulder but, ignoring the pain, he let fly a punch that caught his assailant so squarely in the eye it made him drop his weapon and suddenly think of a very important thing he had to do somewhere else.

Charles, meanwhile, was huffing and puffing beneath his potbellied adversary, who was using his bulk to keep him flat on the ground while he shouted curses at him and dug his thumbs into his eyes. Charles succeeded in freeing one arm and was valiantly trying to tear off one of Fats's ears when Henri ran up with the branch and, inserting it between Fats's back and his school bag, used it as a lever to pry the bully off Charles. The battle was over.

When Rosalie saw Charles through the window of the restaurant, she ran out immediately.

"What in the world happened to you, you poor thing? It looks like you've gone through a snowblower! Have you been in a fight or something?"

"I didn't start it," Charles said, tearfully.

She brought him inside and took him into the washroom, where she gave him a quick wash and put a Band-Aid on his elbow.

"Gracious God in Heaven! And here was me thinking you were such a quiet little boy. Just look at you!"

"I *am* a quiet little boy," Charles sobbed. "Fats Dubé picked on me for nothing. I never did anything!"

Sylvie, who was busy serving a customer, merely wrinkled her eyebrows and went on with her work.

"Go home and change," she told him when he came back into the dining room. "Look at your sweater, it's torn. We'll have to throw it out. I'm ashamed of you. I can't wait to see what your father's going to say when he sees that."

■ ■ ■

Since Charles had been going to school Rosalie's affection for him had blossomed into a deep admiration. The boy came to the restaurant every day after school for his supper, and would sit at an empty table to do his homework or go over his lessons. Rosalie had always wished she had "learned how to write better," and blamed her parents for not making her study harder "when it would've made a difference." At first she thought he was rushing through his work so as to get outside quickly to play with Boff and Henri, but one night she sat next to him and watched what he was doing. The beauty of his handwriting, the ease with which he read his lessons, his skill at addition and subtraction (a skill that even at her age required a great deal of concentration) plunged her into a bottomless well of wonderment.

"He's a genius, that boy," she remarked one evening to Sylvie. "He's got two heads rolled up in one!"

Sylvie smiled as though she were the one being praised, but she couldn't help replying:

"Not hard to tell you don't live with him . . . You'd sing a different song then, let me tell you. Last night I practically had to drag him off to bed."

■ ■ ■

The Fats Dubé episode made Charles do some hard thinking. He discovered to his horror the exact meaning of the word *queer*, and decided he would nip his reputation for being one in the bud. Following Henri's example, he leapt at every opportunity to fight with the other children in his class, even provoking fights when none seemed on offer. As a result, he spent a lot of time in the principal's office. He even managed to punch Fats Dubé in the eye twice, right in the schoolyard, which earned him some respect among his peers and inspired the flatulent virtuoso to find himself another punching bag.

Above all he set about minimizing his scholarly successes in the eyes of the other pupils. He pretended complete indifference towards his studies, which he in fact adored. Mademoiselle Laramée, who saw through this ruse, sighed deeply for him but refrained from stepping in, contenting herself with encouraging his progress without making too great a fuss over it.

Her meeting with Wilfrid at the end of the semester did not leave her with a favourable impression of the carpenter; she found him crude, coarse – and smelling of beer (which to her was the purest essence of debauchery). Wilfrid obviously considered the meeting a waste of time and gave only a cursory glance at his son's report, which she placed on the table in front of him before beginning their discussion. But when she stated that Charles was doing very well in class and even appeared to be an exceptionally gifted pupil, his face brightened.

"We've always had a good head for figures in our family," he said. "Charles is a real Thibodeau."

"I trust you're doing your best for him. A child like Charles is a gift from God, you know."

"Yeah, yeah, we're doing everything we can, don't worry."

Then his eyes went dull again and drifted towards the clock.

■ ■ ■

Ginette Laramée's worst fears were confirmed: towards the end of the school year Charles began to be bored in class. He yawned during the sometimes interminably repetitive explanations she had to give to the class dunces, which he had understood the first time, and he became more and more restless. Or else he fell into an absent reverie, gazing out the window, seemingly soaring off to some faraway land. One day she caught him with a knife, carving a word into the top of his desk: Boff.

Her hand fell on the back of his neck, and she shook the child briskly.

"Exactly *what* is that, young man?"

"It's the name of my dog, Mademoiselle," he replied, smiling angelically. The class broke into loud laughter.

"Very funny. If you go on behaving like this, you'll end up in the doghouse yourself."

And for the first time she made him stand in the corner with his face turned towards the wall.

Out of desperation, not knowing any other way to keep his flagging interest alive, she decided to start a *Class Journal*, and named him Editor-in-Chief. He was given permission to attend to his professional duties during class, as long as he had finished his regular work. She thought that would keep him occupied until June. The day the report cards were handed out – which was also the first day of summer vacation – Charles ended up first in the class, far ahead of the others, despite the extra work.

That afternoon Mademoiselle Laramée handed out small gifts to the students. She also had them draw prizes from a box. Henri pulled out a fluorescent green ball, Charles a small plastic truck. Just before three o'clock the pupils were given permission to leave early; the halls filled with the sound of running feet and the stairwells rang with excited voices. There was a traffic jam outside Mademoiselle Laramée's classroom. Charles was about to thrust his way into it when the teacher called him back.

"Charles," she said, smiling tightly, "I have a special gift for you."

Charles let out a cry of joy and tore at the wrapping. It was a book.

"*Alice's Advan . . .*"

"Adventures," corrected the teacher.

". . . *in Wonderland.*"

He looked up at her, his face smiling but serious.

"Alice . . . that was my mother's name," he said.

"I know."

The woman's face tightened even more, and the corners of her mouth began to twitch.

"Thank you very much, Mademoiselle. It's a beautiful book. I'll start reading it tonight, or maybe tomorrow, but no later than that."

"I think you'll like it. I bought you a children's edition, of course. If you stumble over any words you can ask someone to help you with them. But I don't think there'll be many."

"Yes, Mademoiselle."

The classroom was empty. Henri was impatiently waiting for him out in the hall.

"Have a good vacation. Have fun. And come back to us in September in good health."

With these words Mademoiselle Laramée's face softened, and she gave Charles a warm hug.

Taken aback, Charles retreated several steps, waved awkwardly, then ran out of the room.

8

His second year at Saint-Anselme Elementary was an almost unmitigated disaster. He'd been happily expecting to see Mademoiselle Laramée again at the head of his classroom. Instead, his new teacher was Séverine Cotruche.

Madame Cotruche was of medium build, a bit on the heavy side, with varicose veins in her calves, hair like steel wool tied up in a bun, elbows constantly in motion (often requiring dexterity to get out of their way), and magnificent blue eyes meant to express adoration but more often reflecting a severe and narrow-minded gravity; she was married, the mother of three children, and had the maternal instincts of a telephone pole. She had been a teacher at Saint-Anselme for twenty years, twenty years she considered to have been totally wasted – an opinion that would have been shared by her pupils, if anyone had asked them. Like most of the other teachers, she had heard Mademoiselle Laramée singing Charles's praises, but she had also heard about the boy's tendency to wildness and smart-ass tricks, his ability to turn a classroom upside down if he weren't dealt with firmly and with a great deal of imagination.

"I'll bring him down a peg or two if he tries any of his shenanigans on me," she promised herself the day school resumed, watching Charles as he took his seat and exchanged greetings with his neighbours; when he looked up at her, she was sure she saw a distinct shiftiness in his eyes.

The first days of the school year are generally peaceful; teachers and pupils use them to get to know one another, establish alliances, detect secret weaknesses. In Grade Two, however, the terror of the unknown that had pumped through so many young breasts the year before, had turned so many throats to cardboard and sometimes brought tears to their eyes, were long forgotten. A child of seven or eight already considers himself a veteran and looks disdainfully down upon the timidity of those just beginning their academic careers. Madame Cotruche's reputation had preceded her. Most of the pupils hated her before they even met her, and with the others the honeymoon lasted only a day or two; by Thursday of that first week, her piercing, exasperated voice was already resounding in the classroom.

Charles hated her as much as the other pupils, and he resolved to let her know it. On Friday he had his first detention. On Monday he was sent to the principal's office, and the next day had to copy out fifty times: "I am an idiot who laughs at everything." Three months later his report card showed that he was barely keeping up.

A truce was arranged, organized secretly by Mademoiselle Laramée, who called Charles into her classroom after school one afternoon and tried to get him to control his displeasure. "Listen, Charles," she told him, "in Grade Three you'll have Madame Dupuis and Mademoiselle Deneault, both of whom are kind and good teachers. And they can't wait to have you in their class. Force yourself to be good, my dear. Ten weeks isn't so long." The next day, apropos of nothing, she told Madame Cotruche about Charles's lamentable home life, about which she'd learned from the boy himself, and succeeded in winning her over somewhat by making a few pointed references to the teacher's "vast experience and excellent pedagogical judgment."

In December, Charles checked his headlong descent to the bottom of the class and ended the term with creditable results. But on January 6, 1975, everything came apart.

■ ■ ■

The week started badly. A wave of intense cold descended over the city, and the reports said it would set record lows and last for several days. Every day after school, Charles found Boff half frozen to death in his doghouse and begged his father to let the dog stay inside until the cold front had passed. But Wilfrid stuck to his guns:

"What, so he can destroy the rest of the place? A dog's a dog, it's used to being miserable. He's lived outside for years and it hasn't killed him. I don't want to hear any more about it."

Finally, at the suggestion of Monsieur Fafard, whose son Henri had told him about Charles's problem, Wilfrid agreed to install a hundred-watt light

71

bulb in Boff's doghouse, beneath a false floor, thereby affording the dog a modicum of warmth. With his usual helpfulness, Fafard even chipped in an extension cord. Boff no longer shivered, but he still kept an envious eye on the apartment windows.

The day after the light bulb was installed, coming back from the Fafards' with his young master, the dog found a package of rotten meat in a garbage can and swallowed it in a single gulp. Two hours later he was seized by a sudden bout of diarrhea that threatened to turn him inside out. There was no point in even trying to have the dog stay inside until he was better. Charles stood by the kitchen window and looked down at his pet, slumped in the doghouse in the middle of the snow-covered yard, surrounded by yellowish splotches that bore mute testimony to the violent upheavals that were taking place within the poor spaniel's intestinal tract. Neither was there any use in pleading to take the dog to a vet; Wilfrid had already declared that vets were too expensive.

"If he dies, I'll get you another one. It's not as if there's a shortage of stray dogs in Montreal."

And so it was that when Charles arrived at school he was already in such a state of frustration and worry that it was impossible for him to remain quiet or still for more than two minutes at a time. In order to dispel the anguish that was wracking his guts, he decided to become the funniest kid in the world. His first attempts were received with varying degrees of success, but at nine-forty-five, taking advantage of Madame Cotruche's turned back, he threw a piece of chalk that hit her square in the back of the neck and propelled her into a fit of sneezing that went on for a good ten minutes.

This was followed by an unprecedented flurry of jubilation in the class. Half an hour later, Sylvie received a telephone call from the school principal, telling her that Charles's behaviour in class was causing them more and more concern.

"I would like to meet with you to discuss this problem," he added.

"He's not my kid. Talk to his father. I've put up with enough already."

When Wilfrid arrived home at five o'clock, Sylvie told him what had happened. Charles, shaking with fear, had shut himself in his room. The carpenter's face turned a dangerous shade of red, but he managed to keep himself under control.

"Bring him out here," he said to Sylvie.

Charles stood in front of his father, breathing rapidly, his bowels turning to water, but with a tiny smile of defiance on his lips.

"I promised myself I wouldn't hit you again," his father said in a heavy, almost lazy voice, "but you don't leave me any choice. Come here. I said, Come here!"

And he smacked Charles across the face so hard that the boy was thrown back against the wall.

Charles bit his lip and leaned against the wall, his face scarlet and twisted with pain. Then he burst into sobs and ran back to his room.

Wilfrid sat down at the kitchen table and stared at the counter, a strange expression on his face. Sylvie took the chair across from him and lit a cigarette.

"A bit heavy-handed, don't you think?" she said after a pause. "You're going to end up turning him against you for good."

"He's already turned against me."

"You could find some other way to punish him. After all, he's only eight."

"I don't know any other way to put the pig-headed little bugger in his place. You saw the way he looked at me when he came out of his room! He was mocking me! You said yourself he's been sent to the principal's office three times already this month. When I was his age, my parents woulda beat the living crap outta me for a quarter of what he gets away with. And I toed the line at school. The teachers were hardly aware I was there. I did my homework, I learned my lessons, and I minded my own business."

Sylvie, shaken, nodded slightly and stood up, having remembered that it was time to get supper ready.

Charles appeared at the kitchen door in a state of tearful fury aimed at both of them; his cheek was bright red and so swollen that his whole face looked off-kilter.

"I'm not eating with you! I'm leaving this place! I don't want to see either of you again! Do you understand! I don't want to see you ever again!"

And he turned and ran to the vestibule. Wilfrid jumped up to go after him, but Sylvie held him back.

"Let him go," she said quietly. "He's had his say. The cold will bring him back soon enough."

Charles, crying at full throttle now, pulled on his coat and boots and went slowly down the stairs. The porch steps were coated with ice and a glacial wind wrapped itself cruelly around his tense body, making him feel even stiffer.

But his cheek hurt less in the cold air; a violent shiver went through him, slowing him down a bit.

Reaching the sidewalk, he turned towards rue Ontario, passed the restaurant without looking in, and turned left into the alley that ran behind his building. He soon found himself at the fence at the back of his yard; Boff was on the other side, maybe dying of cold. Lifting a large board, Charles crawled into the yard and ran to the doghouse. Seeing him, the animal raised its head and feebly wagged its tail, not having enough strength to stand.

Kneeling down, Charles wrapped Boff in his arms and cried. Suddenly he came to a decision. He undid the dog's collar, slid his hands under its chest, and, lifting it up, carried it with difficulty to the gate and out of the yard. In a few minutes he was in front of the Fafards' house. He climbed heavily up the front steps and, freeing one hand, pressed the doorbell.

When the door opened, it was Céline, Henri's sister, who was standing there. He barely knew Céline, had spoken to her only two or three times, in the way boys have of showing supreme indifference to girls their own age.

"What do you want?" she asked. "Are you giving us a dog? Quick, come inside. It's freezing!"

He followed her in, his bravado suddenly fading; the warmth made his cheek throb again. There was the sound of voices and laughter coming from the kitchen.

"What's wrong with Boff?" Céline asked, standing in front of him.

"He's sick."

She put her face close to him and then recoiled:

"Phew! He stinks!"

Boff gave a small whimper and shifted in Charles's arms. Charles put him down on the rug.

"I came to see Henri."

Céline looked down at the dog, which was lying slumped on the rug looking half dead, then ran off towards the kitchen. After a moment her father came out to the hallway, an apron wrapped around his waist.

"Well, look who's here! How's it going, Charles?"

"Okay," Charles said, smiling with some difficulty. "But Boff has diarrhea. He's very sick." Then, some of his courage having returned, he added: "Could you keep him here with you for a while, Monsieur Fafard, until he gets better?

My father won't let him in the house. But he's so weak he'll die if we leave him out in the cold."

The hardware-store owner bent down to look at the dog and stopped when he caught sight of Charles's face.

"Great balls of fire! What's happened to your cheek?"

Charles looked away.

"I fell."

Fernand kept looking at him.

"Must have been a strange kind of fall," he couldn't help remarking, but seeing Charles's discomfort he decided not to press it. "Hmm. He doesn't look too-too good, your Boff . . . What's wrong with him?"

"He ate some bad meat he found in the garbage."

"Oh-oh. Maybe he should be looked at by a vet, eh?"

"I don't have any money," Charles said, sobs filling his throat.

"There there there, no need to cry. Makes the devil laugh, as my father used to say. All in good time. First we'll take him down to the basement, let him lie beside the furnace, he'll be snug as a bug in a rug, eh, Boff? Then we'll make a little phone call."

Lucie Fafard came out to the hallway, attracted by the conversation. Seeing Charles she stopped short and brought her hands to her mouth; a discreet sign from her husband, however, told her that it was better to say nothing for the moment.

Boff, his energy renewed by the warmth of the house, had managed to get on his feet and was sniffing the carpet.

"Hey!" cried Henri, suddenly appearing behind his mother, followed by Céline, "what's up with you, Charles? What's wrong with . . ."

"Everything's okay," Fernand cut in. "Right now we're taking care of Boff. He doesn't look as though he's going to do much running around, poor guy!"

And taking the dog in his arms, not without a slight grimace, he made his way down to the basement while his two children stayed upstairs, looking at Charles with some concern but without speaking; Charles followed their father, still fighting back tears.

As soon as he was placed on a blanket, Boff fell asleep, his muzzle resting on his forepaws. While he slept, Monsieur Fafard telephoned the veterinary clinic on de Maisonneuve – the doctor there was one of his customers. Their conversation was rapid and friendly. Both men shared a sense of humour, a love of efficiency, and a horror of small talk.

"Has he thrown up at all, your Boff?" the hardware-store owner asked Charles when he hung up. "No? Good. We'll give him something to drink right away, since his bowels must be as dry as baking soda. Lucie, go look in the bathroom cabinet and see if we have any Kao Pectate. That'll coat the lining of his intestines. And Imodium, too; that ought to put a cork in him."

Gendron, the veterinarian, had said that if the dog was still sick after twenty-four hours, it would require treatment, but that would mean taking it down to the clinic.

A few minutes later, Boff was able to swallow two tablespoons of a grey liquid that he didn't seem to like very much; a bowl of Seven-Up made him forget it soon enough. Meanwhile, Henri ran to the corner drugstore for a package of Imodium.

Charles began to feel better himself; he sat in a rocking chair watching Madame Fafard finish preparing supper. From time to time, when her back was turned, he brought his hand up to his face and rubbed his sore cheek.

Lucie Fafard was as taken aback by the look of profound sadness in Charles's eyes as she was by his face. Smoothing the pan of mashed potatoes with a spatula, she tried to sort out the welter of contradictory thoughts that kept springing up in her head, in order to come to at least a temporary solution to the problems that the boy in her kitchen was facing. He was clearly being put to more tests than one child should have to undergo.

"So, Charles," she said, turning towards him, "would you like to stay for supper? I know how much you like chicken pot pie."

A hungry smile spread over the boy's face, making him forget his swollen jaw, but it soon disappeared.

"I have to ask Sylvie or my father, first," he said. "But I'm pretty sure they'll say it's okay."

"Would you like me to phone them?"

He nodded his head vigorously.

"Just a minute, please," Sylvie said dryly when she heard her neighbour's voice on the phone, "I'll ask Wilfrid."

She put her hand over the receiver.

Lucie tried to make out the ensuing conversation between Sylvie and Wilfrid, but to no avail. She kept her eye on Charles, who was watching her with an anxious look.

"It's all right, he can stay," Sylvie said, "but only if he gets back here by seven o'clock sharp to do his homework."

And she hung up.

"I'll bet he's over there spilling his guts out to the Fafards," Sylvie said to Wilfrid, who, standing at the kitchen window, had just noticed that Boff was gone. "Some reputation we'll have after this! You should learn to control those fists of yours one of these days, eh?"

■ ■ ■

Two days later, Boff had completely recovered and was able to move back into his doghouse. A truce was again in effect between Charles and his father. To Madame Cotruche's amazement, Charles was a model student for a week. With Boff out of danger, Charles's naturally calm nature returned and with it some of his enthusiasm for school. But the smack across the face and the rescue of his dog through the good graces of the Fafards marked a change in his life.

He began to eat more and more of his meals at their house and even, one or two nights a week, got into the habit of doing his homework and going over his lessons with Henri, under Lucie's discreet but efficient eye. After some initial misgivings, Sylvie and Wilfrid ended up accepting the new arrangement. If nothing else, it relieved them of a huge burden.

Fernand and Lucie could easily see that the child was unhappy at home and had probably been the victim of a great many other abuses they couldn't bear to think about. But Charles was incredibly secretive and wily for a child his age, and assiduously avoided their questions. Without proof, they were hesitant to lodge any specific complaints.

Weeks went by. Charles suffered through the inferno of Madame Cotruche's class as best he could. Slaps to the back of his head and banishment to the hallway alternated with scoldings, detentions, all endured to the tune of the teacher's incensed, high-pitched, eternally dissatisfied voice, the voice of one who regarded her tenure as a teacher as a kind of penance, and who had decided to pass her own misery on to her pupils. At times, however, she

77

could achieve an almost miraculous, Sargasso-like calm: for an hour or even two the acid that usually flowed through her veins seemed to have been transformed into human blood. Her voice came down a few decibels, and she seemed patient with and even attentive to her charges. At such times she even displayed a sense of humour!

Thus it was that one morning, on a Friday in March, she brought into the classroom an enormous book with a stiff cover held together by chrome rings, and the children discovered to their stupefaction that their teacher was a passionate stamp collector. "I am a philatelist," she announced with pride. "That means a stamp collector. I collect all the stamps I can find, especially those that interest me."

The previous day, after school, the janitor had placed a large cardboard box on her desk that had had the pupils guessing. Now she opened the box and took out a projector. She asked one of the children to plug it in, then drew the curtains on the two classroom windows (the resulting darkness did not impair in the slightest her ability to see everything the pupils were doing, and everyone knew it), and took the entire class on a voyage around the world and through layers of history that held each of them motionless until recess. Charles bombarded her with questions throughout the whole film, and she even took one or two of them seriously. When the lights were on again, Charles approached her desk.

"When I get bigger, I'm going to collect stamps, too," he said.

"Well, good for you. If you could manage to interest yourself in something intelligent for a change, it would be a pleasant surprise to us all."

"But I am interested in something intelligent," Charles replied, crushed by her remark.

"Oh? Such as what?"

He hesitated, asking himself whether this loud-mouthed slapping machine deserved to be taken into his confidence; then someone called him and he turned on his heels and ran off without bothering to give her an answer.

That afternoon, when he left school with Henri, he was seized with such joy at the thought that the school week was over that he invited Henri into the Chez Robert for a treat.

"On me," he said.

His friend looked at him incredulously:

"You have money?"

"I've only got twenty cents, but watch me. I'll fix us up."

Walking ahead of his friend, he pushed open the door to the restaurant and went in with that air of nonchalant pride that children often show when they have gained a measure of familiarity with certain generous adults. At the far end of the room two women in their forties were leaning towards each other, talking together in low and mysterious tones. Near the window, an elderly man in a tie and with a large birthmark on his right cheek, his coat propped up on the chair across from him, was playing solitaire beside a cup of coffee. Monsieur Victoire was sitting at the counter chatting up Liette, guffawing loudly while she washed dishes, blushing with pleasure. Sylvie, her mind elsewhere, was wiping the counter with a cloth, making large circular movements as though they were part of a dance. Charles walked past her as though he didn't see her, went up to the cash where Rosalie was adding up a pile of receipts, and started a brief conversation with her.

Her eyes opened wide in surprise, then she began to laugh:

"Really?" she said. "The same as you?"

He nodded.

"What does he want?" Sylvie asked, turning towards the restaurant owner.

"Oh, nothing, nothing," Rosalie replied. "We're making a deal here."

A few minutes later, when the boys had taken their seats across from each other in a booth, she brought them two cups of hot chocolate and a plate of oatmeal cookies.

"And here's a little something extra," she added, giving Charles a conspiratorial look. From her apron pocket she extracted two Mars bars. "You'd better eat these outside, though," she said, lowering her voice, "or else Sylvie will be after me for spoiling your appetites before supper. When you're finished up here, Charles," she said, speaking loudly again, "would you mind going to the grocery store and getting me a gallon of vinegar . . . and five boxes of toothpicks? After that I might have a pizza delivery you can make, just to the corner, for Monsieur Saint-Amour."

"You see?" Charles said to his friend when Rosalie had left. "I do a few errands for her, she gives me stuff to eat."

Henri was so impressed that when they left the restaurant, he invited Charles to have supper at his place, even to stay the night if he wanted to, an invitation he also extended to Boff.

They would have to ask their parents for permission, of course. But before that the two boys headed off to the grocery store for the vinegar and toothpicks, then they delivered the pizza. In order to get the pizza to Monsieur Saint-Amour when it was still hot, they ran down the street with Charles holding the large, flat box in front of him. Monsieur Saint-Amour was known for giving good tips. Delicious odours issued from the box as he ran. The old man opened the door before they had even rung the bell. He was a retired hairdresser, living in a minuscule two-room apartment in a shabby building on the corner of Frontenac and Bercy; three or four times a week he ordered a pizza with anchovies that Roberto prepared according to his own particular instructions.

"Ah, good. What's this!" he cried in a curiously strained voice. "Two of you now making deliveries?"

Henri blushed. "No, sir. I'm just tagging along."

"All good, all good," replied the old man, looking from one boy to the other with an expression of deep contentment. "Come in, boys, I left my wallet on the dresser."

Charles put the pizza on a table while the old man shuffled over to the dresser. Henri looked in astonishment about the room, which was jam-packed with boxes, pieces of furniture, and knick-knacks of all sorts. Perched atop an enormous china cabinet was a red, plastic rooster, its eye bright with fury, as though it were waiting for an opportunity to throw itself at the television set that was dominating another corner on a mahogany stand.

"There you go," said the old man, handing a five-dollar bill to Charles. "That's for the pizza, and this, this is for you, and for you," he added, handing each boy a quarter.

"Thank you, sir," they said in unison, amazed at such generosity.

Saint-Amour gave them a wide smile, his small grey eyes never leaving the children. "My pleasure, boys," he said. "See you next time."

And he gave Charles's buttocks a quick, furtive caress through the boy's snowsuit.

■ ■ ■

Henri easily obtained permission to ask Charles to stay for supper and also to spend the night.

"But I'm not the only one who gets to decide," Lucie warned them.

To his great delight, Charles also had no trouble getting Sylvie's approval. It would be the first time in his life he had slept over at someone else's house. A feeling of elation spread through him, as though he were setting out on a marvellous adventure. He had always admired the Fafards' house, with its high ceilings, polished wainscotting, and spacious rooms. It was beautiful compared to his own apartment. He quickly ran home to get his things, and a few minutes later presented himself at the Fafards' doorstep, face shining with happiness, his dog at his side and a plastic grocery bag serving as a suitcase.

"Let's go, let's eat. Quick, quick. Sit down!" cried Fernand. "I could eat a whole horse and its cart tonight. Charles, put Boff in the basement, or he'll be bothering you all through the meal."

His hairy forearms resting on the table, Fernand greedily eyed the roast beef surrounded by a ring of carrots and turnip cubes, flanked by a huge plate of mashed potatoes that gave off a delicious odour of nutmeg and melted butter.

Everyone took their place at the table, and the room was soon filled with the sound of clicking silverware. Fernand chewed thick slices of beef with a loud smacking of his lips, talking all the while, obviously in an impish mood, presiding over the meal with a benevolent, patriarchal air – a bit overdone, perhaps, which brought a tolerant smile to his wife's face.

"Quite the appetite on him for a little fella," he said, watching Charles empty his plate. "He does honour to my wife, who has been doing me the honour for twelve years now. Go ahead, Céline, give the boy some more potatoes, it looks like he'll make short work of them, too. What about you, Henri? Go fetch us some milk, this one's about empty."

Céline jumped up and, smiling sweetly at Charles, scooped an enormous spoonful of potatoes onto his plate.

"What have you got for us for dessert, Lucie?" Fernand asked after a moment, leaning back in his chair, his hand covering his mouth to smother a small belch that made no more sound in the room than a passing train would have.

"Chocolate cake."

"Bring it on."

"I'd wait if I were you. You're going to explode. Why don't we have dessert in an hour or so. We'll enjoy it more."

"All right, whatever you say," he sighed. "You're the one who wears the pants in this family. You just roll them up a bit so they don't show under your dress."

"Mama wears pants under her dress?" Céline asked.

"He's just kidding," Henri drawled, looking at his sister condescendingly.

Charles swallowed his last morsel of cake, heaved a long sigh, and turned to Lucie:

"Thank you very much, Madame Fafard. It was delicious, the best supper I've ever had in my life!"

Everyone burst out laughing.

"Well, I can see he's a kid who knows his manners," exclaimed Fernand. "Anyone'd think he was brought up in a palace."

"You can come here for supper any time you like, Charles," said Lucie, ruffling his hair. "There'll always be a place for you here."

When Charles left the table with Henri to go to his friend's room, he was in such a state of bliss that he forgot all about Boff, who was still in the basement; curled up near the furnace, his ears perked, the dog followed each of Charles's footsteps on the floor above his head, tortured by the wish to bark but not daring to do so, knowing he was in foreign territory.

Fernand had set up a camp cot for Charles beside his son's bed. Charles stretched out on it and closed his eyes.

"I'm going to get a good night's sleep," he said to himself after a moment. "I feel better here than in my own bed at home."

He sat up sharply and slid a hand into his bag of overnight things. "I brought something special," he told Henri, his face taking on a serious expression.

He pulled out the copy of *Alice's Adventures in Wonderland* that Mademoiselle Laramée had given him the previous year. It was an abridged version of Lewis Carroll's book; the full-colour illustrations took up most of the space, but there were about ten pages of text. The story of Alice had for some time been part of his interior world. He had flipped through the book any number of times, lost in contemplation of the pictures, which were executed with a blend of fantasy and high realism. Then bit by bit, line by line, he had worked his way through the text. The huge blocks of type had at first daunted him, but he'd persisted until he'd mastered them all, one after the other, sometimes asking Sylvie, rarely his father, to help him when he became stuck on a word. The pages containing illustrations with only five lines of text beneath were like colourful oases rewarding him for his efforts. The delirious logic of the story completely carried him away, although he didn't quite understand why.

It gave him a great deal of pleasure to think of Alice as his mother when she was a young girl, even though it was difficult for him to imagine her that way. He envied the young heroine her extraordinary adventures and secretly hoped that one day he, too, would run into a rabbit sporting a waistcoat and a pocket watch who would drag him down his rabbit-hole to the centre of the Earth. Several passages had particularly appealed to him, and he returned to them often: Alice's slow descent down the well whose walls were lined with cupboards and bookshelves; the time she almost drowned in a pool of her own tears; the episode of the Cheshire Cat, who disappeared into thin air leaving nothing behind but his smile; and her meeting with the Mad Hatter and the March Hare.

He was particularly taken with the Cheshire Cat. He had convinced himself that Boff, who was extremely smart, could with a little training be taught to smile. Several times he had sat in front of the dog and pulled faces, contorting his lips and uttering the most ludicrous sounds, in the hope that Boff would do likewise. One day he even took off his shoes, and with his socks in his mouth crawled about the room on his hands and knees. The dog watched him, its eyes overflowing with tenderness, but contented itself with wagging its tail. "Don't smile with your tail, Boff, smile with your mouth, like this." He demonstrated, spreading wide the corners of his mouth. But Boff, despite the obvious pleasure he took in Charles's shenanigans, did not once smile.

"If you'd like, I could read you some of it," Charles said, opening the book.

After a moment's hesitation Henri nodded, sensing that his friend's offer was more like an order.

Twenty minutes later, Lucie, intrigued by the quiet coming from her son's bedroom, tiptoed quietly to the door.

"He reads like a grown-up," she said to herself after listening for a minute. "A lot better than Henri. With a bit of luck this child will have a future, as sure as God made little green apples."

With his eyes fixed on Charles, Henri was completely caught up in the adventures of Alice, which he already knew from looking at comic books.

From time to time Charles showed him an illustration and then continued reading. They had arrived at the episode of the croquet game when a series of loud barks from the basement suddenly reminded the entire house that a dog's patience, even a dog as accommodating at Boff, had its limits. Going down to get him, Fernand discovered that the dog had chewed on one of the legs of the high chair in which Lucie had learned to use a spoon when she was a baby, and which had since been used by both their children.

"You try that again, you," growled the hardware-store owner, seizing the dog by its ears, "and I'll dip your tail in turpentine and set fire to it!"

■ ■ ■

Grade Two continued to hobble along for Charles under the iron fist of Madame Cotruche, and he finished the year with mediocre results. He did, however, develop a remarkable capacity for smiling while receiving clips to the back of the head or having his ear pinched. And he knew how to instantly stop the teacher's severest yelling fits with a single word.

"What did Jacques Cartier discover in 1534?" she asked one rainy afternoon in June, raising a menacing index finger above the class.

"The Jacques Cartier Bridge," Charles answered.

"You got the knack, Thibodeau," Fats Dubé said to him afterwards, during recess. "I always thought she had her jaws wired shut, but you really cracked her up, she was laughing so hard."

"Yeah, just lucky, I guess," Charles said modestly.

Lady Luck seemed, without any possible doubt, to be smiling on Charles again when, in Grade Three (he was just about to turn nine), he found that Mademoiselle Laramée was no longer teaching the babies in Grade One but had been assigned to his class.

A few weeks after returning to school, Charles gave her a huge thrill. As the bell rang announcing the end of the last class, he approached her desk with a big smile and brought a book out of his school bag. It was *Through the Looking-Glass*, the sequel to *Alice's Adventures in Wonderland*. He had been given it by Sylvie and Wilfrid as a birthday present.

"I've already read it twice," he said proudly. "But I like the book you gave me much better. It's the best book I've ever read!"

"Oh Charles, Charles," she cried, overcome by a fit of maternal lyricism, "if I'd had a boy of my own I would so much have wanted him to be you, no one but you!"

Flushed with pleasure, she combed his hair with her fingers; but then her pedagogical instincts shouldered their way to the fore:

"You read other things, too, I hope?"

"Uh . . . yes. Comic books, mostly."

"Not other books?"

"Yes, some . . . But I really like *Alice*."

"Yes, yes, that's good, *Alice* is a good book, I agree entirely, that's why I gave it to you. But there are many other interesting books out there. Some of them even more interesting than *Alice*! If you want, I'll take you to the library one day."

Charles nodded politely. At the moment, *Alice*, Henri, Boff, and television were more than enough for him.

As it turned out, the most significant event of that year would have nothing to do with reading: it would involve the diabolical resurrection of Boff.

It happened one evening in April 1976. Wilfrid came home around six o'clock in one of those tired, irritable moods that follow a bad day. That afternoon his foreman, after swearing at him in front of his fellow workers, made him take apart a stairway he'd been sweating over for hours. For the first time in his career as a carpenter, he confided to Sylvie, whom he had chosen as a vessel for his furious outpouring, the threat of being fired was hanging over his head. His whole reputation could be ruined. And why? Because the blueprints were drawn up by some greenhorn architect who'd never held a hammer in his life and who knew as much about construction as a whale's ass. They were so totally incomprehensible he'd had to call the architect ten times a day to figure out what the hell they meant.

Charles was listening from his bedroom, lying on his bed beside Boff, who was asleep. He could tell it was going to be a tricky evening. He'd have to tread softly, and maybe quickly.

"Bring me a beer," Wilfrid called to Sylvie.

"Maybe you should eat something first," she replied, also sensing what was in store. "I kept your supper warm."

"I'm not hungry."

There was the sound of a bottle being opened in the kitchen and Wilfrid guzzling a beer. But instead of bringing on a feeling of benign well-being that would lead to the gradual return of good spirits and eventually plunge him into the arms of Morpheus, the alcohol merely exacerbated his foul mood – as well as his thirst! After an hour, Sylvie tried to encourage him to go to bed, but Wilfrid, waving two twenty-dollar bills, stood up, face red as a beet, lips curled into an ugly sneer, and began looking for his coat. He was going to go down to the corner store for a fresh supply of beer. Just then, Boff appeared in the kitchen and quietly crossed over to his bowl. After lapping up a bit of water, he spied Wilfrid's coat, which had fallen off its hook and was lying on the floor beside the dryer, and decided to curl up on it for a short nap.

The volume of the discussion between Wilfrid and Sylvie had risen alarmingly. Sylvie noted with her usual bluntness that Wilfrid's damaged reputation probably had more to do with his numerous mornings-after than with a few criticisms from his foreman.

"If you drank a bit less beer and got a bit more sleep, maybe you wouldn't make so many mistakes building staircases."

Wilfrid stiffened and sucked in his cheeks at the remark, giving his cheekbones a distinctly menacing prominence.

"When I want advice about how to live my life from a goddamn nothing like you, I'll ask for it! If I hadn't picked you up in the restaurant, where do you think you'd be today? Eh?"

This was met by a burst of mocking laughter.

"Right! Where the hell is my goddamn coat?" he yelled, lumbering around the room in search of it. His eye fell on Boff. "What are you doing, you filthy beast? Get the hell off my coat!"

And he buried the toe of his boot in the dog's side. Boff let out a sharp yelp and scurried out of the room. In his anger, however, Wilfrid lost his balance and fell over backwards, banging his head on the corner of the table.

Charles watched the scene in horror from the kitchen doorway. His father, lying on the floor partly stunned, was staring up at the ceiling, muttering incomprehensibly, a dark pool of blood spreading rapidly behind his right shoulder.

"You big oaf!" Sylvie cried, helping him to his feet. "Look what you've done to yourself, losing your temper like that! Have you split your skull open or what? Come here, I'll have to put a bandage on that. You might even have to go to the hospital, you stupid drunk!"

They made their way to the bathroom without noticing Charles. The boy looked at the pool of blood in the middle of the kitchen floor, then at the trail of spots leading to the bathroom, and then went to find Boff. The dog was in the living room, hiding behind a chair; he stared up at Charles with huge, fearful eyes. When Charles tried to touch him, he began to whimper then crawled on his belly into a corner. Distraught, Charles went back to his room and sat on the side of his bed, listening to the conversation coming from the bathroom.

"Ow! That peroxide bloody well hurts!"

"Good. I hope it burns like hell! In fact, hell isn't hot enough for my liking, you asshole!" Sylvie fumed. "And to think you're the head of this household. What kind of example do you think you're setting for your son?"

"Forget the bloody sermon, will you? Ouch! And get a move on with that goddamn bandage. My legs are giving out on me, you're hurting me so much."

"Maybe this'll teach you a lesson! I can just see you at work tomorrow ... you're going to build a staircase upside down!"

When they returned to the kitchen, the first thing Wilfrid did was put on his coat.

"What?" Sylvie cried indignantly, hands on her hips. "Don't tell me you're going to go on drinking after this!"

He turned to her:

"Shut your mouth! I've had enough of you for one night!"

His expression did not invite a reply. She gave a deep sigh, opened the kitchen closet and took out a bucket and mop to clean up the floor.

"Where's my money?" Thibodeau demanded suddenly, lifting up the newspapers that were on the table. He looked all about, anxiously at first, then becoming more and more agitated.

"It was right here a minute ago. Did it fall on the floor?"

Sylvie, bent over beside him with the mop in her hands, remained silent, having decided to sulk.

Wilfrid searched the kitchen high and low. He scanned the floor, pulled out the chairs, looked in the garbage pail, groped in all the nooks and crannies, even opened all the cupboards.

No money.

Furious, he stalked up and down the hall, although he hadn't been there with the money in his hand. Then, turning his head, he saw Boff chewing on something in the living room.

"What have you got there, you!" he cried, suddenly struck by a horrifying thought.

He had barely entered the room when the dog leapt up, squirmed between his legs, and was gone. Unfortunately, he left behind a fragment of chewed-up paper, irrefutable evidence of his revenge. On the scrap of paper Wilfrid made out a bit of Queen Elizabeth's hair and her left eye, which looked a little sad at having been ripped from the royal face.

The carpenter let out a yelp. He held the piece of banknote up to his eye and then at arm's length, as though unable to believe that the object he was holding was anything but a cruel hallucination.

"He . . . he . . . he ate my twenties!" he finally yelled, so choked with rage that the words came out sounding high and screechy. "Sylvie! Come here and look at this! Come here! That goddamned dog ate my money!"

Sylvie appeared in the doorway and looked at the wad of paper that he shoved in her face.

"My, my," she said, barely managing to keep from laughing. "He's pretty quick, too, I'd say. An eye for an eye, a tooth for a tooth, as they say."

The carpenter stared at her, his face turning purple, his cheeks radish red, and his lower jaw quivering.

"Is that all you can say?" he finally spurted. "Forty bucks down the toilet? Easy to see it wasn't you who earned it! I'll give him an eye and a tooth, god-damnit. Charles!" he yelled at the top of his voice. "Bring that dog out here!"

Charles, still sitting on the edge of his bed, had heard everything. His clammy body had become prickly and his insides gurgled. Holding his breath, he stared in mute anguish at Boff, who sat in front of him as though humbly asking for his protection. But there was no protection from his father's fury.

"Charles!" Wilfrid yelled again, his voice sounding demented. "I told you to bring that dog out here!"

Heavy steps came down the hall towards his room, and Wilfrid loomed in the doorway:

"Are you deaf or what?" he shouted, propping himself against the door frame.

"He . . . he doesn't want to come," the child quavered.

"He doesn't want to come?"

"No."

Father and son looked at each other for a moment. Wilfrid blinked and breathed loudly through his nostrils.

"What are you going to do to him?" Charles asked in a whisper.

"I'm going to get rid of him, goddamnit! He just ate my forty bucks! I don't want him here any more. I'm going to take him to the vet's and have

89

him put down. Right now, this minute! I'm going to teach him a lesson he'll never forget!"

At this Charles burst into tears and threw himself on the spaniel, covering him with his body, hugging the dog tightly.

"No! No, Papa! Please don't kill him! I'll pay you back!"

"Pay me back!" jeered the carpenter. "What'll you pay me back with, eh, a kid like you?"

"Don't you think it's time to come to bed?" Sylvie said quietly to Wilfrid, putting her hand on his shoulder.

"Let me handle this," he retorted, pushing her hand away. "No dog is going to eat forty bucks of mine and get away with it."

He advanced into the room. Boff bared his fangs and began growling. The carpenter tried to grab him by the collar, and the dog sank its teeth into his hand. Wilfrid let out a cry of pain and backed quickly away, then tried to strike back with a swing of his boot, but the dog had scampered under the bed.

Wilfrid looked at his bloody hand where Boff's fangs had made a large gash. For a few seconds the only sound in the room was the steady drip, drip, drip of blood on the floor.

"My, my!" Sylvie said mockingly. "This sure is a night for bandages. Come on, Mr. Dogcatcher, time for another trip to the bathroom."

"Don't let that mutt out of this room," Wilfrid told his son with terrifying calm.

And he left, closing the door behind him. Charles, his face glistening with tears, remained collapsed on the floor. Suddenly he jumped up and looked under the bed.

"Boff," he said. "Come on. Let's get out of here."

But the dog wouldn't budge. Reaching under the bed, Charles pulled with all his strength on Boff's collar. Then, holding the dog beside him, he quietly opened the door, listened, and crept out into the hall. The next instant he was running down the stairs, crossing the street, and heading in the direction of the Fafards', shivering in the humid air redolent with the spicy smell of Macdonald's tobacco. He let himself cry, as though knowing it would give greater power to the plea he was preparing in his head.

■ ■ ■

Sitting in his recliner, slippers on his feet, a doughnut in his hand, Fernand was watching a hockey game on TV and, from time to time, stifling a yawn. He had closed the living-room door so as not to disturb Henri, who was doing his homework on the dining table.

Henri opened the door and came up to him looking frightened.

"Dad, Charles wants to see you. He's got his dog with him again and he's crying."

"Good Lord!" exclaimed Fernand, jumping to his feet. "What's the matter?"

Charles, standing in the vestibule, the dog at his feet, his voice choked with sobs, described what had happened in the apartment as best he could, careful to make it clear that Boff was only getting even for being kicked and that he had never shown the slightest interest in money before, nor had he ever bitten anyone.

Fernand listened, torn between feeling sorry for the boy and wanting to burst out laughing. His son, however, pressed against the wall, listened to Charles's tale with wide eyes.

"And now, Monsieur Fafard," Charles continued, shaking with sobs, "my father . . . wants to take . . . Boff to the vet . . . erinarian to . . . have him killed! You've got . . . to help me . . . Monsieur Faf . . . ard I don't . . . want Boff . . . to die!"

Fernand looked through the window of his front door and saw Wilfrid across the street, coming down the stairs leaning heavily on the handrail. "Hmm," he said to himself, "he looks like he's had a snootful all right. He won't be easy to reason with. And what can I say to him anyway?"

"Your father's on his way, Charles. I don't think he's going to be in a very good mood. Henri, take Boff down to the basement, and then go back into the dining room and finish your homework."

Charles had gone silent, watching his father crossing the street. He backed up instinctively and took Fernand's hand. The latter, surprised and troubled by this, gave Charles a quick glance, then rubbed his own throat, feeling more and more embarrassed.

Heavy footsteps were heard on the porch, and Wilfrid was standing before them in shirtsleeves, unsteady on his feet, a strangely contented expression on his face. Fernand opened the door. Without looking at him the carpenter entered and stood in front of his son.

"I thought I'd find you here! Now you come with me and bring that dog, and be quick about it!"

"Hello, Wilf!" cried Fernand cordially. "Good God in heaven, man, what's happened to you? You look as though you've been in a war."

"You could say I have been," Wilfrid replied dryly.

"Your son has told me a bit of what went on. I –"

"I have nothing to say to you. This is between me and him." He grabbed Charles by the arm. "Call your dog and come back to the house with me."

"Hey, now, Wilf, hold on a minute!" said Fernand, putting his large hand on the carpenter's shoulder. "Let's try to discuss this calmly, just the two of us . . ."

Fernand's massive body and deep voice made the carpenter seem much smaller and thinner than he was – made him, in fact, look puny and miserable. But Wilfrid's black, piercing eyes and tightly drawn lips showed that he was not intimidated. The image he brought to mind was that of a venomous insect.

"I already told you, you and me have nothing to discuss."

"Okay, Wilf, you're right, of course, this is your business, not mine, and I'm the last person to want to interfere, but all the same . . . I've never heard of a dog eating money before!"

"Well, now you have! He ate forty bucks! Now let's go, Charles. Go fetch the dog. We've been here long enough."

"Okay, let's say he ate your money," said Fernand, his voice soothing but a bit desperate. "Look here, if I give you two twenty-dollar bills that should settle it, right?"

He put his hand in his pocket and took out his wallet.

"I don't need your money," replied Wilfrid disdainfully, pushing the man's hand away. "I've got a job and I can manage just fine on my own."

Charles was looking from one to the other with a look of exquisite anguish on his face. Henri's little head appeared behind them, looking equally worried.

"I don't doubt that for a second," replied Fernand, more and more embarrassed, "I wasn't implying anything, I mean it never occurred to me to . . . offer you a handout, good heavens, no. Look," he interrupted himself, "what say we sit down and discuss this over a beer?"

"I won't say no," Wilfrid said after a pause.

"Perfect! Let's go into the kitchen. My wife's out visiting one of her sisters, there's no one here to bother us. You kids, go on in and watch TV."

Charles looked imploringly at Fernand, who, with an urgent gesture, waved him out of the room. But after exchanging a few quiet words with Henri in the living room, he tiptoed back into the hall, torn by anxiety, to spy on the two men in the kitchen. There was a large pine cupboard against the wall in the hall outside the door, in which Lucie kept the linens and towels. By squeezing himself against the side of it, Charles could look diagonally into the kitchen and see his father and Fernand sitting across from each other at the table. He had barely settled in when a sentence from Fernand struck his heart like a block of ice:

"Look, Wilfrid, why pay a vet twenty dollars to give your dog a needle when the SPCA will do it for nothing?"

Wilfrid set down his beer, which was already nearly empty, and spoke in a thickened voice:

"You're right . . . I never thought of that . . . He's already cost me forty bucks, the son of a bitch. That's enough. Where's the SPCA, anyway?"

"On Jean-Talon, in the West End."

"Good enough, I'll take him there," he said, standing up. "Do you know the exact address?"

"What's your hurry? They're open twenty-four hours. Anyway, my friend, I don't want to insult you, but in the state you're in, if I were in your shoes, I wouldn't drive out there. If you got pinched by the cops, or if you had an accident, that dog of yours would end up costing you an arm and a leg, nevermind forty bucks! Why not let me take the dog. We're neighbours, eh? We should be able to do favours for each other."

Wilfrid looked at him for a minute and a suspicious grin slowly spread across his puffy face.

"Oh no, you sly bastard, I know what you're up to. You're trying to pull one over on me . . ."

"Why do you say that, Wilf?" replied Fernand, feigning indignation. "I'm only trying to help, for crying out loud. Do you want to get rid of the dog or don't you? Okay! Get rid of him, then. But when I see that you're in no shape to do it tonight, I offer to do it for you, that's all there is to it. What am I trying to pull? Oh, I see your bottle's empty. Reach back and get another one from the fridge."

Drunk as he was, the carpenter didn't need to be asked twice. In an instant a new mouthful of cold beer was flowing down his throat, which seemed that night to be burning like the sands of the Sahara.

"You really want to get rid of that dog for me?" he asked after wiping his lips with his bandaged hand, slightly out of breath.

"You'll never see it again, I promise you."

"You're going to get them to give it a shot, right there in front of you?"

"I'll ask them. I don't know what they'll say, but I'll ask them."

"If they charge you for it, I'll reimburse you."

"No problem, you can pay me later."

Wilfrid, leaning heavily over the table, thrust his hand out to the hardware-store owner, who took it in the tips of his fingers with a slight grimace of distaste.

"Thanks, Fafard. I owe you one."

A cry of despair rose from the hallway. Charles ran into the kitchen, tears in his eyes, yelling curses and threats at the two men, especially at Fernand, who had betrayed him so cruelly. Then he threw himself down on the floor, curled up in a ball, and continued to wail.

"Little beggar," was all Wilfrid said, with a satisfied smirk. "Where's the dog?"

"In the basement."

"If I had my way I'd go down and finish it off with a two-by-four."

"No, Wilfrid, *your* way is off to bed. You can hardly stand up straight."

"Haha. Whatever you say, Fafard. Whatever you say . . ."

Fernand, upset by Charles's reaction and barely able to conceal the fact, kept glancing down at the boy, impatient for Wilfrid to be gone. But the man was so drunk he hardly seemed able to move.

"I'm going to take the boy downstairs to say goodbye to his dog," Fernand said, getting up. "No, no, no! Not a word, Wilf . . . Give me that, at least, for Pete's sake. You still have a heart in there, don't you?"

"A heart? Of course I have a heart, it's just that . . . Ah, the hell with it . . . Do what you want. Where's the can?"

Fafard pointed to a door. The carpenter got to his feet with the solemn dignity of the drunk and crossed the kitchen, concentrating on walking in a straight line; at one point he pushed off a wall. Charles was still lying on the floor, crying loudly. Fernand wanted to talk to him, but he didn't want Wilfrid

94

to hear. The sound of urine streaming into the toilet bowl lent a grotesque note to the scene. The carpenter emerged from the bathroom tugging at his fly, and Fernand steered him towards the front door, made sure he got safely across the street, and then returned to the kitchen – to find that Charles had disappeared. He found him in the basement with Boff and Henri.

"You're a traitor!" Henri said to his father.

Charles was kneeling with his face pressed against the dog, sniffling in great gulps of air, his posterior sticking up as though to show his contempt for his former ally. Boff, sensing himself in some way responsible for the entire mess, was whining softly and looking up anxiously at Fernand.

"Charles, I hope you don't seriously think that I want to take your dog to the SPCA," Fernand began, ignoring his son's remark. "I only said those things to gain time. But, doggone it, I couldn't very well tell you that in front of your father, could I?"

Charles sat up sharply.

"Is that true?" he said, with a cry of joy.

"Well, what do you take me for, for pity's sake? Some kind of two-faced jackass? When I give my word on something, I give my word. That's always been my way. Ask my wife. But enough talking, it's getting late and we have to find some place to keep your dog until we can think of a way to save its hide."

"Keep it here, Dad."

"You and I both know that your mother is allergic to dogs. She doesn't like them much, either. I can't very well saddle her with this chair-leg chewer, can I? This twenty-dollar-bill-swallower."

Coming from him, the phrases sounded like affectionate compliments; Boff sensed as much and began wagging his tail.

With his hands thrust into his pockets and his brow furrowed in thought, Fernand paced back and forth in the basement making strange noises with his lips. The two boys watched him in silence, not daring to interrupt his cogitations. After looking at his watch, he went upstairs and telephoned his wife to ask her to come home as soon as possible, because he needed the car to go out.

"It's Charles again," was all he told her. "I'll explain later."

When she arrived at the house, Lucie found her husband and Charles in the vestibule with their coats on (Charles had borrowed one from Henri); curled up at their feet was Boff, calmly shredding a newspaper.

"Henri will tell you all about it," said Fernand, hurrying out to the car with Charles and the dog in tow. "I'll be back in twenty minutes."

Charles was once again overcome with anxiety as he sat beside Monsieur Fafard, having installed Boff in the back seat.

"Okay, listen to me," Fernand said in a sudden fit of impatience, "I'm not taking your dog to the vet's to have him put down, but to have him put in a kennel until we find him a home where you can go see him as often as possible. I hope the Good Lord will send me an idea because I've wracked my brains and come up empty. It's like scraping the bottom of an empty barrel."

"It's too bad your wife is allergic," sighed Charles. "Boff would be so happy living with you, and I could come see him every day."

"Well, that's how it goes, my boy. If cows shat caramel, we'd all eat candy."

The Maisonneuve Veterinary Clinic near rue Ontario was housed in an old, two-storey building between a flower shop and a used-car dealer; founded twenty years earlier, the establishment had grown considerably, expanding into the basement and boasting a reception area and individual treatment rooms. Just the week before the beautiful carved wood that had decorated the building's facade had been covered with aluminum siding in the purest "no-maintenance" style that was beginning to crop up everywhere.

"Whoa, whoa!" cried Fernand, waving his arms, when he saw the receptionist getting ready to lock the door.

The woman batted her eyelids (and a young man sitting in the waiting room, obviously her boyfriend, more strenuously batted his), but she graciously let the hardware-store owner in, since she knew he was one of her boss's friends.

Boff, for whom the clinic held very few happy memories, suddenly began to manifest a decidedly fidgety disquiet, as though he'd suddenly remembered a thousand pressing things he needed to do outside. He tried to drag Charles back to the door, and the youngster had a great deal of difficulty restraining him. They said their goodbyes in the basement, where new kennels had been installed, amid a cacophony of barking, scratching, and other displays of chronic discontent.

"I'll be back, Boff, don't worry," Charles said, tears filling his eyes, after stroking his dog's muzzle for the nth time through the bars of his stainless-steel cage.

"We have to go, my boy. I think the receptionist has other plans for tonight." Fernand gave the girl a big smile and she frowned in embarrassment.

Charles climbed back into the car in complete dejection and said nothing for the entire drive home.

"Thank you very much, Monsieur Fafard," he said with a brave smile as he got out of the car. "I'll never forget everything you've done for Boff and me."

"Oh, well, neither will I, I guess," Fernand laughed. "Quite a night, eh? We'll neither of us soon forget it. Well, sleep well, Charles. And don't worry, I'll take care of everything. Your Boff hasn't licked our faces for the last time, believe me." Yes, but how will I take care of everything? Fernand wondered as he watched the boy run across the street and up the stairs to the Thibodeau apartment. Lucie will never allow that animal to live with us.

10

It had been a rough evening, and the night was no less turbulent. Charles, exhausted, slipped into bed shivering, but was kept awake by the gigantic snores of his father, coming to him from the bedroom; they made him think of a huge saw cutting through the house. Suddenly his eyes closed and he sunk into a deep, heavy sleep.

He woke with a start at three o'clock in the morning. His mouth was dry, his throat constricted, and his limbs tingling. He looked fearfully about the darkened room, which seemed strange and vaguely menacing. Light from the streetlamp was reflected on the handle of his door, and its colour made him think of Boff's blond, silky hair. He imagined his dog lying in its cage, its eyes wide open in anxiety and dread, not understanding anything that had happened to it. Suddenly a flood of terrible doubts washed through Charles's mind. What if Monsieur Fafard had tricked him? What if he were more in league with his father than with him? Or, even worse, what if the veterinarian put Boff to sleep by mistake, instead of another dog? And even if that didn't happen, what if they couldn't find Boff a new home in the neighbourhood? Would they give him to just anyone?

He sat up in bed and, sliding his arms under the covers, slipped his fingers between his moist, freezing toes and began tugging hard, as though trying to pull away from the anguish that was tormenting him. He knew that there was no going back to sleep that night.

Stretching up on one side, he lifted the blind and looked out onto the street. Pools of ice glowed softly on the opposite sidewalk, surrounded by fringes of black that meant they were melting.

He was suddenly gripped by an irresistible desire to see Boff. When he'd been at the kennel a few hours earlier, he'd noticed a large basement window facing the row of stacked cages in which they had placed his dog. He wanted to see Boff and he would not calm down until he had.

Breathing quickly out of fear and excitement, he dressed in the darkness, slipped silently down the hall, and, for the second time in twenty-four hours, sneaked out of the house. He would be back in twenty minutes; no one would know he'd been gone.

As he descended the elegant curved staircase to the sidewalk he looked up and stopped in mid-step, in a sort of rapture. A beautiful sky spread out over the city, and hundreds of stars twinkled peacefully, transforming the terrifying blackness of space into a calming blue, and turning the night into a friend and accomplice.

He quickly ran down the remaining steps and along the street, then stopped once again: the silence of the streets, down which a gentle, almost warm breeze was blowing, made his footsteps ring out like gunshots. "Quiet!" he said, addressing the stars. "If you're going to see Boff you have to go softly, softly . . ."

Reaching rue Ontario he saw a pair of headlights turn onto the street in his direction. For some reason he thought they might be from a police car. If they caught him out on the street at this time of night, they'd pick him up for sure and take him back to the apartment. And that would certainly earn him a licking!

He retraced his steps and came out on rue Coupal, a curious, S-shaped street lined by single-storey houses running parallel to rue Ontario. The street would surely be deserted at this hour. Rue Coupal would take him to the rear of the veterinary clinic. First he came to the corner of Fullum. From there, Coupal went in a straight line all the way to Parthenais and ended in the parking lot of the used-car dealer beside the clinic. He crossed the nearly empty lot and stopped at a high, metal, chain-link fence that separated the lot from the clinic grounds. This he climbed without difficulty and dropped to the other side on all fours, scraping his palms on the sand-studded ice.

The next instant he was crouched beside the basement window. In the subdued lighting of the room he saw Boff sleeping on his side. In the cage next to him was a sort of poodle, stretched out on its belly, legs at its sides, its hind quarters trembling.

Seeing Boff looking so peaceful surprised Charles a bit. Was he the only one who was upset? Perhaps Boff had fallen asleep from exhaustion, still in the grips of despair? Surely it would do him a world of good to know that his owner had come to see him in the middle of the night, to reassure him that he had not been forgotten? But to do that he would have to wake Boff up.

Charles spied a large piece of brick lying in a pool of loose ice at his feet. He picked it up and turned it in his hand, his eye still fixed on Boff. After a long pause he tapped twice on the window with the brick.

The effect was instantaneous. An immense clamour of barking, howling, and yapping rolled up from the basement, so loud that Charles looked anxiously towards rue Ontario, afraid that the sound would draw attention despite the clinic's thick walls and closed window. Boff was standing up, barking with all his strength, but he didn't seem to have seen Charles. The boy gently waved his hand and the dog, seeing him, threw himself frantically against the bars of his cage, backing up to rally his forces and throwing himself against the bars so forcefully that Charles was afraid he would hurt himself. Now he was sorry he'd wakened him. He thought he could make out Boff's barking in all the cacophony; Boff's face was so full of despair that Charles turned and backed away from the window. The noise from the clinic increased. Charles stood up and a sob shook him. What should he do? Go home? Stay where he was until the noise died down?

He knelt down again beside the window. Boff was sitting in his cage, howling piteously. Suddenly it was as though something clicked inside Charles, and his hand, which seemed to have a mind of its own, began beating violently against the window with the brick. The glass shattered into a thousand pieces. He jumped back, terrified by what he had done. Now the noise from the basement would surely reach the street and bring someone running. The police were bound to hear. But the foolishness of his act stunned him, nearly knocked the wind out of him, and instead of running he began tearing at the few pieces of glass still stuck in the frame, then slipped through the opening and landed on the cages that were stacked under the window. The floor was barely six feet below him; closing his eyes, he jumped down, deafened by the racket that was now rising to an even greater pitch. He landed square in front of Boff, who was dancing with joy, paws pumping the air, front end rearing up and falling, licking the bars, quivering with love. The cage door opened easily, and the dog leapt out and sat on his haunches in the middle of the room, awaiting instructions from his lord and master. Now Charles was thinking coolly, like a man of action. He saw a table in a corner of the room, swept off the plastic boxes piled on it, and dragged it across to the broken window. Then lifting

Boff onto the table, he climbed up after him. From there, hoisting Boff up to the top of the cages was more difficult, but after a few tries he succeeded, and no sooner did the spaniel find himself at the window than he disappeared through it. Charles was not far behind.

Since he knew he couldn't climb the chain-link fence with his dog, Charles went around the clinic and, with Boff running wildly ahead of him, raced onto rue Ontario, a distance of only a few metres.

The deserted street was profoundly quiet. It was as though nothing at all had happened. Uselessly, enigmatically, a traffic light changed from green to amber, and then to red. Charles continued to run, his eye fixed on the corner where he would turn and make his way back up to rue Coupal, where he knew it would be dark and safe. Boff stopped every ten feet to make sure Charles was still behind him. At the corner Charles stopped, out of breath. Only then did he feel something hurting his hand. He brought his hand up to his eyes and saw that it was bleeding from a long, deep gash that he must have made when he escaped through the window. He stuck his hand into the pocket of his windbreaker and began walking, his legs suddenly stiff and sore, his breath coming in short gasps, his shoulders aching. Boff ran in great circles around him, sniffing the ground, every now and then emitting a small whine to attract Charles's attention. Afraid that the dog would start barking, Charles knelt down and put his arms around him; the spaniel threw itself on the boy, its paws up on his shoulders, and began frantically licking his face.

"What am I going to do with you now, Boff? Why did you eat that forty dollars? Now you can't come home with me any more. My father will kill you."

Boff kept on licking the boy's face as though nothing else mattered now that he and his master were back together.

"Stop, Boff, that's enough, you're getting on my nerves now. Poor Monsieur Fafard," he said, still trying to figure out what to do. "The vet is going to yell at him, and he'll probably call the police, and the police will come to our place. God, what a mess we're in! I shouldn't have gone looking for you, Boff, but I couldn't stop myself, you see, because I love you too much, you stupid old hound."

By now fatigue was making Charles's eyes burn; weariness had so overcome over him that he was tempted to lie down on the ground and go to sleep.

"I have to let Monsieur Fafard know what's happened," he murmured, and began walking. "He'll know what to do."

His wounded hand felt the stub of a pencil in the pocket of his wind-breaker and suddenly everything became clear in his mind. When he arrived on rue Dufresne, he saw a piece of cardboard lying on the street beside a car. He tore off an end and slipped it into his jacket. Walking down the Fafards' driveway, he found himself in the backyard, at the end of which was their garage. The door was not usually locked. He tried the latch and let out a sigh of relief.

While Boff explored the yard, always keeping an eye on Charles, the boy leaned against the garage wall and wrote a note for Monsieur Fafard:

> *I'm very sorry M. Fafard but I was too worried, I went to get Boff from the veterinarian. Please do not call the police I'll pay for the window. But take care of Boff for me, please. I put him in the garage, I don't think he'll be cold in there.*
> *Thank you very much,*
> *Charles*

To his great annoyance Boff was once again shut in after having been warned very seriously to keep quiet; Charles went to the Fafards' front door and slid his note through the mail slot. He then carefully returned to his apartment; vigorous snoring from his father's room told him that his adventure had so far gone undetected. A few minutes later Charles himself was sound asleep, lying fully clothed on his bed.

■ ■ ■

At six-thirty that morning Wilfrid, head throbbing, legs wobbly and refusing to bear his weight, stomach feeling as though it were full of sludge, was sitting at the kitchen table staring lugubriously down at a cup of triple-strength instant coffee made with lukewarm tapwater, wondering whether he had enough strength to lift it to his lips. The idea of getting through the workday ahead filled him with dread; the memory of his binge of the night before brought on a shudder of self-loathing, a disgust made all the more depressing by the knowledge that every five, maybe six days, two weeks at the most, he'd be going through the whole thing again, the beer, the reproaches, the morning-after, for as long as he could buy beer and drink it. The foreman's thinly veiled hints came back to him. He was a hard man who got along with no one, not even the best of the workers. Wilfrid shouldn't take his criticisms so much to heart, because his anger often made him say whatever came into his head. Anyway, the guy had been right yesterday. He really had screwed up those goddamn stairs. Completely misread the blueprints, like an idiot. For some time now he'd had the feeling that he was losing it, that his eye was becoming less sure, his common sense failing him. Was the booze finally getting to him? He'd have to wait and see.

Overcoming a wave of nausea that filled his mouth with saliva, he took a mouthful of coffee and grimaced, then looked at his watch. He'd have to leave in a few minutes.

Suddenly a thin ray of sunshine shone through the dark and murky thoughts that were stuffing his head. Last night he had done one good thing. He'd taught that goddamn dog a lesson. Ate forty bucks! Nearly a whole day's pay! Well, by now he should be mouldering with them in his grave, the bloody money-swallowing son of a bitch!

He smiled with satisfaction, but at the same time felt a slight tightening in the pit of his stomach. His son had wanted that dog for a long time. He'd never heard the boy cry so much. So what? That was life. You can't go around crying over spilt milk, you have to get on with it. If Charles had taken the trouble to train the dumb animal, it would still be sleeping in his bed with him this morning. Wilfrid took a second drink of coffee. It went down a bit better than the first. Then he heard a low sound coming from the back porch, followed by scratching. He turned his head, let out a cry, and spilled half his coffee on his lap.

A dog was looking at him through the back-door window, its mouth hanging open. It was wearing a dark brown leather collar. It was a spaniel. It had to be Boff!

The dog and the carpenter stared at one another without moving. Wilfrid, hand shaking, set down his cup and rubbed his eyes. Was he seeing things? Were his excesses of the night before giving him hallucinations? Or had that goddamn Fernand Fafard made a bloody fool of him?

He jumped up and bounded towards the back door, caught his foot in a chair leg, and nearly went down in a heap on the floor.

A deep sigh floated out from the bedroom.

"What're you doing out there?" Sylvie mumbled sleepily.

With his nose pressed to the window, Wilfrid watched Boff run down the stairs, cross the yard, and disappear under the fence. Rage rushed the air from his lungs. His head began to pound. His neck and throat caught fire. His fingers spread wide open then slowly closed into a fist. He turned around, barely able to gulp in air, and there was Sylvie, standing in the middle of the kitchen, watching him with eyes still heavy from sleep.

"What's the matter with you?" she said, frightened. "You don't look so good."

"That dog . . . he's not dead," Wilfrid managed to croak.

"Who? Boff?"

He nodded his head, his eyes staring crazily.

"He was just looking at me through the door. As soon as I got up he took off. Fafard has tricked me. And Charles, too."

She gave a little pout of disbelief, then tightened her robe as though protecting herself from something.

"But I tell you I just saw him!" he thundered. "What do you think, you think I'm crazy?"

"Okay, okay, I didn't say anything," she replied bitterly, backing up quickly to let him pass.

Wilfrid roared into Charles's room like a hurricane. "Get out of that bed!" he shouted.

The child opened his eyes and stared up at his father for a second, then sat up.

"So," Wilfrid said, crossing his arms on his chest, "you think it's funny, lying to me straight in the face?"

Charles continued to look at him without saying anything.

"Answer me! What did you do with Boff?"

"I . . . I don't know," stuttered Charles, trembling terribly inside.

"You don't know? You're telling me you don't know what you did with him? Well, I've got news for you. Two minutes ago your precious Boff, who should have been dead twelve hours ago, was out on the back porch thumbing its nose at me through the window. What have you got to say about that?"

"I . . . I don't know," repeated Charles.

The carpenter took a step towards the bed, then looked at his watch, stopped, and retreated slowly to the door.

"I have to go to work," he said. "I'm going to be late. But this isn't over by a long shot. I'm giving you fair warning. When I get home tonight, you and I are going to have a nice long chat."

A few seconds later Charles heard his father's heavy footsteps thundering down the outside staircase.

■ ■ ■

Fernand, dripping with suds, sang his own idiosyncratic version of "O sole mio" in the shower while going over in his head his recipe for ham-and-cheddar omelette with maple syrup and green peas, which he was going to prepare in a few minutes. After lathering his cranium, whose smooth, pink surface had been a source of regret for a number of years, he turned his attentions to a more intimate and infinitely more satisfying part of his anatomy, the dimensions of which brought a smile of contentment and pride, consoling him as usual for the ignoble treason that nature had visited upon his shiny pate. He was conjuring up a few naughty memories when he heard a knocking at the bathroom door.

"What is it?" he called out. "What's going on?"

He recognized Lucie's voice. From her halting delivery he could tell she had bad news, but he couldn't make out was it was.

"I'm coming!"

Twenty seconds later, wrapped in a towel, he was walking with great wet steps towards the kitchen, from which he could hear an unusually loud uproar.

Henri, his feet bare, a coat thrown over his pyjamas, was hurriedly shoving his feet into his boots while Lucie rummaged crossly through the refrigerator. Céline, standing on the radiator, was shouting with glee and signalling through the window at something in the backyard.

"Hurry, Mama!" Henri implored. "He's getting away!"

"Boff! Boff!" cried Céline, in an agony of excitement. "Come back, Boffie, come up on the porch. We've got something for you!"

"Boffie?" exclaimed Fernand.

"Yes, it's Boff!" Lucie replied, handing a plate to Henri, who took it and ran with it out into the yard.

She half-turned, picked up a piece of cardboard from the table and passed it to her husband. "I found this in the vestibule, dear," she said.

"Ah, the poor little tyke!" said Fernand after reading Charles's note. "What in the world got into him? He's landed me in doo-doo up to my neck, for crying out loud."

"Henri!" Lucie called through the half-opened door, "get back in here this instant before you catch your death of cold! It's not summer, you know!"

"He's already gobbled up everything on the plate," exclaimed Céline. "He must have been famished, poor Boffie!"

Just then the telephone rang. Lucie answered, muttered a weak "Hmm, hmm," allowed her eyes to widen slightly, then motioned to Fernand to pick up the extension. It was Dr. Roberge, the vet who owned the Maisonneuve Veterinary Clinic, and he'd been in better moods.

"Listen, Paul, I don't know anything about it. It was my neighbour's little boy, Charles Thibodeau, who pulled this stunt. I don't know what he was thinking either, but he's going to tell me, and I don't mean next week. I'll send someone over to repair your window and I'll pay for everything, don't worry. No other damage, was there? Good. But most important, don't go calling the cops, okay? That'll only make things worse. He's a good boy, I assure you: I've known him since he was knee-high to a grasshopper, but he's had some trouble at home, mostly with his father . . . Thanks, Paul, you won't regret it. Thanks."

With the omelette he'd been imagining now a distant dream, as was the feeling of well-being that had come with it, he watched Henri grunting as he pulled off his boots by the kitchen door.

"Were you in on this?" he asked his son, pointing a patriarchal finger at him.

Henri hunched his shoulders with such a gesture of innocence that Fernand's finger sank down and humbly rejoined its colleagues.

"He's leaving!" cried Céline, jumping down from the radiator.

"Don't open the door!" ordered Lucie, blocking her path to the back porch. "Go finish your cereal this instant, and then go get dressed. Ah, what a way to start the day! Gracious God in Heaven, it's enough to make a saint curse."

Fernand, meanwhile, had looked up Charles's telephone number and was about to dial when the doorbell rang. Henri ran to open it, and a few seconds later Charles came into the kitchen, looking red in the face, scared and guilty. Seeing him, Lucie opened her arms despite herself and the boy ran into them, crying, babbling excuses, trying to explain his actions and blaming himself for putting Monsieur Fafard in such an embarrassing position; then in the same breath telling them that half an hour earlier Boff had been stupid enough to show up at their house and his father had seen him through the kitchen door and was furious and had promised Charles he'd give him a real licking when he came home that night.

Lucie and Fernand looked at each other.

"I'll speak to him," Fernand promised. "But between you and me and the gatepost, my boy, you've really put your foot in it this time! If it wasn't for me, the clinic would have had the police on your tail by now! Oh, yes! . . . Don't you trust me? When I say I'm going to do something, by the jumping Jehosephat, I do it. If you'd been smart enough to stay in your bed last night, everything would be going along fine right now. But now . . . the wheels have come right off the hay wagon! Anyway, I'll see what I can do."

He took Charles firmly by the shoulders:

"You know, you've got a lot of guts, no question, my boy!" he said. "I'd hate to see what you'll be like when you're twenty! Holy cow! Wild horses won't hold you back!"

On the verge of tears, Charles started pouring out more excuses, promising that from then on – assuming there would be a from then on – he would follow Monsieur Fafard's word to the letter, take his protector's advice and counsel to heart, and he thanked him over and over for interceding on his behalf with the veterinarian. He spoke with such emotion that both Fernand and Lucie were silenced, captivated, and Fernand was almost sorry he had spoken so harshly.

"But where's Boff?" Charles said suddenly. "Where's my dog? Is he here?"

"He just ran out of the backyard," Céline told him.

"I gave him a big bowl of shepherd's pie," added Henri, "and he swallowed the whole thing!"

Lucie, who had sat down again with her cup of reheated coffee, pulled Charles onto her ample lap.

"Don't worry about your dog, Charles," she said. "I'm sure he'll come back. He knows he has friends here."

She gave him a hug.

"I have to go," Charles said, jumping down. "Sylvie won't like it if I'm away too long. She told me I'm not supposed to come here any more."

"And you came anyway?" said Fernand, surprised.

Charles gave a faint smile that betrayed a wisdom unusual in a child of his age.

"I told her that if she turned a blind eye this time I would do the same for her some day. And it worked!"

■ ■ ■

Just before five o'clock, having shown the colour to the customer and made sure she was happy with it, Fernand hammered the lid back on a can of paint with a rubber mallet and called Clément to come over and fill in for him. He wanted to get home a bit earlier than usual so he could go see Wilfrid Thibodeau as soon as the carpenter returned from work.

He put on his coat and overshoes but left his gloves in his pockets because the weather was getting milder. When he walked out onto the sidewalk, he noticed with satisfaction that it was almost entirely free of ice. "The sun's done a full day's work today," he said to himself. "Another two or three days like this and we'll be able to go outside in just our shoes."

He walked along rue La Fontaine and turned right on Dufresne. His house was a ten-minute walk from the store. Two years before, Lucie had persuaded him to walk to and from work, to help him lose weight. And he was grateful to her for it, since his daily walks, although undertaken primarily for reasons of health, also gave him more time to himself than he'd had before. Time to work out the thousand little problems that cropped up during the day, time to look at all the pretty young women who lived in the neighbourhood, and enough exercise to justify a snifter of cognac every night after dinner.

He felt a drop of rain on his cheek, then another on the tip of his nose. Looking up, he saw that the sky had become heavy and grey and looked about ready to open up. He picked up his pace. A tall, thin man wearing a helmet passed him on a bicycle, looking miserable, a cigarette dangling from his mouth. Fernand felt a connection with him without knowing why, then remembered that two days before the man had come into the store and bought a hatchet and ten pounds of finishing nails, and had launched into an impassioned diatribe against Premier Bourassa, whom Fernand particularly disliked; he'd found the man's eloquence so moving that he'd given him a discount.

The raindrops were falling closer and closer together. Fernand began jogging, but after two blocks he had to stop because flames were shooting up from his lungs into his throat. There came a crack of thunder above his head, and rain started pouring down by the bucketload.

By the time he got home he was drenched. Ordinarily Lucie would have chewed him out for not taking a taxi, then helped him out of his clothes and into a warm bath. She had an inordinate fear of respiratory diseases – her grandfather had died of asthma and her father of pneumonia. But tonight she barely seemed to notice his soaked hat or his dripping clothes.

"Wilfrid just left," she said breathlessly. "He wanted his dog. It's a good thing I saw him coming through the window. I told Céline to hide Boff in the garage, and she stayed there with him to keep him from barking. What on earth are we going to do, Fernand? Playing hide-and-seek like this is fun for a day, but not for a week! Go see him and figure something out between the two of you, for pity's sake. He's waiting for you."

Fernand handed her his coat, which was twice its usual weight. "That's just what I intended to do," he said.

"What are you going to tell him?" Lucie asked.

"God knows and the Devil's not saying," Fernand sighed. "It's been crazy in the store all day, I haven't had a minute to think about it."

"Well, be ready to get an earful, my poor Fernand. He was looking pretty mean. Whatever possessed you to come to that dog's rescue I'll never know."

He looked her straight in the eye.

"I'm not a bit sorry I did it – and neither are you. So there's no point crying over water under the bridge, is there Lucie? Eh?"

Lucie gave an embarrassed smile and looked away. Her husband changed into dry clothes, more thoughtful than ever, and then crossed the street and rang the bell of the Thibodeau apartment. Wilfrid answered the door in his undershirt, a cup of coffee in his hand, his face looking like hell warmed over.

"Ah, so it's you, finally," he muttered. "Come into the kitchen."

They'd gone only partway down the hall when Wilfrid stopped, turned around, and said furiously:

"So tell me, were you giving me the gears last night?"

"No, of course not! It's just my car wouldn't start. Dampness in the wiring or something. I don't use it every day, as you know. And taxis are expensive so I decided to wait. That's all."

"So I guess the car's working okay today, then?" Wilfrid sneered, continuing into the kitchen.

"Like a charm," said Fernand, impressed by his own presence of mind. "I plugged it in."

Thibodeau flung himself onto a chair and gestured towards another for his guest. A deep silence reigned in the apartment. Sylvie must be at work, Fernand thought. But where was Charles?

Wilfrid brought the cup to his lips, threw back his head, and slurped loudly at his coffee. Fernand suppressed an expression of distaste.

"When are you going to bring my dog back?" Wilfrid said, wiping his lips with his bare wrist.

"As soon as I see him."

Wilfrid blanched, then struck the table with his fist so hard a teaspoon danced in the air.

"You're lying to me again!" he shouted. "To my face! Bring back my dog. Now! What I do with it is none of your goddamn business!"

Fernand frowned, stood up, and, placing the palms of his big hands on the table on either side of the carpenter's, said:

"Listen, Wilfrid. I'm not used to being yelled at like that. It could very easily put me in a bad mood. Now, we're going to talk this over calmly, like two grown men, understand me? Without getting our backs up! We can work things out. Okay, I lied to you, and I hope you'll forgive me for that. Your dog is over at my place. I didn't have the heart to have it put down last night because it would have really hurt your son. He's just a kid. You remember when you were a kid, Wilf? No? You don't give a damn? Okay, that's your business. But your boy, don't you give a damn about him either? Don't tell me you don't, Wilf, because it would really lower you in my estimation."

"Oh, well, we wouldn't want that, would we?" sneered Wilfrid, leaning slightly back in his chair.

Fernand smiled as though he'd been given a compliment. Then he sat down again, smiled a second time, and rubbed his hands together slowly. He seemed to have had an inspiration and was looking for the best way to present it.

"Listen, Wilfrid," he said finally, "what is it you want out of this, anyway? Not to have that dog under your feet, am I right?"

"Right. And the sooner you bring it back, the sooner I can get rid of it."

"I've got a better idea: let me buy the dog from you!"

"No. You bring the dog here, and I'll get rid of it myself."

Fernand put his hand in his pocket and took out his wallet. He counted out six ten-dollar bills and laid them on the table.

"You sure you don't want to sell it?" he asked gently. "Sixty bucks for a Heinz 57 you picked up in the street. That's not a bad deal."

Wilfrid stared at the money. He kept his face expressionless, but his right foot was tapping quietly on the floor; he was doing the mathematics in his head: this bloody mutt had chewed up forty dollars, but now here he was being offered twenty bucks more than that. Only a fool would pass up such an offer.

He cleared his throat, then said quietly: "Eighty."

Fafard considered for a moment, then shook his head.

"No. Not a penny more."

There was a moment of silence. Fernand made as though to put the money back in his wallet.

"Okay, it's a deal. But you have to promise me that dog will never show his face around here again."

"In a few days you won't even remember what colour it was."

"If it even thinks about coming over here, I'll grab it and have it killed, and you'll have no right to complain about it."

"I won't even try."

"What are you going to do with it?"

"I haven't the faintest idea."

Wilfrid scooped up the money, put it in his pocket, and held out his hand to Fernand.

"Goodbye. I've got to start making supper."

When Fernand left, Wilfrid went into his son's room. Charles was lying flat on his stomach on his bed, pretending to be absorbed in a *Tintin*, but his face beamed with pleasure. His father saw it in an instant.

"Do you understand what went on just now?"

The boy shook his head and looked away.

"Liar. Your teeth will fall out. You know damned well I just sold your dog. I can tell by your face. Count yourself lucky! You can go see it at the Fafards, but I don't want it in this house again, you get me? If I see it, I'll break its neck. After supper you can get your wagon and take the doghouse back over to Henri's."

"Can't I do it now?" Charles asked, standing up.

"No, I still have a few things to say to you."

111

Charles sank back on the bed and waited, looking at his father's legs.

"Tomorrow you're going to stay home from school."

Charles looked up, astonished.

"You're going to stay here and do some thinking," his father went on, in a curiously pompous and affected tone of voice.

"Thinking?" repeated Charles.

"Yes. You lied to me last night. You were in cahoots with Fatso Fafard." (Charles couldn't help but grimace at that.) "You were both trying to put one over on me. His wife and his kids were in on it, too. You're going to think about that – and about the consequences. The consequences it could have for you in your future life. And I know just how to make you think about that for as long as you need to."

"How?"

The carpenter raised his hand with a self-satisfied smile.

"You'll find out soon enough."

And with that he left the room.

11

For the rest of that night Charles was lost in thought. What sort of punishment could his father possibly have come up with? That smile had not boded well. After supper (a can of pea soup, a can of baked beans, and a few slices of cold ham), he hauled Boff's house over to the Fafards' backyard. The dog, lying on an old quilt in the garage, heard Charles's step and began barking wildly. Charles hurried over to him with tears in his eyes and for a long time the two friends showered each other with affection. Then, obeying his father's order, Charles left the yard without speaking to anyone.

Wilfrid, stretched out on the sofa, was watching television. Charles did his homework in the kitchen, took a bath, flipped through an issue of *Tintin*, then went to bed the minute Sylvie came home from the restaurant. She looked tired and complained of a headache. She and Wilfrid had a long conversation, keeping their voices low so that Charles couldn't make out what they were saying except for one sentence uttered on two separate occasions by the waitress: "Have you lost your mind, Wilfrid?"

Charles slept badly that night. He dreamed that his father was slicing his head off with a circular saw that flew by itself in the air at the end of its cord; the saw then flew after Boff, who barely managed to avoid it. Then the situation was reversed: the dog became furious and began chasing the saw, frightening the tool so much that it sawed itself into a wall, making a huge hole that suddenly turned into a window; the window gave onto a slide that stretched off into the blue sky to the far-off mountains of Russia. Laughing, Charles threw himself onto the slide and was carried along as though by a swiftly flowing river. Then he became scared. He felt himself falling through a vast, dark, menacing emptiness. He opened his eyes. His father was shaking him awake by the shoulders.

"Get up," his father said. "Breakfast is ready."

Charles got up, as wide awake and alert as though he had never been asleep. He took his place at the kitchen table. Wilfrid had prepared his breakfast – which in itself was unusual and disturbing: a bowl of cereal and two pieces of toast with peanut butter on a plate that was too big for them. He began to eat, watching his father out of the corner of his eye. Wilfrid was wolfing down a western omelette. Through the window Charles could see the back of the neighbouring house, still slightly blurred in the cool morning light; inside the house, a fat, bald man in a singlet was walking back and forth, drying a shirt.

The smell of bacon usually made his mouth water, but this morning it turned his stomach.

"I'm not hungry," he said, pushing his bowl away.

"Eat up," said his father. "It'll be a long time before your next meal. And get a move on; I've got to leave in five minutes."

Charles looked at him, suddenly apprehensive.

"What are you going to do to me?"

Wilfrid swallowed a mouthful of bacon and, keeping his head down, carefully wiped his plate with a piece of bread crust, put the bread in his mouth, and chewed energetically. Then he looked up at his son.

"Don't worry," he said, "I'm not going to hit you. Okay, you don't want to eat? Bring your toast to your room."

In the room next to Charles's, Sylvie let out a long sigh that ended in short peeps, like the call of a sparrow. Charles wanted her to get up and almost called to her, but thought better of it.

Wilfrid was waiting for him in his room, standing beside the bed with an electric drill in one hand and a large empty jam jar in the other. The closet door was open. Wilfrid pointed to it.

"Get in there," he said.

"What for?" Charles asked, astonished. He was frightened and amused by the request.

"So you can do your thinking."

His father put the drill under his arm and fished three long screws from his shirt pocket. Then he held the jam jar out to Charles.

"In case you need to pee," he said. His actions were deliberate and businesslike, as though he were performing a tiresome but necessary task. All the same, there was a strange smile of contentment on his parted lips. Charles took the jar and went into the closet.

"How long do I have to stay in here?"

"For as long as it takes you to think."

"But I've already been thinking since last night, Papa. I promise I'll never lie to you again."

"You haven't done nearly enough thinking, as far as I'm concerned," replied his father, pushing Charles deeper into the closet.

The next thing Charles knew the door was closed, and he was enveloped in a strange darkness, half buried in the clothes hanging on their hangers. The electric drill whirred and gave out little spasmodic buzzes as, one by one, screws were driven into the wooden door. Charles was a prisoner in the closet.

"Sylvie will let me out as soon as my father goes to work," Charles told himself, although as soon as he said it he knew she wouldn't do it.

For several minutes he didn't move. He listened to the sounds of the building. Someone in the upstairs apartment was filling a bathtub with water; when the tap was abruptly shut off, the pipes jumped above his head with a metallic shudder.

Stretching out his hand, he leaned against the door and pushed with all his might; it didn't budge. With his arms he spread the garments on their hangers, since their slightly dusty closeness was beginning to suffocate him; then he remembered his toast, which was on the plate at his feet, resting on top of the jam jar his father had given him. He moved several pairs of shoes, a metal truck, a few sections of track from an electric train set, and two cardboard boxes, then sat down on the floor, his eye fixed on the thin line of light coming from under the door. He began to eat. The line of light was comforting. It connected him to the other rooms of the apartment, like a promise that he would soon be set free and able to move about, as long as he stayed calm and quiet in this darkness which, as his eyes became accustomed to it, wasn't so bad.

A shiver went through him and he felt goosebumps on his legs; his father hadn't given him time to get dressed. He was still in his pyjamas, and it was cold in the closet. He stood up, rummaged through the clothes on the hangers until he found a winter coat. It was much too big for him but it would keep him warm; he could even wrap his bare feet in it. He unhooked it and tugged it around himself. A faint but familiar odour of perfume emanated from its lining; it was his mother's coat, which had been hanging forgotten in this closet all these years. He plunged his face into the folds, overcome by a piercing joy, and leaned against the wall hugging the coat tightly about himself, closing his eyes and breathing a sigh of contentment. A feeling of benevolence washed over him, his ice-cold feet began to warm up, and the sense of the strangeness of the situation that had been so frightening until then slowly began to dissipate, as though an invisible presence were in the closet, protecting him. After a few minutes, he fell asleep.

■ ■ ■

A noise woke him with a start. Sylvie had just put the kettle on the stove. Then she took a plate from the cupboard and slid it across the table. In his mind he could follow every one of her actions, which made him feel as though he were in the kitchen with her. Why didn't she come to see if he was all right? he wondered. Did she think he'd gone to school?

He pounded on the closet door with his fist and waited. Steps approached down the hall and stopped at the door to his bedroom.

"Sylvie?" he called, his voice trembling.

There was no answer.

"Sylvie, I'm in here! I want out!"

A moment passed, then the steps moved away. Charles sat down again and wrapped himself in the coat, crying quietly.

"I hate her!" he said to himself, rubbing his eyes. "I hate her!"

He remained seated for a long while, lost in his own unhappiness and anger. Suddenly a door slammed and he heard steps going down the outside stairs. Sylvie had gone to work, leaving him alone in the apartment.

"You bitch!" he shouted at the top of his lungs. "You bloody bitch!"

The words sounded good to him, and he repeated them over and over again in different tones until they became a sort of refrain.

His anger diminished slightly; then he felt an urgent need to pee. He stood up and relieved himself in the jam jar. The odour of warm urine filled his nostrils, and he shoved the jar into a far corner. He was no longer sleepy. He would have to wait until Wilfrid came home to get out of the closet, because Sylvie wouldn't interfere. That meant he'd be there until six or seven o'clock, maybe later. What would he do all that time, with no light, no food, nothing to occupy his mind? Think, as his father had told him? But he had no desire to think.

But of course he did think, curled up in his mother's coat. But his thoughts soon became disturbing. What will I do if my father decides to leave me in here *forever*? he asked himself. Sylvie will never let him do that. But what if she leaves? Or is so afraid of him she doesn't dare do anything? Eventually the Fafards will ask about me. And Mademoiselle Laramée. She always looks for me at the beginning of class. But how many days will it take for them to get worried? Two or three at least. And even then, what could they do? Come and ask my father or Sylvie where I am. But they'd never tell the truth! I'll have to wait for the police to get involved. And how many days will *that* take?

He pictured himself dying of thirst or starvation in the closet, too weak to cry out, exhausted, desperate . . . He remembered hearing a horrible story about a child who was beaten and locked up. Marcel Lamouche, one of his friends at school, had read about it in *La Presse*. Such things happened. They could happen in Montreal! What if . . .

Enough of that! He stood up, trembling and sweating. His stomach was plunging into a tailspin. He felt as though all the clothes had got together and were sucking the air out of the closet.

He threw himself violently against the door, but it still didn't budge. It seemed to be made of steel. And now his knees, hands, and shoulders were sore. He sat down on the coat and tried with all his might to think of something pleasant. It was absolutely necessary to think of nice things, otherwise how could he possibly not go crazy before his father came home?

"Boff! I'll think of Boff! What are you doing about now, my dear friend? Still in the garage? No, Henri or Céline have let you out and you're prancing around the neighbourhood, thinking about me. Oh yes, I know you're thinking about me, you big fat lump of hair! Watch out for cars, Boff! I don't want you getting run over after everything I've gone through for you! I'd go through more than that, though, Boff, more than Alice went through in Wonderland! That's for sure!"

And then a question popped into his mind. What would Alice do if she found herself in this situation? Hmm. Obviously she would explore the closet, just as she explored the land at the bottom of the rabbit hole. Why shouldn't he do the same? The time would go by faster and, who knew, he might even find something interesting.

Creeping along the wall, he edged to the left towards the deepest part of the closet, moving as slowly as possible to give himself the illusion that there was a lot of space. It wasn't clothing that was brushing his head, it was long, soft leaves and vines, maybe even sleeping bats hanging by their feet. The wall was the outside of a huge, fortified castle. Where was he? He was in Africa, in a jungle, and the castle was in the middle of it; he absolutely had to get inside because in the Room of the Giants there was a small, glass table (just like the one Alice saw in the rabbit hole) on which lay the Famous Chocolate Cherry that made anyone who ate it invisible if they took a small bite first and then a big one, while at the same time singing Bloody Bitch. He needed the chocolate because he had no weapons and was being chased by a band of thieves, the Clumpfart Brothers with their poisonous giraffe that could stretch its neck out a thousand feet.

Charles bumped into something blocking his way. The object resembled a series of small tables stacked one on top of another, but closer examination revealed it to be a ladder with which he could climb up to the top of the castle wall.

He began scaling the wall. It wasn't easy! The ladder was hard to hold on to, and strange obstacles kept forcing him to lean way back and risk falling, and his sweating hands were too slippery to hold on to the rungs (shelves, actually), but finally, after much effort, he was at the top, out of breath, glistening with sweat, the arches of his feet aching, and proud of his accomplishment.

But wait! His troubles were far from over. From the top of the wall a thin branch stretched out over the void (a terrifying gulf) leading to the window of the Room of the Giants. The branch was curiously hung with leaves, vines, and sleeping bats, and it was difficult and dangerous to work his way along it. Charles was able to push some of the obstacles along the branch (some of them fell, and after a long while he heard them hit the ground with a faint thud), and then holding on with his hands and knees, his head dangling, he managed to advance slowly, jerkily, towards the Room of the Giants and the Famous Chocolate Cherry, which he couldn't wait to sink his teeth into, because for the past several minutes his stomach had been growling like a washing machine.

Charles had now arrived at the middle of the rod suspended in the closet. The back of his knees were hurting slightly, but he smiled as he hung there in the darkness, the tips of his toes touching the ceiling; with his left hand he continued pushing the clothing that was blocking his advance, but it was becoming more and more difficult, and eventually he had to let them fall to the ground. But to do that he first had to raise the hangers off the rod, and that was extremely difficult. He wiggled and wriggled, arm outstretched, panting for breath, feeling as though his head were swelling up like a balloon, his cheeks were about to explode, and his blood would start pouring out through his eyes – when suddenly Crack!, the rod bent in the middle and became detached from the walls, and Charles tumbled ass-over-teakettle to the floor, landing on a pile of clothes that fortunately broke his fall, although he did manage to scrape his neck on a coat hook.

He lay without moving for a moment, flat on his back, thinking about the consequences of his accident. His father would be furious and would punish him again, this time even more severely because he'd interpret this mess as an act of revenge, a revolt.

He got up, picked up two sections of rod and tried to fit them together. No use. It was like trying to stick a tail back on a cat. It would have to be replaced with a new one. Whose stupid idea was it for him to act like a monkey in a closet?

Then a thought so horrible struck him that he let out an involuntary cry. He hurried over to the side of the closet, his hands feeling in the darkness, expecting the worst. But no, the jam jar was still standing up in the corner, and still contained the urine that made his nose wrinkle, all the more so because he knew it was his own.

Charles began carefully piling the clothes in the corner opposite the jar in order to give himself more room to move about. Not that he had any particular reason for moving here rather than there, lying down or standing up, stretching out his legs or keeping them bent. It was total boredom, the perfect punishment; his father must really hate him for thinking up something like this.

And so he was back where he started in his thinking. What fate awaited him? Luckily, his acrobatic antics had tired him out, and fatigue even more than hunger so dampened his spirit that he curled up again in Alice's coat, closed his eyes, and went to sleep.

A faint noise under the door woke him up. Opening his eyes, he saw two chocolate bars sliding through the line of light.

"Sylvie? Is that you?"

A dark shadow divided the line in half; the shadow wavered back and forth as though whoever was making it was trying to make up her mind.

"Not a word to your father, okay?" she said finally in a low voice. "And don't leave the wrappers out where he'll see them, either."

He heard another faint noise. The floor creaked and she was gone.

Feverishly, Charles unwrapped one of the bars, ate it in two bites, unwrapped the second bar, ate that in two more bites, then lay back on the pile of clothes with a contented sigh. He didn't feel quite so alone any more. Someone had thought of him. He was sorry for calling her a bloody bitch. She wasn't as bad as he'd thought. She really was very kind underneath, in her own way. But she was probably afraid of his father. Just as he was. And anyway, how could she love him, seeing as she wasn't his mother?

Charles thought about it for a while, his eye on the thin line of light as it began to fade, then realized that his mouth was dry and his throat stinging. All that chocolate had made him thirsty. Sylvie probably hadn't thought of that, and anyway what could she have done about it if she had? She couldn't slide a bottle of water under the door!

He worked his jaws and ran his tongue around the inside of his mouth, hoping to find a bit of saliva. His tongue had become thick and heavy. Again he was overcome by anger, and he took a violent swing at the door with his foot. The door resonated loudly but did not give.

"I want out of here!" he shouted at the top of his lungs, but his voice echoed hollowly in the empty, darkening apartment. His only reply was the sound of a fly buzzing around the room, aroused by the promise of an early spring.

■　■　■

Around five-thirty Wilfrid, who had come home from work earlier than usual feeling a bit uneasy in spite of himself, removed the screws from the closet door. Charles was sitting on the floor, stunned and blinking in the harsh light from the ceiling fixture.

"You can come out," Wilfrid said without seeming to notice the piled clothes and the two pieces of rod leaning against the wall.

Charles stood up slowly, walked unsteadily to the centre of the room, and then stopped. He turned his back to his father.

"Are you hungry?" Wilfrid asked, his voice curiously solicitous.

Without turning around the child nodded, yes.

"Good! Then let's eat. I brought you some Chinese food. You like that?" he asked.

There were two beige cardboard boxes on the kitchen table, tied up with string. Charles went straight to the sink and drank two large glasses of water, then, after looking at the boxes without apparent interest, let his gaze travel about the room as though seeing it for the first time; gradually his expression became more animated.

Wilfrid cut the strings, took the food out of the aluminum wrappers, and began setting the table.

"I stopped off at the Jade Garden on my way home from work," he said cheerily. "You remember we went there last summer with Sylvie?"

Charles said nothing. He took his place at the table and waited for his father to serve the meal. After the two chocolate bars he had little appetite.

They ate in silence. The kitchen smelled of deep-fried sugar. Charles thought of Boff, wondering where he was and sorry he couldn't share his food with him. Wilfrid ate noisily, smacking his lips, from time to time looking across the table at his son.

"You're not hungry?" he said after a while.

"No."

"Why not? Oh, I don't suppose you got much exercise today, eh?"

He was trying to speak lightly, but Charles remained cold. The carpenter's face tightened with annoyance.

"I know what you're thinking, Charles, but you shouldn't be angry with me. What I did I did for your sake. You needed to be taught a lesson that you would remember for a long time. It's a serious thing to lie to your father and to laugh at him behind his back with the neighbours. Parents deserve their children's respect, don't you ever forget that."

Charles hung his head and squirmed in his chair, saying nothing.

Wilfrid watched him for a few seconds.

"It's too bad you're not hungry," he said in a syrupy voice. "I got it especially for you because I know how much you like this stuff."

Charles stared at him, open-mouthed. His father had never spoken to him in such gentle tones before. Wilfrid smiled, then stuck his finger in his mouth to pry at a piece of meat with his fingernail.

"Stop staring at me like that, for Christ's sake," he suddenly shouted. "You look like you want to skin me alive!"

■ ■ ■

That night Charles went to see Boff at the Fafards'. He fed him, gave his house a good cleaning out, put in a new square of soft carpet, checked that the light bulb under the floor was working, talking to him all the while, teasing him and covering him with hugs and kisses. Everything he'd gone through for Boff's sake only seemed to increase the love that the child now felt for his dog.

"My little Boffie," he said, embracing him, "I love you more than if you were my brother!"

"I'd trade him for my sister anyday," laughed Henri.

Several weeks went by before Charles could bring himself to tell Henri about the punishment his father had inflicted on him, and which he'd been warned not to tell anyone about. His friend heard him out, his mouth hanging open in amazement, arms dangling, as though Charles had suddenly turned into a giant bird or a fire hydrant.

"The whole day?" he said when Charles had finished. "You spent the whole day locked up in a closet?"

"Yes," Charles said with a kind of stoic pride. "And I wasn't scared a bit."

Henri shrugged his shoulders and gave a skeptical laugh.

"Don't tell me you weren't scared, Thibodeau. I bet you cried. Didn't you? A whole day locked in a closet? It's like waking up in a closed coffin, or under a pile of rubble after an earthquake! Holy Moley! I'd've lost it for sure. And I bet you lost it, too."

"Nope. I made up games. I didn't even notice the time passing. The first thing I knew it was six o'clock at night and my father was opening the door. Maybe I was a bit thirsty."

Henri laughed, half-closing his eyes like a lawyer who didn't believe a word the witness was saying. Then he became serious.

"Why did he do that? Because of Boff?"

Charles nodded. Henri looked him in the eye.

"He's crazy, your father is," he murmured, looking very serious. "If I were you I'd go straight to the police! No question about it!"

Charles said he'd think about it, but made Henri promise in the meantime that he would keep the story to himself.

"Of course," said Henri, almost offended. "What do you take me for, a blabbermouth?"

But keeping such an important thing secret took an extraordinary amount of willpower. Henri had enough to last him about three hours, forty-two minutes, and eighteen seconds, which took him up to suppertime. At the table he broke down and gave a vivid description of the ordeal forced on Charles by his father. Fernand and Lucie listened to him, petrified.

"The whole day locked in a closet!" cried Céline in her thin, clear, little-girl's voice. "I'd be dead! Poor Charles! I'll bet he nearly died!"

Fernand slowly ran his fingers through his non-existent hair. Red splotches appeared on his face, evidence of the extreme agitation taking place just beneath the surface.

"I'm going to speak to Wilfrid about this right now," he said in the voice he used for important occasions.

"That's a good idea, dear," Lucie nodded. "Oh, Fernand, before I forget," she went on in a voice so light and carefree that Henri stared at her in astonishment, "can you come into the bedroom for a minute and help me hang up those curtains? I can't do it myself. You know how dizzy I get standing on a ladder."

Fernand gave her a quick look, got to his feet, and left the kitchen in two strides. Céline shrugged her shoulders, surprised by all the sudden leave-taking in mid-meal.

Henri leaned towards her. "It's because they don't want us to hear their conversation," he explained. "They're going to talk about Charles."

"If I were you," Lucie said, closing the door behind her, "I'd think twice before going over there to talk to Wilfrid. He might take it out on his son. This is a matter for the police, Fernand."

"I'm going to speak to him in any case. By the time I'm finished with him he won't dare take it out on anyone, believe me."

"Fernand, this is way out of our league. If I were you . . ."

"What kind of Christian," Fernand thundered, to the great satisfaction of the two children sitting immobile in the kitchen with their ears trained towards the bedroom, "would treat a nine-year-old boy like that, tell me? No, no, and no. I'm going to have a talk with him! There's only one way to deal with a bully like that – make him afraid!"

"He won't be afraid of you."

"We'll just see about that!"

He rolled his terrible eyes, turned around in the room, and repeated in an even louder voice:

"We'll just see about that!"

"Papa is very angry," said Henri, smiling at Céline. "I think he's going to go over there and clean Monsieur Thibodeau's clock for him!"

"But then they'll put him back in jail," said Céline, horrified.

"Let's say he is afraid of you," said Lucie, motioning to her husband to keep his voice down. "After three or four beers his fear will disappear, and who knows what he'll do after that?"

Fernand was stopped for a moment by the logic of this argument, but the righter-of-wrongs in him demanded immediate punishment for such insupportable behaviour; a raging bull wouldn't stop him from achieving his end.

"Don't worry, Lucie," he promised. "I'll take time to think before going to see him. I'll make sure I know what I'm going to say. But put yourself in my place, for crying out loud! – I can't just stand around with my arms folded with things like that going on."

"You are not the police, Fernand. It's not up to you."

"Hey!" called Henri from the kitchen, "we're starving to death out here! Can't you talk about this after supper?"

"Oh well, do what you think best," sighed Lucie, leaving the bedroom. "If you ask me, there's a much better way to deal with this problem."

"What's that?"

"We can talk about it later."

Shrugging her shoulders, she went back to the kitchen. Fernand headed down the hallway towards the front door, but the delicious smell of lasagna-au-gratin suddenly reminded him that a stomach deprived of food could transmit its emptiness to the brain, and so it wasn't until after he'd had two huge helpings followed by a slice of blueberry pie and a cup of syrupy tea that he put on his overcoat and left the house.

12

Fortune smiles on the brave. When Fernand crossed the street, Wilfrid was working on his front staircase, prying off a rotten board with a crowbar. Fernand kept his eye on the carpenter's back, walking quickly and breathing deeply, trying to keep calm. But the sight of his neighbour's long, thin hands and angry, drawn face, reddened by the cold but looking flushed with anger as he applied his weight to the tool with sharp movements that made the board shriek in protest, made him forget his resolution and feel the bile well up in him.

"Wilfrid!" he called out. "I need to speak to you!"

Wilfrid hadn't heard Fernand coming up behind him and nearly jumped out of his skin. The crowbar fell from his hands and clattered down the stairs.

"What do you want?" he said nastily, eyeing Fernand up and down.

"You know darn well what I want," growled the hardware-store owner, standing at the foot of the stairs and motioning for the carpenter to come down.

Thibodeau curled the corners of his lips in a show of bravado and turned his back, then, fearing his refusal to come down would be taken as a sign of cowardice, he descended, but slowly, only a few steps, until only a metre separated him from his interlocutor.

"It's not right, Wilfrid, what you did to your son the other day."

"What are you talking about?"

"Don't play the innocent with me! I know everything. You don't lock a small kid in a closet for a whole day, without light or food or anyone to keep an eye on him. It's a lousy thing to do! What if he hurt himself? Did you stop to think what such a thing might do to him psychologically?" he added, tapping his temple with his forefinger.

"What business is it of yours? What are you, his father now?"

125

"No, of course not, but speaking as a simple citizen . . ."

He stopped, not knowing how to finish the sentence. His embarrassment brought a mocking smile to the carpenter's lips, rendered vaguely sinister by his thin mouth and yellow teeth. Emboldened, Wilfrid came down another step.

"I have the right to raise my kid any way I see fit, you got that, Big Mouth? I don't go sticking my nose in your business, so don't come around here sticking yours in mine. Understand? Do I need to draw you a picture?"

Fernand looked at Wilfrid for a minute, staring at him strangely, then his heavy cheeks began to twitch. His hand suddenly shot out and grabbed Thibodeau by the shoulder, making him grimace in pain.

"You listen to me, fella," Fernand said. "If I ever hear that you've mistreated that boy again, I'll rip off your arm and shove it down your throat, you miserable little excuse for a human being!"

And he shook Wilfrid so hard the carpenter had to grab the handrail to prevent himself from falling backwards.

"Ow! Let go of me, you fucking idiot!"

Enraged beyond control, Fernand continued shaking Wilfrid, seemingly unable to stop himself. His eyes narrowed, his mouth tightened, his nostrils flared; his whole face seemed to be closing down, a terrifying sight. It certainly frightened Wilfrid, who went on whining in protest. Suddenly, he delivered a violent kick to his assailant's stomach, succeeded in freeing himself, and dashed up the stairs as though all the demons from hell were at his heels. At the top, he turned and looked down at Fernand, who was bent over, holding his stomach with both hands and trying to catch his breath.

"You try that on me one more time," shouted the carpenter, rubbing his shoulder painfully, "and you'll be back in prison before you can count to ten, you jailbird!"

"Prison, is it?" Fernand managed to get out in a strained voice. "Well, we'll be in there together, then, my friend, because I'll report you to the police."

With those words the two men parted. "Well, now you've done it, you big idiot," Fernand told himself as he returned to his own house. "You should have given it more thought before barging over there and sticking your big foot in it like that. Now you'll never see the little guy again at your place. Instead of helping him, you made it worse for him – maybe even put him in serious danger. Maybe I should lodge a complaint after all."

He talked it over with Lucie for a long time. Her advice was to wait a few days to see what would come of the incident.

■ ■ ■

As Fernand predicted, Charles didn't show up at the Fafards' the next day; Boff waited patiently for him, emitting little plaintive barks until late into the evening. But the next day the child appeared as though nothing had happened, saying to Lucie, who was surprised and relieved, that his father had calmed down and everything was back to normal.

In fact, once the carpenter had had time to work through his anger and think about it, he'd realized that the Fafards' attachment to his son presented certain benefits to himself, relieving him of a good part of his responsibilities, even allowing him to save money on food bills, and that the situation was also satisfactory from Sylvie's point of view; she had never shown much interest in the boy, considering herself to be completely separate from him. The deception Charles had subjected him to, plus the humiliating scene on the staircase, had distanced Wilfrid from his son even further, if such a thing were possible. The threats Fafard had made frightened him, however, and he didn't dare punish his son for his behaviour. But he began to regard the boy with a deep, insidious hatred, the extent of which was unknown even to himself. It continued to deepen and fester, and would have serious consequences for Charles later in the boy's life.

■ ■ ■

Spring arrived without further incident. The snow eventually melted, leaving little clumps of dirt that the street-cleaners smashed into powder and scattered to the four winds. The air warmed up, became almost sweet, filled with unfamiliar odours that caused some people to dream and others to wince. The lawns and waste spaces exhaled a stench that smelled like vomit, making Charles hold his nose as he walked past. The sweet effusions from the Macdonald's Tobacco Company floated in the air from morning to night along every street in the neighbourhood. Henri began smoking in secret and tried to get Charles to join him. After taking a few puffs and nearly choking to death, Charles stomped on the cigarette in disgust and vowed he would never try it again, no doubt in rebellion against his father and Sylvie, both of whom smoked like chimneys.

Winter clothing was packed away in closets and stored in cardboard boxes sprinkled with mothballs. Everyone, emboldened by the fine weather and impatient to take advantage of it, dressed as though it were already full summer. For the first time, Charles began to notice girls' legs, since short skirts were the fashion of the time. Some legs attracted him with a mysterious, almost irresistible force; they moved, intrigued, and delighted him, and he joked about it with Henri, who confessed to having the same urges as Charles and who told him three extremely dirty stories, at least dirty to them, that made them both laugh.

One day, towards the end of the afternoon, finding himself with nothing to do, Boff wandered over to the Thibodeaus' yard and ended up face to face with Charles's father, who had just finished repairing Monsieur Victoire's clothesline. Seeing the dog, the carpenter threw his hammer at it, hitting it hard on the haunch; the dog, howling, escaped through a hole in the fence, ran down the alley, and, crossing rue Dufresne, came within a hair of being run over by a delivery truck. Charles, who'd been watching, was horrified, and ran to shake Boff roughly by the collar, scolding him for his carelessness; then he saw the wound on the dog's leg.

"Who did this to you?" he cried in alarm.

Then his father appeared at the apartment door, and Charles guessed the truth. Crouching down beside Boff, he whispered:

"Let this be a lesson to you, you big dummy. This is not your home any more. Don't ever forget it."

■ ■ ■

Towards the end of May, Wilfrid, off work because of a fractured wrist, announced to his son that he was cutting off the boy's weekly allowance, seeing as how Charles was making enough to get by on running errands for the corner restaurant.

"I think it's better to *think of your future*," he explained in strangely accented tones (he'd been drinking). "You never know, you might want to go on to *further your education* . . . we'll need the money more, then."

It didn't take long for Rosalie to hear about this new arrangement. She was outraged. Like everyone else in the neighbourhood, she knew all about the episode with Boff, and she thought Wilfrid Thibodeau's decision was just another example of his cruelty. She talked it over with Roberto.

"The poor kid! He'd be better off with no father at all than with one like him! I'm going to give him some deliveries at Frontenac Towers from time to time. He's a bit young yet, but he's smart. I don't think Gilles will mind that much: he's often got too much as it is."

Charles was delighted when Rosalie told him that his territory would henceforth include the Towers. The three huge apartment blocks, built a few years earlier on rue Bercy, were home to a large number of people who were crazy about Roberto's pizzas and club sandwiches and hot chicken sandwiches, not to mention his incomparable poutine. They liked to consume vast quantities of them in the comfort of their own apartments, and they were famous for being generous tippers.

■ ■ ■

His first delivery took place that Friday night at seven, and it left him with mixed feelings. He started out by losing fifteen minutes (and no doubt a big part of his tip) by going up the wrong tower; then, when he at last found the right address, he was hit by a fire alarm the moment he stepped off the elevator on the seventeenth floor. The horrible sound of bells going off and the toneless, metallic voice coming from the loudspeakers telling everyone to proceed in a careful, calm manner, threw him into such a panic that he ran up and down the corridor like a rat spattered with nitric acid. The air seemed hard to breathe, and he was sure he could smell smoke. He thought of firemen's ladders, of people in flames throwing themselves out of windows, their faces twisted in terror. He ended up crashing heavily into a door, crying. The door opened and he nearly tumbled into the apartment. A young blond boy considered him in silence. From Charles's position on the floor, the boy looked like a giant, but when he stood up he saw that he was about his own size; he even seemed vaguely familiar.

"What are you doing?" asked the boy.

A man's voice came from within. "Shut the door, Michel! We have to keep the door closed! Didn't you hear the instructions?"

At that second the alarm went off.

"I'm lost," Charles said piteously.

"Who's the pizza for?" asked the boy.

"Apartment 1759."

"Another false alarm, I guess," grumbled the man's voice, and there was the sound of someone dialing a rotary telephone. "Shut the door, Michel," the voice said again, this time with much less urgency.

"It was a false alarm, Papa!" called the boy. "Just like before!" Then he turned to Charles. "Do you want me to show you where it is? It's not far."

Charles put his hand on the pizza box, which was almost cold by then, and nodded.

"Ah, good!" said the man's voice into the telephone. "Another false alarm? It's getting on our nerves, Madame! I've even got cramps in my legs. Yes, yes, I understand. Good luck!"

Michel closed the door and moved rapidly down the corridor with Charles. As he walked, he told Charles that his last name was Blondin, that he had until recently been going to the new Champlain School on rue Logan, but since moving into the Towers he was going to start at Saint-Anselme, where he'd be in Grade Three, in Madame Robidoux's class.

"Oh yeah? I'm in Mademoiselle Laramée's."

"I know," replied Michel, smiling. "I saw you in the playground during recess. Here we are, this is it."

With his heart pounding, Charles rang the bell. The door was opened by a huge woman with grey hair and a mauve dress, whose silver glasses seemed to shoot out lightning bolts. She crossed her arms and, looking furious, stood there saying nothing.

"It wasn't his fault, Madame," said Michel, giving her a slight bow. "He was caught by the false alarm. He was quite frightened by it, as you can appreciate."

Charles thought it prudent to accompany Michel's story with a smile that expressed his regret at having arrived with a pizza that by then would have to be re-heated.

"Well, I guess it's all right this time," grumbled the woman, taking the box. She handed Charles an envelope. "But aren't you a bit young to be delivering pizzas? Is this the first time you've been up here?"

"It's the first time I've been to your apartment, Madame," Charles replied, evasive without being aware of it. "But I've been working for Chez Robert for two years now."

The woman shrugged and pursed her lips in what could with generosity be described as the beginning of a smile, and closed the door.

"Thanks," Charles said, leaving his guide.

"See you tomorrow," Michel replied, and ran off towards his own apartment.

Afraid that his lateness would lose him his precious Frontenac Towers, Charles ran back to the restaurant as quickly as he could, where there would no doubt be more deliveries waiting for him. There were, as it turned out, and Rosalie was just about to telephone the customer to try to track down her delivery boy. Charles told her about the false alarm, didn't try to hide from her how frightened he'd been, and promised to display a little more sang-froid in the future if something like that ever happened again.

"Well, this time don't leave anyone waiting. It's for Monsieur Saint-Amour. As usual, he likes his anchovy pizza piping hot. As soon as you get it, you run like a rabbit, okay?"

Charles took off at a run for rue Frontenac, where the former hairdresser lived, the one with the over-stuffed apartment and the slightly strange ways.

The evening was to have more emotional adventures in store for him.

■ ■ ■

When he entered the apartment building, he saw a bag of dog food in the ground-floor hallway, lying half-split open with some of its contents spilled out over the unwashed linoleum floor. It seemed to have been just left there. "I'll take that for Boff," he thought, happily. "Monsieur Fafard will be happy." (The hardware-store owner had graciously taken over the feeding of the dog.)

He turned to the door to Monsieur Saint-Amour's apartment and knocked. There was no response. He knocked again, louder this time, eager to be taking a closer look at the bag. A very soft tread could be heard coming from within the apartment, like that of a person walking carefully, followed by a sort of snap, then a long, floating groan. Charles felt his face turning red and his hands becoming suddenly moist.

"Oooooh! Oooooh!" cried a man's voice, struggling, it seemed to Charles, with unspeakable pain.

131

"Monsieur Saint-Amour!" Charles called out. "Can you hear me? It's me, Charles, the delivery boy from Chez Robert."

"Come in, Charles," said the voice, sounding faint. "The door is open."

The child entered the apartment. In the centre of a kitchen so tiny that a fly would have had a hard time flying more than twenty centimetres in a straight line, he saw the former hairdresser stripped to the waist, collapsed on a black leather recliner with his head thrown back, staring up at the ceiling with every sign of being on the very threshold of passing into the next world.

"What's wrong with you, Monsieur Saint-Amour?" cried Charles, horrified. He put the pizza box down on a table that also held an electric heater and several other cardboard boxes.

"Aaaaah! Aaaaah!" repeated the man, without seeming to have heard Charles's question. "It's my ... stomach ... It's killing me ..." he finally gulped. He brought his trembling hand up and rested it on his belly, which was grey and flabby and covered with white hairs and hung out over the top of his belt.

"Come and rub me, my boy," he begged in a whisper, emitting another groan.

Charles hung back, torn between disgust and pity, then stepped hesitantly forward.

"Where do you want me to rub, Monsieur?"

"Here, on my ... just below the stomach ... Yes, there, near the belt ... maybe a bit under it, that's right ... aaaah, these damned stomach pains ... they'll be the death of me ... yes, there ... don't stop, dear boy ... it feels so good ... a bit to the left ... now a bit to the right, there ... yes, yes ... and a bit lower down ... my intestines are so delicate ... ever since I was a lad ... such pain ... comes on without warning ... it's pure torture ... Oh, yes, keep rubbing ..."

A moment went by.

"I'm getting kind of tired, Monsieur Saint-Amour," sighed Charles, who had just noticed a strange bulge in the front of his customer's pants that made him feel increasingly uneasy.

"You'll get your ... reward in a few minutes ... dear boy. Aah! It feels much better ... already ... Faster, faster ... it's almost gone ... There! Oh! Oh! Oh, thank you so much!"

The man gave a slight jump, then closed his eyes, and sank back into his chair, his body completely relaxed.

"Step back a bit now," he said to Charles without looking at him. "I'm feeling much better. You can leave . . . There's an envelope on the table beside the heater, take it . . . Wait," he added suddenly. "I want to tell you something."

His voice had returned to its usual strength and clarity; he sounded almost joyful. He sat up straight in the chair and looked hard at Charles, his eye sparkling maliciously while his mouth fought to keep a serious expression.

"Don't go telling anyone about my stomach trouble, if you don't mind, my dear boy. People will laugh at me and I won't have the courage to order any more pizzas from Chez Robert . . . And that would be too bad. You'd lose your tips . . . When you open that envelope you'll see that tonight's is an extra generous one . . . You promise me this will be our little secret?"

"I promise, Monsieur Saint-Amour," Charles replied, turning red.

"Next time you come I'll have a surprise for you, something that will give you a great deal of pleasure."

Charles headed for the door, impatient to be out of the apartment. Then suddenly he turned around.

"Monsieur Saint-Amour, do you know who owns that bag of dog food in the hall?"

"Oh! It belonged to two Jamaicans who lived in the apartment next door. They left it there this morning when they moved out. You can take it if you want. It'll give your dog strong teeth."

Charles hurried down the street carrying the bag, which was heavier than he'd expected it to be. He felt sad and uneasy without really knowing why. The scene in the apartment had disgusted him and made him feel ashamed, but he didn't think he had done anything wrong. He'd only done what the man had asked him to do.

When he arrived at the restaurant, he opened the envelope: there were two dollars in it, the largest tip he'd ever received in his life. But it gave him no pleasure. He stuck the money in his pocket and thought no more about it.

The next night, Monsieur Saint-Amour ordered another pizza, but Charles refused to deliver it.

"What's got into you?" Roberto asked, greatly surprised.

"I don't feel like going."

"Putting on airs, now, are we?" said Sylvie, passing with a carafe of coffee. "Better be careful, they'll show you the door."

Rosalie, however, was curious. She looked at Charles for a second, then, shrugging, turned to a tall, skinny kid with a black moustache who had just come in twirling a ring of keys on his index finger.

"Gilles," she said, "take this pizza over to Monsieur Saint-Amour."

Charles gave a sigh of relief and went to join Boff, who was waiting for him outside the restaurant.

■ ■ ■

Charles would have liked to have confided in Henri, since the incident of the stomach pains continued to torment him, but he felt bound by having given his word. He was sorry he had given it, because he felt he had dirtied himself.

In the end he took the two-dollar bill to the Woolworth's on rue Ontario, bought a pretty plastic doll in a blue tulle dress, and gave it to Céline. He knew it was exactly the kind of gift that would please a six-year-old girl. Overjoyed and delighted, she threw herself in his arms and kissed him on the cheeks.

"A doll for me? But it's not even my birthday!"

"That doesn't matter, I felt like giving it to you."

He liked Céline very much. She reminded him a bit of Henri, rowdy and boisterous, always thumping or tugging at him; there were certain advantages to being the friend of the best fighter in the third grade at Saint-Anselme Elementary, but it was also sometimes exhausting. Céline, however, was a girl, and that made a world of difference. Sometimes when he was in the Fafards' living room watching television with Henri, she would slip in between them on the sofa and lean ever so slightly against him. Charles pretended not to notice, but he liked it very much.

■ ■ ■

Charles and Michel Blondin, the boy from Frontenac Towers, quickly formed a friendship. Michel was a quiet, even-tempered child, meticulous as a three-legged turtle yet also a dreamer, although that didn't stop him from being an excellent pupil. He soon gained a leadership role among his friends, for two reasons: his interest in others, and his talent for settling minor disputes. Three weeks after his arrival at Saint-Anselme he was on good terms with one and all, and despite his dubious status as a newcomer no one thought of him for a moment as an outsider.

One day, when two pupils were shouting insults at each other and seemed on the verge of coming to blows, Michel went over to them, calm and smiling, and the following scene unfolded:

MICHEL:

Hey, guys! Don't get yourselves in a knot. If the supervisor sees you, you'll both end up in the principal's office.

FIRST PUPIL:

He called me a dirty pig!

MICHEL:

You're not a pig and as far as anyone can tell, you're not dirty, either. (*To the second pupil*) Why did you call him that?

SECOND PUPIL:

He said my sister smells like piss.

MICHEL:

(*Frowning*) Well, *does* she?

SECOND PUPIL:

No! I mean . . . okay, maybe sometimes she does (*general laughter from the onlookers*). But (*shaking his fist at the first pupil*) it's none of his goddamn business!

MICHEL:

(*Unmoved*) And that's what you were fighting about? It's no big deal! When I eat a hamburger, I smell like onions. So what?

FIRST PUPIL:

(*Sarcastically*) Better to smell like onions than piss!

MICHEL:

(*Turning on first pupil*) Once, when I was in Grade One, I had diarrhea (*renewed general laughter*), and my teacher sent me out of class because I had an accident (*more laughter, cries of Phew!*). I cried then, but now it doesn't bother me! (*To first pupil*) Tell your mother to pay more attention to your sister, make sure she washes a bit more often, the whole thing will blow over. (*Back to first pupil*) When you were a baby, you smelled like piss, too. So did I. Everyone smells like piss at some time in their lives. It's really nothing to get excited about.

135

■ ■ ■

Everyone called him Blonblon; it was a slightly mocking nickname, but it also held an appreciable dose of affection. Madame Robidoux, his teacher, called him "the diplomat," or sometimes even "the priest" or "the missionary," which always made him wince. He had a sister who was much older than he was, just finishing high school. His mother was a real estate agent and the sole supporter of the family, since his father, who suffered from multiple sclerosis, had been confined to the home for many years; it was perhaps from having grown up with a handicapped parent who required constant care and attention that he had acquired his penchant for looking after others and making sure that harmony reigned, hardly a common trait in someone his age.

More than once Charles was on the point of telling him about the scene with the stomach pains, but each time the words stuck in his throat. He had Blonblon over to his house two or three times, but his father's unpredictable behaviour – he had by then lost his job completely and dwelled in a world full of foul moods in which his dependence on alcohol had become more and more obvious – discouraged Charles from making it a habit. He settled for seeing Blonblon at Henri's house, where Blonblon, with his good manners and his preference for quieter games, was an instant hit with the Fafard parents. He had a calming influence on their own son, and even on Charles.

■ ■ ■

Charles's route to and from school was always along rue Bercy. At a certain point his attention had for some time been drawn to a brass plaque attached to the front of one of the nicer houses, on which could be read:
PARFAIT MICHAUD
NOTARY
The plaque intrigued him for several reasons. How could anyone go around calling himself Parfait? Even if his parents had had the ridiculous notion of calling him Perfect when he was born, he surely could have changed it when he grew up! And then what was a notary, anyway? To judge by the house this Parfait Michaud lived in, whatever he did for a living must bring in a fair amount of money; which again was strange, because he'd never seen anyone either entering or leaving the premises. The whole thing was a mystery to him.

"What's a notary?" he asked Sylvie one day.

"Someone who pushes paper for a living," she replied.

"What kind of paper?"

"Oh, you know, contracts, wills, things like that."

"What's a will?"

"When a person dies . . . Oh, I'll explain it to you some other time. I'm not in the mood today."

"Madame Laramée, what's a notary?" he asked his teacher the next day, unsatisfied with Sylvie's reply.

The teacher told him that a notary was someone whose work consisted in putting things down on paper that two parties had agreed to, especially important transactions such as buying or selling houses, transferring money, debts, loans, and so on.

Charles concluded that being a notary must be an extremely uninteresting way to make a living, and that anyone who even came near such a person would immediately drop dead of boredom.

Which was a completely erroneous conclusion, at least in Parfait Michaud's case.

One morning as Charles was walking to school, an incident took place that made him change his opinion.

He was walking with Henri and four more or less skeletal dogs that had been following them for a while despite the fact that he had nothing to give them except two miserable crusts of bread, the only food he had in his pocket that morning. But his charm seemed to compensate for the meagreness of his offerings. He had just stopped to pet a large, black, mastiff-like dog that was particularly affectionate when the animal let out a howl of pain and took off down the street. A stone had hit it in the paw.

Fats Dubé appeared from behind a hedge on the other side of the street, accompanied by his two henchmen, and began to laugh.

"You asshole!" shouted Charles in fury. "Leave my dogs alone!"

"Your dogs stink!" one of the henchmen yelled back.

"And so do you!" added the other.

A volley of stones made the other three dogs take off, also howling in pain.

One of the stones struck Henri on the forehead. Unmindful of the blood that was staining his shirt, he chased after the boy who had thrown it, who lit out like an arrow for the safety of the school grounds. Charles remained

137

where he was, without his protector. He picked up a stone and threw it, hitting Dubé on the elbow. Fats let out a cry and vigorously rubbed his arm. Not finding any stones of his own, he ran towards Charles, his second henchman close behind, intent on giving Charles the beating of the century. Charles threw another stone, missing his target, then stood stoically awaiting his destiny. There was no question of running away. His honour was at stake. In seconds the two bullies had stripped him of his school bag and emptied it onto the sidewalk; then Fats Dubé sat on Charles and calmly began strangling him while his henchman stood beside them kicking Charles in the ribs. Fats began experiencing difficulties with his left ear, because Charles was attempting to detach it from Dubé's head with his teeth. Nonetheless, his attempts to suffocate Charles were bearing fruit; he was on the point of claiming complete victory when he suddenly felt a sharp pain on his backside that made him let go of his quarry. Someone was whipping him! Charles disentangled himself and the two boys stood up, panting. Dubé's henchman had run off. A tall, thin man in a dark blue, pinstripe suit, holding a fishing rod, grabbed Charles's assailant by one arm and shook him.

"You hooligan! Don't let me catch you at it again! Torturing animals, and then fighting two against one! You should be ashamed! Go smartly, now. I've got my eye on you! Next time, I'll call the police!"

The scene had taken place before the notary's house. On the doorstep, with the door wide open, stood a small woman wearing a purple turban, nodding her head approvingly. Charles guessed that the unknown man was her husband, and also the notary.

Fats Dubé had ran off, sheepishly, although he turned round from time to time to cast furious looks at the man with the fishing rod.

Charles would have preferred tasting his victory without having had help, but he nevertheless bowed towards his deliverer.

"Thank you, sir," he said, dusting off his jeans and windbreaker. "And the dogs thank you, too."

The man smiled and held out his hand.

"You strike me as a good little guy," he said. "I've seen you passing the house a good many times with your herd of wild dogs. Are they all yours?"

"No, sir. My own dog stays at home."

"Where do they all come from?"

"I'm not sure, sir. From all over, I guess."

"In any case, they seem to be fond of you. You feed them, I shouldn't wonder?"

"Not always. When I can. I didn't have much to offer them today."

"Then they must like the way you are with them. I can see why they feel safe with you. Have they been following you about for a long time?"

"Yes, sir. Excuse me, sir, but I have to go now or I'll be late for school."

"If those hooligans bother you again, just ring my doorbell. My name is Parfait Michaud. I'm almost always home."

"And when he isn't," called the turbaned woman from the porch, "I am."

■ ■ ■

Weeks went by and summer came. Charles finished second in his class, to Ginette Laramée's consternation; she would have liked him to have finished first. On the last day of school, just before the class was dismissed, she gave him a present, as she did to each of her pupils. It was an illustrated edition of the better-known fables of La Fontaine. The cover showed a fat crow perched in a tree with a piece of cheese in its beak, staring down at a perky red fox who was winking up at it.

Charles thanked her with a smile, which pleased her greatly; then, in a rush of affection, he took her hand; the gesture made her weak in the knees, like a convent girl receiving her first kiss.

"Wait a bit," she said, "there's something I want to show you."

She finished distributing her gifts, wished each of her pupils a good vacation ("Be careful, have a lot of fun and come back to us in one piece"). Then, when everyone but Charles had left, she opened her desk drawer, took out a parcel wrapped in brown paper and gave it to Charles.

"A little something extra for you. I bought it for my nephew," she explained, which was a white lie, "but he's grown so much it's much too small for him. I hope you like it."

It was a blue cotton shirt, very smart, with shiny, dark-blue buttons. Charles looked at it, surprised and a bit embarrassed, suspecting that the nephew was a fiction.

"Thank you, Mademoiselle Laramée," he said with a somewhat forced smile. "It's very nice. I promise to take good care of it."

She leaned towards him and kissed him on both cheeks, a highly unusual gesture for her.

"Off you go, my boy, and have a good holiday. And keep reading every day. It's a good habit to get into."

And with hasty, awkward movements she began to arrange the papers on her desk.

13

Charles guessed that the blue shirt had been the result of an impulse of pity. For some time he had been what modern specialists might call clothing challenged: shapeless socks, thread-bare elbows, underwear about to give up the ghost. Wilfrid's financial problems had been transferred to his son in ways that were becoming increasingly visible, and it was apparent that the state of Charles's clothing was no more important to the carpenter than it was to his companion. Lucie Fafard often brought up the matter with her husband, but neither of them dared become involved for fear of rubbing their neighbour's fur the wrong way.

Wilfrid was supplementing the money he was collecting from Unemployment Insurance by doing odd jobs under the table around the neighbourhood. A large portion of his earnings, however, were translated into alcohol. Towards the middle of July, a violent argument broke out between him and Sylvie. As he was sitting in the kitchen, beer in hand, she told him she was "fed up with supporting a drunkard," that it was "high time you got up off your ass and looked for a job," and that, if in two weeks' time nothing had been done about it, she'd be "out of here so fast you won't see my tail lights for dust!"

Depressed by her relentless criticism, he decided to go down to the Amis du Sport, an institution he'd been supporting for the past few years, to think things over.

It was there that, after drinking three beers (in an excess of heroism he'd decided to limit his daily intake to that number), he made the acquaintance of a certain Gino Guilbault, known to his friends as Loose Lips; he was an affable, dapper man who looked upon the world with an energetic optimism. Complaining, deep sighing, stomach ulcers, insomnia, all of that he left to the world's defeatists, hypochondriacs, and other professional depressives. The first time Wilfrid noticed him in the bar he liked what he saw: marine-coloured suit with yellow stripes, sky-blue silk tie shot with gold threads, thick, lustrous hair swept back from his temples. A big, red-faced man who glowed with health and self-confidence, he was sitting by himself with six draughts of beer on the table in front of him, drinking them one by one with deliberate satisfaction. A large, red boil shone softly on one of his cheeks, but, unlike most blemishes, this growth lent his face a sympathetic and unpretentious air, drawing attention from the slight asymmetry of his mouth and its quivering lips.

He glanced up at the carpenter and smiled, said something pertinent about the state of the weather, and invited him to join him at his table. Wilfrid didn't need to be asked twice. The promise he'd made to himself about the three beers didn't extend to those he got for free.

Introductions made, Gino Guilbault smiled warmly and declared that the beer sitting before them on the table was their common property.

"A nice, quiet spot," he added after a contented sigh, his arm sweeping the bar in an all-inclusive gesture. "A fella can come in here and drink his beer in peace and be left alone with his thoughts. You come here often?"

"When I have the time," Wilfrid replied cautiously.

"You have to make the time! Make the time, I say!" replied Guilbault joyously. "We only live once! Even if we had three lives, time would still be a precious commodity!"

To this Guilbault added several other philosophical considerations of a similar profundity. Then, after apprising himself of his companion's trade and expressing his deep and abiding admiration for carpenters, he began to speak of his own occupation. Gino Guilbault ran a small charitable company. He sold chocolate bars and gave the majority of his profits to organizations dedicated to the welfare and protection of youth, such as the Boy Scouts, 4-H Clubs, various camps for handicapped or destitute children, sports organizations for the underprivileged, and so on and so forth. Children, both boys and girls, sold the chocolate bars for him, and his company – a modest affair, he hastened to make clear – was at that time in the process of recruiting new salespersons.

Wilfrid's eyes lit up. "How much do these kids make?" he asked.

"Twenty-five cents a bar. It may not seem like much, but an enterprising boy or girl can make up to ten dollars a day. Girls make a little more, in fact. Do you have children?"

"One, a boy."

"How old is he?"

"Nine."

"A good age. Not too old, not too young. Smart kid?"

"Too damned smart," Wilfrid said with a puff of paternal pride accentuating his red nose and cheeks. His face, softened by alcohol, took on an expression of grave solemnity. He launched into a flattering description of Charles, doubtless for the first time in his life.

"Perfect, perfect, just the kind of employee I'm looking for. He'll make a lot of money, just you wait and see! It'll be good for him, good for me, good for everyone."

He searched the inside pocket of his jacket and gave Thibodeau a card.

CHOCO CHARITIES
Society for the Aid of Destitute Youth
738-9014
"We work hard at doing good"

"Tell him to give me a call tomorrow. His hours will always be after school and on weekends. We don't want to interfere with his studies, naturally."

"Don't you have an address?" asked the carpenter, surprised.

"No, I'm always on the move. I spend my days on the street, at my suppliers, in the metro stations, places like that. But I have a secretary who takes all my messages."

Wilfrid finished his own beer, and Guilbault told him to help himself to the glasses sitting so invitingly under his eyes, and even nudged one of them towards the carpenter's hand.

When Wilfrid arrived home that night around eleven, a bit rubbery in the legs, the apartment was completely dark. He made his way as silently as he could towards his bedroom and stood for a moment leaning in the doorway. A gentle light came in through the parted curtains and fell on the sleeping Sylvie. Because of the heat and humidity, she had thrown off the sheet and blanket, and was lying on her back with her legs apart, snoring lightly. Wilfrid smiled, went over to the bed and slid his hand under her nightgown to caress her breast. Her eyes opened suddenly, and she pushed his hand away, grumbling.

Disgruntled, he went out into the kitchen and discovered that there was no more beer in the fridge. He flopped down on a chair, leaned back against the table, legs outstretched, and suddenly remembered there was a heel of scotch left in a bottle in the cupboard above the fridge. The next moment he had the bottle out and made the happy discovery that it was a third full; he drained it in one long, satisfying guzzle. A deep sense of well-being spread through his body, and he looked around the kitchen with a benevolent eye.

Despite his fatigue he did not feel like sleeping. A vague desire welled up within him, a sort of purposeless and causeless elation that also contained an element of piercing sadness and even anger that had to be held in check at all costs, by constantly moving about, by acting, by doing something, anything.

He stood up with difficulty and went into Charles's bedroom and sat down heavily on the side of the bed. The boy breathed a deep sigh and smacked his lips, but didn't awaken. Wilfrid looked at him in the orange light from a Mickey Mouse nightlight installed in the plug beside the dresser; every so often the boy's eyelids fluttered, or his lips contracted slightly, or his head turned from side to side. But he remained on his back, one arm hanging over the side of the bed, hand open like that of a beggar. He had always slept like that, and it had always bothered the carpenter; he felt as though the hand were there as a reproach to him.

"Charles!"

The boy sighed and turned on his side.

"Charles, wake up! I got something to tell you," said the carpenter in a slightly louder voice.

He shook the boy roughly by the shoulders.

"What? What's the matter?" sputtered Charles, sitting up in the bed.

He looked at his father with a terrified expression.

"I got you a job, my boy. You're going to sell chocolate bars!"

The child kept staring at him silently, pushing himself back to the head of the bed. His father's breath, his slouched and somewhat puffy posture, and his narrow eyes, staring and slightly feverish, all spoke eloquently of his condition. Anything could happen. Charles held his breath and waited.

"Aren't you happy?" Wilfrid demanded, returning his hand to his son's shoulder. "You're going to make us a lot of money! Five bucks a day! D'you hear that? Five bucks! Aren't you glad?"

Charles nodded his head rapidly.

"Tomorrow you're going to call a Monsieur Guilbault. You'll go and meet up with him and he'll tell you what you have to do. It's as easy as pie. He gave me his card."

He lifted his slightly trembling hand to his shirt pocket and succeeded in taking out the small card, which he held out to Charles. The boy took it without even glancing at it and put it down beside him, his eyes still on his father.

"You don't look too happy about it," Wilfrid said jokingly. "But I just did you a good turn, my boy. Money don't grow on trees these days . . . When you get a chance like this you gotta jump at it without asking too many questions . . . S'true I just woke you up," he added, placing his hand on his forehead as though to prevent it from exploding. He began breathing in irregular snorts, and his head bobbed gently on his shoulders.

"Yes," said Charles.

"So say thank you! Christ's sake! I just done you a big favour, you know."

Charles pushed farther back in his bed and managed a tight smile: "Thank you very much."

Satisfied, the carpenter nodded once and yawned deeply. When he tried to stand up, however, he discovered to his stupefaction that his legs had decided to detach themselves from his body, as though they wanted to follow their own separate destinies; they no longer did what he told them to do. He couldn't let his son see him leave the room on his knees or, even worse, on all fours. No, he must avoid that at all costs.

"Tired's the devil all-va sudden," he slurred, struggling to make his swollen lips move in their normal fashion. "Think I'll jus' lie down here furrabit. Don' mind me, jus' go backta sleep."

And under the astonished gaze of his son he slid down to the floor, leaned his head against the end of the bed and closed his eyes.

Charles waited a long time before lying back down. He turned his back towards his sleeping father, curled up into a ball hugging Simon tightly, and pulled the blanket up over his head. He imagined himself in a bubble, gently floating high above the city. Boff was in the bubble with him, snuggled up against his chest, and he felt he was in the best of all possible worlds.

His father's snoring woke him in the morning; he was sleeping with his mouth open, still stretched out on the floor.

The night before, Charles had forgotten to close the blind before going to bed, and now the morning sunlight flooded into the room, pushing the night's fears deep into the corners of his mind.

With his shirt half-unbuttoned, his hair sticking up on his head, and his jaw hanging open, Wilfrid was not a pretty sight. Sitting in his bed, Charles studied his father's mouth, a huge, dark cavern that reminded him of a drain-hole in a bathtub or a sink; he imagined a leak in the ceiling through which a thin trickle of water would fall into his father's mouth with a quiet gurgle. The idea made him laugh, then he stopped, slightly ashamed of himself. There was nothing funny about what he was looking at. His father was drinking so much these days that he couldn't keep a job; one day, something terrible was sure to happen to him.

Quietly he got out of bed, gathered up his clothes, and went out into the living room to get dressed. Sylvie was still asleep. He decided to go to the Fafards' for breakfast. Lucie and Fernand always got up early and would welcome him with pleasure, as they always did. He'd hardly closed the door and begun descending the staircase when he heard Sylvie's furious voice rising from the apartment:

"What the hell do you think you're doing there, you! Sleeping on the floor in your son's bedroom! Drinking like a pig again last night, were you?"

Charles crept silently down the stairs and ran across the street. In the Fafards' backyard, Boff heard the boy's footsteps and began barking.

■　■　■

Gino Guilbault got out of his purple Lincoln, rubbed his stomach absently with a circular motion, and walked towards the entrance to the Frontenac metro station, singing *You are my sunshine, my only sunshine*, softly to himself. His new shoes squeaked satisfactorily, a fresh stick of cinnamon-flavoured gum was sweetening his breath, Angèle, his secretary, had recently sweetened his day with never-to-be-forgotten pleasures, and sales of chocolate bars had never been better. In short, life was good.

A small but steady crowd was coming and going in front of the metro station. Two men were handing out advertising pamphlets; a city worker wielding a jackhammer was busy demolishing a section of sidewalk next to a drinking-fountain, closely watched by a gaggle of children. Guilbault slowly scanned the area until he saw Charles leaning against the station wall, holding out Guilbault's business card. He made a quick sign for the boy to come over.

"Are you Charles Thibodeau?"

Charles nodded, staring in fascination at the man's crooked mouth and the huge red boil in the middle of his cheek, both of which gave him a slightly comical appearance.

Guilbault looked the boy up and down, nodded his head and murmured, "Okay, okay, okay . . ." with an air of contentment.

"Follow me," he said. "We'll talk in my car. It's too noisy out here, that thing's making my ears ring."

Charles stopped respectfully beside the Lincoln, then, at Guilbault's invitation, climbed in on the passenger side. For a moment the splendour of the car's interior took his breath away.

"You okay, kid?"

"Yes," replied the boy in a barely audible voice.

The businessman gave a little chuckle of satisfaction.

"Not a bad heap, eh? I'm on the road a lot, you know, so I need to be comfortable. Okay, Charlie my boy, as you know I ran into your father the other day and he told me you were a clever young lad, a good worker, good with people, and you wouldn't be against having a few bucks in your pocket. Is that right?"

"Yes, sir," Charles replied, blushing.

"Would you like a Coke, Charles?"

The child hesitated a moment, then nodded, his eyes shining in anticipation. The man turned brusquely in the seat (his bulk forcing a long sigh from his lips), stuck his hand in a bag lying on the floor behind him, and took out two cans, each of which he opened with a flick of his thumb.

"There you go, my boy. Pleasure. In this bloody heat you have to keep your guts wet or you'll shrivel up like a kernel of corn left out in the sun!"

He took a long drink and wiped his fleshy, pink lips.

"I've got a job for you, Charles. It's easy and it pays well. I'll show you the ropes and you'll pick it up in no time. All you have to do is sell chocolate bars. You like chocolate, I guess?"

"Yes, sir, I do."

147

Guilbault patted Charles on the shoulder. "I like your style, my boy. You come across very well mannered. That's perfect for our business, you know."

Sweat had begun to bead on the man's forehead. He turned the key in the ignition and flipped on the air conditioning, then described to Charles the exact nature of the business. Charles heard him out, becoming more and more interested. The idea of earning easy money (and it sounded as though there'd be nothing to it) while at the same time helping other kids in need was very appealing. One by one, Guilbault revealed to Charles the secrets of salesmanship, his voice rising and falling with enthusiasm.

"First important point: your clothes shouldn't be either too good (how can you inspire pity when you're wearing good clothes?) or too raggedy (which attracts scorn). The clothes you're wearing now are perfect. Next important point: you have to offer your merchandise confidently, but not arrogantly. A good salesman looks the prospective customer straight in the eye, and with a big smile explains the purpose of the sale in as few words as possible: We're trying to raise funds for the Saint-Eusèbe Recreation Centre, or, We want all the needy children in Hochelaga-Maisonneuve to have a nourishing breakfast, whatever. Depends on the day. If you get a refusal, your smile should get even bigger, because the passerby might change his mind, either right there on the spot or maybe later. Final important point: always address the prospective customer with respect. Make it clear you're asking for their help, but don't exaggerate or they'll think you're putting it on. A good salesman takes absolute care with the money he collects, so that it doesn't get lost or stolen, in which case, you are responsible for replacing it."

Charles listened attentively, nodding his head and practising smiling at an imaginary client.

"Is all that clear, my boy?"

"Yes, sir."

"Call me Gino. We're like friends now, you and me."

Charles cleared his throat in embarrassment.

"Could you tell me how much . . . er . . . what my salary would be?"

"Two bits a bar, the same as I get. The rest goes to good causes. Okay? Perfect. Now listen: every Monday night between eight and nine o'clock I'll come over to your place and bring you more boxes of bars and collect the money you made the previous week. Got that? I'll give you some special forms for keeping track of everything."

With his eyes riveted on Guilbault, Charles nodded to show he understood. Then his eyelids fluttered, as though an unpleasant thought had just occurred to him.

"Do I have to ... do I have to work very often, sir?"

"Gino, call me Gino, like I told you. From now on you and me we're on the same team. Right? If you want to make good money, my friend, you have to put some effort into it: weekends and at least two or three evenings after school, let's say between six and eight. You got a problem with that?"

"It's just that I already have a job."

"What job's that?"

"I do deliveries for the restaurant down the street from our house."

"And how much do you make doing that?"

"Um ... nine or ten dollars a week, about. Depends on the week."

Guilbault smiled, and because of his strangely asymmetrical face Charles couldn't tell if he was expressing disdain or amusement. His words, however, removed all doubt.

"Listen to me, Charlie my boy. You put a bit of oomph into your work with me, you could bring in two or three times that much. D'you understand what I'm saying here? Twenty, thirty dollars! A week! I got a little girl up in the Plateau makes twenty bucks a week, regular as clockwork. She's a hard worker, I'll give her that, and she's not one to hang back, like. But you've got the goods, I can tell just by looking at you, and your Dad tells me you've got a good tongue in your head; I have no doubt that you could easily do as well as she does, maybe better."

Charles blushed and looked down. Guilbault twisted around again and plunged his hand into the bag. He took out a cardboard box, which he placed on Charles's lap.

"You feel like maybe getting started right away? You're in a good spot, right here at the entrance to the Frontenac station."

Charles hesitated, then nodded. Guilbault opened the box, took out a bar, and passed it under Charles's nose; the boy's nostrils attracted by the smell of chocolate.

"These bars here, they're for the Baie-Saint-Paul Youth Club, they want to go to Quebec City in the fall to visit the Museum they got there. An excellent cultural initiative ... You sell 'em for a buck a bar, not a penny less. Just stand over there by the entrance and give it a try. I'll hang around for a while

149

and watch you from the car, make sure everything goes okay, but I can't stay long: I got three other meetings to make before six o'clock."

Charles read the inscription on the back of the bar wrapper two or three times to himself, in order to memorize it, then slid over on the seat and opened the car door, nerves clutching at his throat. But he managed a smile. Guilbault gave him a little encouraging pat on the back.

"Good luck, Charlie my boy. It'll be a piece of cake, just you wait and see. You look just right! Sincere, and a good little gent to boot. The women'll gobble 'em up! Oh, by the way . . ." he called as Charles was moving off, "if you know of any other kids who might want to sell chocolate, give me their names on Monday, okay?"

A few minutes later Charles sold his first bar. Fighting off an impulse to jump for joy, he waved the dollar bill towards the purple Lincoln. Guilbault gave him the thumbs-up, then pulled rapidly away from the curb in a whirling cloud of blue smoke.

■ ■ ■

Towards six o'clock, feeling sad but resolute, Charles turned up at Chez Robert to tell Rosalie and Roberto that he'd been offered a new job and wouldn't be delivering pizzas for them any more.

"What job? What are you doing?" Rosalie asked in astonishment.

"I'm selling chocolate bars."

"Twenty-five cents a bar?" she muttered when the boy had left, shrugging her shoulders. "Poor little tyke! He'll be back in no time, you wait and see!"

■ ■ ■

Boff was miserable. He spent most of the day dozing in his house beside the Fafards' garage, ignoring the other neighbourhood dogs that came to visit from time to time. He almost never left the yard. Not even the odoriferous rear-end of a beagle with whom he had, in the past, enjoyed a few torrid afternoon adventures was enough to draw him out of his sad state. He missed Charles. Curled up in a ball, head poking out of his house, he dreamed longingly of those halcyon days when he'd slept at the foot of Charles's bed, spent entire days with him, and run his tongue up and down the boy's cheeks just about any time he'd wanted to. Now those days were long gone. His whole reason for living had flown out the window. He could no longer go across the street to see him (a lesson he'd learned the hard way!), and on the rare occasions when Charles came to visit him he never stayed long enough and seemed tired and distracted. He came, he left, God knew where he went off to. In fact, Boff was beginning to suspect that the boy no longer loved him. The very idea of it killed his appetite, turned his paws into jelly, made his head moan like an empty seashell. There was nothing he wanted to do but sleep, sleep and never wake up . . .

Once in a while Henri, worried about Boff's condition, went out to see how he was doing. Henri was not the kind of person who did things by halves. What he liked were energetic, rapid solutions to problems. He'd grab Boff by the collar and haul him out of his doghouse, attach a leash to him, and, ignoring the dog's whining, quick-march him around the block a few times "to keep him in good shape and build up his appetite."

"That's not what he needs," Lucie said one night after watching them anxiously from the kitchen window. "What he needs is Charles. That's all."

But Charles was selling chocolate. He was selling it six days a week (he took Mondays off), from eight o'clock in the morning till nine o'clock at night. He sold chocolate in his sleep; he sold chocolate as he was getting dressed in the morning; he sold chocolate while he was brushing his teeth, while visiting Boff, night and day, selling chocolate. He would have liked to have sold a bit less and been able to take a break, see his friends, whom he was beginning to neglect. But Gino Guilbault smothered him with so many compliments, phoned him nearly every night encouraging him to do better than he'd done the night before: "Charlie, my boy, you keep it up like this you're going to be my best salesman, bar none. You're going to out-sell my little Ginette in the Plateau. You're a natural, no kidding, I'm prouder of you than I know how to tell you! But don't slack off, now! You haven't shown me half of what you're capable of doing!"

Charles redoubled his efforts, his charm, his cleverness. Smiling with his lips – a smile that sometimes betrayed his weariness – he held out his chocolate bars to passersby, constantly coming up with new ways to make himself more noticeable, to attract more and more of their sympathy. He would return home late in the evening totally exhausted. He began getting headaches for the first time in his life, his legs would ache, and the soles of his feet would feel as though they were on fire. He'd broadened his sales base, adding the Berri-de Montigny station to the Frontenac site and expanding into the Place Versailles shopping concourse and all down rue Ontario, as well as other spots. Guilbault drove him all over the city in his purple Lincoln, picking him up from various places with exemplary punctuality. Often Charles would travel with other children; their drained faces and unwillingness to talk (perhaps because of the Big Boss's presence) made him thoughtful.

Charles worked himself to the bone to spread happiness throughout the land by the sale of chocolate bars – also to make himself a bit of money. Because of his efforts, he believed, children from Baie-Saint-Paul were being better educated; Scouts from Verdun were able to clear the city air from their lungs on camping trips; young polio sufferers (how that word *polio* made him squirm!) at the Institute Notre-Dame-du-Rosaire were able to buy the equipment they so badly needed. He was overwhelmed by good causes, limitless in their diversity, each need as pressing as the next and the next. A million lives like his wouldn't make a dent in them!

Lucie and Fernand forbade Henri to become involved in selling chocolate bars for charity and blamed Wilfrid for having pushed his son into the life of a street vendor.

"He's wearing himself out, the poor kid," Fernand grumbled whenever he saw Charles leaving his apartment, arms loaded with boxes. "And for who? For a bloody crook, I'll bet any money. Not to mention the risk! Montreal's a big city. All kinds of low-lifes in it. Who's to say what could happen to him?"

In early August, Blonblon joined Guilbault's team, but he quit after three weeks, discouraged by the hard work. When Charles worked the Frontenac metro station, Blonblon would sometimes keep him company, run errands for him. But Charles was so caught up in his work he barely paid attention to his friend, and the visits trailed off and eventually ended altogether.

In any case, Charles soon stopped going to the Frontenac station. Monsieur Saint-Amour had spotted him there. Charles saw him coming down the street one day, walking slowly, his shoulders hunched over, his eye sweeping the sidewalk in front of him; in his shapeless brown suit, bulging here and there in odd places, he looked like a sack of potatoes with feet. His face was dark and creased, also like a potato, an old potato someone had forgotten in a corner somewhere, over which had grown a thin layer of mould, separated down the middle by a furrow.

"Charles, dear boy! What are you up to these days? No longer working at Chez Robert, I've noticed."

"No," the boy replied coldly.

"Ah, that's too bad. My pizzas are cold by the time I get them now . . . I miss you, you know. You must come to see me one of these days . . . And – have you forgotten? – I still have that little surprise I promised to show you. Will you come?"

"I'll try," he said evasively, "but I have a lot of work to do, you know."

And turning away, he put on his forced smile and approached a large woman who was walking with the candid yet slightly stiff air of a nun.

Saint-Amour turned up every day in the early afternoon and bought a chocolate bar, always taking advantage of the situation to hold Charles's hand a little too long, or to pat his back; then, standing off to one side, he would watch the boy with his creepy eyes. By the fifth day Charles was so put off by these attentions that he told his boss he wanted to move to a different location, because a stranger was making advances to him. Guilbault was out-raged; he said he'd go for the pervert "from zero to sixty in three seconds flat!" He'd run into those "little carrot-lovers" before, he said. But Charles, having little confidence that such methods would actually settle the matter, politely refused Guilbault's offer, saying the stranger hadn't really done him any harm, and that for the time being he'd just as soon work somewhere else.

As September drew near, Charles was earning twenty-five dollars a week, sometimes more. He took Lucie's advice and opened a savings account at the Saint-Eusèbe Credit Union. Wilfrid had been following his son's career with a great deal of interest for some time, and one fine morning demanded that Charles pay him half of his earnings, since he himself was still out of work and could no longer make ends meet. From then on, he said, Charles should be "paying for his keep."

"I'm the one he should be giving money to," Sylvie declared in a voice that brooked no reply. "After all, who do you think pays for everything around here?"

Wilfrid grumbled a bit but didn't dare argue with her. And so every Monday night Charles gave Sylvie part of his earnings. At least she used the money for the household, and sometimes even secretly returned some of it to Charles.

"I wish I could give it all back to you, Charles," she said to him one day, giving him a rare peck on the cheek, "but the way your father goes through money, I really need it."

School was about to re-open. Charles was going into Grade Four. One night, while he was eating dinner (again!) at the Fafards', Fernand set down his cutlery on his carefully wiped plate (he ate at the same rate as Napoleon) and asked him, apropos of nothing, if he intended to go on selling chocolate bars for much longer.

"I'd like to stop," said Charles, his face clouding over, "but I'm not sure my father would let me."

"Hmmm," said Fernand, frowning. "It's funny, though, isn't it . . . You know, with your studies and everything . . . at least . . . You can't serve two masters and all that . . . Something to think about, anyway."

He looked at his wife helplessly.

Guilbault had been thinking about the same problem for some time. It always came up when school started in September, and he always had to find individual solutions to it. Usually he let his average salespersons go without making much of a fuss, but he went to great lengths and exercised much ingenuity to hang on to his best sellers for as long as possible.

Two days before Charles and Fernand had their somewhat short conversation, Guilbault was walking along rue Ontario with Charles in search of a nourishing but inexpensive lunch, when Charles stopped suddenly at a bicycle-store window and gazed ecstatically at a superb ten-speed in metallic blue, equipped with pedal traps. A light bulb went on in the businessman's brain.

"You like that bike, Charlie?"

"Do I ever! Mine's pretty busted up and the gears don't work too well . . ."

"It's a beautiful bike, that's for sure . . . Hey!" he said as though struck by a sudden inspiration, "why don't I buy it for you? You can pay me back, a little bit every week. That way you don't have to wait to buy it."

Charles turned to him with a look of burning desire.

"I don't know what my father would say . . . It's seventy-nine dollars!"

"I'll fix it with your father, don't worry about that. Come on! Gotta raise your gun when the geese are overhead, eh? Otherwise all you get to eat is baloney . . ."

When Charles left the shop, he was walking on air. The shop-owner had put the bicycle aside for him until the next day; Guilbault had arranged to speak to the carpenter about it that very night.

"So, you're happy?" asked the businessman with his crooked smile.

Charles looked at him without speaking, too emotional to say anything.

"Thank you, Monsieur Guilbault," he finally managed. "You have done me a great favour. Thank you, thank you so much!"

Guilbault gave a little coo of satisfaction and put his hand on the boy's shoulder. "If there's ever anything else I can do for you, Charles, don't be shy about asking!"

They walked along the street talking animatedly, like two friends. Charles was already riding his new bicycle in his mind, and the businessman was calculating how many weeks it would take for his little salesman to pay off the debt. With a bit of luck he might be able to make it last until mid-winter, maybe longer. His smile broadened, and a saucy little smile played at the edges of his lips.

The rupture, however, was fast approaching. And it would be brutal.

14

School started on the seventh of September. Charles gave it all the attention his job as an itinerant salesman would allow, which meant not
much. In fact, it took almost all the energy he had just to stay awake in class.
His teacher, Madame Jacob, who was new to the school, pigeonholed him as
a professional slacker and relegated him to a place among her least promising pupils.

She was a woman in her mid-forties, nervous, very emotional, and slightly
out of sync with the other teachers at Saint-Anselme Elementary. She wore
makeup like a supermodel, dyed her hair blonde with platinum highlights, kept
it in a style of meticulous disarray, dressed in flamboyant outfits, with enormous, diamond-studded rings on fingers tipped with false nails painted pink.
Twenty times a day she peered anxiously into her compact, as though looking
for signs of slow decline in her overblown beauty. Within three days her pupils,
in their usual cruel and perceptive way, were calling her Minoune – a term that
could mean either a somewhat plump and pampered cat or an old car that has
outlived its usefulness.

They thought they'd found in her the ideal outlet for their overflowing
energy. Minoune quickly disabused them of that notion. She may have been
a hypersensitive coquette, but over the years she had nonetheless developed
an incredibly efficient means of self-defence; the gaze with which she swept
the class seemed to be all-seeing. She could hear the slightest whisper, and
her false fingernails would sink like talons into the arm or neck of an undis-
ciplined child.

Charles had never before met a woman who was so much the *grande
dame*. He imagined she must have been enormously wealthy, and wondered
what she was doing teaching school. A few days after school started, he

gathered up enough courage to go up to her during recess and try to sell her some chocolate bars. She gave a shy, almost disdainful laugh and bought three, which confirmed Charles in his suspicion that she was rich.

"'For the Support of the Sainte-Justine Hospital Centre for the Hearing Impaired,'" she read on the label. "Do you have hearing problems, Charles?"

"No, not at all, Madame."

"So why are you selling these bars?"

"To help those children who do have problems, and also to make a bit of money for myself."

"I see. Do you sell very many?"

"I do all right," he said with a modest smile. "Last weekend I sold eighty-seven."

She looked at him a moment, fiddling with one of her rings, then adopted the condescending, slightly detached air with which adults sometimes address future low-income earners (and what country doesn't need them?).

"Well, don't waste too much time on them," she said. "You have to keep up with your studies, you know."

Charles had recently changed his opinion on that subject. What was most important to him from now on was to make money, as much money as possible. With money you could buy a bicycle on credit. You could treat your friends. With money you could help your father (a bit), who was on Unemployment. Of course he didn't have much choice in that matter, as Sylvie had made sufficiently clear.

But school didn't solve any real problems, nor did it give him any real pleasure, or at least very little. Only money did that. And to make money, he had to work.

The next Saturday morning he dashed joyfully down the staircase and into Gino Guilbault's purple Lincoln, which was parked in front of his building. In the back seat a young girl was squeezed in between two enormous boxes of chocolate bars.

"Hi there, Charlie my boy!" cried the businessman happily as Charles took his place in the front passenger seat. "You look in fine fettle this morning! Sleep well?"

"Very well, Gino."

"Well, let the Devil fart in my nose if you don't sell forty bars today!"

"I'll do my best."

"Charles, I want you to meet Josiane. She's new. She's still a bit nervous, so I'm going to put her in a spot not far from you so you can help her out if she needs anything, okay?"

Charles turned around and said hello in his friendliest voice. "There's nothing to it, you'll see," he added. "All you have to do is be nice to people, that's usually all it takes. And you're a girl. It's even easier for girls."

Josiane gave him a tight-lipped smile, pressed her knees together, and looked away. The boxes on either side of her made her look tiny. Charles felt sorry for her, and told himself he'd help her as much as he could.

By lunchtime he had already sold eighteen bars, while Josiane had sold only three. Charles went over to her and was busy teaching her a few tricks of the trade when the purple Lincoln pulled up in front of them. When he heard how few sales the girl had made Guilbault frowned, but quickly hid his annoyance behind his affable demeanour.

"Hey, hey, Josiane," he said, patting her on the head, "what's with the long face? You're going to frighten off the pigeons! Let's see you smile, you'll get the hang of it" – or else you'll go back to the welfare centre so fast it'll make your head spin, he added to himself. "Come on, the two of you, I'll treat you to a couple of hot dogs at the Greek place across the street. You'll work better on a full stomach!"

It was in the greasy spoon that events suddenly took an unexpected turn. After making short work of a club sandwich, which unfortunately came with a chicken bone that almost got caught in his throat, Guilbault excused himself from the table to make a phone call. A few seconds later, Charles also got up to go to the washroom.

The washrooms were down a narrow hallway in which the payphones had been installed. Charles had to pass the businessman, whose back was to him and who was absorbed in a serious conversation. Charles went into the washroom and took his place before the urinal – and heard his name being mentioned by Guilbault as clearly as if the man were standing beside him. He listened in on the conversation.

"I tell you, my friend," the businessman was saying warmly while Charles listened, wide-eyed, "if I could lay my hands on two or three more kids like little Thibodeau I could retire in five years and live like a king in the lap of luxury. Not a word of a lie, that kid makes me an average of a hundred bucks a week! Can you believe it? But what am I going to do?" he sighed. "How am I going to find more like him? I have to look, and who's got the time for that? . . . Why not? Right now I've got thirty-four kids, Serge! Do you have any idea what that means? On any given day this one quits, that one gets sick, another one can't keep his money straight, another one goes to the wrong street, another one has a breakdown, and another one is stealing bars from me. I'd need two heads and eight arms . . . On the other hand, if you came in with me, Serge my boy, I'd have more time to recruit better sellers . . . Everything's in place, I tell you! I'm beginning to get the hang of it, after all this time! And then, my friend, we'll be rolling in more dough than the guy who invented rubbers."

Quietly, Charles left the washroom, overcome by a feeling of dread, the cause of which he only vaguely grasped. He passed Guilbault, who was still on the phone, and sat back down at the table. He looked without appetite at his cold hot dog. Had Josiane been left alone too long? She was looking at him silently, her mouth twisted and her eyes shining with tears.

"Is something wrong?" Charles asked her.

She shook her head, but two tears rolled down her cheeks and into her mouth, where they joined a paste of mustard-coloured hot-dog bun. Then Guilbault came back rubbing his hands together.

"What's the matter, kids?" he said, surprised by the long faces. "You get run over by a hearse or something?"

Charles pushed his plate away and said he wasn't hungry. Josiane did the same. The businessman looked from one to the other, more and more mystified.

"'Fess up, you two. Have you had a falling out?"

It was only after Guilbault had left with the sobbing Josiane – she'd insisted on being taken home – that Charles knew without a shadow of a doubt that for the past two months he'd been working for peanuts for a crook who was filling his own pockets, and that the only needy children he was helping existed in the businessman's imagination. He was overcome by rage; his back broke out in a cold sweat and his shoes felt as though they were red hot. He went on selling chocolate bars as though nothing were wrong, however. After a few minutes his rebellion gave way to a cold, calm determination to get revenge. He would have the perfect opportunity that same day.

■ ■ ■

At six o'clock the sun was setting and the city was bathed in a cool breeze. By that time there were few pedestrians on the streets. Charles shivered and suddenly felt extremely tired. His stomach had been grumbling for an hour, and he decided he'd call it a day. He'd begun outside the Frontenac station, then, after Josiane left, he'd gone door-to-door up and down the neighbouring streets (a good strategy on weekends) and now found himself at the corner of Logan and de la Visitation. He bought a bag of potato chips to stave off his hunger and began to walk home, hoping that Sylvie would be there and that supper would be waiting for him. He balanced his nearly empty chocolate bar box on one finger and felt his pocket bulging with bills and coins. "He's not going to get a penny of it, the bloody thief!" he told himself between clenched teeth for the twentieth time that day.

He had just turned onto rue Ontario when the purple Lincoln pulled up and kept pace beside him as he walked.

"Come on, hop in!" Guilbault cried happily. "Save some shoeleather."

Charles hesitated a second, then climbed in when Guilbault insisted he take his place in the car. Prudence cautioned him to hide his anger, but he didn't know if he had enough strength.

"Where were you off to?"

"Home."

"You're quitting early!"

"I'm tired," Charles said without looking at the man.

"It's true, it's tiring work," agreed Guilbault, patting the boy's knee sympathetically.

A small explosion, like a gunshot, accompanied the final syllable of Guilbault's sentence. Charles looked at him. Guilbault had stopped at a red light; his face had taken on a greenish tinge and was stretched out of shape, contradicting the sympathy he was trying to show. His left hand alternated between his stomach and his mouth, massaging the former in large, circular movements, and at the same time trying to cover the latter, from which erupted a series of deep, cavernous burps.

"It's that goddamned club sandwich I had at noon," he finally said. "Doesn't want to stay down. That bloody chicken was an old hen when my grandfather was being ... 'scuse me ... potty trained ... It's sitting in my gut like a lump of cold porridge ..."

He tried to whistle, but gave it up.

"How many bars did you sell today?"

"Forty-four."

"That's good, Charlie my boy! And it's only ten after six! A little more . . . 'scuse me . . . effort and you might beat your record of fifty-one, eh? What say we go to a restaurant? We can put a little lead back in your wings, and I can have a cup of hot tea. Help clean out my system. What do you say?"

"No thanks. I don't feel like it."

Guilbault, still rubbing his stomach, looked at the boy out of the corner of his eye. He was surprised, but he didn't say anything. His instinct told him it was better not to insist.

"Okay, whatever you say . . . Nothing like a good home-cooked meal prepared by your . . . urrrp! . . . mother."

"I don't have a mother," Charles couldn't help saying in an acid voice, still looking straight ahead.

Guilbault looked at him more carefully.

"Yeah, right, sorry I forgot, big dummy that I am. Listen, Charlie my boy," he went on, belching and covering his mouth with his hand, "you look fairly . . . wiped out. Maybe it would be . . . good for you to have a quiet night at home. If it's . . . all right with you, though . . . we'll just swing by the office for a minute and I'll give you tomorrow's merchandise. After that I'll . . . give you a lift home. Okay by you?"

Charles nodded, his anger dissipating, replaced by the sweet enjoyment of seeing Guilbault feeling so badly; a particularly sonorous burp shook the man's shoulders, and Charles had to clench his teeth to keep from laughing.

A few minutes later the car stopped on rue Parthenais in front of a small, one-storey brick building that looked as though it had seen better days. It was squeezed between a run-down boarding house and a restaurant from which swung a sign in the shape of a pipe. Whatever was afflicting Guilbault had spread from his stomach down into his intestines. The businessman jumped out of the car with sweat on his forehead and his nostrils flaring; he took out a large key-ring and ran to the front door.

"Hurry up! I can't . . . I've got to go!" he called to Charles in a barely recognizable voice.

And he disappeared inside the building, leaving the door open behind him.

Grinning contentedly, Charles strolled into a large, half-empty, neon-lit room containing an imposing oak-panelled desk in need of repair, an olive-green metal filing cabinet that appeared to have been violently attacked by a large carnivore, and two varnished wooden office chairs. A narrow hallway opened at the back of the room. Portraits of Pope Paul VI and Cardinal Paul-Émile Léger hung on the wall on either side of the desk, welcoming visitors with an unctuous gravity into a room that smelled nauseatingly of cheap chocolate.

Charles stopped in the middle of the room and looked around for his boss.

"I'm in the john," Guilbault called out in agony. "Have a seat . . . I'll be . . . out in a minute."

The room filled with the grotesque sounds of explosive defecation coming from the end of the hallway. Charles leaned against the desk, laughing into his hand. The sounds were amply accompanied by sighs and stifled groans. The club sandwich seemed to be passing through Guilbault's entrails like a horde of barbarians armed with pikes and axes.

Charles sat in one of the chairs and swung his legs, more and more delighted with the turn of events. Things seemed to bode well for revenge. His eye fell absently on Guilbault's cardigan, hanging crookedly on a coat hook; one of the pockets was partially open, and seemed to contain an object of some weight. He found himself staring at the bulge in the material with no particular idea forming in his mind, occupied as he was with the heroic combat Guilbault was fighting in the bathroom; it was as though his boss's intestines had been transformed into a giant tuba and were playing an obscene tune.

"Everything okay in there, Monsieur Guilbault?" Charles asked as seriously as he could manage.

"Yeah, I think so," came a supplicating voice.

Charles was still staring at the cardigan pocket, only now his look was sharper. Without taking time to consider the consequences of his act, he walked over to the coat hook, reached into the pocket, and took out a wallet. At the sight of the enormous wad of bills the wallet contained he felt as though he had been kicked in the stomach. Here was his revenge, he was holding it right in his hand. With a swift, precise gesture he divided the wad in half, stuffed one of the halves under his windbreaker and returned the other half to the wallet and put the wallet back in the cardigan.

His first instinct was to run, but he quickly realized that that would be the end of him. He went back and sat on the chair and waited. His limbs were trembling. He squeezed the chair arms and crossed his legs to hide his anxiety. Every now and then he looked down at his windbreaker to see if there was any tell-tale bulge. A minute before he'd been hoping that the swindler's torture would go on forever, but now he wished it would end as quickly as possible. He brought his hand up to his cheek, which seemed to be burning. Was he red in the face? How would he explain that to Guilbault if he noticed it? From the hallway came nothing but silence. Then the flushing of a toilet indicated that the man's torments were at least temporarily suspended. Quick steps came down the hallway and there he was, looking as though he had just given birth.

"Ah, my boy . . . I thought I was going to die in there! It was like I'd swallowed an orangutan . . . Nevermind, I'm going to sue that bastard for selling food poison! He'll have to explain himself to the judge!"

He stopped when his eyes fell on Charles's face. The boy was looking up at him, sitting stiffly on the chair.

"What's the matter? You don't look too good yourself."

"I don't feel well."

"Ha! A bloody epidemic! Come on, I'll drive you home."

He tried to put his cardigan on but suddenly his eyes lost their focus and he had to lean on the desk with one hand.

"My head's spinning like a top, for Christ's sake . . . He really poisoned me, that bastard . . ."

He took a deep breath, then pressed his hands to his stomach.

"Christ, I feel like death warmed over . . ."

"Me too."

"As soon as I get better I'm going straight to a lawyer, that's it! I'll get that son of a bitch! I'll make him eat dog hair, that crap vendor! Okay, here we go . . . that's one sleeve . . . that's the other one. Oh, it feels good to have a little cloth to cover me. The back of my shirt's like a wet dishrag."

Charles's heart leapt to his throat as Guilbault slid his hands into his sweater pockets.

"Okay, let's go, Charlie my boy. I'll drop you off and then straight to bed . . . A little nap'll do me good . . . Tell me, your head's not spinning, is it?"

He'd suddenly remembered his Lincoln's interior. "You don't feel like throwing up or anything, do you?"

"No," replied the boy, walking awkwardly towards the door. He was deathly afraid that the banknotes he'd stuffed into his windbreaker would slide out and flutter down to the floor.

"Hmm," said the businessman, watching him, "you definitely look under the weather. I'm not going to risk it. I'll put you in a taxi. You've got enough money, haven't you? I'll pay you back tomorrow."

Charles was already out on the sidewalk fighting off a furious urge to run like a rabbit.

"Hold it a minute!" Guilbault called after him. Charles froze. "I forgot to give you your bars for tomorrow. Although judging from the way you look now . . . Oh well, you never know . . ."

He went back into the building; a door creaked and an instant later he reappeared carrying two cardboard boxes, each one labelled:

EXTRA GOURMET CHOCOLATE WITH ALMONDS
QUEBEC PRIVATE DAYCARE COALITION

Five minutes later a taxi appeared and Charles got in stiffly – part of the wad of bills was protruding from the windbreaker and slipping down his thigh. Guilbault nodded through the window, looking concerned.

"Good luck, Charlie my boy!"

And he waved him off.

■ ■ ■

As he turned towards the daycare, Charles noticed a plastic bag fluttering at the edge of the sidewalk. He grabbed it, slipped it in his pocket, and quickened his pace. He'd had the idea near the end of the taxi ride and had asked the driver to keep going as far as rue Lalonde. If he got off in front of his house he'd run the risk of bumping into people he didn't want to meet just yet.

He'd transferred the wad of bills to his left armpit, between his skin and his cotton T-shirt, where there was no chance it would escape, but because he had to keep his arm stiff he was afraid of drawing attention to himself. He cast a quick look around, stepped into a small yard, knelt down behind

164

a garbage pail, and slid the bills into the plastic bag, then continued on his way.

As he'd hoped, the daycare was closed and its grounds completely deserted. His throat tightened slightly when he saw the old cherry tree at whose feet the little yellow dog was sleeping. He remembered the circumstances surrounding its death with such extraordinary clarity; it was one of the landmarks of his childhood. He sat between the tree's roots and gently patted the grass. The little yellow dog was right there and would look after the money. Charles was sure of it.

He looked carefully about him, then took the bills from the bag and began counting them. There were tens, twenties, and fifties (which he now saw for the first time in his life), all brand new, crisp and crackling, still at the beginning of their life's journey.

"Three hundred and fifty dollars," he murmured, flabbergasted.

He was seized by a wild joy. He leapt to his feet and jumped up and down, waving his hands. What a perfect revenge! What a way to teach the dirty exploiter a lesson! Now all he had to do was bury his loot, keep his mouth shut and his head down until Guilbault gave up looking for the thief and resigned himself to putting the incident behind him. He'd never dare file a complaint with the police, of that Charles was certain. People like him avoided the police at all costs.

He found a small shovel in a sandbox and used it to dig a hole about a metre from the little yellow dog. He made it just deep enough, put the bag of money in it, then filled it in, and carefully replaced the sod.

By the time he got home he was weak with hunger. Sylvie had a macaroni and cheese casserole in the oven, which was just about ready to come out. The succulent, slightly sweet odour filled the apartment and reminded him of the time Alice moved about in the same rooms, a time when he'd been so happy. His mouth filled with saliva, and he felt deliciously sad. Alice's macaroni was much better than Sylvie's, but Sylvie's wasn't bad.

"Home already?" the waitress greeted him in surprise.

Charles almost told her he was no longer working for Gino Guilbault, but held himself back, afraid of giving too much away.

"I was so hungry, Sylvie," he said. "Is it going to be ready soon?"

She opened the oven door, decided the casserole was cooked, and served him a large portion. Charles poured himself a glass of milk, and the two of them ate in silence. Wilfrid was out, God knew where, and Charles preferred not to ask any questions.

The emotions of the day had exhausted him. He watched television for a while, spoke briefly with Blonblon on the telephone, then went over to see Boff. When he got there, Henri was vacuuming out the doghouse. By eight o'clock Charles had had his bath and was in bed. His father came in soon after that and, in his loud and imperious after-tavern voice, demanded his supper.

Charles was just drifting off to sleep when the doorbell rang. An unpleasant presentiment make him sit up in bed and hold his breath, and he soon recognized Guilbault's dry and haughty voice, asking to speak to him. There was a short conversation between the two men and Sylvie, but his blood was pounding in his ears so loudly he couldn't make out what they were saying. Still trembling, he lay back down and pretended to be asleep, although acid kept climbing up into his throat, making him cough. He bitterly regretted his impulsive act of the afternoon and prepared himself for the worst. He didn't have long to wait.

The bedroom door burst open and banged against the wall, the ceiling light was switched on, and his father was standing beside the bed, livid with rage:

"Get up!" he shouted.

Rigid with fear, Charles stared at him without speaking; his father's head appeared to be scraping the ceiling.

"Get up, I said!"

Seizing the boy by the shoulders, he pulled him from the bed.

"What have I done?" sputtered Charles, instinctively raising his arms to shield his face.

The carpenter grabbed him again by the shoulders, spun him towards the door, and gave him a violent shove, projecting him into the hallway.

They had shown Guilbault into the living room. He was sitting in one of the sofa chairs, legs crossed, hands folded on one knee, wearing a silk tie, shiny shoes, his pudgy face heavy with an episcopal seriousness only slightly compromised by his crooked mouth. He gave a small inclination of his head in Charles's direction as the boy appeared before him, barefooted and still in pyjamas, looking terrified. Sylvie was sitting on the sofa; she gave him a quizzical look, but didn't dare open her mouth.

"Monsieur Guilbault has a few questions for you," Wilfrid announced, standing behind his son.

Guilbault looked at Charles through half-closed eyes. Charles had never seen anyone so evil-looking. His hatred for the man rose up inside him and he stopped trembling.

"Was it by accident that you went through my wallet this afternoon, Charles?" the man asked in an almost comically affected voice.

"What wallet?" the boy murmured.

"This one," Guilbault replied. He picked up his cardigan, which was folded over the arm of the chair, and slowly withdrew the wallet from one of the pockets.

"No," Charles said.

His firm, almost insolent tone brought a fleeting frown to the philanthropist's pink lips without detracting from his overall air of solemnity.

"Is it not true that you were in my office this afternoon while I was … indisposed?"

"Yes."

"Did anyone else come into the office while you were waiting for me?"

"No."

"So," Guilbault went on, "no one apart from yourself was in my office between a quarter past six and six-thirty, is that right?"

"Not that I saw."

"Right. Then explain something to me, Charlie my boy. How is it that, when I went into my office at six-fifteen and hung this sweater on the coat hook, my wallet had seven hundred and twenty dollars in it, and when I left that same office, where, as you have just admitted, you were the only person in it with me, my wallet contained only three hundred and seventy dollars?"

"I don't know."

"Tell the truth!" Wilfrid growled, squeezing the back of the boy's neck.

"I am telling the truth."

"You have no idea?"

"If I knew, I'd tell you. But I don't know. So I can't tell you."

"Talk more politely, you," growled his father, increasing the pressure on his neck until Charles groaned with pain.

"In that case," sighed Guilbault, straightening the crease on his pantleg, "I have no choice but to go to the police. The police will come here, and believe you me, they won't go as easy on you as I have. Do you understand me, Charles?"

"Yes."

The child stared directly into the man's eyes. Guilbault thought he detected an almost imperceptible expression of bravado in the look, and the corset of respectability within which he had bound his rage suddenly flew apart; his face turned purple and a speck of foam appeared at the corner of his mouth. He leapt to his feet and reached an arm towards Charles.

"Now you listen to me, my little friend! You're not going to get away with this! You're going to find yourself in reform school! Is that what you want? And as for you two," he said to Wilfrid and Sylvie, "don't forget you're responsible for this child. If he refuses to return my money, it's you who'll have to pay me back!"

With that he stormed towards the door like a buffalo, nearly knocking the carpenter over. The latter hurried after him, sputtering promises Guilbault wasn't hearing. Guilbault went out and was halfway down the stairs when he stopped, turned around, and came back into the vestibule, where Wilfrid was standing with his arms hanging by his sides.

"My boxes of chocolate!" he shouted.

"Your what . . . ?"

Guilbault stared at the carpenter's dismayed face. Then, in a falsetto voice his suppressed rage poured out in an uncontrolled torrent.

"*Go get them*, you idiot! Wake up! The two boxes of chocolate I gave your son this afternoon! Do you think I'm stupid enough to leave them here with a thief?"

■ ■ ■

Sylvie sat Charles down beside her on the sofa and was patiently and gently trying to get him to admit to having stolen the money. He continued to deny everything, crying hot tears and using his large round eyes to great effect. She'd told Wilfrid to keep out of the way, and he was pacing back and forth in the kitchen, beer in hand, muttering to himself over and over.

"Three hundred and fifty bucks! Where are we going to lay our hands on that kind of money, for the love of Christ?"

After a quarter of an hour, moved by the child's sobs and not knowing what to think, Sylvie went into the kitchen.

"Listen, Wilfrid," she said. "I don't think he took it. We don't know anything about this Guilbault. Maybe he's trying to put one over on us."

Wilfrid stared at her for a second in astonishment, then slammed the beer bottle down on the table so hard beer splattered everywhere.

"Is that what you think? Well, I never thought you could be so stupid! Have you lost your memory, is that what you're telling me?"

He stretched his trembling arm towards the living room.

"The fast one that little asshole pulled on us last spring, have you forgotten that? When he snuck out of here in the middle of the night, broke a window at the vet's clinic to get his goddamn dog out, and you think he's not capable of going through someone's wallet? I *know* he did it, goddamnit, I know it was him who took the money. And you can be goddamn sure that little Christer is going to pay back every last penny of it!"

Picking up his bottle, he left the kitchen and went into the living room. For the next minute or two, father and son shouted at each other in unison, the one accusing and the other denying, their voices hoarse and strident, carried away by the same vehemence and equally aware that they were playing for keeps; that this battle marked a turning point in their relationship.

They were stopped by a sudden knock on the floor. Monsieur Victoire had had enough; he was demanding a truce. The carpenter calmed down immediately.

"Okay, you don't want to talk? It's up to you. Tomorrow I've got a little surprise in store for you. Go to bed."

Curled up in his bed with Simon, Charles's whole body shook as he thought about the surprise. He knew what it was. He could see the closet door beside him, still with the three screw holes in it. He'd be kept a prisoner behind that door, and not for just a day, either, but until he confessed to his crime. He knew his father was capable of keeping him in there for a long time, such a long time that Charles might not even be conscious when they came to let him out.

His neck was stiff and sore and burned as though someone had poured scalding water on it. His clenched jaws ached all the way up to his ears. Despite every effort, Simon was unable to comfort him. His first sojourn in the closet hadn't been that hard to bear, because he knew how to kill time. But the prospect of another one filled him with terror. Especially since he had no intention of returning the money. That money belonged to him. He was the one who had earned it, not that crooked-faced thief in his tacky Lincoln.

Charles turned on his back and stared at the ceiling for a long time, then let out a sigh: he had made up his mind. He would wait until the middle of the night, then get up, get dressed, and sneak out of the house like he did before, and go over to the Fafards' house. To do that he had to be absolutely sure that his father was asleep. He could still hear him stomping around in the kitchen, muttering to himself; the radio was on low, and every now and then a *pffsssst!* told him that another bottle of beer had been opened.

To save time and because he couldn't just lie there keeping still, he took off his pyjamas, folded them, and put them under his pillow, and got dressed. Knowing that he was ready to go made him feel better. He got back into bed and this time Simon found the right words to reassure him: "You won't have to put up with him either, Simon," the boy whispered into the bear's ear, "because I'm going to take you with me. Would you like that?" "Are you kidding? You bet I would," Simon replied. "I've never liked that man." Gradually, Charles's fear diminished and was replaced by an immense fatigue that settled into his limbs. The burning in his neck also subsided. Maybe he should sleep a bit in order to have a clear head when the time came to run away and leave this place behind forever, where he would never in his life be happy. Slowly his eyelids closed despite his efforts to stay awake . . .

■ ■ ■

A violent blow knocked him out of bed. He found himself on the floor, at his father's feet, half blinded by the light from the ceiling.

"What are you up to this time, eh?" shouted Wilfrid, standing with his legs spread and his arms weaving dangerously as he tried to keep his balance. "Come on! Answer me!"

"I . . . I was cold," blubbered Charles, hiding his face in his hands.

"Get up, you little liar! Get in the kitchen! I want to talk to you."

There was no mistaking his heavy, slurred speech; he hadn't stopped drinking since Guilbault's visit. Charles turned and directed a silent appeal to Simon, who'd been thrown to the floor as well and was staring at his master with a hopeless, appalled expression.

Charles got up with a grimace and followed his father.

"'S a good thing I thought of waking you up," muttered the carpenter, leaning one hand against the hallway wall. "'S plain as the nose on my face, for Christ's sake."

In the kitchen he slumped down on a chair, legs spread out before him, and gestured for his son to stand a few feet in front of him.

Charles obeyed, casting a furtive look at the door of the bedroom where Sylvie was sleeping. It was closed. The apartment was totally silent.

"You're gonna stand there like that, 'thout moving," Wilfrid said slowly, "until sush time as you tell me where you put the money. You got that? I'm in no hurry."

And grabbing a bottle from the table, he took a long swig, then placed the bottle on the floor and crossed his arms, giving his son a smile that oozed hatred.

Charles looked at his father's face. He'd never seen it looking so mean, with its thick lips hanging slightly down, its eyes swollen almost shut, nearly disappearing into the folds of skin around them and so full of anger that they looked almost blind. Something terrible was taking place behind them. He started to cry.

"No, no, no! No blubbering," shouted Wilfrid, sitting up. "You're not gonna get around me like that!"

Leaning forward he took a swipe at the boy but merely managed to clip his cheek; then he flopped back onto his chair.

"'S not blubbering I want from you," he said again after taking another drink. "'S information! We'll see who's boss around here, goddamnit!"

He crossed his arms.

"Where'd you put the money?"

Charles worked hard at holding back his tears. He tried to wipe his cheek with the palm of his hand, but his father leapt to his feet.

"Don't move, I tole you!" he shouted. "I tole you not to move! You move when I tell you to move, not before!"

Charles lowered his head and kept silent. The carpenter stared at him, swaying slightly on his feet, then placed his hand flat on the table and sat back down.

"Still don' feel like talking?" he said after a moment. "Take your time, I'm in no hurry."

Several minutes went by. Wilfrid stood up, went to the refrigerator, and returned with another bottle of beer. For a few long seconds he seemed to have forgotten his son's presence in the room, lost in his own gloomy and confused thoughts. Then, shooting a sudden suspicious look in Charles's direction, he assured himself that his instructions were being followed. Charles was breathing quickly and becoming more and more uncomfortable. His arms hung down, his hands felt swollen and covered in pinpricks. He was struggling against an almost irresistible urge to move about the room; sharp pains shot through his lower back and down his legs. Every so often he lifted his head slightly and looked around the kitchen; the walls had lost their solidity, they'd begun to undulate. He was getting dizzy.

He realized then that there was only one way out of the situation; he would have to explain himself to his father.

"He's a crook, that Guilbault," he murmured hoarsely.

The carpenter jumped.

"Whass that you say?"

"He's a crook. The money he makes from chocolate bars doesn't go to people in need. He keeps it all for himself. I heard him talking on the telephone yesterday at lunch. He was telling someone all about it, how he makes us children work for him for practically nothing and he fills his own pockets. He's nothing but a crook. I'm going to tell the police."

The boy's words appeared to have penetrated to the bottom of the carpenter's drunkenness. The lines on his face hardened and a look of attention and cunning replaced the animal stupor that had been there before.

"What's this you're telling me?"

The surprise and interest in his voice encouraged the boy. He repeated the details about the conversation he had overheard in the restaurant.

His body bent forward, one hand on his knee, Wilfrid nodded his head. "Okay, okay, okay," he muttered thoughtfully. "I never woulda guessed . . . He looks like such a clean-cut guy . . . Did you take his money?"

Charles hesitated a second, then nodded, then instantly realized he had fallen into a trap.

"Where'd you put it?"

There was a threat in the question. Charles clenched his teeth, bowed his head, and didn't answer. His heart was beating so hard that a small, dry cough tore at his chest. The carpenter rose slowly, his hands outstretched.

"What'd you do with the money, you stubborn little bastard?" he repeated more loudly. "Where'd you put it? You want me to force it out of you?"

He grabbed Charles and began shaking him violently.

"No! I'm not telling you!" cried the boy without knowing what he was doing. "You'll take it from me! It's mine! I earned it, not you!"

And he began to fight back, terrified; inadvertently he plunged his fist into his father's stomach; the carpenter groaned and relaxed his grip slightly. With a sharp twist of his shoulders, Charles succeeded in breaking away, stumbling backwards a few steps until his back came up against a wall.

Wilfrid let out a roar and stood stock-still for several seconds, his face in convulsions. A horrifying expression appeared in his eyes; he turned to the counter. The black-handled paring knife was lying near the sink; it had a short blade that came to a sharp point. With a yell he grabbed the weapon and turned on his son, who watched him petrified. Something strange took place in Charles at that moment. He suddenly saw the face of his father transformed into that of a green, warty toad, with grotesque mouth, and with enormous shiny eyes turning softly on themselves like gold-threaded marbles; the child was seized by a convulsive fit of laughter; he raised his hand, one finger extended, and tried to speak.

A loud shriek saved him. Sylvie was standing in the doorway, staring at Wilfrid, who had stopped a few paces from Charles. She screamed again, the piercing sound invading every room of the apartment like a cold wind that took the breath away; the paring knife fell to the floor with a clatter. The carpenter, looking haggard and contrite, gulped slowly, then babbled something inarticulate, collapsed on the chair, and stayed there, motionless.

"You were going to kill him!" the waitress shouted in amazement. "You were really going to kill him! You've gone crazy, I swear it! Crazy! Completely crazy!"

15

Charles flew down the stairs under the astonished eye of Monsieur Victoire, who had come out onto his balcony in his pyjamas. He ran down the sidewalk without knowing where he was going, turned a corner, and found himself in the tiny park off rue Coupal. As though this were where he had been headed all along, he threw himself straight under the bench, curled up as tightly as he could, trying to make himself as small as possible, in fact trying to disappear altogether in the dead leaves strewn about the ground. Jolts of energy shot through his body, he couldn't stop his eyes and mouth from opening and closing, and such a clanging was going on in his head that he couldn't formulate a single thought. If anyone had asked him where he was, he wouldn't have been able to answer. There was an unpleasant coldness between his legs, which told him he had wet his pants. Shudders wracked his body, he gasped for breath, feeling bruised and exhausted. If only he could go to sleep, right there under the bench! But the chaos that had taken over his brain made sleep impossible. Minutes passed. Traffic picked up on rue Ontario. Somewhere a clock struck. Suddenly the angry growl of a garbage truck rolled over him. The ground under his thigh and shoulder became hard and cold. He would have crawled out, but the strength to do so had drained out of him.

Then he heard a familiar bark coming from far away, and he was visited by a miraculous clarity. It was Boff, in the Fafards' backyard. The dog must have recognized his steps on the staircase and was calling him. In an instant Charles was on his feet and running back towards rue Dufresne.

At the corner he paused and looked carefully at the door to his apartment, trying to see if a human form lurked behind the glass, but he couldn't see anything because of a reflection from the streetlight. He raced across the street and rushed into the Fafards' yard. Boff saw him and instantly stopped barking, then began pulling on his chain and shaking his head, choking. Charles released him and signalled to him to follow. He'd changed his mind; he would not hide out with the Fafards. That would be the first place his father would look for him. Who could say he wouldn't succeed in getting him back to the house? The idea filled Charles with horror.

He left the yard and soon found himself on rue Ontario. The store windows glowed palely in the orange light from the streetlamps. Boff pranced around him, ecstatic at being taken for an unexpected early-morning walk. Charles moved quickly, looking anxiously up and down the street, afraid that a police car would suddenly appear; they would surely stop and take him home despite all his protestations. In the distance he saw a tramp crossing the street, carrying a huge sack. Twice a car slowed down beside him; each time the driver gave him an appraising look, then picked up speed and moved off.

Suddenly he spotted a vaguely familiar figure a hundred metres ahead of him, a man pacing back and forth at the corner. Charles continued walking and recognized Monsieur Saint-Amour, wrapped in a heavy brown overcoat that reached all the way down to his ankles, his hands thrust deep into its pockets and a dented felt hat jammed on his head down to his ears. Who could he be waiting for at this hour?

The old man hadn't seen him. Charles turned and doubled back, took a side street, and made a wide detour to avoid running into him. After a few minutes he was in front of his old daycare on rue Lalonde. No one would think of looking for him there, and he had to come there anyway to get his money, which now he would certainly need. The cherry tree stood in the bluish light of early dawn, its crown half bare of leaves, and a mysterious peace seeming to hover in the air around it. Charles sat at its feet and ran his hand over the dried grass, greeting the little yellow dog. As though sensing the solemnity of the occasion, Boff lay down at his side. Charles breathed a sigh of relief. He now had two dogs to keep him company. He began rubbing the spaniel's back and the thick hair warmed his icy fingers. His pants were nearly dry. He had regained most of his spirits, and now if he was still shivering it was because of the chill in the morning air rather than out of fear. Nevertheless, he was still plunged in gloom, feeling hopeless. He did not know what to do or where to go.

He put his arms around Boff and closed his eyes. The dog's warmth, which gave off a deep and familiar odour, was a profound comfort to him. His trembling slowed down, then disappeared altogether. Was he asleep? He couldn't say. After a certain time had passed he felt a faint light penetrating his eyelids. He raised his head. The sky was brilliant. Boff moved one foot but continued to snore lightly. The shimmering leaves of the cherry tree, now bathed in light, rustled gently and the sound, blending with the other noises of the awakening city, was extremely pleasant. It must have been the little yellow dog who had taught the tree to make such pretty music. Charles stared at the spot on the ground where he had buried the dog and a smile rose to his lips; suddenly, with wonderful precision, he had thought of the perfect solution to his problem.

■ ■ ■

Parfait Michaud, the notary, sat by himself in his dining room, turning a spoon in his cup of coffee with a pensive air. Living with a hypochondriac was not easy. His wife was sick again, or at least believed herself to be. The previous afternoon she'd gone to the jeweller's to pick up a bracelet she was having repaired, and, while handing it to her the jeweller had unfortunately coughed in her face. That was all it had taken. She'd returned to the house pale as a ghost, swallowed aspirin after aspirin and taken handfuls of Vitamin C, felt a death of a cold coming on, taken to her bed, and buried herself under two duvets with a hot-water bottle at her feet, already shaken by spasms and aching all over. He'd gone up to see her between clients. "Amélie, for the love of God, why start suffering before you get sick?" But as usual his little pleasantry had not had the slightest therapeutic effect.

And this morning, of course, she'd come down with a high fever. It would last two or three days, leaving him to make all the meals, bring her infusions of this and that, glasses of fruit juice, finely chopped salads, and all because somewhere in her brain there lurked a device that allowed her to fall sick at will. The only time it left her in peace was when she was busy with something, when she couldn't afford to waste time in bed. Alas, such moments were rare; for years she had believed herself to be suffering from an energy deficiency that prevented her from doing anything that could even remotely be described as too much work.

The notary lifted his cup, took a sip of coffee and smacked his lips appreciatively: the espresso was particularly good this morning. The Italian on rue

Jean-Talon had not been lying after all; the machine he'd sold him had been worth every penny.

A second warm thought followed the first and brought a small smile to his lips: it was Sunday, a day of rest, a respite from clients; he could listen to his favourite LPs in peace, then settle down to read *L'homme rapaillé*, a collection of poems about which he'd been hearing a lot of good things.

Was that his wife's voice? No, she was asleep and probably wouldn't wake up until ten. Her glass of orange juice was ready on the counter, along with two multivitamins and a jar of Scotch marmalade of which she was particularly fond and which he had been lucky enough to find yesterday. Everything was in place, at least for the time being.

Suddenly the doorbell gave out its strangled vibrato. He looked at his watch and made a face. Who would have the nerve to turn up on his doorstep at five after nine on a Sunday morning? That tramp he'd given money to on Thursday? Jehovah's Witnesses? He would convert them to silence!

Tightening the cord of his dressing gown, he went into the vestibule, his slippers flip-flopping on the hardwood floor. Through the door's window he saw a small boy standing on the porch beside a dog, gazing straight back at him with a determined look.

"What can I do for you, my little friend? Ah, it's the boy with the dogs," he said, recognizing him. "Heavens, but you're up and about early this morning. Don't you know it's Sunday?"

"It's just that I need to speak to you, sir," replied the child. The dog, sitting on the porch, wagged his tail gently.

"What about?"

"A business matter," said the boy. Then, seeing the astonished look on the notary's face, he added, "It's important."

"Can't you come back tomorrow?"

"It can't wait that long, sir."

The boy gave him a smile that was warm enough to melt a snowbank. Michaud caught the look of supplication in his shining eyes.

"All right, come in," he sighed, stepping aside to let him pass. "But the dog stays here. My wife's allergic."

The boy told his dog to stay and followed the notary into the house. The latter opened a door that gave into a small waiting room, then turned to the boy with a stern look.

"I hope this isn't about selling me some raffle tickets or anything of that sort, is it? I have no intention of buying anything like that today, I'll tell you right off."

"No, sir. It's about something a lot more important than that."

He led the boy through the waiting room, with its chairs, its newspaper rack, and small table stacked with magazines, into a large, sombre-looking room with an enormous carved-oak desk at the centre, like a casket. Drab beige curtains flanked a large window through whose Venetian blinds Charles could see rue Bercy. A sullen row of olive-green filing cabinets lined the left-hand wall. On either side of the door, framed diplomas solemnly declared the competence of the master of the premises.

The notary brought over a chair for his young visitor, sat behind his desk, and, steepling his long fingers, pronounced the ritual opening phrase of any client interview: "What can I do for you?"

Charles reddened and shifted slightly in his chair.

"I want to get a divorce from my father," he said.

"You want to . . . Can you say that again, please?"

"I want to get a divorce, from my father. I have enough money . . ."

And he took a fistful of banknotes from his pocket.

The notary considered the boy's lively, intelligent face, his polite manners; he had just withdrawn a seemingly large amount of money from his pocket, and Michaud wondered how on earth he would approach such a curious affair.

"I'm not sure I understand you . . . By the way, what's your name?"

Charles gave him his name and forestalled what was obviously the next question by telling him his age.

"But I'll be ten in one month," he explained.

"Fine, fine . . . First of all, Charles, you should know that a divorce can take place only between a man and his wife. I gather you no longer want to live with your father, is that the way of it?"

"Yes, that's it."

"And what about your mother?"

"My mother's dead. She died six years ago. My father lives with Sylvie. She's a waitress at Chez Robert. She's not so bad, but I don't want to live with her any more, either."

"I see. Good. You don't get along with your father, Sylvie hasn't been able

178

to settle things between you, and so you've decided you want to live with a different family."

"Yes, that's it exactly."

A look of profound relief spread across Charles's face, and he slid the money under his thigh in order to have it handy when the time came to pay the notary.

Michaud parted his lips and tapped his teeth with the nail of his index finger, as was his habit when presented with a particularly knotty problem. He would have to proceed tactfully; it seemed a serious matter, and he had little experience with such cases.

"I must also tell you, Charles," he said after several small coughs, "that notary publics don't, as a rule, handle these kinds of problems. It's usually up to lawyers."

"Oh," said Charles, with a little pout. "Do you know a lawyer?"

"Yes, of course, I know several. But first, with your permission, there are a few questions I'd like to ask you."

Charles clasped his hands together and rested them on his knee, waiting for the questions. His pleasant, forthright manner, and the clearness of his gaze, pleased the notary very much, and the furtive idea flitted through the latter's mind that if he had had a child, despite all the inconveniences such an occurrence would entail, his life would have been a happier one; but the time for such an undertaking had obviously passed.

"May I inquire," he said, nervously scratching one of his elbows on the arm of his chair, "as to what it is that has come between you and your father?"

Charles blushed again. "We don't get along," he said.

"I can see that. Does he hit you?"

"Sometimes."

"Is he . . . does he show violence towards you?"

Charles looked away and frowned. "Sometimes," he said. Then he looked down and murmured, in a voice that was both overwhelmed and brave, added: "I don't like my life."

A moment passed.

"I see," said the notary.

The rubbing of his elbow against his chair arm had become audible. On the porch, Boff gave a sharp, imperious bark, signifying that his waiting had gone on long enough.

"It's just that the law is very clear, Charles," Michaud went on. "A child cannot leave his parents without very good reasons. Do you understand? Reasons that put his health or his life in danger."

But Charles was becoming increasingly guarded, and Michaud knew that for now he could go no further. He reached out his hand towards a porcelain candy dish, then leaned forward and offered it to the boy.

"Would you like one? Raspberry-flavoured."

The speed with which Charles popped a candy into his mouth made one thing perfectly clear: the boy was starving. The notary laughed.

"Have you had breakfast, Charles? You look like you could eat a horse!"

"No, not really. I wanted to see you first."

"Well, what would you say to some toast, or a bowl of cereal? Come on, I can tell you'd like something but you're too shy to ask for it. Nevermind, we'll go into the kitchen."

Charles slid off his chair and followed the notary. They went through a door with a frosted pane on which a very self-satisfied-looking peacock was spreading its fan of feathers. They passed through a large room with burgundy walls, which Charles took in with a respectful gaze, then an even more impressive dining room, with its long walnut table surrounded by a solemn circle of chairs, and entered a kitchen lined with huge walnut cupboards, an even nicer and bigger room than Madame Fafard's kitchen, which had been until then Charles's *ne plus ultra* of kitchens. A corridor opened to the left down which he could make out a door that was slightly ajar.

The notary pulled out a chair and Charles, feeling shy, sat down at a large table of blond wood.

"So what do you feel like?" Michaud asked. "Toast? Cereal? Both? Maybe with a cup of hot chocolate?"

"Who's here?" asked a woman's voice.

"A young friend who has come to pay us a visit, Amélie. His name is Charles. He didn't have time to have breakfast this morning, so I'm making him something."

"Bring him to me."

Michaud made a sign for Charles to follow him, and together they went through the half-opened door. At first all Charles saw was a heap of blankets and quilts on top of a huge bed, then a head appeared with black hair and a

180

red nose; it raised itself up and peered at him intently for a second with large round eyes.

"A nice-looking boy. Don't come too close, for mercy's sake, or you'll catch my cold. And it's a doozy, believe me. What did Parfait say your name was?"

"Charles Thibodeau, Madame."

"And why are you here, Charles Thibodeau?"

"He has come to consult me about a small problem," the notary replied, "but for the moment he's too hungry to concentrate, I believe, so we're going to have breakfast together first."

"*Bon appétit*," sighed the woman, then let out a sneeze that ended in a high, resonating wail like that of a muted trumpet.

Charles ate five slices of toast spread with peanut butter or strawberry jam; he also downed all of two large cups of hot chocolate and a bowl of Rice Krispies generously sprinkled with brown sugar. While sipping his own cup of hot chocolate, the notary chatted with him about nothing in particular. From certain allusions dropped by Charles, Michaud understood that the boy was very much afraid of returning to his own home, that he would rather sleep on the street than go back to his father's apartment. But he could not find out exactly what had taken place between the boy and his father; Michaud had the impression that the child was too ashamed to say. But it must have had something to do with the pile of banknotes Charles had brought with him.

As for where he'd got the money in the first place, Charles was much more loquacious. He happily recounted the story of his misadventures selling chocolate bars, and the way in which he had taken his revenge, which in the notary's considered opinion was not a question of robbery – at least not in the usual sense of the word.

"Well, what's your plan, Charles? Where will you sleep tonight if you don't go back to your own house?"

Charles replied that he would be all right at his neighbours' house, a family called Fafard, which was like a second home to him. Except that that was where his father would certainly look for him. That was why he had thought of getting a divorce.

"I could call Blonblon," he said worriedly. "He's one of my friends. Maybe his parents will put me up for a while. Does it take a long time to separate from your parents?"

"Hmm . . . I'm not sure. I suppose in serious cases things can be moved along fairly quickly. But you still haven't told me your exact reason for not wanting to go home, Charles. Nothing says you have to tell me, of course," he added quickly, seeing the child's face cloud over.

Charles looked down at his empty cereal bowl for a moment as though he hoped something would leap up out of it. They heard Boff give a long, mournful howl from the porch.

"I have to go," he said, getting up off his chair. "My dog is tired of waiting. Can you tell me where the lawyer is who can help me?"

"You won't be able to see him today, unfortunately. It's Sunday, you know. I think I mentioned that earlier."

He brought his hand up to his mouth and coughed two or three times.

"Tell me, Charles . . . I don't mean to interfere, and as I say you are under no obligation to answer me, but . . . how much money do you have on you?"

A look of pride spread across the child's face.

"Three hundred and forty-eight dollars and twenty-five cents."

"That's a lot of money for a nine-year-old to carry around."

"I'm almost ten," Charles told him again.

"Yes, of course, but even so . . . What would you say, Charles – you know you can have complete confidence in me, I can assure you – what would you say to letting me keep some of it for you in an envelope with your name on it? It's not a good idea, you know, to go about the city with such a large sum . . ."

Charles thought about it for a moment, then said: "I'd like that. It's a good idea."

And while Boff broke into a long, lugubrious serenade that seemed to express all the accumulated sufferings of his life as a dog, Charles took the wad of bills from his pocket, extracted a twenty for walking-around money, and gave the rest to the notary with a wide smile.

"Whose dog is it howling like a banshee out there?" Amélie called from her mound of quilts.

"It belongs to our young friend," replied the notary. "Don't upset yourself, my dear, Charles is going out to him right away."

"At least let it into the vestibule. I find the noise terribly upsetting. You know very well a dog's barking has always given me the shivers."

182

Charles hurried towards the front of the house, followed by the notary, and opened the door. Boff burst into the vestibule in an explosion of delirious joy.

"Well," Charles said when he'd got the dog to settle down, "so when can I see the lawyer?"

"Tomorrow, probably. I'll have to make some phone calls first. I don't want to send you to just anyone. But before you go I want you to give me this Blonblon's phone number – that's his name, isn't it? The home you're going to? We may have to get hold of you between now and tomorrow. And while you're at it you should probably give me the number of those neighbours of yours, the ones you like so much."

Charles gave him the numbers quickly. He felt as though each number were a life-line tossed between himself and this tall, thin man, who talked a bit strange but was also very kind, and who was going to rescue him from the huge emptiness he'd been drifting in since the previous night.

Michaud watched from the vestibule as Charles disappeared down the street, Boff leaping wildly and licking the boy's hands. His fingernail tapped on his front teeth with a low sound that rose into his skull and reminded him of his visits to the dentist. What was his responsibility in this affair? Should he call the police? A priest, perhaps? The Sisters of the Convent of Transubstantiation? But he had no precise facts to give them, other than that the boy had run away from home, refused to go back or provide any reason for his flight. On top of that, the whole business was complicated by the theft of a fairly large sum of money. There was clearly much food for thought here.

Whistling the overture to *Lohengrin*, he went back into his office and began flipping through the telephone book, every now and then reaching his hand out to the candy dish.

■ ■ ■

As he walked along the sidewalk, Charles chewed his lip thoughtfully. What was he going to do with Boff? He didn't dare try taking him back to the Fafards for fear of running into his father. And to turn up at Blonblon's with a dog and ask him to take them both in would surely be asking too much.

Arriving at the corner of Ontario, he turned in the direction of home, walking more and more hesitantly, feeling more and more distraught. Suddenly he gave a shout of joy: Henri had just turned the corner of rue Poupart. He called his friend and waved his arms wildly.

"What're you doing out here?" Henri asked, trying to catch his breath. "You're supposed to be sick. I was just at your house, and your father said you were in bed with the flu."

Charles told him about the fight he had had the previous night with his father, and his decision to spend the night outside. He evaded most of his astonished friend's questions about the incident, and asked him to take Boff back to his yard, because he had decided to spend the next few days at Blonblon's, until he had had time to make other arrangements.

"Why don't you come to our place?" asked Henri, a bit put out.

"My father would find me there in two seconds!" Charles replied.

Henri watched him walk off for a moment, a frown tugging at the corners of his mouth, holding the poor, whining spaniel by its collar. Boff, too, stared after his master, devastated by this second desertion in less than an hour.

Boff's mournful cries were still in Charles's ears when he turned the corner of rue Bercy and headed towards Frontenac Towers. He was in for a setback: there was no answer to his ring at Blonblon's apartment. He left the building not knowing where else to go. He was beginning to feel the effects of his nocturnal escapades; his legs were weak, his eyelids drooped, and he dragged himself along the street looking in every direction for somewhere to sleep.

At the Frontenac station he had an idea. He bought a few metro tickets, boarded the subway and found a seat in one of the corners. Within minutes he was dozing off, lulled by the rumbling of the wheels that enveloped him like a down-filled blanket; loudspeakers announced each stop, the subway doors slid open and closed, the movement of the car rocked him gently; passengers, respecting his look of exhaustion, the slight twitching of his lips, kept their distance. He felt and heard nothing, plunged as he was in the most blissful sleep, finally shielded from the most terrifying day of his entire life.

Fifteen minutes later a young woman shook him gently by the shoulder and told him they'd pulled into the Atwater terminal. He got out, took the train going the other way, and thus began making the journey from one end of the line to the other, staggering from one stop to another like a sleepwalker, finding a seat in which he could fall asleep for another precious quarter of an hour. He was reassured by the sense of being in perpetual motion, and therefore in a continuous state of flight. His only concern was to gain enough time for his friend the notary (for he now counted Monsieur Michaud among his friends) to get him out of this predicament.

The previous night's scene filled him with shame, as though he had somehow been the cause of his father's behaviour. In a sense, he was. Maybe he should have reported Guilbault instead of stealing his money? It didn't matter anyway, though, because his father would have found fault with him no matter what he did, would always take the other's side against him, the side of that fat thief in his Sunday suit who lived like a millionaire on money belonging to poor children. Why couldn't he have a decent father like other kids? What had he done to make his father so bad? Alice had never been like that. Alice had loved him, simple as that. When he had been with her, he had felt like a normal kid, no better and no worse than any other kid, and that had made him happy.

But at the thought of his father a black and ugly feeling spread through him, which made him terribly afraid. He would never reveal to anyone, not even to the lawyer, what his father had tried to do to him that night. But what had his father wanted to do, really? Kill him? *Him*, Charles? It hardly seemed possible, and yet that was the word Sylvie had used after giving out that terrified scream: kill. And that was the word that continued to fill him with insupportable shame, as though he had been the one to put the paring knife in his father's hand, and then pushed him beyond all endurable limits, until that ugly toad's look had appeared on his father's face. . . .

He was having trouble sleeping now, his head was so full of disturbing thoughts flashing endlessly through his mind. He was also opening his eyes at every stop to make sure he didn't find himself alone in a car that had been taken out of service, which would surely land him in another mess.

Sometimes, however, sleep overcame him; his head would flop forward onto his chest, his arms would relax, and he would slip into a profound sleep. On one such occasion he suddenly felt a hand rubbing his knee. He opened his eyes and there, hovering above him, was the smiling face of Monsieur Saint-Amour. The car was nearly empty.

"Leave me alone, you old pig!" Charles screamed at him as loudly as he could. And he pushed the man away with his foot.

16

Parfait Michaud sat looking about his office for several minutes, his fingers tapping on the telephone directory, then decided that the first thing he had to do was find out more about Charles. He called the Blondin number, then, receiving no response, dialed that of the Fafards.

It was Fernand who answered, wearing slippers and a bath robe, a copy of *La Presse* tucked under his arm, still in a state of indignation over Trudeau's remark about the Québécois "tribe," and the "separatist dreamers" among them. A half-hour earlier Henri had told him about his encounter with Charles on rue Ontario. The carpenter's lie about the boy's illness had intrigued Fernand, as had Charles's decision to ask the Blondins to put him up for the night. He, too, had tried unsuccessfully to connect the two puzzles, and was looking for an excuse to go over to the Thibodeaus' to find out what was going on. The news he was now hearing from Michaud raised his anxiety to an even higher pitch. Charles's visit to the notary's office, the amount of money he'd been carrying around, and the terror the thought of going back to his father seemed to have inspired in him, all convinced Fernand of the seriousness of the situation. The two men agreed to meet in Michaud's office. Fernand had used the notary's services in the past, and knew him to be an eccentric and even slightly absurd character, but amiable and competent for all that.

By eleven o'clock in the morning, Fernand having informed him of the carpenter's curious (to put it mildly) behaviour regarding his son, Michaud had put forward two or three highly pertinent moral observations, but the affair had advanced not a whit since no one knew where Charles was. Fernand decided to pay Thibodeau a visit, to beard the lion in his den, face to face, and to pluck the whiskers from his jowls one by one until he was willing to talk. The notary, for his part, undertook to call the Blondin number in thirty minutes, in the hope that Charles would eventually show up there.

Stepping out onto the street, Fernand noticed a purple Lincoln parked in front of the Thibodeau building; a man in a maroon hat was descending the staircase; he was pudgy, wore a number of flashy rings, and had a red face and a crooked mouth.

"If he thinks he's going to put me off like that for long, he's got another think coming," the man muttered menacingly to himself as he passed Fernand without looking up, completely absorbed in his anger.

Fernand returned to his own house and took up a position behind a curtain in the living room, but there was no sign of life in his neighbour's apartment.

Lucie, who had been brought up-to-date on the affair and was extremely worried, put on her overcoat, put Boff on a leash, and walked with him through the neighbourhood, in the hope of running into Charles. Michaud sat in his living room listening to his record-player, trying in vain to concentrate on a Schubert quartet. He turned the machine off, brought dinner in to his wife (who was surprised at being served so early), got into his car, and drove down rue Saint-Denis to the National Library. A dispiriting light spilled from the wells of the reading lamps and windows in the huge room with beige walls, where the readers bent over the long oak tables seemed to have come to escape all the passions of the world. The notary settled under the halo of a brass desklamp and read meticulously through the Laws concerning the protection of children, got up a few times to call the Blondin number again, still without getting a response, then left the library, hardly any wiser than when he had gone in. As he turned towards his car, he suddenly felt a craving for a good, strong espresso, and went into the Picasso, a café across the street from the library. He was served by a beautiful petite waitress, as lively and jolly a brunette as he could have wished, with legs that would make a saint's mouth water. Since the café was almost empty he struck up a conversation with her and got the impression that she didn't find him hard to look at either. Half an hour later he left with her telephone number scribbled on a corner of his napkin.

■ ■ ■

Charles quickly left the subway at the next station, then got on another one a few minutes later that took him to the Berri-de Montigny station. There,

187

hoping to lose the hairdresser, he changed lines, going down from the east-west train to get on the north-south. He was less familiar with this line and made his first trip keeping his eyes open, figuring out how long it took to make the complete run and memorizing the names of the stations at each end, so as to be sure to get off at the right times. The trip took a bit longer, allowing him to stretch out his naps; he stayed out of empty cars and always sat near another passenger so that he would have someone to turn to if he needed help. Gradually the fatigue that had overwhelmed him began to fade. His mind cleared, and his situation began to seem almost pleasurable; he had become the hero of a kind of detective story, except that in his case it was he who controlled the action rather than being the victim . . . at least most of the time. . . .

Around two o'clock in the afternoon he was awakened by hunger pangs. He got off at Berri-de Montigny and went into a restaurant in the station, where he ordered a bowl of chicken soup, fries and a hamburger, keeping an eye on everyone who entered; he had already tried phoning the Blondins at least six times and was beginning to worry that some unexpected tragedy had forced them to leave the city. At three, however, Blonblon's happy and triumphant voice echoed in the receiver.

"Aha, you at last!" he said. "Get over here right away! We've been waiting for you. Where the heck are you?"

Charles hardly had time to reply when he heard a man's voice on the line.

"Hello, Charles? I'm Michel's father. Are you okay?"

"Yes, sir."

"No problems?"

"None at all."

"You sure?"

"Yes, yes."

"Good. Michaud, the notary, just called. Everything is arranged. Don't worry about a thing. Do you want my wife to come to get you?"

"There's no need, Monsieur Blondin. I'm in the metro, only three stops from your place. I'll be there in ten minutes."

As he was leaving the Frontenac station, he saw Blonblon standing beside the exit. He ran towards Charles and hugged him.

"Hello! About time you showed up! Everyone's worried sick about you. My folks almost called the cops!"

Charles pulled away quickly, pleasantly surprised at his friend's unusual display of affection. Blonblon looked at Charles closely. "Were you really in danger, Thibodeau?"

Charles nodded but almost immediately regretted it; Blonblon's curiosity increased.

"What happened? Tell me!" he said, grabbing Charles by the arm.

Charles's embarrassment increased; he tightened his lips and frowned. Blonblon wasn't interested in him, only in what had happened to him. He wouldn't tell him a thing. To hell with nosy busy-bodies.

"Well, aren't you going to tell me?"

Blonblon stopped and stood in Charles's way. Charles almost told him to get lost, and almost said "Get your nose out of my business!" But Blonblon's eyes were fixed on him, and they shone with such emotion, such warmth, and his face expressed such sympathy and friendship, without a trace of pity, that Charles suddenly felt a kind of melting take place inside him; he felt as though the immense and frigid emptiness inside him was receding, and tears welled up in his eyes and his voice, when he spoke, trembled and cracked.

"My father tried to kill me, Blonblon."

His friend kept his eyes fixed on his own with the same smiling intensity. Then slowly a look of incredulity and horror spread across his face:

"Really?" he said softly. "No kidding?"

"With a paring knife," Charles added despite himself. "He was going to stab me with it, but Sylvie screamed and he stopped. Then the bitch grabbed him and made him sit down. That's when I got out of there, fast."

He gave a nervous laugh, then took his friend by the arm and shook it as hard as he could with a fierce expression on his face.

"Never repeat what I said to anyone, Blonblon, do you understand?" he said through clenched teeth. "If you ever tell anyone, I'll smash you one and it'll be all over between us. Promise me! Promise!"

"I . . . I promise," Blonblon said, speaking like an automaton.

"It's my secret, Blonblon, and you're the only one who knows it. Don't forget what I said. Not even Henri knows, and he never will!"

They began walking and for several minutes neither of them spoke.

"This isn't a joke, is it, Thibodeau?" Blonblon said in a changed voice. "You're perfectly serious?"

"Yes."

"It's a serious thing," he said, adding, as though to himself. "You must never see your father again."

"Don't worry, I don't want to see him again. Ever. I just came from Michaud, the notary, to ask him to separate us."

Blonblon nodded with a faint smile; that explained the call from the notary that had so intrigued him. An idea occurred to him with such sudden force that it stopped him in his tracks.

"You know, Charles, you really must go to the police! He's a dangerous man! He might try to kill someone else."

They were at the entrance to Blonblon's apartment tower. A fat woman in a red scarf pushed open the glass door and came slowly towards them pulling a white chihuahua on a leash. The dog's mouth was twisted and it had a large welt under its left eye; pulling against its chain, the animal ran up to Charles, smelled his shoe, and tried to climb up his leg.

"Down, Martin!" the lady scolded. "Where are your manners!"

She gave a great tug on the leash and pulled the animal away. Turning its head towards Charles, the chihuahua gave a short, sharp bark.

Charles waited until the woman was some distance away, then put his mouth to Blonblon's ear: "Let me worry about the police, all right?" he whispered menacingly. "This is my business, not yours. I'm not going to the police and I don't want anyone else going, either, understand? You think I want to grow up a prisoner's kid?"

And clenching his teeth to keep from crying, he turned his back on Blonblon and walked with determination towards the building.

A problem was waiting at the Blondin apartment, however. Fernand had just arrived, and absolutely insisted on taking Charles home with him. The notary's phone call, the arrival of Fernand, and the excitement generated by Charles's disappearance had made him the centre of attention. Edith Blondin, a tall, thin woman with elegant yet casual features and a loud laugh, who barely listened to anything anyone said and rarely stopped fidgeting, insisted that Charles spend at least a few days with them. Sitting slightly hunched in his wheelchair, her husband, Marcel, questioned Charles in a serious, calm voice about the reasons for his flight, without succeeding in breaking through the boy's reticence. In the end Charles became annoyed and joined Blonblon, who was in the kitchen filling a bowl with potato chips for the guests. The invalid signalled Fernand to come closer.

"What we need to know, Monsieur Fafard," he said with the pensive expression of someone who is used to spending all day thinking hard, "is what actually happened. My son will know how to talk to him. They're great friends, and Michel is very good with people. We'll keep Charles with us for a night or two. He'll sleep in Michel's room. That'll give them a chance to talk on their own. I'm sure the whole thing will come out."

Fernand, who was beginning to think of himself more and more as Charles's second – and would soon come to think of him as his only – father, was unable to suppress a small frown of displeasure. In his opinion, the boy would be safe nowhere but in the Fafard household. He turned to Charles, who had just reentered the room.

"So tell us, my boy, what have you decided? Do you want to come with me or stay here?"

"Stay, Charles, do," Edith said in a tone that was half serious and half playful. "I'm making a big batch of spaghetti tonight and Michel will go out and get us a cake at the bakery."

Blonblon smiled at Charles and nodded his head, gently encouraging him to say yes. Charles, who always wanted to please everyone, turned from one to the other, greatly embarrassed by the superabundance of attention he was receiving. He knew Fernand's bland look hid his true feelings, and it made Charles feel even more uncomfortable. A thought came to him. He reddened noticeably and took the hardware-store owner aside.

"Has my father been to your house?" he asked quietly.

"No," Fernand said, sensing the fear that lay behind the question. "And if he does come, I won't let him in. No need to worry on that score!"

Charles looked relieved. He went over to Madame Blondin and said in his most gracious manner:

"For today, Madame, I'll go with Monsieur Fafard. Tomorrow, if you like, I could come back here."

"We can't force you to do anything, Charles," she replied a little coolly. "You do what you like."

■ ■ ■

Wilfrid Thibodeau was terrified by the outrage he had almost committed the night before. He shut himself off from the world, refused to answer the telephone or the door, and hadn't spoken five words the entire day. Sylvie stayed in the bedroom, either asleep or pretending to be. Stretched out on the sofa, he watched television in a distracted haze and hadn't had a drop of alcohol since waking up, which went a long way towards indicating the state he was in. He figured his son had gone to seek shelter at the Fafards, and for hours after the boy's flight he had prepared himself resignedly for a call from the police. No such call came, however, and he no longer knew what to think. Life seemed to have drained out of him, as though he were a barrel that had lost its bottom. Should he wait it out? Run away? Stay put? Try to forget the horrible events of that night? These were the only solutions that went through his chaotic mind. When, a few hours earlier, he had seen Gino Guilbault's Lincoln pull up in front of the building, it was the final straw. The crooked salesman was all he needed to finish him off.

He got up and took a shower. Then he ate some leftovers in the kitchen, succumbed to a single beer from the refrigerator – but just the one – and stood for a moment staring at the bedroom door, which remained obstinately closed.

He went back into the living room and had just managed to evince a modicum of interest in a game show when the doorbell rang repeatedly. There followed the sound of fists pounding on the door. He knew who it was: that bloody Guilbault again. How could he get rid of him? Would he have to move?

The pounding continued for a while, then there was an ominous silence. The squealing of tires told him that the salesman had taken his anger off somewhere else. Shortly after that the telephone rang again.

"Tomorrow I'm gonna have to get outta here early," he said to himself. "The bastard'll for sure be trying again."

He fell asleep on the sofa and found himself in a boat in the middle of a lake. His father was in the boat with him, and night was falling. He could no longer see the shore. The old man was wearing his mechanic's cap backwards, for some reason, and was lying on his back in the bow, his long, thin legs stretched out in a V. The boat was rocking; the dry sound of waves smacking the hull were becoming louder and more menacing. He looked about for the oars, but there weren't any.

"Papa, where did you put the oars?"

192

The old man neither moved nor answered. Then he realized with horror that his father was dead; a thin dribble of blood ran from his mouth onto his threadbare jacket.

The closing of a door startled him awake. He must have been struggling in his sleep, because he was lying crosswise on the sofa, his feet on the floor. Early-morning light filled the room, making the objects in it look curiously dusty and indistinct. It must have been six o'clock; Sylvie had no doubt gone out to work. He would see her again at the end of the afternoon, and they would talk this whole thing out. Her silence worried him, but the important thing for now was to get the hell out of the apartment before that goddamn chocolate salesman showed up again.

Without bothering to wash or even change his clothes, he put on his coat and left. Passing Chez Robert he thought briefly of going inside for break-fast; he might get a chance to have a word with Sylvie, find out what kind of mood she was in. But he wisely kept going. Who knew? Guilbault himself might drop in to find out where he was.

He'd barely turned the corner when Sylvie left the restaurant and headed quickly back to the apartment. Half an hour later a taxi pulled up in front of 1970 rue Dufresne. What followed looked like a hasty evacuation. The driver, who'd been given a ten-dollar tip, moved as though his life depended on it. The taxi was soon loaded to the brim with piles of clothing, suitcases, and garbage bags stuffed with everything the waitress could carry with her; all she'd left behind were an ironing board, a chest of drawers, and an old, dilap-idated sofa chair. In exchange she took a toaster, the electric kettle, and the small television set, which was practically brand new.

By seven-thirty she was gone and Rosalie, fit to be tied, was on the phone looking for a new waitress.

Wilfrid returned just after five, having carefully inspected the street for the presence of his creditor. Sylvie was gone without a word of explanation. He wandered from one overturned room to another, shattered, furious with himself for having been the cause of her unhappiness, then took himself down to Chez Robert. He was received coolly; no one knew where Sylvie had gone to hide. He sought refuge in the Amis du Sport and didn't get home until well after midnight, bent over like a badly driven nail and drunk as a skunk that had fallen into a vat of beer. He spent another night on the sofa in the living room; the sight of the big, empty bed was too painful to contemplate. During the entire day the idea of finding out where Charles had gone had not occurred to him once.

■ ■ ■

The next morning, Blonblon woke with a pressing problem on his mind, one that needed to be resolved as quickly as possible. Hunched over his bowl of cereal, he reflected on it with all the intensity a nine-year-old could muster, his face contorted from time to time with unusual frowns. They finally attracted the attention of his father, who was sitting across from him with a cup of coffee.

"Something bothering you, son?"

Since his father had become sick four years ago, Blonblon had a ready answer for such a question.

"No, nothing's bothering me, Papa."

Blonblon protected his father. He had decided that multiple sclerosis was more than enough for one man to have to deal with, and that it was his job to shield him from everything else.

"You're keeping something from me, son," Monsieur Blondin pressed.

"No I'm not, Papa," Blonblon replied, hurrying to finish his cereal so as not to give himself away. "It's just that I have some homework to finish before going to school. Excuse me, I've got to go to my room."

He got dressed, then sat down on the side of his bed to give the thing more thought. His mother might have been able to help him see the problem more clearly, but she was still sleeping. Her job as a real-estate agent often kept her out late at night.

Blonblon rubbed his feet together and frowned again, this time without trying to hide his agitation; he felt himself torn between two obligations: on the one hand was the promise he had made to Charles, and on the other, the sense that he had to intervene in order to save his friend from almost certain death, a danger of which Charles himself seemed entirely unaware.

He left his room, schoolbag on his back, hugged his father and headed off to school. Henri would probably already be in the schoolyard, since he always got there early. A thought quickened Blonblon's step: maybe Charles had let

194

Henri in on the secret. That would release Blonblon from his promise, and he would be free to save Charles's life.

In the schoolyard he saw Henri playing ball-hockey with some friends; Charles was leaning against the fence, watching them but looking deep in thought. He turned towards Blonblon and waved his hand. Blonblon approached him, struck by the pale, exhausted look on Charles's face.

"Where's your hockey stick, Blondin?" Henri called over.

Charles merely gave him a sad, intent look, the kind spies gave to their contacts when they wanted to warn them about something. Henri noticed nothing, and went on playing hockey as though everything were normal.

Blonblon chatted with Charles about this and that until the bell went. But just as they were about to enter the school he managed to get beside Henri and give him a light elbow in the ribs.

"So?" he asked, giving his voice a mysterious cast.

"So what?" asked Henri.

"Is there something you want to tell me?"

"Like what?"

Blonblon looked at him for a moment, then pointed a finger at his temple.

"Wheels grinding a bit slowly this morning, are they?" Then he shrugged: "Forget it," he said, and moved off.

The problem tortured him throughout the morning. Madame Jacob told him three times to stop daydreaming, and the third time her admonition was accompanied by such a vigorous pinch on the arm that he cried out in pain, to the great enjoyment of the entire class. But at least the pain produced a salutary effect: his ideas quickly took shape in his mind and he finally was able to come to a decision. At noon, on his way home for lunch, he went by way of rue La Fontaine and stopped in at the hardware store owned by Fernand Fafard. Monsieur Fafard was deep in an impassioned conversation with a small man in a grey hat who was holding a huge catalogue in his hand, waving it about in front of him in a menacing way. For some time now tempers in Quebec had been flaring up, ever since rumours began spreading that the Bourassa government was going to call an election in order to block the rise of the Independence movement.

"Bourassa!" Fernand Fafard was saying in disgust. "Come on, Roland! He's like an empty hand puppet! We'll never get anywhere with him in power!"

"Farther than we'll get with your Separatists! Lévesque and his bloody theories, he's nothing but a Separatist and you know it!"

"You sound like Trudeau, Roland! Shame on you! All we want is to have control over our own affairs! You'd like that, wouldn't you, to be able to control your own affairs? What would you say if I stuck my nose in your business, like the English in Ottawa have been doing to us since the very beginning?"

The argument escalated. The sales rep's face became as red as the feather that adorned his hat band; Fernand's face was an even darker crimson.

Suddenly both men became aware of Blonblon, whose feverish eyes had been on them for several long minutes.

"What can I do for you, my lad?" Fernand asked, trying with little success to separate himself from the vehemence that he felt.

"It's about Charles Thibodeau, Monsieur Fafard."

The child's voice expressed such anguish that Fernand turned to his opponent. "You'll have to excuse me, Roland: I've got to talk to this young lad. You'll bring my order on Tuesday?"

He signalled to Blonblon to follow him into his office and, with his stomach churning from the passion of his speechifying, took his chair behind his desk and unscrewed the cap from a thermos bottle, from which arose the mouth-watering aroma of beef-and-carrot stew.

"Okay, so what's happened?" he asked, spreading a napkin on his lap.

With his fork suspended in mid-air, Fernand listened to Blonblon with such a serious expression that Blonblon wondered if he had angered him.

"Well, to tell you the truth I'm not surprised," Fernand said when the boy had finished. "A paring knife! The man's crazy in the head! You did the right thing by coming to me, my friend. Don't worry, I'll take care of it."

Satisfied, and with the smell of beef stew pricking his appetite, Blonblon hurried home. Meanwhile, after a long telephone conversation with his wife, Fernand called Parfait Michaud and asked the notary to come to meet him in his office as soon as possible.

"This is serious, very serious, much more so than I thought," murmured Michaud, rubbing his chin. "The child is definitely in danger."

"Let me get my hands on his father and he won't be for long," said Fernand, who had taken on a proud, military stance reminiscent of the Lambert Closse statue on the monument to de Maisonneuve in the Place d'Armes.

The two men went to call on Wilfrid Thibodeau. By chance, the carpenter was standing at his living-room window looking discreetly up and down the street before risking going out, and he saw the hardware-store owner and a stranger climbing his staircase. They were surely coming to talk about his son. Something serious must have happened. He felt obliged to let them in.

The meeting was brief. Fernand introduced the notary, who impressed Wilfrid greatly. Then Fernand said he knew the whole story of what had happened the other night, every horrific detail, and that he had taken the liberty of speaking about it with Parfait Michaud, whose opinion agreed perfectly with his own: Thibodeau was skating within a hair's breadth of going to jail. His only hope to avoid it was to accept the proposition they were about to make and which he should look upon as an undeserved godsend.

Lucie had been urging Charles to come to stay with them for several weeks, and now Fernand was offering to raise the boy as his own until Charles reached the age of majority. And unless the child expressly asked, Thibodeau was not to try to see him. The carpenter was to sign a consent form to that effect, and furthermore would undertake, in writing, to give the Fafards a monthly sum of money for the boy's upkeep, the exact amount to be adjusted according to the carpenter's income. And finally, Charles was to get immediate possession of all his clothes and personal effects.

Wilfrid was in such a state of discomposure that he agreed to each term without a murmur, and even helped his neighbour gather Charles's things together. His hands shook as he filled bags and cardboard boxes: two decampings in such short order seemed to have completely unnerved him.

Michaud, embarrassed by the proceedings, looked on in silence. He arranged with Thibodeau to come to his office the next day to sign the appropriate papers.

"Good luck, my dear sir," he said, giving the man a stiff, formal bow.

Wilfrid merely stared at him with his mouth open.

"My dear Fafard," Michaud said when the two men were back on the sidewalk, loaded down with bags and boxes, "you are a man of extraordinary generosity! I don't know anyone like you. You should be made a saint."

Fernand laughed, flattered. "What else could I do?" he said. "I had no choice! If I hadn't done what I did, what would become of Charles? One day we'd pick up a copy of the *Journal de Montréal* and there he would be, on the front page. That's what would happen, my friend . . . Anyway, it wasn't me so much as my wife. She'd've boxed my ears for the rest of my life! She loves that boy as if she'd carried him in her belly herself."

Wilfrid did not show up at the notary's office the next day. A few days later, Monsieur Victoire told Rosalie over his morning coffee that the carpenter had skipped out during the night without paying his rent. A few weeks later, Fernand heard from one of his suppliers that Thibodeau was working in a logging camp up on James Bay.

It would be a long time before Charles saw his father again.

■ ■ ■

For years, despite Premier Bourassa's attempts to calm things down, Quebec had been in a state of agitation and turbulence. Bourassa was accused of being weak, but weakness was simply one of the masks he put on to hide his determination, which was unshakeable. In his view, the security of la Belle Province required that it remain part of Canada, under the control of the federal government in Ottawa. According to his adversaries, such a policy would keep the province standing in the wings of the stage of world history, and condemn it to perpetual decline.

Within days of Charles moving in with the Fafards, the government, worried by the inroads the sovereignty-association movement was making in the minds of the people, called an election. There followed one of the hardest-fought campaigns in the history of Quebec. Despite the protests of his wife and plain good business sense, Fernand had two gigantic Parti Québécois posters plastered across the front of his house, one with a photograph of René Lévesque, the other with one of Guy Bisaillon, who was running for the PQ in the riding of Sainte-Marie, where the Fafards lived. Lévesque criss-crossed the province talking tirelessly of the "normal country" his compatriots must seize for themselves or else risk losing their patrimony. Fernand wore out a pair of shoes going from door to door with Bisaillon, leaving the running of the store to Clément Labbé, his right-hand man, who was delighted to be given the opportunity to ask for a raise in salary at the end of the year. Despite her initial misgivings, Lucie spent several evenings a week in the candidate's office, checking voters' lists and taking phone calls; she also organized a series of kitchen meetings, inviting neighbours who she thought might be willing to discuss changing their allegiances. One of the meetings featured none other than Pierre Bourgault, the man with the white eyelashes and the acid tongue, who could lift a crowd as easily as others could lift a teaspoon.

Far from feeling left out, Charles was caught up in all the excitement, especially since it took his mind off the unpleasantness he had recently gone through. It also freed him from the pitying attentions the others had been lavishing on him.

On November 15, 1976, the Parti Québécois formed the new government, and a gust of fresh wind blew through Quebec. That night Fernand and Lucie took their children to the Paul Sauvé Arena, where a huge rally was taking place. Even though Charles went to bed very late that night, he still found it hard to sleep; his brain tingled with the sound of ovations, just as his stomach ached from too much potato chips and pop.

17

When subjected to a surfeit of sudden happiness, the mind can sometimes rebel, as though incapable of digesting too much change at one sitting. A daily portion of suffering eventually conditions those who are forced to undergo it; slowly, inevitably, pain becomes the medium through which the sufferer perceives life. Such is the strange and somewhat sad way that Nature, in its determination to endure, has found to withstand the vicissitudes of existence. Experts call it the adaptation instinct.

For several days, Charles felt like a prisoner who had been yanked from a dark, dank basement and thrust unceremoniously into the sunlight. His eyes blinked, his head spun, he couldn't breathe the unaccustomed air, and he didn't quite know where he was.

What a change he had undergone. He would suddenly find himself being hugged for no reason, he who had known so little gentleness since the death of his mother. The Fafards maintained a calm, safe, normal household, built on a foundation of good humour whether they were squabbling or simply discussing something animatedly. There was the assurance of three meals a day. The family displayed a friendly and affectionate interest in whatever he was doing (sometimes excessive and even a bit annoying). He had become a star. His mildest jokes were met with bursts of laughter. Every night Lucie or Fernand would help him with his homework; even Henri, ordinarily so wild and scatterbrained, gave him a disconcerting amount of attention. As for Céline, she was always beside him, smiling angelically. Even Boff got into the act: in an historically significant decision, Lucie disregarded her allergies and allowed the dog to spend nights in the house with Charles, and every evening the poor thing exhausted itself trying to show his master how overjoyed it was at this arrangement, to such an extent that getting undressed and into his pyjamas had become an arduous operation for Charles.

As in his previous home, Charles had his own room. Until his arrival it had been the guest room, but as though by a magic wand it had been transformed into his. Lucie had helped with the redecorating, using all the things Charles had brought with him. A framed photograph of Alice, smiling, sitting at a picnic table with a glass of lemonade, sat on a desk that Fernand had salvaged from the garage and on which Charles was supposed to do his homework (in fact he did it with Henri on the dining-room table); on one wall was a poster for *Once Upon a Time in the West*; a small bookshelf near the window had had its collection of *Reader's Digest*s removed to make room for Charles's toys, including a magnificent firetruck with a moving extension ladder, a siren, and a searchlight, which his father and Sylvie had given him for his seventh birthday and which had miraculously survived two years of hard use; on the top shelf, in plain view, were the two volumes of *Alice in Wonderland*, the only things Boff was not allowed to sniff at nor even to approach. Simon the Bear was enthroned in one corner on a small chair to which had been added a blue cushion decorated with stars.

If Charles were asked what he'd been feeling since coming to live with the Fafards, all he would have been able to say was that he had never felt anything like it before. It almost made him feel bad to feel so good. Such a wealth of happiness sometimes made him anxious and uncomfortable; his first night in his new room he had cried bitterly without really knowing why, and the presence of Boff – a somewhat astonished Boff, for obvious reasons – had been extremely precious.

He might have been expected to be calmer in school, more attentive, but in fact he was the opposite. His joy was so intense, so new, he had no way of knowing how to contain it, and it seemed to make him as fidgety as his former unhappiness had. He laughed at everything and anything, played the clown more than ever, concentrated on nothing for more than three minutes at a time, and shot into raging fits of inexplicable anger that took everyone by surprise. One day he entertained himself by dumping a garbage pail into one of the bathroom toilets! The toilet flooded, a plumber had to be called in, and Charles, thanks to an informer, received two weeks of detentions. In desperation, Madame Jacob scolded and pinched him mercilessly, and ended up writing him off as a deeply disturbed idiot. It would take him a long time to disabuse her of that notion.

Wilfrid's disappearance didn't seem to have affected him at all, but in fact he went to great lengths to hide his shame. He never mentioned his father and did not like anyone speaking about him. When he absolutely needed to talk about such a painful topic, his only two confidants were Boff and Simon. And he was even reserved with them.

Sometimes he watched Fernand play his fatherly role, to which he brought a great deal of energy, authority, and imagination. Why couldn't Charles have had such a father? What had he done to deserve one who behaved so odiously towards him? His own father's image haunted his mind like a wound. Thinking of him was a sort of bottomless pit, an obscure weight that tore at his insides so cruelly that sometimes he had to leave the company of his friends and sit by himself in a corner, looking dispirited and dejected, scowling at everyone. Or else, bent over his desk at some task, he would suddenly look up with a terrified expression, his twisted mouth gaping open and closed so grotesquely that the other children would snicker and Madame Jacob, for want of anything better to do, would fetch him a smart smack on the back of the head.

He developed an almost servile attachment to Fernand. When the hardware-store owner came home in the evenings, Charles would stop what he was doing and stand in a corner, looking devotedly on as Céline threw herself into his arms and Henri, with his hands in his pockets, told him about some important event in his day. Then Fernand would signal Charles to come over.

"And what about you, my lad," he would say to Charles, ruffling his hair. "Everything going well?"

Charles would lower his head in bliss, not knowing how to reply.

On Saturday mornings, instead of sleeping in he would get up at eight and go with Henri to work in the store. "For free," as he was always careful to say; Fernand was touched by the gesture, but didn't always know how to take advantage of it. He would find little ways to keep the boy busy, teach him a bit of the business, give him small tasks such as tidying up the small storage shed in the yard beside the shop. Charles sometimes got under Clément Labbé's feet, but as Fernand dryly remarked to him one day, it was the patience one showed to children that ultimately determined whether a man had a good heart.

Fernand tried to use the influence he had over Charles to convince him to improve his conduct at school, especially after his wife, disturbed by the episode of the flooding toilet, began talking about taking the child to see a psychologist.

"If you start showing me better grades," he said to Charles in Clément Labbé's presence, "I'll let you work behind the counter."

At which the assistant pulled one of his more eloquent faces.

Lucie joined her efforts with those of her husband. One evening, when Charles despite his acute embarrassment allowed her to wash his hair while he was taking his bath, she spoke to him in her tenderest voice. "Charlie, you'll never guess who I ran into the other day in the grocery store. Your former teacher, Mademoiselle Laramée! My goodness, is she fond of you! She told me what a fine pupil you were, the best in her class, she said, the very best, so eager to learn and so kind to the other pupils . . ."

"With her it was easy," Charles said simply, his eyes squeezed shut to keep out the soapsuds.

"Oh? And with Madame Jacob it isn't?"

"Madame Minoune . . ." Charles said, and began to laugh, then complained that the rinse water was too hot.

"What's so hard about getting along with Madame Jacob?" Lucie asked when she had turned the hot-water tap down.

Charles fell silent. He kept his head down, letting the water run down his neck and over his shoulders, and Lucie thought he simply didn't want to respond to her question. But then suddenly his voice shot up and he spoke rapidly, in clipped sentences, as though a pressure-valve had been released.

"She doesn't care about me at all! All she ever does is laugh at me, or punish me, or pinch my arm! When I ask her a question she either doesn't hear me or she gives me a stupid answer, like I've interrupted her or something. She thinks I'm an idiot and she can't wait for the year to be over so she can be rid of me. Madame Minoune . . ."

Then he laughed again and held his arms out in front of him, fingers spread wide, as though admiring imaginary rings and bracelets.

"Would you . . . would you like me to speak to her?"

"No! Everyone'll think I'm a cry-baby."

After a moment he opened his eyes and asked for a towel to dry his face.

"But Charlie," Lucie went on in her gentlest voice, "don't you think it may not be entirely her fault if she's impatient with you? Maybe if you were a little . . . calmer in her class and at recess, she would eventually change her mind about you, and realize like Mademoiselle Laramée, and like me and Fernand, what an intelligent, good-natured young man you are?"

Her honeyed tones didn't work with Charles, who lifted his head and looked her fiercely in the eye.

"She doesn't like me and I don't like her, and there's nothing anyone can do about it."

■ ■ ■

It was Parfait Michaud who, without knowing it, would be responsible for mending the fences between Charles and his teacher. One Saturday morning when he was in his library looking for a book, his eye suddenly fell on a bookcase holding one hundred and fifty-seven volumes of *Acts of the Historical and Research Institute of Ile-de-la-France*, a collection whose usefulness may have been questionable but whose weight was undeniable. It was no doubt the latter, combined with the inherent weakness of wood, that had over the years pushed the bookcase into a hazardous angle that seemed about to prove the axiom that a little knowledge is a dangerous thing. The most sensible solution to the problem would have been to pitch the collection, which he had never once consulted, but Michaud had inherited them from one of his former professors, a scholar whom he had venerated, and to get rid of them would have been tantamount to sacrilege. Not to mention that the *Acts* also performed the very useful function of concealing behind their dusty dullness a rather stunning collection of nude photographs and etchings, which he had yet to draw to the attention of his wife, who could be somewhat churlish about such things. He therefore decided instead to anchor the bookcase firmly to the wall, and called Fafard's Hardware to find out if they sold the appropriate screws and braces. Charles walked through the door of the hardware store just as Clément Labbé was taking the call, and the manager, seeing an opportunity to rid himself of the child's presence for twenty minutes, sent Charles to deliver the articles to the Michaud residence.

It was Amélie who answered the door; she was wearing a long, mauve, satin dress and mauve pumps, and half a dozen rings sparkled from her fingers; these reminded Charles of the heavily bejewelled hands of Madame Jacob, and a slight frown of disapproval registered on his face.

"Ah, look who's here! Our famous Charles!" the woman cried. "Come in, quickly, I can't stand fresh air. To what do we owe this pleasure?"

She looked at him with kindly curiosity. Her wrinkled doll's face and her heart-shaped mouth quivered with mischievous delight.

Charles held up a paper bag. "Monsieur Michaud ordered some things from the hardware store."

"Oh, well! You'd better take them to him. He's in the library, third door on your left. Don't get lost, now!"

And off she drifted, laughing merrily. Charles knocked on the door and waited to be invited in, then looked about the room with a slow, stupefied expression. He had never seen so many books in all his life! Every wall was covered with them, floor to ceiling. Two large tables at either end of the room each supported a mountain of books that rose to what seemed a dangerous height. Between them, seated in a soft leather chair, the notary smiled at him, surrounded by piles of journals that enclosed him in a kind of semi-circular wall.

"You look surprised, my boy."

Charles nodded, still inspecting the room. "Are all these yours?" he asked.

"Most assuredly they are."

"Did you buy them?"

"Some of them were my father's, but yes, most of them I bought myself."

"You must be rich!" Charles exclaimed.

His face expressed such innocent admiration that Michaud burst out laughing.

"Not really!" he said. "Not rich. I pick them up here and there. It's amazing how quickly they add up to a fairly good collection. I love books . . . as you can see!"

"There's more here than at my school," Charles said.

"Which mainly goes to show how poorly equipped your school is. In any case, what have you brought me?"

He stood up and emptied the bag on one of the tables, nodding his head with satisfaction. Then he pointed to the emptied bookcase that had held the

Acts. "Lucky for me I have a good eye, eh? That thing was about to crash down on my head! It would have flattened me thinner than one of these slim volumes . . . and the world would have lost a great poet!"

He laughed. Charles laughed too, out of politeness, not because he understood the joke. Michaud went over to the bookcase and examined it, first on his knees, then standing up, then leaning over to one side. His tall, thin, lanky body reminded Charles of a giraffe prancing about on its long legs.

"Well, Charles," he said, turning towards the boy, "could you spare a few minutes to give me a hand?"

It was the first time in his life anyone had spoken to him in such a manner. The request pleased him greatly, filled him with a delicious feeling of importance that was increased tenfold by the admiration he felt for the man who had asked for his help.

"I could use your help in getting these brackets in place," Michaud continued. "It'll save me a lot of time."

Charles replied that he was in no hurry and he would be happy to make himself useful. The notary left the room and returned with a drill, a wooden stepladder, a tape measure, and a screwdriver. The work began; Charles held the brackets against the wall while Michaud drilled and fixed them in place. As they worked, Michaud questioned Charles lightly about how things were going, how he liked living at the Fafards', what the neighbourhood was like, how he was feeling, how he was doing at school. He even asked about his dog, whose operatic talents he had so admired. Feeling emboldened by the closeness, Charles chatted easily and, without really being aware of it, gradually opened some of the hidden recesses of his heart. He talked of his difficulties with Madame Jacob, the warmth with which he'd been received by the Fafard family, and even hinted at the deep sadness that overcame him from time to time for no apparent reason, especially at night, and kept him lying awake in his bed. He didn't mention his father. Michaud listened, secretly moved, pleased by the boy's candour but not quite knowing how to respond to it. When the bookcase was firmly in place, he took out his wallet and handed Charles a dollar bill. Charles adamantly refused to take it.

"No thank you, Monsieur Michaud. I didn't mind helping you. I didn't have anything else to do. No, I don't need the money, really."

What he would have liked to have said was that after the notary's generous help at an extremely difficult time of his life only the most heartless brute would have taken a single penny, but he didn't quite know how to put it into words.

"Come, come, Charles. How else can I show you my gratitude? I'm not in the habit of making people work for me for nothing, you know!"

Unnoticed by Michaud and Charles, Amélie had come into the room and was watching the scene. Only she noticed the look that escaped from the corner of Charles's eye and landed on the rows of books, along with the slight trembling of his lips from which no sound emerged.

"I think he's interested in your library," she said loudly.

Both the others nearly jumped out of their skins.

"Dear God, Amélie, what are you playing at, ghosts and goblins? You're going to end up giving me a heart attack! Well, Charles?" he went on, smiling as though he had already forgotten the incident. "You're interested in books, then?"

"I've read *Alice's Adventures in Wonderland* . . . and *Through the Looking Glass*, too," Charles said proudly.

"Have you? Splendid! In that case, my friend," he said, leading Charles deeper into the room, "I think I may have a few things that would interest you. For some inexplicable reason I still have the novels I read when I was about your age . . . I, too, loved to read when I was a young man like yourself."

He bent before a shelf and ran his fingers along the spines of a row of books, taking one out and replacing it, then stopping at the next, abandoning it as well with a small frown.

"Let me see, let me see," he murmured, a serious expression on his face, as though he were about to commit an act of incalculable significance.

Amélie had come up behind them and was watching her husband, while with a teasing smile on her lips she ruffled Charles's hair. Completely intimidated, Charles stood as stiff as a fence-post.

"Let him have *Treasure Island*," she said quietly. "I just re-read it myself last week and it's still every bit as good as it was when I read it the first time."

"Excellent choice!" cried the notary with boyish enthusiasm. "Here you are, Charles," he added, handing over a large volume with a slightly frayed cardboard cover. "Pictures and everything! I must have read it ten times! Robert Louis Stevenson was a great storyteller! Let me know what you think of it."

Charles looked at the cover illustration: a young boy not much older than himself, standing on the deck of a sailing ship with his arms held in a very theatrical pose, staring in terror at a pirate with a wooden leg who was advancing upon him, pistol in hand and a fierce, man-eating grin on his face.

"Once you start it," said Amélie, looking straight at Charles, "you won't be able to put it down. You'll see."

Charles thanked Michaud, promising to take great care of the book, and returned to the hardware store, where he imagined his long absence was beginning to be noticed.

┌─────────┐
│   18   │
└─────────┘

H e worked for the rest of the morning in the stockroom, sorting screws and nails, then dusting the shelves. At noon he went home for lunch with *Treasure Island* wrapped in a plastic bag. When he got up from the table, he decided to have a quick look into the book, and was not seen at the hardware store for the rest of that day. At two in the afternoon, Henri poked his head into Charles's room to see if he wanted to play baseball with Blonblon and a few other friends in the schoolyard. Charles was lying on his bed, reading. He looked up, said he didn't feel like going out, then went back to his book. He read until supper, ate quickly with an abstracted air, barely responding to questions, and returned to his room. A few minutes later, out of a sense of duty, he returned to the kitchen to help Lucie tidy up while Céline and Henri engaged in a lively discussion about whose turn it was to do the sweeping. When his chores were done he hurried back to rejoin young Jim Hawkins and Long John Silver, whom he had left glaring at each in the midst of a ferocious quarrel. The next morning at ten after ten, after a somewhat abbreviated night's sleep, he closed the book with a sigh of regret.

■ ■ ■

Over the next few weeks, thanks to Parfait Michaud, who was delighted at having kindled a literary flame in the heart of his young protégé, Charles devoured *Kidnapped* and *The Black Arrow*, both by Stevenson, then plunged into novels of lesser merit but which nonetheless fed his growing hunger. He spent the winter in the company of the characters from *Nobody's Boy*, *The Princess's Jewels*, *Escape from Sirius*, *The Caravan of Death*, and *The Pontinès Castle*, then, entering the world of Jules Verne, found himself journeying to the centre of the Earth, travelling twenty thousand leagues under the sea with the enigmatic Captain Nemo, charging on horseback across the Russian Steppes with the courageous Michael Strogoff, and marvelling at the inventiveness shown by the inhabitants of the Mysterious Island as they soared in a hot-air balloon through the eye of a terrible storm.

The seed that had been planted somewhat haphazardly by Mademoiselle Laramée was now, after a long period of germination, blossoming into a magnificent, multicoloured flower. As he explained one day to Blonblon, he was "enjoying himself in his head"; whole worlds, entire centuries, stretched out before him to a limitless horizon, and he felt he had been given a miraculous gift: he could cross oceans, clamber over frozen ice fields, traverse jungles and deserts, struggle through fierce blizzards, explore wild, strange, barbarous, incredible countries, and at the same time make the acquaintance of an infinitude of characters, all without risking a single scratch. In fact, he could be anyone, anywhere, at any time. It was total freedom.

Reading also played another role in Charles's life: that of refuge. If, for one reason or another the world became too much for him, he had merely to open a book to escape from it. Except for the times he was at school he could make his getaway easily and discreetly, by day as well as at night.

Movies and television worked in a similar fashion, but were never quite able to bewitch him as much. Their magic was all too fleeting, and they did not fire his imagination the same way.

At first, reading cut him off almost completely from his friends. Eventually his body adapted to this sedentary life. His face rounded out, his arms became plump, an absent expression dulled the sparkle in his eyes and softened the contours of his face. He became silent and almost invisible, constantly stretched out on his bed or curled up in a chair with his nose in a novel. Reading rendered him deaf. Calls to meals or to do his homework or to come to the telephone were lost in internal space. He had quickly come to feel at home in his new family, and so he now monopolized the bathroom or the living-room sofa. The outside world became anathema to him: it was either too cold or too windy, and he arrived either too late or too early to join in his friends' games, which in any case seemed insipid to him compared to the adventures he was missing in his books. His friends began to complain. One day, Henri even called his interest in books "girlish," an observation, overheard by Lucie, that earned him an hour in his room to contemplate the deeper implications of language. Only Boff seemed to know how to take part in Charles's new life. Curled up against his master, he revelled in the warmth of his body and dozed for hours, emitting occasional deep sighs of bliss.

■ ■ ■

Without actually articulating it to himself, Fernand was of the opinion that there was a connection between a passion for reading and certain forms of mental illness. It must be said that his temperament and tastes were singularly resistant to the charms of literature. The only novel he had read in his entire life – the product of one of his cousins, a secular priest in Trois-Rivières who had had it published at his own expense – had taken ten months of laborious effort (most of it in the bathroom), and by the time he'd arrived at the end he had completely forgotten the beginning. And so he began to worry about Charles. A child "who didn't move," as he put it, and was neither yelling nor pestering someone, who preferred to stay indoors, silent as a stone, shut up tight as a clam, was, in Fernand's eyes, a child in desperate need of help, of the kind that, delivered as energetically as possible, would put the child into some kind of motion, since without motion the body stiffened, the joints fused together, the patient gained weight, grew up deformed, and, what was worse, risked becoming prey to certain bizarre and disquieting states of mind that would end up with his frittering away his entire life.

Fernand's fear of books, however, dwelled alongside a deep respect for learning. Books represented both Knowledge and Danger, the one not being found in Nature without the other, a fact that complicated everything. The fundamental thought that underlay all his other concerns was this: a certain amount of ignorance (not too much, mind) made for a simple, healthy life, not unlike a good bowl of mashed potatoes with real butter and whole milk. On the other hand, it had not gone unnoticed that even after a dozen or more years of schooling the need for diligent, prolonged study did not seem to diminish, and it was becoming more and more difficult to get a decent-paying job without having first handled an extraordinary number of books on a wide variety of subjects. On still another hand, he had also noticed that it was mostly women who were great devourers of novels (his own wife usually read one or two a month). Was Charles somehow hormonally deficient? When he mentioned this concern to Lucie, she laughed in his face, which did not reassure him in the least.

Fernand thus found himself in a state of great confusion with regard to Charles. His conscience urged him to remain even-handed, since he was in many ways the boy's father, at least for the time being. As a result, after two weeks of observation and reflection, he decided to adopt an ambivalent position based on equal amounts of tolerance and coercion. When Fernand was at home, Charles could read in peace for an hour or two, and then Fernand would suddenly storm into his bedroom or the living room, voice raised, arms flapping, shouting in his brisk, resolute voice:

"Come on, let's go, hop-hop! Outside, Charles my lad, you need some oxygen, I can tell by your face. Come on, now, hurry, hurry. Stop dragging your heels!"

Or:

"Okay, okay, okay, enough reading for now! Lucie needs a quart of milk! Do her a favour and go to the store. The fresh air will do you good! I don't want to see you back in the house for at least an hour, understood?"

Charles would get up, perturbed but obedient, and leave the house to go for a walk around the block, or join his friends who were shouting themselves hoarse in some game in the freezing air.

Sometimes, however, the compulsion came from within himself. After hours spent among the Kurds of the Victorian era, or in the jungles of Vietnam, bullets whizzing past his head, or in the shadowy slums of east-side Chicago, he would suddenly be overcome by a feeling of claustrophobia, as though his brain were stuffed with images that seemed to be trying to squeeze out through his eyes and ears, and a raging hunger for the real world would suddenly come over him. He would toss his book on the floor, run out of the room, and start teasing Céline, or find Henri and Blonblon and spend the rest of the day taking part in their fantastical activities.

■ ■ ■

Late one afternoon, after having read an article about coffee in a back issue of *Reader's Digest*, Charles decided to try an experiment on Boff. In a quiet corner of the basement he mixed four tablespoons of instant coffee with an equal amount of vanilla ice cream that Blonblon had smuggled out of his own house, poured a cup of corn syrup over it and gave it to Boff, who lapped it up in three slurps. Half an hour later the animal exploded into an state of intense misbehaviour. He raced from room to room, yowling and baying, seemed to settle down when called but then jumped up on people without warning, climbed up on the furniture, pulled rugs across the floor with his teeth, slammed into doors and pulled down a curtain in the living room, became tangled up in it and struggled to free himself while the children doubled over with laughter, albeit somewhat worriedly – until Lucie appeared, having returned from a visit to a neighbour's.

Boff had to be tied up in the yard, where he threw himself into an operatic cycle of barking before digging deep holes in the frozen ground. When it was time to go to bed, Charles, distressed at the thought of his dog spending the night out in the cold, begged permission to put him in the basement.

Around two o'clock in the morning, Fernand was roused from a deep sleep by a strange noise. He got up, went into the kitchen, and turned on the light. A sound of crunching was coming from the basement. He opened the door. Boff scurried down the steps in a cloud of splinters; the bottom of the basement door had been chewed to the thinness of cardboard. Another fifteen minutes and the dog would have escaped into the house.

"As far as coffee is concerned, Charles," he said the next morning at breakfast, with a slightly mocking smile, "would you agree that you have pursued your experiments to, let's say, their logical conclusion?"

Charles's reading produced other results. One day while Lucie was busy tidying the basement, Charles, inspired by the adventures of *Kim Barsac at the North Pole*, persuaded his friends to build an enormous snow-fort on the slightly inclined roof of the shed, which would give them control of the entire neighbourhood. Henri and Blonblon carried up huge blocks of snow by means of a ladder, while Charles put them in place and cemented them with water. They had just finished building the fort when a loud crack came from the roof, which slumped significantly in the middle. The boys made an emergency call to Fernand and, to their great disappointment, the hardware-store owner dismantled their fort as quickly as he could to avoid a complete collapse, then had to hire a carpenter to spend a day repairing the roof joists.

On both these occasions, Fernand sensed that his precautions against too much reading should be cut back; at least books, he thought, had the advantage of keeping Charles out of trouble.

■ ▩ ■

It had not escaped Madame Jacob's notice that a profound change had taken place in her pupil's behaviour. The sudden improvement in his marks in dictation was her first clue. Was he cheating? Close observation revealed nothing. Then one morning she became convinced that Charles was borrowing his knowledge from some other source. She'd asked the class to write a ten-line composition on the theme of a trip to the country. Inspired, Charles wrote sixteen fully imagined lines almost without a single grammatical error. Set in the centre of the piece was the following astonishing phrase: *Clouds of dust hovered over the road.* Clouds of dust hovered over the road? There was about as much chance that a small boy from an over-crowded neighbourhood in east Montreal, a boy near the bottom of the class, no less, would understand the meaning, let alone the orthography, of the verb "to hover" as there was that he could recite elegies in classical Greek.

Pointing a finger at the suspect verb, she said to Charles:

"Nice work, this composition. Where did you copy it from?"

"Pardon?" Charles replied, turning red. "I didn't copy it."

"All right, then, what does 'hovered' mean?"

"Hung in the air over the road, I guess."

Madame Jacob eyed him for a moment without comment, a look of deep suspicion on her face. She slowly flexed her ring-encrusted fingers, and an expression of cruel cunning curled the edges of her pinkly painted lips.

"Do you mind if I look in your desk?" she asked.

Charles, more and more embarrassed, shook his head. The room was as silent as if a blanket of snow had fallen over it. The pupils watched bright-eyed, not moving a muscle, and the smile curling the teacher's lips could also be seen on many of the faces throughout the room.

The search of Charles's desk produced nothing.

"Where did you learn that word, Charles?" asked Madame Jacob, beginning to lose patience. "I have never used it in this classroom, and I doubt very much that anyone else has ever used it in your presence."

"I read it in a book . . . I don't remember which one."

"*You* read books?"

"Does he read books!" snorted Blonblon, coming to his friend's aid. "He's read hundreds of books. He hardly does anything else these days."

Madame Jacob told him to keep his comments to himself and turned back to Charles. "What books, Charles?"

He rhymed off a list of books that astonished her.

"You've read all those?"

Charles, sensing victory, nodded his head and tried to maintain a look of modesty so as not to annoy his teacher.

"Right to the end?"

"Yes, right to the end."

"He even reads in his sleep!" Blonblon added quickly, fascinated by the turn the conversation had taken.

"No one's asking you!" she hissed, striking out with reptilian suddenness. Her hand swept empty air, to the great delight of the class.

But from then on her attitude towards Charles changed, albeit gradually. Her opinion of him as a ne'er-do-well, destined to a life of obscure dullness, began to crack and fade, and the somewhat malicious indifference she had always shown towards him evolved into astonishment; a faint hint of inter- est, perhaps even a certain level of affection, was born in her for this larva about to sprout the wings of a beautiful butterfly; fragile, diaphanous wings that would lift him, she began to imagine, above the mediocre circumstances of the life for which his lowly birth had prepared him.

■ ■ ■

His reputation as a reader of Olympian stature spread as far as Chez Robert. He had been going to the restaurant much less frequently since his trans- fer to the Fafard family. Now that he no longer worked as a delivery boy or as a commissioned salesman, his adoptive parents wisely considered it more important that he focus his energies first and foremost on his school work. Nor did he go so often as a customer, given that Lucie made sure that all meals were prepared on time and that Charles had as free access to the refrigerator and cupboards as anyone else in the household. But he had kept in touch with Rosalie and Roberto, who, without knowing the details of the scene with the paring knife, certainly knew that a tremen- dous rift had taken place between father and son, even that Charles's life had been in a certain amount of danger; their affection for the child had increased accordingly.

One afternoon in March, on his way home from school, Charles dropped into the restaurant with Henri for a hot chocolate and a Joe Louis, as had been his former habit. They sat at the counter and amused themselves with elbow jabs to the ribs while the hot-chocolate machine gave out its little businesslike hum as it filled the porcelain cups with a layer of sweet-smelling froth.

"Well, Charlie," said Rosalie, setting the cups and cakes before them, "how goes the battle?"

"Fine, Madame Guindon. Everything's great!"

"How about your reading? You still enjoying it?"

"He hardly enjoys anything else," teased Henri, giving Charles another jab in the ribs, which caused a miniature tempest in his friend's cup.

"Easy, there," Rosalie scolded, handing Charles a paper napkin to wipe up his spill. "It wouldn't hurt you to take up a bit of reading, Henri. Might calm you down a bit. Boys!" she sighed, pinching his nose to take the sting from her reprimand, "they say every one of 'em gets ants in their pants the minute they come into this world! But it doesn't matter, we love 'em just the same! So tell me, what are you reading these days, Charlie?"

"*The War With the Salamanders.*"

"*The War With the . . .* what?" said Rosalie, flabbergasted.

Just then Roberto showed his head at the kitchen door.

"Salamanders," explained Charles gravely. "They're kind of like frogs, only very intelligent. They know how to use dynamite."

"Sweet Mother of God!" exclaimed Rosalie, taken aback.

"It's just a story, Madame Guindon," Charles hastened to add, while Henri burst into laughter at her naïveté.

Roberto came to the counter. "You mean *djou* can read books like that?" he asked incredulously.

"Of course. I even have it in my school bag."

He rummaged through the deep recesses of his bag and produced the Karel Capek novel. It was a soft-covered book, a bit worn, on which was depicted a photograph partly consumed by flames, showing a young man and woman smiling enigmatically.

"Could djou read us a bit of it?" asked Roberto.

Charles hesitated for a second, then opened the book and began reading the first page.

"If you look for the little island of Tana Masa on the map, you'll find it smack on the Equator, just to the west of Sumatra; but if you were standing on the bridge of the *Kandong Bandoeng* and asked Captain J. van Toch about the island off which he'd just dropped anchor, you'd first be rewarded with a string of curses, then with the information that it was the meanest corner of the Sonde archipelago, an even more wretched hole than Taba Bala . . ."

His clear, young voice contrasted comically with the roughness of some of the expressions in the book; he articulated each word without hesitation, stumbling only over *Kandong Bandoeng*, but is wasn't so much the ease and speed with which he read that impressed his audience as the sense he imparted that they were actually witnessing the beginning of a fascinating story that could keep them enthralled for hours on end. Roberto and Rosalie, mute with astonishment at the strange words coming from the mouth of a child they'd known since he was in diapers, who had taken his first steps on the sidewalk outside their restaurant, looked as though they'd suddenly found themselves in the presence of the Holy Ghost.

Two young girls, students from the local high school, had left their Cokes and moved silently close to Charles, and were listening to him with smiles of ecstasy; a furnace-oil deliveryman, his cap a bit askew and his chin stubbled with a three-day growth of grey whiskers that emphasized the fatigue showing on his face, also approached, entranced. Charles looked up, saw that everyone was listening to him, turned beet red, and stuffed the book back into his school bag. There followed a long silence.

"Well," sighed the deliveryman, "now I've seen everything."

While everyone was complimenting the boy, Roberto put his hand in his pocket and handed Charles a two-dollar bill.

"Here," he said, "djou can buy a few books with this. Books, I said, no cigarettes or bubble gum, eh?"

Charles was dumbfounded. He hesitated a moment before accepting the money. Henri watched him enviously. True to the code of polite conduct that had been instilled in him, Charles thanked Roberto profusely, promised to use the money as directed, and even said he would bring the books to the restaurant to show him.

"I wasn't so wrong after all," said Rosalie. "You're going to go far, my dear!" In her entire life she'd read only two Harlequin Romances (that was when she'd been laid up in hospital). As for her partner, even that exploit remained in the realm of the unthinkable.

That day marked the beginning of Charles's second period of glory in the neighbourhood. His first had been for the way he had with dogs; now he enjoyed a reputation as a boy wonder, someone who knew a great deal more than anyone would expect from a child his age. Rosalie and Roberto were certain that their numerous friendly customers were aware of the privilege they were enjoying, just being in the presence of someone who was perhaps going to put their neighbourhood on the map.

One Saturday morning, on his way back from shopping, Charles dropped into the restaurant to show Roberto three books he had purchased with the money; he'd been to a used bookstore on rue Ontario with Lucie.

"Good timing!" said Rosalie. "Someone was just here and left something for you."

She handed him a parcel carefully wrapped in craft paper.

"Who's it from?" Charles asked, surprised.

"Open it and see."

With some difficulty, Charles finally managed to get the wrapping off. The parcel contained a superb children's edition of *1001 Arabian Nights*. Tucked inside the front cover was a card with a few words written on it:

To my little Charles, who keeps on growing and growing.
    Happy reading!
    – Conrad Saint-Amour.

■ ■ ■

Months passed. Charles had at last found peace. His relationship with Madame Jacob had changed radically; she actually displayed a certain warmth towards him. More and more often it was Charles she selected at the end of the day to clean the blackboards (which was considered a signal honour), and one day – a red-letter day – she even asked his opinion about something: her memory, she said, had failed her as to the respective positions of the letters *y* and *i* in the word *olympic*. Even so, Charles felt little friendliness towards her, and continued to treat her with mistrust.

However, his quasi-chummy relationship with the teacher was not lost on his classmates. One morning Fats Dubé planted himself in front of Charles in the middle of the schoolyard and, after twisting his face into a series of astonished grimaces, much to the delight of his henchmen, asked him if he liked licking a schoolteacher's arse, and what did it taste like? Charles, who had over the past two years acquired a certain amount of self-confidence, not to mention strength, turned as red as if he had been slapped in the face and threw himself at his enemy, landing a punch on Dubé's nose that caused him to lose half a cup of blood and stopped the laughter that had sprung up around him in its tracks; his reputation from then on was as someone it was better to insult from a safe distance.

One afternoon, as he was leaving school, he ran into Mademoiselle Laramée in the corridor. She was walking slowly, shoulders a bit hunched, holding a black notebook with frayed corners in her arms. Her body was thinner than seemed possible, and her austere, thoughtful expression made her look like a tired, old woman who was going to have to rally her strength just to become a habituée of doctors' waiting rooms. Upon seeing Charles, however, her face lit up with pleasure, a radiant smile smoothed the wrinkles on her face and instantly had her looking like a young woman again. She turned quickly towards him.

"How are you, Charles? I'm hearing a lot of good things about you. Madame Jacob never stops singing your praises! She says you're the highlight of her career!"

She discreetly brushed his hair with her fingers. Charles smiled modestly, slightly embarrassed by the mocking looks he was getting from the other pupils in the hallway, who slowed down as they passed. The teacher understood his unease.

"Come on, let's have a little chat in private."

She went into an empty classroom, waited until he had joined her, and then shut the door behind him.

"Is everything going well, Charles?" she asked, sitting on one of the desks in order to put herself more at his level.

Her voice, which normally sounded a little harsh, had taken on a sweet, almost syrupy softness that Charles found intimidating.

"Yes, very well, thank you, Mademoiselle."

"Are you happy at the Fafards'? I've been hearing about the problems you had with your father. Don't feel too badly about that, such things often happen," she added when she saw his troubled expression. "Honestly, I could tell you a few things you wouldn't believe."

"Yes, they're very kind towards me. Much kinder than my father was!" And he gave a strange little laugh that caught in his throat.

"Madame Jacob tells me," she said, placing her hand on his shoulder, "that you have become a great reader."

"That's thanks to you, Mademoiselle," Charles declared with sudden exuberance, as though the idea had just occurred to him.

And for the first time in the history of their acquaintance he gave her a broad smile, a golden, lucid smile that gladdened the heart of the fifty-year-old. She laughed and, taking Charles by the shoulders, gave him a peck on the cheek.

"You know I've always been very fond of you, don't you, you little rascal!"

Just then the door opened noisily and the janitor came in, a clumsy, loose-jowled, unshaven man pushing a huge vacuum cleaner in front of him. For a second he stopped and contemplated the scene with a stupefied expression, not knowing whether to enter the room or back out.

"It's all right, Monsieur Duquette, you can come in," the teacher said in a slightly pinched voice. "We're through here."

19

Charles had started taking an occasional look at the newspapers. Fernand was a great devotee, and they were often scattered around the floor of the living room, to the consternation of Lucie, who threw herself into indignant fits of tidying up which ended just as suddenly when she came upon an article that interested her. The two of them talked politics frequently, sometimes vigorously. Both were in favour of Quebec's independence, but Lucie thought her husband was "slightly fanatical about it," while Fernand considered his wife to be "a tad too fond of the English." Charles would listen to them without understanding much of what they were on about, but some of their ideas sank in and produced a small glimmer in his mind. Fernand never failed to let fly at any politician ill-advised enough to show his or her loathsome mug on the tiny screen of the Fafard television; so it was that Pierre Trudeau, Jean Chrétien, and Gérard D. Lévesque, Bourassa's boring successor as the head of the Quebec Liberal Party (Bourassa himself had resigned after the party's defeat, and hadn't been seen since) were often subjected to harangues that would have turned them forever off public life had they been able to hear them.

Parfait Michaud held René Lévesque in a kind of mystical awe. One day, when Charles was at the notary's house and an announcement came on the radio promoting the law regarding the financing of political parties, Michaud took the boy by the shoulders and looked deep into his eyes with an intense, burning expression.

"Remember this day, Charlie boy," he said. "Lévesque is the saviour of Québec. One day you'll be able to brag that you lived at the same time as him."

After that, whenever Charles saw the politician's photograph in a newspaper or read his name in a headline, he would pick up the article and read it.

■ ■ ■

That year Charles grew six centimetres. His features became firmer, losing something of their childish softness, but he retained his frank, naive, and open expression, his easy laugh and unalloyed joyfulness that so easily gained him friends and had made him such a wizard at selling chocolate.

Lucie had developed a deep affection for him. Sometimes, during one of his rampages through the house, she would grab him in the hallway and hold him close to her, smothering him with kisses.

"Oh you, you, you," she would say. "With a little mustard and ketchup I could just eat you up!"

He would allow himself to be doted on, delighted and slightly intimidated by it, under the thoughtful gaze of Henri, who seemed to be a bit uneasy at this erosion of his status as only son.

He was bonded to Céline, who was now eight, by a secret complicity. Despite her brother's teasing, she continued to snuggle up against Charles when the two boys were watching television. Charles had passed on to her his love of reading, and he was very proud of having done so. He helped her with her homework and never failed to take her side in any argument she might be having with Henri. From time to time she and Charles would go for long walks around the neighbourhood under the guise of "exercising the dog," since Boff was, at the time, looking a trifle overweight.

Once or twice a week Charles would show up at Parfait Michaud's; he enjoyed the notary's somewhat affected but charming mannerisms and his often unpredictable comments. He also respected Michaud's vast knowledge, and he didn't say no to the many little treats he was offered at the house. But what gave Charles the greatest pleasure was that Michaud spoke to him as a grown-up. On those occasions Charles felt such an intense bubbling up of joy in his soul that he could barely refrain from leaping into the air and click-ing his heels; of course he restrained himself, not wanting to be seen acting like a child. Michaud continued to lend him books and even, sometimes, made him a gift of one or two. And recently he had been initiating his young friend into the intricacies of chess.

Charles's feelings for Michaud's wife Amélie were more ambiguous. He found her strange and unpredictable; when she was out of sorts, a condition that seemed to form the basis of her life, she could be frankly unpleasant. But she was also capable of showing surprising thoughtfulness.

One day Charles told her about his weakness for raspberry pie. On his next visit, she brought him into the kitchen with a mysterious air and gave him two huge slices of a raspberry pie she had made the previous night especially for him.

One afternoon, when he'd finished a game of chess with Michaud (Charles was proving himself to be a formidable adversary) and was about to take his leave, she came up to him in the vestibule.

"Do you have a minute?" she asked him casually. "Good. Come with me, there's something I want to show you."

She was wearing her purple turban (she claimed it helped to ward off her migraine headaches), a velour dressing gown of the same colour, pink slippers with white fur around the edges, and her hands were weighted down with a large number of shining, multicoloured rings. The boy found her outfit rather ridiculous.

"Where are you two off to?" asked the notary when he saw them passing his office.

"I'm going to show him my happiness cocoon."

"Oho! Lucky boy, Charles! You're one of the privileged ones. They're as rare as bilingual kangaroos."

They crossed the kitchen to a narrow hall that led to the back of the house.

"Close your eyes," Amélie ordered, stopping before a door painted a deep, soft blue. "Don't open them until I tell you to."

Charles heard the rattle of keys, then Amélie took his hand and drew him forward several steps.

"Are you keeping your eyes closed?"

More and more intrigued, Charles nodded.

Amélie let go of his hand and he heard a few slight sounds which he was unable to identify. Then there was a brief silence.

"Okay. You can open your eyes now."

Charles gave a cry of astonishment.

He was standing in front of a magnificent Christmas tree, decorated and lit with regal magnificence. A pile of beribboned presents wrapped in silver or gold paper lay at its feet, beside an illuminated crêche comprised of delicate figurines of painted porcelain. A music box, perched on a small pedestal table, began playing "Silent Night."

A delicious half-light filled the room, decorated as it was with garlands, huge stars cut from golden cardboard, stuffed bears, and the rubicund faces of various Santa Clauses. Dark-blue star-covered blinds covered the two windows, cutting out the light of day and giving the room a surreal atmosphere. A large rocking chair piled high with thick cushions had been placed before the tree, ready for someone to sit down to contemplate the room full of marvels.

"It's beautiful," murmured Charles, heaving a sigh of ecstasy.

"Not bad, eh? I put a lot of time and money into this room. The crèche figurines come from Vienna – ho-ho! – and they're nearly a hundred years old. They're from Conrad Kreutzer's workshop. Means nothing to you, I see. You can sit in the rocking chair if you like."

Charles climbed into the chair and sat with his legs dangling, looking at the Christmas tree.

"Why have you done all this?" he asked after a moment.

"Can't you guess?"

"Because you like Christmas?"

"Everyone likes Christmas. Guess again."

"Because you want Christmas to last all year?"

"Warmer."

"Because . . . because being here makes you happy."

"That's it. This room is my happiness cocoon, as I said. It's like an antidepressant for me. Whenever I feel sad or upset, or a problem is giving me a headache, or simply when I'm bored, I come in here, sit in front of my tree, and everything just tumbles into place. If you ever feel extra sad, you have my permission to come here. On condition that you don't tell another soul about it."

The music box had switched to "While Shepherds Watched Their Flocks By Night." Charles remembered one Christmas Eve when Alice had gently awakened him and taken him into the living room to see the tree, a tree as wonderful as this one was, he thought. In front of the crèche had been a fantastic cowboy outfit, complete with a ten-gallon hat, a holster, and two six-shooters.

He looked up at Amélie. "I have a secret place to go to that makes me happy, too," he said.

■ ■ ■

About six months after Charles moved in with the Fafards, Wilfrid Thibodeau began sending Fernand small monthly sums. He was still working up at James Bay, and Fernand concluded that the carpenter must have kicked the booze, at least for the time being.

On May 12, 1977, when he came home from school, Charles found, to his great astonishment, a letter addressed to him on his bed. It was from James Bay. His father had sent him a ten-dollar bill wrapped in a piece of paper on which was scribbled:

Some pocket money for you. Good luck,
  Your father,
  Wilfrid

The letter gave him not the slightest amount of pleasure. He deposited the money in the Credit Union as though he wanted the bill to be lost among the bank's thousands of other banknotes.

He rarely thought about his father. He'd pushed the unhappy years he had spent with him far to the back of his memory. He even experienced a pang of annoyance mixed with fear when Fernand told him that Wilfrid had started sending a small sum every month to offset some of his expenses; it was as though the money represented a link between himself and a man he no longer wished to see and to whom he felt no goodwill.

"Am I going to stay with you always?" he'd asked Lucie one night when she was going over his homework with him.

She had laughed. "As long as you like, Charlie! And your dog, too, as long as he keeps his nose out of the living room."

But the next day she called Parfait Michaud to ask him what was involved in becoming a child's legal guardian. He advised her to see a lawyer.

"Don't waste your money on a lawyer!" Fernand exclaimed when she asked his opinion on the matter. "You know Wilf as well as I do: he no more wants anything to do with his son than he wants a tail in the middle of his forehead! I'll wager you a thousand dollars that we never set eyes on him again! And even that would be too soon for me!"

■ ■ ■

One afternoon in June, Charles was walking down rue Ontario, his school-bag on his back, having just got out of school. A small stray dog was following him on its short legs; it had taken a liking to the boy and was constantly jumping up on him. Suddenly a vigorous tapping on a plate-glass window beside him made him look up.

On the other side of the window was Sylvie. She was smiling and waving at him, seated at a restaurant table beside a man Charles didn't recognize. He had black, curly hair and looked younger than Sylvie, and he too was watching Charles and smiling. Charles hadn't seen Sylvie since the night of the paring knife, and as he looked at her he had a vague presentiment that this chance meeting did not augur well. The young woman motioned him into the restaurant. He felt like running as fast as he could, but the imploring look in the eyes of his father's former girlfriend made him push open the restaurant door, leaving his new canine friend on the sidewalk. The dog looked after him for a second, disappointed, then took off down the street.

Sylvie stood up and waited for him beside the table.

"How big you've grown!" she cried after giving him a big hug and two loud kisses on his cheeks. "I hardly recognized you!"

Charles tilted his head from side to side, not knowing quite how to respond to such comments, which kids always find so boring. Unexpected exuberance like this from a woman who had never shown anything but coldness and reserve towards him made him feel shy and uncertain. Her breath smelled strongly of beer, which explained everything. She turned to her companion.

"This is Charles, my ex's son. He gave me a pretty hard time, the little rascal, but he's not a bad kid underneath."

The man half-stood and held out his hand.

"Pleased to meet you, Charles. My name's Gilles. Come and sit with us for a few minutes."

The child hesitated slightly, but Sylvie pushed him gently towards the table.

"Come on, let's have a chat. I'm so happy to see you again! We haven't seen each other for nearly a year!"

Charles sat on a chair with his hands joined together on his lap, looking about as comfortable as a cat in a bathtub. Sylvie took her beer bottle and refilled her glass.

"So," she said, watching the glass fill with foam, "how's your father?"

"I don't know. I don't live with him any more."

And he briefly told her about the great changes that had taken place in his life.

"I'm happy for you, Charles. That man was not meant to bring up a child."

"What man is?" asked her curly-headed friend, with a big smile. He emptied his glass in two gulps and signalled the waitress to bring two more.

Charles didn't like him. His red, glistening skin, his bright, expressionless eyes, his small, thin, meticulously trimmed moustache, his slightly creased cheeks sloping down to a square jaw, all gave an impression of indestructible hardness, as though with a single head-butt he could burst through the thickest of walls as though they were made of paper.

"And I don't think, if you don't mind my saying so," Sylvie went on in a sad voice, "that he liked you very much, my poor little Charles."

"I don't think so, either," Charles replied.

"What a family!" exclaimed Gilles, laughing again, a loud, mocking laughter that seemed to hold both father and son in the same disapproving light.

Charles rubbed his knees together and looked longingly at the door.

"But are you happy living with the Fafards?" Sylvie asked.

"Yes," Charles said. "They love me very much. And I'm doing well at school."

He tossed these last words like a challenge at the man, whom he was disliking more and more.

"Tell me, Charlie, what's your pleasure?" Gilles asked. "It's on me. Anything you like."

Charles looked at him coldly.

"No, thank you. I have to go."

"Well, aren't you the independent one! Come on, come on, I'm paying. Ask for something!"

"Come on, Charles, have something," Sylvie insisted. "Have a Coke. Or a Seven-Up. As a favour to me, Charles. Oh yeah, I remember: hot chocolate! You love hot chocolate, don't you? It just came back to me."

Charles still shook his head and, sliding to the side of his chair, placed one foot on the floor.

"How about a beer, then?" said Gilles, grabbing him by the arm. He looked straight in the boy's eyes and laughed openly. "But no, of course not," he said, answering his own question. "You're just a little raggedy-assed kid that's not man enough to drink beer, aren't you?"

"Raggedy-assed yourself – I'm as much a man as you," Charles spat out, furious.

And he grabbed one of the bottles in front of him and brought it to his lips. Sylvie cried out in protest.

At first the ice-cold liquid with its slightly acid taste, which was entirely new to him, and the explosion of bubbles that prickled in his throat like a mouthful of needles, contracted his chest and forced a burping sigh up into his mouth, to the great amusement of Gilles, who nodded his head approvingly. Charles took two more large swallows and put the bottle back on the table to catch his breath.

"Well, I'll be a son-of-a-gun! You're a real man, after all!" exclaimed Gilles, holding back Sylvie, who was trying to reach out and take the bottle from Charles.

"Gilles!" she said under her breath, looking anxiously about the restaurant to see if anyone was watching. "Cut it out! He's just a kid!"

"A kid? No he ain't! He's a man like me! Ain't you, Charles? Ain't you a man like me?"

Charles nodded. Flattered though he was by the compliment, he also wanted to show up the slobbering idiot who was not even trying to hide his disdain.

"What'd I tell ya?" cried Curly-Head, turning to his girlfriend. "The boy says he's a man. Down the hatch, my man, you gotta still be thirsty. Two, three more guzzles. Don't listen to Syl – *ouch!*"

Sylvie had punched him soundly in the ribs. Silently, with a feline grace, he grabbed her arm with both hands, keeping it out of harm's way, and at the same time steered her towards the back of the restaurant so that what he had to say to her would be confidential.

Meanwhile, Charles picked up the bottle again, and, his eyes bulging out of his head, tried to swallow as much beer as he could.

228

"Atta boy, kid!" Curly-Head said encouragingly, coming back to the table. "You're a real connoisseur! An honest-to-God connoisseur! You'd think he was born with a beer in his hand, this guy! No kiddin', Charlie my boy, you're the champ!"

Sylvie suddenly broke her arm free of his grasp and, nearly leaping over her chair, wrestled the bottle from Charles's hand.

"Get out! Get out of here! This is no place for you!" she told him quietly, pushing him towards the door. "I should never have waved at you, you poor kid."

Charles, proud of his defiance but burdened nonetheless by the unpleasant feeling that he'd been an object of ridicule, left the restaurant with Gilles's guffaws ringing in his ears. Curly-Head, enchanted by his own wit, waved goodbye to Charles through the window while Sylvie, once again seated beside him, looked the other way.

20

Charles took several steps along the sidewalk; he was filled with an immense joy, the cause of which he could not determine. He felt light on his feet, not a care in the world, wanting more than anything to talk to someone without having anything in particular to say. His feet, however, were having trouble moving in unison, and the weight of his school bag was pulling him over backwards, nearly making him lose his balance. He tried to shuck it up higher on his shoulders, but the manoeuvre seemed complicated and confusing. He turned to a young girl in a blue dress who was walking in his direction.

"Hey!" he called to her happily. "Could you give me a hand? I can't seem to get my school bag . . . I just need you to lift it . . ."

The girl stopped, a little disconcerted, then came up to him and adjusted the leather straps on his shoulders; but the bag nearly fell to the ground, and he grabbed it at the last minute with his left hand. As she walked away she turned two or three times to check on his progress, and he, oddly enough, did the same, waving his free hand.

"Thank you!" he called joyfully. "You are very kind!"

He was now having more and more trouble walking in a straight line. The street and its buildings had begun to wobble gently, as though they were trying to bend over and hug him; he suddenly felt an enormous tenderness towards them. His eye fell on a brick wall that looked particularly warm and inviting. Cutting sharply across the sidewalk he nearly bumped into an old man coming in the opposite direction, who looked disapprovingly at him and grumbled something. Charles broke into laughter and made faces at the man, but they were friendly, one might almost say affectionate, faces, because he also felt an enormous sympathy for the old man, despite his impatient gestures, and if he hadn't been so far away Charles would have loved to have had a little chat with him.

Leaning against the brick wall he let its delicious warmth spread through his body. He half-closed his eyes (he couldn't close them entirely or everything would start spinning). That Gilles and his beer had taught him a lesson! But why? "To make fun of you, you little jerk," someone inside him said, and he saw Sylvie's indignant face with its sad, worried eyes. "Because you're a man, a real man," said another voice, and Sylvie's face morphed into that of her companion. Charles admired his moustache – so neatly trimmed – his strong, cheerful voice, and the curly hair hanging down over his forehead. "Yeah," chimed in the first voice, mocking now, "a real man, just like your father." He knit his brows; he didn't like that comparison at all. Even though he was now in the same state he'd so often seen his father in . . . Had he become like him? Was he going to fall into the same habits and mannerisms as his father?

Time passed and he began to feel a sudden tiredness come over him. His vision blurred, his legs turned to rubber, and all he wanted to do was stretch out along the brick wall. But he knew that wasn't a good idea. He had to keep walking, he had to get home, or at least to the home of those people who, fortunately, had taken him out of his own home. He shook his head to rid it of such complicated and embarrassing thoughts, then noticed that a man was standing in front of him. He blinked and squinted his eyes a few times and finally recognized Monsieur Saint-Amour, who was looking at him and smiling. To his great surprise he felt not in the least bit afraid of the man; on the contrary, he felt the same friendship and tenderness towards him that he felt for everything in the world at that moment.

"Hello, Charles. How are you?"

"I'm very well, thank you, Monsieur Saint-Amour."

He could hardly move his lips. They seemed to have turned into lead. But rather than feel embarrassed by this, he was greatly amused.

"I've had a bit to drink," he added. "I've been drinking beer."

Saint-Amour looked at him for a moment, thoughtfully, then with an affectionate solicitude, said:

"Yes, I can see that. I can see that you're not your usual self. It feels good to get outside yourself once in a while, doesn't it? But you look tired, my boy. Wouldn't you like to come inside and lie down for a while?"

Charles turned his head and saw that, to his surprise, he'd been leaning against the front of the building in which Monsieur Saint-Amour lived. A definite need to lie down came over him. The old man's voice sounded so gentle, so warm, that he was tempted to accept the invitation. But a small remnant of mistrust, half-dissolved in the alcoholic haze, still stirred inside him.

"Thank you, Monsieur Saint-Amour, but I have to be getting home."

The old man gave a frank but cordial laugh. "Surely not, Charles?" he said. "You can hardly walk. Everyone will make fun of you!"

It was this last argument that swayed him. Saint-Amour looked warily about him, then led Charles into the building, even taking him by the hand to help him down the few metres of corridor that brought them to the door of his apartment. He took out his key chain and looked around again to make sure they were quite alone. Charles noticed the tremble in the old man's hands when he opened the door, but he attached no significance to it, thinking only of how pleasant it would soon be to lie down for a few moments on a sofa or in a bed and go to sleep.

"Did you like my book, Charles?" asked Saint-Amour after gently closing the door behind him.

"Yes, I liked it very much," said Charles, feeling more and more tired. He leaned back against the edge of a chair that was piled high with old magazines. "I read nearly all the stories. Thank you very much for giving it to me."

Then he was shaken by a sudden fit of laughter.

"Jeepers but your kitchen is stuffed with junk, Monsieur Saint-Amour! There's enough stuff in here to sink a ship! You should clean it up sometime!"

"Yes, yes, you're absolutely right, I should do that," replied the old man, wandering about the room with a furtive air, looking here and there. "Ah, here it is."

He returned with a large, yellow plastic cup and leaned towards Charles with a paternal smile.

"Here, drink this, my boy. It'll make you feel better. You look so tired, I'm almost afraid you'll be ill."

His wrinkled, large-knuckled hands were trembling more than ever, and the amber liquid danced in the cup. Charles looked into the old man's eyes and felt another surge of mistrust pass through him, but the warmth and friendliness he saw there reassured him once again.

The liquid was slightly syrupy and acidic at the same time, and Charles could not hide a grimace as he drank it, but obeying the advice of his friend he drank it to the last drop; almost immediately he was seized by an immense feeling of well-being. He chatted easily with Saint-Amour, who responded with great bursts of laughter and an invitation to step into his tiny bedroom.

From that point on, Charles's memory became very confused. He later remembered sitting on the edge of a bed, still feeling happy but almost overwhelmed by a crushing need to sleep. He remembered the soft, caressing voice of his host.

"Perhaps slip off your trousers, Charles. You'll be much more comfortable."

After that it was as though his memory simply refused to function. Tiny bits of images floated in his mind, but in such a strange swirl that it was impossible to see them clearly. For a fraction of a second he saw Monsieur Saint-Amour hovering above him, mouth half open, and his own legs sticking up in the air while someone did something to him, he couldn't say quite what but it amused and disturbed him at the same time, and then he remembered a cry. Was it his own voice? Someone else's? Then he was back in the corridor with a strange taste in his mouth, and he was vomiting. He vomited twice in the corridor and again on the sidewalk in front of a young man in a bicycle helmet who laughed at him. Then he was running (his legs suddenly working properly), crossing a street at an angle, down an alley, and ending up to his amazement in the little park on rue Coupal. He crawled under a bench, exactly the same park and the same bench where he'd hidden after the terrible scene with the paring knife. He curled up into himself, his eyes closed, breathing hard from running. A horrible headache nearly split his head open. But the worst of his suffering came from shame, a vague, imprecise but profound sense of unbearable humiliation that poured over him like warm, stinking grease. After a time he started to cry, but the tears, far from comforting him, increased his rage and despair, the rage and despair of someone who always feels at the mercy of those who are stronger and more evil than himself.

■ ■ ■

He returned home at seven, looking deathly pale and haggard, thin-lipped, dragging his feet. Lucie was standing by the door, looking up and down the street like a nervous bird. When she saw him she let out a cry.

"Gracious God in heaven! What in the world has happened to you, my poor child?" She threw open the door, banging it against the vestibule wall. "Nevermind the phone, Fernand. He's here!"

Then she ran and took him in her arms. His clothes, the smell that he gave off, and most of all the devastated expression on his face told her that something serious had happened. After having dozed for a while under the bench and vomiting a few more times, and then being chased from the park by a gang of kids who had gone there to play, Charles had set off for home, preparing as best he could for the interrogation he knew he would receive once he got there; he had decided to tell only half of the truth.

"I ran into Sylvie while coming home from school," he admitted, crying. Lucie and Fernand seemed bigger and more frightening than ever. "She was with a man in a restaurant on rue Ontario. They asked me to join them at their table and the man made me drink beer and it made me sick . . . I'm so ashamed! I'm so ashamed! You don't know how ashamed I am!"

Five minutes later Fernand, crimson-faced, his biceps bulging in volcanic rage, stormed into the Valencia restaurant intent on breaking a chair over the head of the vile human wreck who had amused himself in such a disgusting way with his little Charles. Fortunately Sylvie and Curly-Head had already left the premises and no one in the restaurant knew them.

He returned home feeling a little sheepish, his anger subsided, humbled by his own impotence. He took the telephone book and looked up this Sylvie Langlois who kept such dubious company, but not one of the dozen S. Langloises he questioned was the one he wanted, and three of them told him so in no uncertain terms.

Meanwhile, with Henri and Céline looking on in amazement, Lucie took Charles into the bathroom, as he was in great need of a wash. He refused to let her undress him, insisted that she leave the room, and he locked the door when she had done so. Twenty minutes later, when he reappeared, he looked a hundred times better; he did not want dinner, however, and went straight to bed.

The next morning he was miserable, running a fever and aching all over. He asked if he could stay home from school. Lucie kept an eye on him all day. He watched a bit of television, then lay down on his bed beside Boff, barely responding to her questions, ate practically nothing, seemed to have his mind elsewhere and be preoccupied with dark thoughts. "Something else happened to him," Lucie thought, "I'm certain of it. But how can I find out what it was?"

"Try getting him to talk, just about anything," she said to her husband on the phone. "He trusts you. Something happened yesterday that was much more serious than he told us, I'd bet everything I have on it!"

"Not everything, I hope," replied Fernand. "Save some for me. I didn't marry you just for your fine thoughts, you know. Okay," he went on more seriously, "I'll do what I can, but you know me: I don't like anyone pussy-footing around trying to get something out of me, and I'm not very good at pussy-footing around someone else, either."

When Céline came home after school she invited Charles to share her snack with her, and he accepted. They ate alone in the kitchen. From time to time she placed her hand on his, smiling at him as she chattered away, and after a while Charles's face cleared perceptibly. He suggested they go for a walk with Boff, who'd been sitting by the table eyeing their cookies like a castaway on a desert island. Their walk lasted almost until suppertime. Céline's care-free happiness, her naive and sometimes ludicrous comments, were a comfort to Charles, and one of her remarks even made him burst out laughing. Curiously, however, he was almost cross with her when she suggested walking down rue Ontario. The very idea nearly made him throw up.

Two days later Lucie and Fernand felt they more or less had their old Charles back. But despite all his subterfuges – some of which, it must be said, were a little ham-fisted – Fernand never succeeded in finding out exactly what had happened between the time Charles left school on that afternoon in June and his arrival at the house. He resigned himself to not knowing; Charles's life was his own, after all, and no one had the right to go through another person's dirty laundry.

He had no idea how apt his metaphor was.

A few weeks after these events, Charles was leaving Chez Robert with Blonblon when he found himself face to face with Monsieur Saint-Amour. It was then he realized that their roles had been reversed. Now it was Saint-Amour who was afraid of Charles. The old man turned white, babbled a few words, and ran blindly down the street, even though it was obvious he had been going into the restaurant.

"Wow!" whistled Blonblon, "you'd almost think he was running away from you! What did you do to him?"

235

Charles shrugged and said nothing. He watched the fleeing old man, sick at heart about the secret that he shared with the pederast.

That week he encountered Saint-Amour twice more, and each time the old man seemed stricken with terror and scuttled off down the street. One afternoon, however, when Charles was on an errand for Lucie, he was walking up and down the aisles of a supermarket looking for a can of stewed tomatoes when he ran into Saint-Amour for the third time.

They were alone. Charles turned on his heels, but Saint-Amour grabbed his arm and held him.

"Don't be afraid," he said breathlessly, "I don't mean you any harm. I just want a word with you."

In the man's shrivelled, yellowish face Charles saw only his huge, protruding eyes rolling back and forth like terrified billiard balls. He fumbled feverishly in his pocket and took out his wallet, then handed the child a twenty-dollar bill:

"Here, take it, there's more where that came from, if you know how to keep a secret."

Charles threw the money in the old man's face and ran out of the store, to the great surprise of a cashier and a clerk who exchanged long, suspicious looks.

He ran down the sidewalk, frightened and furious, so filled with self-loathing that tears welled up in his eyes. He ran and ran, crossing a dozen streets before he remembered that Lucie was waiting for the stewed tomatoes. He stopped and looked down the row of shops until he saw the front of a small convenience store displaying, along with tins of fruit salad with their faded labels, a pile of overripe bananas on sale.

Calm returned to him as he walked home. Shuffling slowly along, the groceries in his arms, slightly tired from running, he went over his latest encounter with the former hairdresser in his mind. A cruel smile appeared on his lips. He knew how he was going to get his revenge.

21

A t the beginning of August, Lucie fell ill with a mysterious intestinal dis-
order and had to be taken to the hospital. Fernand was upset by her
absence because he couldn't take time away from his business. He looked
around for a sitter for the children, then decided that the best thing for everyone would be to pack them off to a summer camp. Despite the lateness of the
season, he found one on Lake Mailhotte, in the Lanaudière region, about forty
kilometres from Joliette. It was an all-boys' camp; Céline went off to visit one
of her aunts who lived in an ancient, dark, Victorian house on Boulevard
Gouin, in Montreal's Sault-au-Récollet district.

One Tuesday morning around six o'clock, Charles and Henri climbed
sleepily into the Fafards' car. Fernand yawned expansively behind the wheel,
his mouth stretched wide, and loud, bovine noises issuing from his throat as
a devastated Boff watched their inexplicable departure with his feet up on
the living-room windowsill.

In order to coax the boys out of bed, Fernand had promised them breakfast at a restaurant, anything on the menu they wanted. And to underscore
the adventurous nature of this early-morning trip, instead of taking them to
Rosalie and Roberto's, he chose The Night-Owl, a restaurant on St. Laurent
near the Metropolitan Autoroute. It was one of those greasy spoons open
twenty-four hours for those who were too busy to go somewhere else, or who
couldn't sleep, or who preferred eating alone, or who liked genuine home-
style fast-food cooking.

They entered the place during a rare moment of calm. There were only
two other customers, both sitting at the counter: an old man with a pointed
chin contemplating his fingers before a cup of coffee, and a young woman
with purple lipstick and a baby on her lap, flipping through a copy of

237

Montréal-Matin and eating a piece of toast. A fly circled the room, landing here and there without staying long in any one place, in the melancholy way that flies have.

Charles and Henri slid into a booth feeling they were momentarily entering the realm of adulthood, and watched while the waiter finished washing the dishes. He was a short man with thinning black hair and a long, funereal face, who gave the impression of having been somewhere else on the day of his own birth. He smoked small, thin, slightly crooked cigarettes, and sighed constantly with sharp movements of his shoulders.

Fernand succeeded in cheering him up a bit with a few pleasantries delivered in his strong, clear voice that thundered in the small restaurant like cannonfire on a holiday. He ordered a cup of coffee and an omelette.

"And what will the young gentlemen have?" the waiter asked morosely, his face half-hidden behind smoke from his cigarette.

Despite the tone, the expression pleased the two boys. After once again checking with Fernand that they could order anything they wanted, Charles opted for pancakes with maple syrup, an apple turnover, and a glass of chocolate milk. Henri chose poutine, a hot dog, and a Coke.

"Go on, you'll never eat all that!" said the woman at the counter, her mauve lips expressing amused condescension.

Charles and Henri proved her wrong. The baby stared at them wide-eyed without moving, as though astonished by such a display of piggishness.

Back in the car, the boys didn't talk much between themselves. Their well-rounded bellies combined with the abbreviated night's sleep so effectively that within five minutes their snores were buzzing about Fernand's head as he pulled the car into the passing lane.

■ ■ ■

They were awakened by a series of sudden jolts. The car was bouncing along a country road. A crow was cawing above a field of beets, staring down at the ground a bit myopically, as though it were too old to see properly; a stand of trees spared by the plough shook in the wind, teeming with mysterious life; a sign announcing *Eggs and Honey For Sale* peeked modestly from behind a bush, no sooner seen than vanished; in the distance, exhaust from a tractor inscribed a smokey question mark into the still air; an abandoned farmhouse was quietly turning grey, falling in on itself, dying.

"Where are we?" murmured Henri, his mouth hanging open.

"Almost there," replied Fernand. "Sleep well, you two? You'll be full of beans this afternoon!"

Charles and Henri looked thoughtfully out the window, as though it had suddenly dawned on them the degree to which their lives were about to change.

They passed between a spruce-log house, all gables and skylights, and an immense, freshly painted barn with a bright red Purina sign on one wall, then drove along trampled fields strewn with stones and covered with scraggly, twisted brush. The pavement ended abruptly, the road took a long curve, and they came to a hill that looked as though it were infamous in the region. Because of the steepness of its slope, a series of concrete ribs had been laid across it. Fernand whistled when he saw it, then backed the car up to get a run at it, while the two boys gawked in excitement.

"Holy Cow!" Fernand exclaimed. "I wouldn't want to have to go up that thing in the winter!"

He put the car in first gear and the Oldsmobile attacked the hill with its motor cursing as though it were being asked to tackle something it knew was well beyond its powers. The gears chewed ferociously, suddenly struck by an uncontrollable urge to grind themselves down to filings, and sinister popping noises emerged from the undercarriage. Charles and Henri fell silent and looked fearfully out the back window at the countryside slipping so slowly away beneath them, as though the car had become an airplane, albeit an old, tired, asthmatic one that could barely get off the ground.

"Aha!" cried Fernand when they had reached the top of the hill. "We made it, by the jumpin' Jehosephat! Phew! I was sure the old heap was going to blow a gasket!"

After a few minutes they came to a rustic arch made of pine poles fastened roughly together. A sign at the top of the arch told them they had arrived at Camp Jeunenjoie.

The camp was run by the Christian Brothers. Each summer the camp took in boys of seven to twelve years of age, in groups of fifty or sixty, for two weeks at a time. Religious communities in general had been falling rapidly out of favour for several years in Quebec, but some had nonetheless managed to maintain the illusion of vitality and importance. Three brothers, with the assistance of monitors recruited from the colleges, worked "for the good of youth," the idea being to turn them into good Catholics through sports, fresh air, wholesome food, short homilies followed by outdoor "return to self" sessions, and daily morning mass. A chaplain saw to the spiritual and moral well-being of the little colony. Camp Jeunenjoie was comprised of a dozen hastily erected buildings, a chapel, bunkhouses, a dining hall, a communal centre, and so on, situated on the shore of Lake Mailhotte at a spot where a former farm had been more or less reclaimed by the surrounding forest.

The car travelled along a narrow road bordered by sparse woods, then stopped at the centre of a kind of public square amid a scattering of buildings. The two boys got out and looked about them, sniffing the breeze, which smelled of pine needles and fields baking in the sun. Below them they could see the surface of a lake glinting through a filter of trees. The distant water, mingled with the echo of laughter and shouting, created a surprising impression of lightness and transparency. The building directly facing them seemed of a more elaborate construction than the others, and was the only one that had a front porch. From it emerged a fat man wearing a blue shirt and khaki pants, and carrying on his shoulder a curious, small animal with black rings around its eyes.

"Well, well, I'll be darned!" Fernand exclaimed. "A raccoon. Where did you find it?"

"Its mother stepped in a bear trap a couple of days ago and we had to put her down, poor creature," said the fat man, coming towards them and looking sideways at the animal. "Her babies were still around her, and we managed to catch this one. It's fairly tame already! You are Monsieur Fafard? I'm Brother Marcel, the camp director."

Brother Marcel held out his hand – it looked chubby and warm and was covered with grey hairs, like an extension of his face, which was also chubby, almost babyish, the face of a fifty-year-old to whom life had been extremely kind, a lover of pastries and café-au-lait. The raccoon shied away from them, trying to hide behind the monk's ample neck.

Fernand introduced the two boys and the monk spoke to them in a friendly enough manner. Charles and Henri were barely listening, fascinated by the animal as though it had cast a Medusa-like spell on them. Their chins were raised and they hardly breathed.

240

"He's beautiful!" murmured Charles ecstatically, and slowly, cautiously, he raised his hand towards it.

The animal, curled on the monk's shoulder, began emitting a series of curious whistling noises through its nostrils. Its eyes became fierce and its lips curled to reveal a row of small, needle-sharp teeth.

"Whoa, whoa, not so fast, my friend!" said the monk, laughing. "He's not used to you yet! Give him a day or two and you'll be able to take him wherever you like, as long as you're patient and gentle with him. Raccoons are nervous animals at the best of times, and this one is still traumatized by the loss of its mother."

"Poor creature," said Charles with heartfelt compassion.

"What's its name?" Fernand asked after a quick glance at his watch.

"We call him Frederic. After Chopin."

"After who?"

"Chopin. The composer. You know, the Polonaise and so on."

"Oh yes, the Polonaise. I see," said Fernand, completely at a loss. He walked back to the car and took out two suitcases and a canvas bag. He hugged the boys, told them he would be back to pick them up in two weeks and that they were to behave themselves and be careful.

The monk, his face half-hidden by the raccoon's tail as the animal twisted round to face a suspicious noise, laughed confidently. "Oh, I don't think we'll be having any problems with these two," he said. "They seem like good little boys to me."

■ ■ ■

Once Fernand had left, Brother Marcel put Frederic in his office, which for the time being was doing double-duty as a kennel, and then showed the boys to the "senior bunkhouse" to assign them their beds.

Charles could hardly lift his suitcase. The monk picked it up.

"What the devil do you have in here, my friend? A piece of Saint-Joseph's Oratory?"

"I brought some books."

"He's always reading," declared Henri a bit sarcastically.

"But that's good! Reading is very good!" said the fat man, with the air of someone who is praising an activity he does not himself indulge in.

241

The bunkhouse was a large room with exposed beams, walls, and floor of rough-sawn lumber, and two lines of single beds covered with grey blankets. It seemed even larger to the two boys because of its crudeness, which turned it into a kind of adventurer's hideout. They were disappointed to learn that their beds would not be next to each other.

"It's better this way," declared the monk, cryptically; he had had long experience of bunkhouse mayhem.

After showing them where to stow their personal gear, the monk expressed the opinion that a short swim was better than no swim at all, and sent them off to the washroom to change into their bathing suits. A few minutes later they were walking along a gravelled path through the woods that brought them to Lake Mailhotte. Dozens of children were running about and playing in a small bay bordered by a narrow beach, on which other campers were lying in the warm sun. A monitor, standing in water up to his waist, was giving swimming lessons to a young boy; another was standing on the beach, scolding a tall, thin boy who was listening with his head down, holding a tree branch.

Charles's eye swept the breadth of the glinting lake, edged in the distance by a dark bank of forest, then peered into the fresh shadows of the forest itself. The trees rustled deliciously in the slight breeze. His gaze finally came to rest on the overexcited bathers around him, and raising his head to Brother Marcel, he gave him a knowing smile, the smile of a small, street-wise kid who had just been set down in paradise. Lucie's sudden illness, which had darkened his summer, had in fact ushered him through the door to a new world, one that until then he had only been vaguely aware of; his soul was suddenly and wonderfully stirred.

"Go, go, what are you waiting for?" Brother Marcel urged with a laugh. "You'll have to hurry if you want time to get a good soaking."

The two boys, shy and smiling, ran down the beach's slight slope. A monitor saw them and moved in their direction. The next instant they had hit the water and joined in the fun with their fellow campers with the natural ease of children.

■ ■ ■

Charles threw himself enthusiastically into the camp's daily routines. He had lunch in the dining hall, where he gobbled up wieners, mashed potatoes, coleslaw, and caramel pudding. Lunch was followed by a "nature discovery" walk that ended in a return-to-self session led by Brother Martin, who in his sharp, nasal voice exhorted the young campers to take advantage of the benefits of prayer. After that there was baseball – Henri scored two runs and became instantly popular – then firewood detail, in which everyone went off into the woods to collect dead branches for the evening bonfire. Then another trip to the lake for swimming, and then dinner, at which time the camp chaplain, Father Beaucage, appeared fresh from the long drive from Joliette.

Father Beaucage was a tall fair-haired man in his thirties. He looked like an athlete, and had confident, quick gestures, a piercing gaze, and a smile always on his lips. But there was also something vaguely false about him, as though his good humour were a duty imposed on him by his position. Brother Albert introduced him to the two newcomers when they arrived at the table.

"Welcome, my friends," said the priest, vigorously shaking Charles by the hand. "You're from Montreal? Which parish?"

"Um . . . I don't remember the name of it," babbled Charles, caught off-guard.

"Saint-Eusèbe," put in Henri confidently.

"Aha . . . Montreal East . . . not an easy place to live . . . Oh well, the next time I ask you," he said, looking at Charles, "you'll know what to say, right?"

And he laughed while Charles, red in the face, turned and took his place at the table.

But his embarrassment was soon forgotten during a fracas caused by the appearance of Frederic, attracted by the smell of food. His domestication seemed to be progressing minute by minute. Despite being called back by Brother Marcel, the animal walked under one of the dining room's long tables and was soon devouring a banquet of bread and crackers. One of the twelve-year-olds finally picked it up; it squirmed in his hands without much conviction, a bread stick jutting from its mouth.

"Bring it here," ordered Father Beaucage. "You should get rid of it," he said, handing the animal over to Brother Marcel with a smile. "Raccoons often have rabies."

This was met by thunderous protest. Standing at the door to the kitchen, enormous Brother Albert, the camp cook, showed his disapproval by slowing shaking his head, which made the deep, greasy folds in his neck tremble with indignation. The priest raised his hands in a gesture of submission and took his seat.

Charles wolfed down his cream-of-turnip soup while discussing with his neighbour to his left, a thin, pimply-faced boy with a curiously pointed nose, the possibility of Frederic having rabies. Every now and then his glance fell on Father Beaucage, who was sitting at the end of the table discreetly following a conversation between two campers seated near him, while with his long, manicured fingers he reached out for the butter that was half-hidden behind a basket of bread. For some unknown reason, Charles did not like the man, and he resolved to have as little to do with him as possible.

The priest, to divert attention from his earlier suggestion regarding the raccoon, began telling humorous anecdotes about camp life. The campers laughed politely. Then one of the monitors, Marc-André, who was spending his third summer at Camp Jeunenjoie, stole the show with a story about something that had happened the preceding year and had caused a great flap.

Early in July, the local butcher had mistakenly delivered eighty pounds of wieners to Brother Albert, who had ordered only twenty pounds, and the butcher had steadfastly refused to take back the surplus. Since there wasn't enough room in the freezer for so many wieners, the cook, after giving the matter much thought and many deep sighs, had resigned himself to using them up as quickly as he could; that week the campers were subjected to a veritable festival of wieners: hot dogs and buns, grilled wieners, boiled wieners, wieners and beans, wieners and onions, wiener casseroles, wieners floating in soup, wieners prepared in every form and combination known to man. Every time another wiener slid onto another plate there was a chorus of groans and complaints, until finally the campers became so sick of wieners they launched a formal protest. There was even talk of going on a hunger strike.

"Our very fingers were turning into wieners!" attested Marc-André, holding up his hands.

One of the campers piped up with a risqué reference to wieners that drew a spurt of laughter from the audience (although Father Beaucage contented himself with a wry frown), then someone reminded them that just that day they had been served wieners at lunchtime. There followed a great banging of knives and spoons, and Brother Albert was called from the kitchen. The monk emerged, raised his arms in the air, and swore that after a few more days wieners would never again appear on the camp menu.

"Swear! Swear by Saint Wiener!" shouted Marc-André.

"I SWEAR!" replied Brother Albert, to thunderous applause.

╔═══════╗
║ 22   ║
╚═══════╝

After supper, each camper was given free time to spend on his own, and the first day Charles and Henri returned to their bunkhouse to unpack their personal effects into the small trunks that were provided at the foot of their beds. Beside his pile of clothes, Charles carefully placed the eight novels he had brought with him, although after his first day in camp he was pretty sure he wouldn't have time to read even a quarter of them. The previous night, before going to sleep, he had had to give up in the middle of a pulse-racing episode in *The Mystery of the Yellow Room*, by Gaston Leroux. Now, sitting on the side of his bunk, he returned to find Rouletabille still, nearly twenty-four hours later, trapped in the same desperate situation.

"Are you coming?" asked Henri, on his way to the door.

"I'll be there in a minute."

Henri shrugged and left the bunkhouse.

It was dark when Charles finally had to quit reading. Looking up, he saw a light switch near the door but did not dare turn the light on for fear of the mockery and sarcasm that would come from the other campers. He got up and, walking cautiously in the dark, made his way towards a large patch of light across from the community building, where campers were piling up firewood for the campfire; he heard their voices coming from that direction.

As he passed the dining hall a dark shadow loomed suddenly in front of him.

"Well, well, it's my little altar boy!" said Father Beaucage in his deep voice. "Where are you coming from? Why aren't you with the others?"

"I was in the bunkhouse."

"The bunkhouse?" the priest repeated, placing his emphasis on the last syllable.

"I was putting my things away."

"So, you're a loner . . . Come, we should get a move on. Brother Martin must be about ready to start the campfire."

And placing his hand on the boy's shoulder he led him quickly towards the fire area, asking him various questions along the way in his brusque but jovial manner. Charles replied only in monosyllables, still feeling vaguely sullen and shy.

■ ■ ■

A small crowd had assembled around the impressive pile of branches, logs, and cordwood, waiting impatiently for Brother Marcel to signal to Brother Martin – nicknamed Little Foot because he was not much bigger than a dwarf – to put a match to the crumpled newspaper that he had cleverly placed beforehand beneath the pile.

With the sun no longer out, the forest had suddenly become a black, impenetrable, and menacing mass. Its humid cave-breath made the campers suddenly aware of the thinness of their cotton sweaters. With thoughts of summer's end in their minds, each of them looked forward to the comforting warmth of the fire.

There was a short whistle. Little Foot, half-crouched with a lighter in one hand, began running around in his lopsided way trying to light the newspaper; a low crackling sound was heard, then the pile gave a great shudder as little curlicues of smoke from the still unseen flames licked along the bottom branches and then flew up, trying to reach the summit of the pile; a kind of whoosh came from the centre of the mass and then there was fire everywhere, big, pulsing, orange-coloured flames throwing their flickering light on the campers' faces, making them look oddly Oriental. A mounting heat spread from the pyre; tiny explosions mixed with the crackling, and the nearest campers had to back up a bit. Everyone stopped talking and fell into a thoughtful contemplation of the fire; the ancient fascination was upon them. Charles had never seen anything so magnificent, except perhaps once, on Saint-John-the-Baptist Day, in a park a long way from his house.

He turned to a camper – the boy with the big lips who'd sat across from him at dinner – and they exchanged a smile. Suddenly Henri appeared at his side. Happy to see him, Charles gave him a friendly poke in the ribs.

"Pretty nice, eh?" his friend said quietly.

"Yeah, it's great! I think we're going to have fun here. Of course," Charles added quickly, "we'd have a much better time if your mother weren't sick."

"Oh, she'll be all right," Henri replied confidently. "My father knows all the best doctors."

Charles gave a deep sigh, whether of sadness or contentment he didn't know. The coals were glowing red and orange and he couldn't take his eyes off them. A feeling of gentle laziness slowly spread through his body, as though his veins were lined with velvet and his body were floating imperceptibly above the ground. He felt calm again, at peace with himself, as happy as the day his father had allowed him to bring Boff into the house. "I hope Lucie gets better," he said to himself, suddenly disquieted by Henri's nonchalance. He remembered Alice lying in her bed in the hospital, saying her final goodbye.

He looked to his left and saw Father Beaucage sitting ten feet away, watching him. The priest nodded; his flashing, domineering smile reminded Charles of a sword. He tried to respond politely, but his lips refused to move except to make a sort of twisted smile, and he returned his gaze to the fire.

They began to sing: "Crocuses in the Meadows," "The Abbot Lights the Fire," and even an Iroquois lullaby, "*A ni cou ni.*" Sitting outdoors at night at the edge of a forest beside a huge fire was a wonderful antidote to Charles's misgivings; it filled him with that delicious giddiness that always accompanies new experiences. He knew none of the songs, but they were all repeated two or three times and after a while he was singing parts of them with all his heart. Henri, too, came under their thrall, and soon was rocking gently back and forth, carried away by happiness. Suddenly the small, pimply-faced boy with the sharp nose, who'd been sitting next to Charles at dinner, slid down next to him.

"You want to hear something funny, Thibodeau?" he said excitedly. He told Charles that an hour ago two boys had been caught jerking off behind the outhouses.

"The priest is going to talk to them in a few minutes. Man, I wouldn't want to be in their shoes!"

After the fire there were snacks in the dining hall, followed by a short period of prayer and reflection in the chapel.

During snack, the absence of Lalumière and Doré was duly noted. They were two of the "big kids," much admired for their wispy beginnings of a

248

moustache and their encyclopedic knowledge of the songs of Robert Charlebois. Wicked rumours began to circulate as to what had happened to them.

On their way to chapel, some of the campers had seen two rigid silhouettes on the blind covering of one of the windows of a small building adjoining the chapel, which was the priest's quarters. There were a few muffled laughs, but also a few sighs of commiseration.

When prayer was over, Father Beaucage rose and, standing before the railing with a gravity no one had seen on his face before, launched into a detailed description of their day, emphasizing that the dominant theme throughout had been purity, "that one virtue God has placed above all others, and the key by which we may open the door to Heaven"; he warned his young listeners against falling into evil practices, succumbing to "the Devil's smile, which works with all its evil force to draw us into sin and eternal damnation."

These stern and terrible words were curiously at odds with the priest's age and bearing. Among certain campers, however, they went straight to the depths of their souls; these boys sat, faces rigid with dread, thinking of the numerous sins they had already committed and of the even more numerous sins they would certainly, alas, be committing in the future. But it was perhaps a sign of the times that most of the boys listening to the priest received his admonitions with marked indifference, their minds elsewhere, stifling yawns, secretly nibbling on cookies snatched from the dining hall, and looking forward to the warmth of their beds. Charles's mother had instilled in him a somewhat frightened respect for the old man in the white beard whom everyone referred to as God, and a naive and sentimental affection for the Baby Jesus and his sainted mother, the Blessed Virgin; he listened to the priest with rapt and vaguely troubled attention, protected though he was by his youth from the pangs of remorse and the tightened chest of fear.

During this time Frederic, who'd been shut up in Brother Marcel's office and evidently felt he was missing out on his rightful nighttime romp in the forest, had succeeded in pushing a chair to a window and, having climbed up on it, was peering over the sill at the immense cloud of smoke rising from the campfire as Brother Martin was putting it out with a hose. From time to time, whenever the raccoon turned its head towards the nearby forest, shivers ran through its body and its claws moved across the windowpane with long, almost imperceptible squeaks.

■ ■ ■

The next day Lalumière and Doré did not show up for breakfast. They had left camp at dawn so quietly than none of their bunkhouse mates had awakened. Brother Marcel's sad, pensive expression suggested he was less than satisfied with the solution that had been brought to the problem. Some of the older campers felt that under Father Beaucage's jovial, dynamic exterior there lurked the soul of a serpent, and they resolved not to trust him.

Three days passed. The weather remained pleasant, windy but warm and sunny, as though summer had found new reserves in its battle against the onset of autumn. Charles adored camp life. His ease with others and his gift for being the life of any gathering quickly allowed him to make new friends, although it somewhat weakened his bond with Henri. And the way he used certain unusual words picked up from his voluminous reading (though he used them in moderation) gave him a reputation as an "egg head," for which he was admired by many but also mocked by some others.

After dinner, he liked to go back to his bunkhouse to read for a while before campfire. He was usually there alone, although sometimes he shared the room with one of the campers who had caught a cold, or was letting off steam after a quarrel.

One night, as he lay on his bunk, chin supported by his hand, absorbed in one of Arsène Lupin's adventures, his tongue sticking out between his teeth (a sign of intense concentration), a shadow fell over him and he looked up. It was Father Beaucage. He had slipped into the bunkhouse as silently as the night air and was looking down on Charles with a smile but also a question in his eyes.

"Tired, my little altar boy?"

"No," replied Charles, surprised, "I was just reading."

"May I see?"

Trying to hide his annoyance, the boy handed over his book.

"*Arsène Lupin, Gentleman-Burglar* . . . Hmm, hmm . . . Quite enjoyable little stories, as I recall. I seem to remember reading one when I was fifteen or sixteen . . . Nothing but trifles, of course . . . But you seem a bit young, nonetheless, to be dabbling in them. Are you sure you can understand them?"

"Pretty sure," said Charles, dryly.

"Amazing, amazing . . ."

The priest returned the book and nodded with a curt laugh, then looked about for a way to change the subject. His eye swept the bunkhouse, searching the shadowy corners as though in the hope of finding some more plausible explanation for Charles's interest in reading. Although this particular night he was there by himself, apparently.

"Do you like it here at camp, Charles?" he asked in a friendly tone.

"Very much." Although a voice in his head added: Except when I'm with you.

"This is a very precious time in your life, my lad, a time you can share with others, that allows you to open up and make important discoveries. Are you aware of that?"

"Yes."

The priest stood up and patted the child's head.

"So, why not put it to better use, eh? Reading is all very well, of course, but surely you could choose a better time for it, don't you think? Here it merely cuts you off from your fellow campers, and you know as well as I do, Charles, that solitude is not always the best counsellor."

The remark was made amiably, but there was a warning in it.

With a wave of his hand, Father Beaucage strode briskly out of the bunkhouse. Charles went back to reading. But after a few minutes he realized that he wasn't taking much in. With a sigh he replaced the book in his trunk and went outside to join his comrades.

The previous night, as he'd passed the cabin in which the monitors slept, he'd seen Jean stretched out on a chair by the door, reading a novel. Why was it all right for others to read, but not him? And why was something that earned him congratulations in Montreal, even brought him a certain measure of prestige, seen as reprehensible by this priest, who pretended to be young with his jogging suit and his great, hearty laugh, but who was really nothing but an old lobster with a magnifying glass in his claws?

■ ■ ■

The following morning, Charles was awakened by a heavy, silken sound coming from the roof of the bunkhouse. Rain had transformed the metal roof into a kind of gigantic harp and was playing a symphony of muffled notes that Charles found deliciously peaceful. He stretched languorously under the covers, peered sideways at his sleeping neighbour, then closed his eyes again hoping he had awakened early and it would be a while yet before Jean, the monitor in charge of waking them up each morning, would make his rounds.

Since the forecast was for two days of bad weather, the directors of Camp Jeunenjoie took appropriate steps to keep their high-spirited charges occupied. Charles was assigned to a small group under Brother Martin, whose assignment was to organize the workshop where the monk exercised his manual dexterity in his own haphazard fashion.

Charles had become fond of the little monk, who wasn't much taller than he was and who laughed at everyone's jokes, even those he didn't understand, and who – perhaps because of his size – hung around with the campers as though he were one of them. Little Foot, with his rough-hewn face, his mouth hanging loosely open, his broken nose, and his eyes set deep in the shadow of his heavy eyebrows, possessed all the qualities of a perfect Sad Sack, but he was friendly with everyone and took all the gentle teasing that the campers threw at him with good humour. And ever since Charles had overheard him talking to a monitor about the hasty departure of Lalumière and Doré he had held the little monk in even higher esteem. "Father Beaucage?" Little Foot had said a little too loudly. "I don't like him very much. Too headstrong! A lot of principles, but nothing in his heart. Not good, that." From that moment, Charles always greeted Brother Martin with a big smile and laughed at all his antics, even the least amusing of them.

That morning, Little Foot took Charles and the thin, pimply-faced boy with the pointy nose, whose name turned out to be Patrick Ricard, to the back of the workshop where there was a shelf with an immense jumble of screws and nails on it.

"I want you to sort all these, okay my friends? I'll go get some pots from the kitchen."

The job took two hours and lasted until lunchtime. It was still raining, a slow, grey, steady downpour that tore the still-green leaves from the trees and stuck them in the mud, where they lay soiled and sad-looking. After lunch, there was meditation and a return-to-self in the chapel, conducted by Brother Marcel in the absence of Father Beaucage, who had gone back to Joliette. Perhaps it was the rain, the dampness that had infiltrated all their clothing, making them feel clammy and out of sorts, but Brother Marcel seemed totally uninspired that day, and the reaction from his audience was of two kinds: from some came light snores, and from others muffled laughter in discreet bursts. The monk wisely cut short his homily and handed his young listeners over to the monitors, to whom fell the redoubtable task of keeping the campers busy and in good spirits until bedtime.

He then went to the kitchen where, with Frederic on his lap, he drank a cup of coffee with Brother Albert, thinking apprehensively about the second day of rain that had been forecast. His colleague, who'd been humming to himself as he iced two enormous cakes, looked up at him.

"You look worried," he said.

In response, Brother Marcel gestured towards the window, where they could see water cascading off a red pickup truck that seemed to be foundering in a vast, empty sea, then gave a deep, discouraged sigh.

The cook finished icing the cakes, gave his spatula a loving lick and handed it to the raccoon, who soon had it looking as shiny as a new penny.

"I just had an idea," he said suddenly.

The good monk had long ago given up the fight against calories and bore the evidence of his defeat philosophically – the pot belly, the stretched navel, the lower back pains, the varicose veins in the legs, the shortness of breath, but also the perpetual joviality and the head swimming with ideas, some of them harebrained but others divinely inspired.

"Why not organize a drama festival? We could divide the campers into teams and the winners will get an entire meal of desserts. There could be consolation prizes, too, of course. I could be on the jury."

Brother Marcel stared at his colleague in astonishment, then drank his coffee in two large gulps, threw on his raincoat, and ran out to announce the festival to the world.

23

Half an hour later the campers had been divided into four teams, each under the supervision of a monitor, and each assigned to a location – the senior bunkhouse, the junior bunkhouse, the community hall, and the dining hall, the latter being a source of great pleasure to Brother Albert, who was a great listener at doors.

Charles found himself in the community hall team, and was given the role of scriptwriter, because he was the one "with all the ideas." His supervisor, Jean-Guy, a six-foot-one-inch sixteen-year-old who was still growing, considered sports the only human activity worthy of consideration, and was not shy about letting Brother Marcel know what he thought about a drama festival. He therefore gave carte blanche to his young scriptwriter and took himself off to a corner chair, where he sat with his arms crossed chewing a stick of gum that had long ago lost its flavour; every now and then he looked absently over at the members of his team, who were sitting cross-legged on the floor talking animatedly and breaking out into regular bursts of laughter.

Charles had decided to be the spokesperson for the campers' general annoyance at Father Beaucage's moral strictness. After choosing a storyline and jotting down a few notes on a bit of paper, he began taking his team through their lines. Jean-Guy watched the goings-on for a few minutes, suppressed a series of yawns, reprimanded two or three campers when they appeared to be getting too excited, then announced that he was going out for a short break (to smoke a cigarette under a tree). Charles turned out to be a demanding director and had his team members rehearse their play without a break until dinner time; two of them had been delegated to be in charge of props, and had brought back all kinds of bizarre objects to the community hall, to the curiosity of the other campers.

At seven-thirty, Brother Martin finished constructing a small stage in the dining hall, and by ten to eight a super-excited audience was waiting for the action to begin. The grapevine was humming with news; the sketch mounted by Charles Thibodeau was going to be a tour de force and sure to win first prize. At eight o'clock sharp the jury – Father Beaucage, Brothers Marcel and Albert, and two of the monitors, Jean and Marc-André – entered the room and took their places in the front row.

In order to involve as many people as possible, each team was composed of an impressive array of theatre professionals: soundmen, props managers, dressers, prompters (even though there were no scripts), lighting engineers (whose sole job was to turn the hall lights on and off) as well as, of course, the actors, limited to five per sketch because of the size of the stage and its dubious ability to withstand jumping, chasing, and other forms of energetic theatricality.

The order of presentation was determined by lots. Charles's team would be third.

The first sketch recounted an excursion into the countryside during which a camper suffered the horrifying torment of stepping into a cow pat. This was met by mild laughter and polite applause. The second sketch depicted a bank robbery, with Henri in the role of bank clerk. The ingenious way in which he foiled the robbery and escaped from his kidnappers – with extremely impressive facial expressions as he ducked under their gunfire – was a great success.

The applause died down and silence fell, the peculiar kind of silence that reigns in a room full of expectant people. There were low murmurs, slight coughs, muffled laughs, and shuffling feet. Then the two actors to whom Charles had given the principal parts, both dry of mouth and rubber of leg, appeared before the sheet that served as a backdrop, and the action started.

FIRST CAMPER
Ah! Camp life! So much fun, isn't it!
(*Sounds of birds chirping, thanks to the soundman, who was an accomplished whistler.*)
SECOND CAMPER
Oh, yeah. No end of fun!

FIRST CAMPER

We can do anything we want.

SECOND CAMPER

As long as the Brothers don't see us!

FIRST CAMPER

Or the monitors . . .

SECOND CAMPER

The monitors never see anything.

(*General laughter.*)

FIRST CAMPER

There's only one thing that bothers me.

SECOND CAMPER

What's that?

FIRST CAMPER

I get so hungry at night. I never seem to be able to stuff enough cookies in my pockets after snack.

SECOND CAMPER

I snuck ten out last night.

FIRST CAMPER

You pig! You could have given me a few. I'm still hungry tonight.

SECOND CAMPER

Me too. Why don't we go see what's in the kitchen?

FIRST CAMPER

Good idea. The cook has just gone to bed. We can make ourselves some sandwiches.

(*Scene change. Two stage hands drag a table to the middle of the stage while a third brings out a chair. The cook appears; he has a paper bag on his head for a toque, a ladle in his hand, and a cushion under his T-shirt giving him a huge belly. Much laughter from the audience and from Brother Albert.*)

COOK

Boy, am I ever tired! Eighty-seven cod-liver-oil cakes today. A hundred gallons of radish soup. A hundred and ten roadkill steaks, slightly off! I'm going to have to change the menu . . . The campers will start complaining and I'll have to eat all that stuff myself . . . (*He moves towards the chair.*) I'll just sit down for a minute to rest my poor legs. (*He sits, goes to sleep, and begins to snore like a furnace.*)

FIRST CAMPER

He's asleep! Hurry! Get in! We'll go through the fridge.

SECOND CAMPER

You grab the roadkill steaks. I'll get the jam.

FIRST CAMPER

Hey, you think I'm crazy?

SECOND CAMPER

(*Points to the cook.*) Shh! You'll wake him up.

(*They tiptoe to the invisible fridge and open the door.*)

FIRST CAMPER

Wow! Wieners!

SECOND CAMPER

Nothing I like better than a good wiener.

(*Tittering in the hall.*)

FIRST CAMPER

Come on, we'll eat them outside. (*Points to the cook, who is still snoring.*) He could wake up any minute.

SECOND CAMPER

Good idea. Let's go down to the lake. No one will see us there.

(*Much amusement in the audience. Brother Marcel's eyes widen in puzzlement; Brother Martin smiles; Brother Albert brings his hand to his mouth; Father Beaucage looks stern; the two monitors exchange surprised looks.*)

FIRST CAMPER

Let's go.

(*A stagehand pours water from one bucket into another, imitating the sound of waves; the soundman, hidden by the curtain, howls like a coyote.*)

SECOND CAMPER

Yum, yum. These are good wieners.

FIRST CAMPER

I'll say.

SECOND CAMPER

Hey, your wiener is bigger than mine.

FIRST CAMPER

Yeah, but yours is cuter . . .

(*Guffaws from the audience, although the jury members react in various ways. Stimulated by their success, the actors risk a few suggestive gestures,*)

257

to the increased enjoyment of the audience. Meanwhile, Charles, who had saved the role of Camp Chaplain for himself and was anxious to take his turn under the lights, pulls on an immense black overcoat that trails down to the floor and appears at the far end of the stage, a prayerbook in his hand.)

CHAPLAIN

My, what a lovely evening ... The Good Lord is good indeed to send us such good weather. I think I'll take a good stroll ... (*He walks about the stage taking deep breaths. Suddenly he stops, puzzled.*) What's that strange sound I hear? I've never heard sounds like that before. I'd better go take a look.

(*He turns towards the lake, lifting his feet as though walking through burning embers. Thrusting his head forward, he spies the two campers.*)

(*In a deep, wrathful voice.*) What are you doing with those wieners?

(*Huge laughter.*)

(*Paralyzed with fear, the campers say nothing.*)

FIRST CAMPER

(*Terrified*) We're just ... playing with them.

CHAPLAIN

And who gave them to you?

SECOND CAMPER

(*Whining*) No one ... we stole them.

FIRST CAMPER

We like playing with our wieners. It feels good.

(*Silence falls in the hall. Father Beaucage jumps up as though stuck in the behind by a pin and sweeps out of the room. Charles is too caught up in his role to notice.*)

CHAPLAIN

So help me God, I'll teach you two a lesson. Go from this camp. I never want to see you here again! You can steal wieners in the city. But remember one thing: one day your wieners will fry in Hell, you pigs!

The actors remained at centre stage for a moment, bowing self-consciously, amazed and a bit daunted by the audience's reaction – the spectators had recovered from their shock and were shouting, whistling, hooting, stamping their feet, and banging on their chairs. Radiant and triumphant, the team returned to their seats, enthusiastically slapped on the back as they passed the other campers.

Brother Marcel had hastened to join the chaplain outside. The two men came back in just before the start of the fourth sketch. Father Beaucage had recovered his composure and sat down, a tight smile on his lips and his eyes darting furious looks about the room like poisoned arrows; one of them lodged in Charles's cheek without his knowing it.

In fact, Charles was oblivious to nearly everything. He would have been embarrassed if anyone had asked him what the fourth sketch was about. He watched it without seeing it, still exhilarated by his success, his lips already smacking at the thought of Brother Albert's dinner of desserts that surely awaited him and the other members of his troupe; he could imagine sitting at the table, stuffing himself while acknowledging the congratulations of the entire camp. He knew he was the one responsible for the triumph, but good diplomat that he was, he was prepared to share the limelight with his co-actors, Jean-Louis and William, whose talent was nearly equal to his own.

The final sketch ended in a burst of warfare so intense that the sheets forming the stage's wings fell off their rods. While the actors struggled to extract themselves, the jury members retired to the back of the hall to make their deliberations.

After a few minutes, the audience began to be impatient. Henri came over to sit next to Charles.

"They can't agree on a winner," he whispered into Charles's ear. "But you'll win for sure. That bit with the wieners, man, I nearly bust a gut. Nadeau was sitting behind me, and he almost fell off his chair he was laughing so hard. Save me a piece of cake, okay?"

"Your sketch was pretty good, too," Charles replied, although in truth he'd found it fairly humdrum. He turned to watch the back of the room, where the jury was still talking in low voices.

Charles and his team did not win the prize. It was Henri's team that was crowned. But the festival was to continue the next day, and the Grand Prize would be awarded the day after that, so as to give Brother Albert time to prepare his dinner of desserts.

Charles walked back to the dining hall for evening snack with the other members of his team, feeling like a dog with a broken leg. The others were muttering to each other. Other campers came up to them to offer their condolences, saying that if it had gone to a general vote Charles's sketch would have won hands down.

"We've still got tomorrow, eh, Charles?" said Patrick Ricard, putting on a brave front. "We'll win the next one for sure."

Henri promised his friend he'd save him three portions of dessert if his team won the Grand Prize. Charles couldn't even manage a smile. He was sitting alone in his corner, nibbling on a cookie and looking downcast, when Father Beaucage appeared before him, flushed, fresh and smiling, and handed him a glass of apple juice. Charles turned his head.

"Uh-oh! In a bad mood, are we, my little altar boy? Sore loser?"

The child turned bright red and said nothing.

"Your sketch showed a certain amount of imagination," said the priest, suddenly serious, "but you and I should have a little talk. There are certain things we have to get straightened out. Tomorrow morning after breakfast all right with you?"

"I have nothing to say," Charles murmured.

The priest laughed aloud.

"No matter, I have a lot to say to you, as you can well imagine! See you tomorrow."

Charles left the dining hall and crossed the rain-sodden field to the bunkhouse, where Henri found him fifteen minutes later.

"What are you doing in here?"

"What does it look like I'm doing? I'm reading."

Henri leaned against a wall and watched his friend stare at a book with somewhat suspect intensity. He sighed two or three times, changed position against the wall, and scratched his neck.

"What are you reading?" he finally asked.

"None of your business."

Henri leapt forward and grabbed the book from Charles's hands. "Okay," he said, "but you don't have to be mad at me. It wasn't my fault you didn't win! I promised to give you three desserts, what else do you want me to do?"

Charles sat on his bed with his arms crossed, staring at the tips of his shoes. He heard the rain pattering on the bunkhouse roof. He felt something break inside, and something else rise to take its place, something sad and familiar; he thought the feeling had gone for good, but no, there it was again, tagging along beside him with cruel fidelity. Seeing how unhappy his friend was, Henri felt his own anger subside. He sat down beside Charles and put his hand on his shoulder.

"It's because of the wiener story, Charles. Everyone in camp knows that's what it was. The priest was fit to be tied. He's the one who made sure you didn't win. If you ask me, I don't think he's all that fond of you."

Charles looked up. "You think I don't know that?" he said.

And to hide his tears from Henri, he shrugged Henri's hand away, got up, and, opening the lid of the trunk at the foot of his bed, began rummaging through his clothes.

■ ■ ■

Although not particularly religious, Charles had taken communion almost every morning since his arrival at Camp Jeunenjoie. Partly because it was part of the routine, partly to blend in with the others – and partly out of hunger, because every morning when he woke up he was ravenous, and the small, delicate-tasting flake of white biscuit that melted so agreeably in his mouth was like an hors-d'oeuvre to the hearty breakfast he knew would follow the mass. But this morning he remained in his pew in the chapel, casting disapproving glances at the members of his team who dutifully waddled up to the Holy Table and opened their beaks like little nestlings for the chaplain, who in his black soutane looked for all the world like an old crow. All during mass he stared furiously at the priest, promising himself he would not show up for their little talk.

As soon as breakfast was over he gathered his team together, determined to get his revenge, and hurried them into the community hall to get down to work. Two surprises awaited them: Jean-Guy, their supervisor, had been replaced by Michel-Noël, one of the "old" monitors – he was eighteen – who had been working at Camp Jeunenjoie for three summers. Their new supervisor immediately announced that, "in order to give everyone an equal chance," they would be rotating responsibilities within the team; from scriptwriter/director, Charles was moved to sound man. It quickly became apparent that the new director would be none other than Michel-Noël himself.

This Michel-Noël was not popular among the campers; tall, dry, and blond, with black glasses, he was about as much fun as a funeral notice. He always managed to sit beside Father Beaucage at mealtimes, gazing adoringly up at the priest with his magnified cow's eyes, drinking in his attention, nodding in agreement at everything he said, laughing first and loudest at his idiotic jokes and constantly on the lookout to pass him the salt or the pepper or the butter. The campers called him the Beadle.

When he was told of his demotion, Charles turned pale, but out of pride said nothing. For fifteen minutes the meeting dragged on, dull and boring as dishwater, with the Beadle vainly trying to instill a bit of life into the group. Then Father Beaucage appeared at the door and signalled to Charles to join him.

"Our meeting this morning?" he said to Charles, smiling broadly.

"I forgot," Charles lied, blushing.

"I'm going to borrow him for a few minutes," the priest called to his disciple.

He gave a small laugh, took Charles by the arm, and marched him out of the building.

Their progress to the priest's lodging was interrupted several times. On each occasion the priest stopped, asked a question, said something he thought was funny, gave a pat on a shoulder, always with that air of false and over-familiar cordiality that reeked of condescension, an air that Charles, for reasons he couldn't explain, detested with every fibre of his being.

The priest opened the door and stepped back. "After you, my little altar-boy," he said.

He directed Charles to a divan near the back of the room. The priest's eye fell on the partly opened door of a side cupboard, behind which glinted a row of bottles, and he hastily stepped over and closed it. Charles had also seen them.

"Well, my little altar-boy," the priest said, sitting down in an easy chair across from the child, "are you having a good time here at our camp?"

Charles's face darkened; his lips tightened and he stared down at the floor.

"I don't like you calling me your little altar-boy," he said quietly, after a moment.

"Whyever not?" Father Beaucage laughed. "It's not just a joke! Things like that are part of camp life. But okay, no problem, you don't like it, fine. I'll stop. No more nicknames. I'll even ask you to forgive me. Happy now?"

Charles nodded.

"You see, my lad, how important it is that we have these little talks, you and I? Something I was doing was bothering you. If we weren't having our little talk this morning I never would have known about it, and I wouldn't have been able to rectify it. Now there's something I, too, would like to mention."

Charles's attention was drawn to a small table behind the priest. On it lay a large book bound in black leather. Sticking out from between its pages was a red bookmark, like a blood stain.

"Are you listening to me, Charles?" asked the priest with a tinge of impatience.

Charles nodded again. His heart was beating so wildly he felt as though someone were pounding under his chin with tiny fists. He could barely swallow. Never again would he set foot in this room. Never again would he talk to this man. He lowered his head and stared down at his forearms; he imagined them growing bigger and bigger, and sprouting huge, black feathers. He had turned into one of the crows that sat at the top of the pine trees all day, cawing loudly. Spreading his wings, he flew through the priest's window and high up into the sky, way above the camp whose buildings now looked like tiny matchboxes. He glided, then beat his wings and climbed higher, away from everything, where nothing at all could ever reach him.

"I'm told that it was your idea to mount that little sketch your team put on last night," said the priest. "Is that true?"

"Yes."

The priest's lips tightened. He was no longer smiling. His glowing, pink skin, his shining blond hair so carefully combed, his cold, blue eyes, even his earlobes, had taken on an extraordinarily hard and impenetrable look, as though all the life had drained out of him and left nothing but its glistening shell behind.

"Well, I didn't like your sketch, Charles. I didn't like it one bit. Do you know why?"

Charles shook his head.

"Oh, yes you do. You are far too intelligent not to know why I didn't like it."

"Because of the wieners?" Charles ventured, fighting off the beginnings of a smile.

"Exactly that. Because of the wieners. And what, exactly, was it about the wieners I didn't like?"

"It was just to make people laugh."

"That's right, to make people laugh. To make people laugh at sin, Charles. Because you and I, we know very well what those wieners were meant to represent, don't we? You knew from the very start, and you left no one in any doubt about it, neither the other members of your team nor anyone else in the audience. And so you see, Charles, with your little sketch, you were making people laugh at sin, and not just any sin, but the most serious sin of all, the sin of impurity, which enters into us like a worm and ends up rotting our bodies and our souls. Your sketch was an occasion for sin, first for yourself, then for the others in your team, and then for all the other campers. Do you appreciate the seriousness of your act, Charles?"

Charles remained silent, not knowing how to reply. He hated to admit his guilt because he was not sorry for what he had done. At the same time, a disquieting feeling was building up inside him at the thought that he had done something reprehensible. But what seemed most obvious to him was that the man sitting in front of him, despite his paternalistic and protective airs, did not like him and knew that the feeling between them was mutual. He therefore decided to play his cards carefully.

"I never thought about any of what you're talking about," he said. "We were just having fun."

The priest gave a tight smile, one that expressed such haughty, disdainful disapproval that Charles became frightened and lowered his gaze.

"You're still young, Charles. You probably don't know yet what terrible power sin has, even though it is at this moment acting inside you – as it acts inside all of us. But I've been watching you for some time now, observing your attitudes, your behaviour, because I saw right away that you are a special child, interesting, a strange boy, in a way. And I have come to the conclusion that you are not as innocent as you would have people believe. You didn't take communion this morning, did you?"

"No," replied Charles, his cheeks burning.

"Why not?"

"Because I didn't feel like it," he said, averting his eyes.

The priest leaned over and stared deeply into Charles's eyes, and with an oily, velvety voice full of sickly sweet insinuations that gave Charles the impression that a warm, thick viscid liquid was running over his body, spreading in putrid streams.

"Wasn't it more likely that you didn't take communion because you knew you were not in *the proper state* for it? Because you were afraid of *committing sacrilege*?"

At the word sacrilege, of whose meaning Charles was only dimly aware, Charles shuddered. "No! It wasn't because of that," he blubbered. "It's because . . . because I was in a bad mood."

"A bad mood?" said the priest, surprised. "About what?"

Charles's face hardened; he wanted to get out of this, but he couldn't back the words.

"About you!" He swallowed, then continued. "Because it was you who wouldn't give us the prize last night."

The priest laughed loudly, but not with real laughter; it was unpleasant to hear.

"Is that so? Well, I must say, you don't mince words, do you. What are you going to be like when you're old enough to grow a moustache!"

Charles wanted to reply that he would never grow a moustache because he didn't like them, but he kept that thought to himself. He felt he had already reached the limit of his freedom of speech, and that for the time being it would be better to listen.

Father Beaucage studied him with a severe expression.

"I still think you couldn't take communion this morning no matter how much you wanted to. I think that last night, perhaps without fully appreciating the consequences of your actions, you instigated a scandal. By which I mean," he explained, responding to the puzzled look that had come over Charles's face, "that you incited your companions to commit bad acts. You are old enough and certainly intelligent enough to see that. Because you are intelligent, much more so than a good many others. Do you not wish to confess your sins? I can hear your confession right now, right here. Perhaps you have committed certain impure acts, either by yourself or with others; if so, now is the time to ask for forgiveness, to disburden your heart. No? Nothing to confess? No bad thoughts? No bad touching? God pardons all sinners, as you know, so long as they confess their sins and repent of them."

The next instant Charles was on his knees before the chaplain, hesitantly reciting the ritual formula for confession. But when the moment came to confess his sins, he stopped, not knowing what to say. His throat felt constricted. If he could, he would have jumped up and run out of the room.

"Repeat after me," the priest instructed in a low voice. "Heavenly Father, I accuse myself of having drawn others into the sin of impurity by my actions and my words, and to have taken pleasure from it."

After receiving his penance, Charles stood up, humbled, eyes lowered, and moved quickly towards the door. His confession was incomplete. He should also have confessed to feeling hatred for this man, enough hatred to make him want to claw out his eyes.

"Have a nice day, Charles," said the chaplain, smiling broadly. "Have fun. And think about what I've said."

Charles turned to leave, but a sudden compulsion made him turn around. "Was it you, then, who made sure I didn't write any more sketches?" he asked.

It was an insolent question, although he hadn't intended it that way. Father Beaucage gave a frown of annoyance.

"No, Charles, it wasn't me. It was the monitors who came to that decision at this morning's meeting. However, I believe it was a wise decision, because it allows each camper to exercise his talents in a variety of roles."

And with that he waited for Charles to close the door behind him.

24

A cold, steady rain continued to beat on the ground, driving away all heat and light and more and more leaves from the trees. Still green, they littered the muddy earth as though autumn had crept up and slain them unawares. Greyish-green puddles spread everywhere, some of them surprisingly deep, so that navigating about camp was a tricky matter. According to the radio the bad weather would persist until the next day. Brother Albert stirred a pot of caramel sauce as he listened to the news; he gave a deep sigh, plunged his wooden spoon into the steaming liquid and took a huge mouthful, his eyes a misty blend of pleasure and misgiving.

At about two o'clock, Frederic stuck his nose out through the partly opened door of the office, inhaled the damp air deeply into his lungs and walked heavily down the steps, making his mournful way through the downpour, wagging his rear end and stopping here and there to sniff at a puddle or ponder the tip of a branch. Thanks to the Brothers' kind treatment and abundant food, the animal had completely lost interest in life in the forest. He stopped in front of the community hall and, hearing a murmur of voices within, decided to investigate. His arrival was welcomed joyfully by the small troupe that had been languishing for an hour under the lethargic direction of Michel-Noël. Charles jumped to his feet and ran to greet him. Frederic, somewhat taken aback, stopped dead in his tracks at centre stage and began snorting menacingly, his way of giving notice that he felt threatened and was not happy about it. But after being stroked a few times he allowed himself to be picked up, and even snuggled into Charles's shoulder.

Patrick Ricard came up to Charles. "Let me have him a minute."

"Boys! Boys!" called Michel-Noël, "back to work! We haven't got anywhere since lunchtime. Charles, put the raccoon down and come and sit."

"Let me have him," Patrick said again.

Pretending not to hear him, Charles began scratching the animal gently behind the ears. Two other campers got up and tried to take the raccoon from him. Michel-Noël shoved them aside, grabbed Frederic, and set him down on the floor; the animal scurried back out through the door. Patrick gave Charles a surreptitious jab in the ribs and Charles turned on him to complain.

"You like that, don't you, rubbing your hands in its fur," said Ricard, smiling suggestively. "We know you. You like stroking things, don't you?"

He sniggered and returned to his place amid the complicitous laughter of the others in the troupe.

Charles stared after him in alarm. Over the past few hours an inexplicable change had come over Ricard. From being a friend, he had suddenly turned into an adversary, an enemy with a cold, malicious eye who pounced on any opportunity to harass or mock him. Charles didn't like playing games, and so responded more or less calmly, but inside he felt his anger building up. At lunch, Ricard, who had been sitting beside Charles since his first day in camp, had taken a seat five or six places away, across the table, and several times during lunch Charles had caught him whispering something into his new neighbour's ear and pointing his finger in Charles's direction, his small, pointed teeth bared in a malicious smile. Even the pimples on his thin face seemed to wiggle in a way meant to annoy him.

And worst of all, his cold mockery now seemed to have become contagious. Charles had begun to notice that some of his friends were beginning to shun him; he'd caught one of them, a member of his team who had been friendly until now, making faces at him behind his back. And when he passed a group of campers after lunch, their conversation suddenly became hushed and whispered. What was going on? What did they want from him? He went to find Henri to ask him, but Henri knew nothing about it, even made fun of his concerns, saying that all those novels he'd been reading were making him "funny in the head."

With Frederic gone, the team returned to work, yawning. Their sketch, chosen by Michel-Noël, was about all the different ways there were for a person to be of service to others. They were cross-eyed with boredom. Charles's job was to beat on a jam jar with a stick to indicate the beginning and end of each scene.

"We'll never win anything with a stupid sketch like this," sighed one of the campers after the rehearsal as they made their way to the dining hall for supper.

The Meal of Desserts would be served to the two winning teams the next evening in the kitchen, and already it was causing lips to smack and tongues to wag.

"Oh, I don't know about that," said Patrick Ricard, as though he had some special information on the subject. "I think we have a pretty good chance, especially with a good soundman like Charlie, here." He gave a small, spiteful laugh as he turned towards Charles.

"Okay, that's enough! What have I done to you?" Charles cried, his voice choking. "You've been picking on me all day ... You want a fight? Is that what you want? Well, just keep it up and you'll have your fight, I'm warning you!"

All Pimple-Face did was stick out his tongue and run off to join another camper; then he whispered something into the other's ear and they both laughed.

■ ■ ■

Normally, Charles ate enough food to choke a horse, but that night he barely touched his plate. It was the inexplicable malevolence that seemed to be floating around him; he was exasperated by it, and overcome with a terrible sadness. He deliberately took his time going to dinner to avoid having to talk to anyone, and he did not want a confrontation with Ricard and his gang; all during the meal Pimple-Face kept staring at him, as though trying to provoke him into something, then he would get up and whisper into someone's ear. Charles never learned what was being said, but whatever it was must have been funny. Just before dessert, the priest received a telephone call and had to leave the dining hall, and as he passed behind Charles he laid a friendly hand on the back of Charles's neck; the boy turned his head to look up, surprised and a bit wary.

"How's it going, Charles?" he said with that crisp, radiant smile of his that always made Charles uneasy.

Charles shrugged his shoulders and looked away.

As soon as he had taken his last mouthful he decided to get up and do some reading in the bunkhouse until it was time for the sketches. Then he changed his mind: he thought it would be a better idea to find Henri, his only true friend and someone everyone else respected. But as he was leaving the dining hall, a loud "Ahem!" from the back of the room made him stop.

A smiling Brother Albert was standing in the kitchen doorway, his apron stretched over a belly on which he could have easily balanced a salt and pepper shaker. With a flick of his spatula he signalled Charles to come over to him.

"Ahem! Let's see, now . . . young Thibodeau . . . I just wanted to say that that sketch of yours last night . . . er . . . very naughty, of course, no getting around that . . . put a few people off their feed, apparently . . . but anyway, I just . . . It was pretty well done, quite imaginative, I have to admit, and you did make us laugh, you little scoundrel! Anyway, I thought I'd ask you and your teammates to come into the kitchen tonight after snack . . . I made up some special desserts. Would you like that?"

Charles stared at him, speechless with delight.

"Well, I'll take that for a yes!" Brother Albert said, laughing. "Tell your buddies, but keep it to yourselves, eh? Don't want to make the others jealous, you never know."

"Thank you very much, Brother Albert," burbled Charles, stepping up to shake the monk's hand.

The monk laughed heartily and pinched the end of Charles's nose, then returned to his kitchen. Charles pulled up the hood of his raincoat, pushed open the screen door, and went out into the rain. Above the pitter-patter of raindrops on his hood he heard all kinds of other wet sounds: the heavy drumroll of rain on the shingled roofs, the lighter ratatat on the foliage, and the crystalline tinkling coming from the water puddles, which were still getting larger and deeper. From the centre of the empty square came the soft, wet sound of rain hitting a sugar maple, darkening its trunk and running down its bark in long rivulets to disappear among its roots. Charles was making his way slowly towards the bunkhouse, soothed and somehow consoled by this music, when a stone struck the side of his raincoat; he stopped and turned around to see where it had come from. A second stone hit him in the back, and then suddenly he was being pelted left and right by a volley of missiles, accompanied by muffled laughter. Frightened and furious, he ran over to a large bin made of rough-hewn lumber in which the garbage pails were protected from bears and raccoons. Behind it were Patrick Ricard and

two of his friends, all three standing innocently enough but smiling idioti-
cally at him. He heard steps splashing in the mud behind him and two more
boys ran up, one of them his neighbour in the bunkhouse, to whom he had
lent his flashlight the previous night.

"Why are you picking on me all the time?" Charles shouted, beside himself
with fury. He planted himself squarely in front of Ricard, whom he was certain
was the ringleader of this little ambush. Ricard looked at his companions as
though to build up his own fading courage, then gave a nasty laugh.

"Take it easy, Stroker. We were just having some fun."

Charles went white.

And, gathering up his own courage, he delivered a thundering punch to
Pimple-Face's nose.

"I'm just having fun, too!" he yelled, jumping back to avoid a retaliatory
punch that never came. There followed a short exchange of punches and
kicks. At one point Charles was down, rolling in the mud, when a third stone
hit him just above the eye, but he managed to struggle to his feet without
much damage being done. The bloody state of Ricard's nose seemed to have
intimidated his assailants, and they judged it better to express their aggres-
siveness by yelling insults at him from a distance.

"Stroker!"

"Jerk-off!"

"Go eat some wieners, why don't you?"

"Jerk yourself off, you pig!"

Charles walked off in a daze, forcing himself to move slowly in order to
show his disdain and contempt for his enemies.

Ricard staggered over to lean against the garbage bin, his shoulders shaking
with sobs, holding his nose in both hands and snorting strangely. A bright
red streak ran down the front of his yellow raincoat, diluted slightly by the
rain. It was from him that Charles received the comment that brought him
up short.

"Father Beaucage is right!" Ricard managed to shout in a quavering voice.
"You are a bad influence! You have brought evil into this camp! You're rotten
to the core!"

Charles turned around and stared at him, thunderstruck.

Suddenly he understood the source of all the sneaky rancour that had been
dogging him all day. The priest who hated him had seen to it that everyone

else hated him, too. That was it! He was a bad influence, someone to be avoided. He was dirty, smeared with invisible filth he could never wash off, because it was his self that was dirty. That's what Monsieur Saint-Amour had seen in him, and why he had done those disgusting things to him.

He turned and ran to the bunkhouse, flung open the door at full speed, and threw himself, raincoat and all, on his bed and cried. Lying with his face on his pillow he tried to rid himself of this new pain that was pulsing through his body, a pain more terrible than any he had yet experienced and which he was now condemned to carry around for the rest of his life. How could he get rid of himself? How could he go on living if his very soul was abhorrent to him? Father Beaucage must be right. No matter how hard he tried to be good, he was wicked, the son of a wicked father and made in his father's image, and nothing could ever deliver him from his own wickedness. Evil flowed through him like the very blood in his veins.

■ ■ ■

After a while the pain began to subside, and he began to doze off. Suddenly he heard the door open and footsteps approach his bed.

"Aha! Here you are," said Henri. "What's the matter? Are you sick?"

Charles shook his head, still lying face-down on the bed.

"So, what is it? Come on, the sketches are starting."

Charles shook his head again.

"What happened to you?" Henri said, sitting down on the side of the bed. "Someone beat you up? Was it that little shit, Ricard? You want me to settle his hash for him?"

"I want to go home," Charles murmured thickly, almost inaudibly.

"We are going home, in three days," replied Henri, smiling at his friend's sudden childishness.

"I want to go home now. Call your father, ask him to come and get me."

"Are you crazy? Papa has too many other things to do. Mama just came out of the hospital, and you know as well as I do that Papa has to do everything around the house. She's still sick, Charles. Very sick."

Charles started crying again into his pillow. His friend watched him uneasily.

"Come on, let's go," he said, laying a hand on Charles's shoulder. "The first sketch has already started. It's that Ricard who's turning everyone against you, isn't it? I saw him doing it during dinner. Don't worry, I'll put that little asshole in his place."

Charles wanted to tell Henri that he'd already done that, but he was sobbing too much to talk. To his unhappiness was now added the shame of crying like a baby in front of Henri.

His friend sat there for a moment, then stood up, shrugged and left, promising himself he would find Pimple-Face and clean his clock for him.

Twenty minutes later the bunkhouse door opened again, and this time it was Brother Marcel who came in, looking anxious.

"What's happened, Charles? Are you not well? Rumour has it there was an incident earlier. That you were in a fight. Is that true?"

Charles was kneeling by his trunk, feeling a bit calmer, but the appearance of the camp director brought everything to the surface again. He threw himself on the bed and buried his face in his pillow, ashamed of his puffy eyes and burning cheeks, and of his reputation for being a cry-baby that seemed to be circulating about the camp. Brother Marcel observed him for a while, still wearing his raincoat.

"Who did you fight with, Charles?"

"With Ricard . . . and . . . his gang," Charles said, his words punctuated by sobs.

"And why did you fight them?"

Charles's only reply was to dig his face deeper into the pillow. A shudder seized his lower jaw and it opened and closed uncontrollably – his fish-mouth was back. Had he not suffered enough humiliation without that? The idea of Brother Marcel seeing his horrible facial tic filled him with terror.

"Come, come, my lad," said the monk, rubbing Charles's shoulder sympathetically. "Calm yourself, I implore you. You can talk to me, no need to be afraid. I'm here to solve problems, not make them."

But no matter how much he cajoled, trying to console the child with his somewhat awkward pleasantries and caressing him with his rough, bachelor's hands, Charles refused to talk. Finally the monk, convinced of the seriousness of the affair but aware that his insistence would get him nowhere, decided that a good night's sleep would do more for the child than all the comforting in the world; Charles would no doubt be more disposed to empty his heart in the morning. In the meantime, he would conduct his own investigations.

"You look tired, my poor boy . . . Why not get into your pyjamas and try to sleep? You'll see things in a different light tomorrow morning, I'm certain of it. Good night and pleasant dreams."

"Poor kid," he said to himself as he returned to the community centre. "What can we possibly do to help him now?"

25

A long time passed. Every so often the sound of distant shouts and laughter reached the bunkhouse before being drowned out by the rain. Charles had turned on his back and was lying with his fists clenched, staring into the darkness with a fierce intentness, as though expecting a glowing angel to drop down and, with the faint touch from her wingtip, relieve him of the pain that wracked his mind. But no angel appeared and the pitiless pain continued to eat away at him. If only he could press himself against old Boff! How much better that would make him feel! (Was it pure chance? At just that moment, Boff, asleep on his blanket by the kitchen door, suddenly opened his eyes and gave a long howl that wakened Lucie, who was lying on the sofa in the living room; she stared at the silent figures moving about on the television screen for a few moments, then sighed and went back to sleep.)

Suddenly Charles sat up in bed, flushed with indignation. He saw again Father Beaucage's terrible smile, with his white, perfectly aligned teeth, his pink, clean face, his aristocratically straight nose, his cold eyes; he felt again the pressure of those fingers on his neck. Shivers of disgust ran down his back. What a hypocrite! That he could smile and pretend to be friendly after speaking so meanly about him to Ricard. Anger quickly dissipated the pain. He now had only two desires: to get his revenge and to leave. To leave this very night, but first to show everyone what it meant to be a bad influence – to make a dramatic response to the schemes of two-faced chaplains who were foolish enough to believe that no ten-year-old could see through them.

He jumped out of bed, took his flashlight out of his neighbour's trunk, put on his raincoat, and left the bunkhouse. Rain beat against his face and made him feel better; he took a deep breath of the rain-laden air, swelled with the scent of wet earth, leaves, and pine resin; it clarified his ideas in a flash.

The rest of the campers were in the community hall; he had the rest of the camp to himself. He swiftly crossed the quadrangle, stumbling over the occasional root, and made his way towards the chapel. As he had hoped, the door to the priest's lodging was unlocked. He crept into the dark room, keeping his ear tuned to the slightest noise, suddenly seized by a panic that froze him in his tracks and made him lose some of his grip on reality; shadows shifted around him, expanding and moving about; a creaking floorboard sounded like a crack of thunder. He turned to the door, on the verge of fleeing, when suddenly something clicked in him; he remembered the gleam that had emanated from the small cupboard when he had been here earlier that day, and the suspicious haste the priest had made to close the cupboard door. Something told him he had found his means of revenge. He went over to the armoire, opened it, and saw a row of bottles. He took one out, removed the cork, raised the neck to his nose and quickly recoiled; it was "the hard stuff," as his father used to say. His mouth twisted in a satisfied grin. So Father Beaucage liked to drink, did he? But in secret, like the hypocrite he was . . . Good! after tonight it would be a secret no longer!

His eye fell on the sofa, then drifted about the room as he tried to find the best means of effecting his revenge. There was a door at the back of the room; he pushed it. It opened onto the bedroom: a dresser, a prayer stand, a small desk, a bed. He went over to the bed and on it he emptied a bottle of cognac marked with big Xs. The odour rose up to his nostrils and nearly suffocated him, but he kept his head, filled with a hateful joy that allowed him to find pleasure even in his sorrow. He returned to the armoire and opened a second bottle, which he poured over the sofa. This time he poured the alcohol to form the letters of his name, but ran out at the letter r. The fumes began to make him feel fuzzy-headed, but joy rose up within him, a lively, sharp, crackling joy. His vengeance enchanted him more and more. Raising the empty bottle he brought the mouth to his lips. A thin trickle ran into his gullet, tracing a line of burning fire as sharp as a razor down his throat. He coughed and his eyes filled with water, but after swallowing a few times he felt better. A warm glow spread through his chest. Suddenly he heard Brother Marcel's voice in the yard, coming through the rain.

"I don't know! He's not in his bunkhouse. I hope he hasn't gone down to the lake!"

"When you find him, bring him to me," called Brother Albert. "I've got something that'll put him in a better frame of mind. You'll see."

Half dead with fear, Charles closed the lodging door silently and made his way to the camp entrance, stopping every ten feet to see if he was being followed. As he passed a huge, rounded rock something bumped against his leg and nearly made him cry out. The animal stopped a few paces from him and began digging in a small pile of leaves: it was Frederic, making his regular rounds despite the rain. Charles bent down and called the animal softly, suddenly taken with a mad desire to pick it up in his arms and, why not?, take it with him. The raccoon looked up at him without moving. Then it stood up on its hind legs and snorted in short bursts, as though fending off a threat.

Voices sounded nearby. Charles started running. He ran through the arch of pines that formed the front gate of the camp, and disappeared into the night. He soon had to slow down, out of breath. In order to hear better he had pushed back the hood of his raincoat. Water ran down the back of his neck like long, cold worms. The rain had already soaked his pantlegs and was now getting into his running shoes. The euphoria that had seized him during his vengeance was now drained out of him. He walked slowly, shivering, along the tree-lined road, stepping around potholes full of water, among dark, looming, indecipherable, vaguely menacing shapes, wondering where he would spend the night. He remembered that when they had arrived at camp they'd passed a long line of fields and pastures without seeing a single house or barn. "No problem!" he told himself with forced bravado. "I'll sleep under a tree. It'll be fun!"

And so saying he stepped into a puddle so deep that his foot was soaked up to the ankle.

Almost at the same time he heard a car behind him; a yellowish halo appeared at the end of a curve a hundred metres away, illuminating the crooked posts of an old fence that lined the road. Stepping over a patch of tall grass, he threw himself headfirst into the ditch and lay down in a pool of water.

A moment passed, then the car bounced into view and stopped. Through the grass he recognized Brother Marcel's blue Chevrolet. One of the windows was down.

"Charles! Can you hear me?" It was the shrill voice of Jean-Guy – he always sounded like he'd fallen prey to a violent emotion. "Brother Marcel wants to talk to you! Everything will turn out okay! Don't be afraid!"

The throaty voice of Brother Marcel also came from inside the car, but Charles could only make out the end of one sentence:

". . . in the fields, but we'd need a searchlight, the little worm!"

The car moved slowly off, jolting over potholes like an exhausted bull, then returned twenty minutes later. Charles hadn't dared move from his hiding place. He gritted his teeth and sighed at the thought of his flashlight, now lying underwater beside him and no doubt dead as a doornail. When the Chevrolet passed he almost jumped up in the ditch and waved his hands, ready to give in to whatever fate had in store for him, but shame and pride kept him pinned to the ground.

When silence and darkness once again descended, Charles climbed back onto the road and began walking, numb with cold, heavy with guilt, unable to understand the folly that had taken hold of him. Questions flooded his brain. How would Lucie and Fernand take this when they heard of it? Would they still let him live with them? Would Brother Marcel call the police? Would they throw him in prison?

The only sound was of rain in the fields, and rain spattering in the puddles that flooded the road. Somewhere in the distance a cow lowed. Charles sat down on a rock, lowered his face into his hands, and began to cry as he thought about the desperate fix he had placed himself in.

Suddenly he heard a movement in the woods behind him. He looked up.

■ ■ ■

Fernand signed the check with a flourish, carefully tore it from his cheque book, and handed it to Brother Marcel.

"There you are, paid in full. Once again, I hope you will excuse him . . . I am truly sorry for all the trouble."

The apparent civility of his remarks contrasted strongly with the look of controlled fury on his face, but it was, for the moment, a fury without an object to dwell on; it had gone off in search of a guilty party but hadn't found one anywhere, so it came back empty-handed and grumpier than ever, thirsting for a head-on collision, a scathing denunciation, a face to spit into. Finally, exhausted by its own impotence, it had slumped into a dark corner and begun gnashing its teeth.

Fernand heaved a deep sigh. The two men regarded each other and both coughed at the same time.

"Are you sure you won't have a cup of coffee?" asked Brother Marcel for the fourth time. "After all, to get up in the middle of the night and drive all this way . . . not to mention the worry . . . Some coffee would help, don't you think?"

The monk gave him a smile that came on in stages, showing first his natural goodness, then his desire to be agreeable, then his sadness at finding himself in such a situation, and finally his conviction that coffee was a good idea. It made Fernand feel he was being a pain in the neck, and the resolve with which he had fortified himself – to take nothing from these people, not so much as a toothpick – began to weaken, leaving behind a pinch of dry dust.

"Well," he said, "on second thought I suppose I could have a quick one. It's going to be a long drive back . . ."

"Excellent!" cried Brother Marcel triumphantly. He got up from his rocking chair. "I'll just run over to the kitchen. Won't be a minute."

He was gone eight minutes, but he came back carrying a fresh pot of coffee and a plate of cookies, cakes, and confections that had been part of Brother Albert's Meal of Desserts.

Fernand took a sip of coffee, raised his eyebrows slightly to indicate his contentment, waved off the plate of biscuits when it was held out to him, then relented and took one.

Brother Marcel had called Fernand at midnight to inform him of Charles's disappearance. Fernand had arrived at the camp an hour and a half later, alone – he had not wanted his convalescing wife to accompany him – and practically bent double with anguish; he was all for organizing a search party immediately to scour the surrounding woods. The police, who had also been called in, explained to him that such a thing was impossible in the middle of the night. Better to wait until sunrise; in any case, it was much more likely that the boy had stuck to the road, and that by this time he had probably found some dry place to sleep. On the other hand, they were working on the theory that he might have drowned, and there was nothing to stop them from dragging the lake right away. They had brought the necessary equipment with them.

On hearing this Fernand's eyes widened as though he had swallowed a large rock; Henri burst into tears. Two monitors and three police officers, accompanied by Little Foot, went off to the lakeshore where the police launches were waiting. Fernand wanted to go with them but held back, unable to face the idea of seeing Charles's dripping body being hauled up from the murky depths of the lake. Instead, he went over to the director, who was pacing back and forth in the clearing, Brother Albert following him and waving his arms, his shirt half pulled from his trousers.

"What happened?" he demanded to know in his terrible voice.

The two men went into the director's office and began to conduct a formal inquiry. Henri was called, then Patrick Ricard, who confessed tearfully that it had been because of the chaplain's condemnations that he and the others had started picking on Charles.

"Get Father Beaucage in here!" thundered Fernand, jumping to his feet and turning purple with rage. "Get him in here this instant!"

Unfortunately the priest, forced to leave his sodden quarters, had decided to spend the night at his sister's house in Joliette – in the circumstances he had not felt that his presence in camp was needed, and besides he had a meeting at the bishopric the following afternoon; but he had promised to keep in touch with the camp by telephone.

Fernand had already learned about Charles's revenge with the cognac; the chaplain had been furious and not a little embarrassed, and had sworn Brother Marcel to secrecy. But thanks to the large ears of Brother Albert, the whole camp had heard about it within half an hour.

"Just let me get my hands on that whisky priest!" Fernand roared, gripping the arms of his chair. "I can't wait. I can't wait to get him in my sights! I'll break every bone in his body! This is all his fault, his fault entirely! No one else's! My boy" – for now Charles had become his son – "a bad influence, you'd have to be a nutcase to think such things about him! Such a gentle boy! Such a hard worker! So friendly! You'd better pray no harm has come to that boy, Brother Marcel, because I'll drag that Nazi priest of yours into court by the hair, if I have to! Where does his sister live in Joliette?"

"I'm afraid I have no idea," said the director prudently.

■ ■ ■

Morning came. It had stopped raining. Since dredging the lake had revealed nothing, the searchers organized a sweep of the forest. Fernand decided to drive around the area in his car.

He drove for half an hour, keeping his eyes peeled. His hands were moist, his feet felt like ice, and he was tortured again by the abominable cramps that made it hard for him to breathe. Several times he was sure he saw a child's silhouette in the distance, but each time it turned out to be a vision born of his own anguish.

Exhaustion overcame him. His eyes blurred, his mind turned to mush. Twice he almost drove off the road into the fields. He decided to pull over and sleep for a few minutes. He stopped the car on a small side road, leaned his forehead against the steering wheel and was soon dead to the world. He was awakened by the cawing of a crow; the bird had landed on the hood of the car with a loud beating of its enormous wings; Fernand took it for a terrible omen. According to his watch it was six-thirty, a sinister hour. He drove quickly towards Camp Jeunenjoie in the grip of a terrible presentiment of disaster; he felt this would be a day he would hate for the rest of his life.

The Provincial Police were leaving the camp just as he arrived. Henri ran towards him; a farmer had just telephoned Brother Marcel saying he'd found a small boy sleeping in one of his outbuildings. The boy was lying naked in a pile of straw, with a flashlight in his hand and his clothes hanging from an old harrow. At first he seemed frightened and wouldn't answer any questions, but finally he identified himself and said he had run away from Camp Jeunenjoie and refused absolutely to ever set foot in the place again. He had begged the farmer to bring him into the house so he could phone his parents to come and get him.

Brother Albert came out of the cookhouse with a dishcloth over one shoulder, stepped heavily off the porch and made his elephantine way towards Fernand; anxiety and sleeplessness had transformed him into a sort of grey, slightly gelatinous, quivering mass, and the announcement that Charles had been found had not yet calmed him down. He shook Fernand's hand vigorously, and the smell of lemon-scented dish detergent filled the humid air around him.

"What a mess! Our director has just gone down to the lake to call off the dredging. As for those out searching the woods, well, I suppose the fresh air will do them good. Lord of Lords! All's well that ends well, but some things are better if they never get started, eh? I haven't closed my eyes all night!"

Fernand turned to get into his car, but Brother Albert took his arm.

"Don't be too hard on the boy. I've been keeping an eye on him, and he's not a troublemaker. Far from it! In the thirty years I've been with the community I've seen a few boys, believe me. Maybe he was just bored and it went to his head, you never know about such things . . . Boredom or . . . something like that," he added, not daring to say what he was really thinking. "You must talk to our director."

"Boredom!" Fernand replied, turning the key in the ignition. "What are you talking about? I know what happened! Tell me, where's this farmer live?"

Ten minutes later, after having put his car's axles in peril several times, he stopped before a small house done up with aluminum siding, whose flashiness bestowed a kind of nobility on the grey-board buildings that surrounded it. He found Charles sitting at a table in the grimy kitchen, surrounded by stacks of old newspapers, in the company of an old man with a crumpled face, shirt-tails hanging out, to whom twelve years of solitary widowerhood had given a slightly wild expression.

"Gimme quite a turn s'mornin', kid o' yours did," said the farmer, scratching the small of his back.

Charles gave an embarrassed smile. Although his hair was mussed and contained pieces of straw and his eyes were wide and bright, he seemed calm enough – as Lucie remarked, between sobs of joy, when Fernand called her on the farmer's telephone.

"Well, you little scallawag! You gave us all quite a turn," said Fernand, without quite being able to hide his happiness at finding the boy safe and sound. "The police have been looking for you! Everyone's been beating the bushes! They even dragged the lake! Gracious me, we've been turning the whole world upside down looking for you!"

"Sorry, Fernand," Charles replied seriously, turning red. He stood up from the table where he'd been eating a bowl of porridge. "But I had my reasons."

And leading Fernand out onto the porch, where the farmer graciously left them on their own, he tearfully recounted the entire story of his stormy relationship with Father Beaucage; he didn't downplay his own part in the fracas, but his simple and pointed narrative brought out the dominating, hypocritical character of the chaplain.

Fernand listened attentively, making Charles repeat the episode of the sketch in minute detail; he listened with clenched fists, nearly bursting with indignation.

"Okay," he said, standing up when Charles was finished. "Let's go get your stuff. I might as well bring Henri home, now that I'm here. But before we leave I want to have a word or two with this Father Beaucage."

He went back into the kitchen to thank the farmer and to offer him five dollars for his trouble; the old man nimbly pocketed the money, then went over to Charles, grinned at him toothlessly, and solemnly shook his hand. The white hairs in his five-day beard shone like silver in a shaft of sunlight.

"Come back any time, my boy," he said. "But try the house next time!"

There was a small welcoming party waiting for Charles at the camp. They raised a shout of joy, a few of them clapped their hands. His little adventure and the business with the cognac had made him a hero. Everyone wanted to speak to him at once. Heads were thrust through the car windows. He smiled, a bit taken aback, replied to a few questions, but refused to get out of the car. Standing a few feet back, Little Foot, gesticulating more than ever, declared to a monitor that having grand principles was one thing, but they weren't worth a pinch of raccoon shit if you didn't have the judgment to know when and where to apply them.

Brother Albert rang the breakfast bell and everyone hurried off to the dining hall. A few minutes later a boy came out carrying a small cardboard box, a gift from the cook, which he handed through the car window to Charles. But the young fugitive, exhausted by his night on the run, fell asleep in the back seat without even opening it.

■ ■ ■

Meanwhile, Fernand was waiting for the chaplain in the director's office. He sighed loudly in his chair, his obstinacy and anger having returned full force, much to the chagrin of Brother Marcel, who tried to calm him down by singing Father Beaucage's praises – his dynamism, his devotion to duty, his unalterable cheerfulness, the enormous efforts he'd made to adapt the teachings of the Church to the mentality of modern-day youth. All to no avail. It was like trying to put out a forest fire with an eye-dropper. In the end he resorted to commiserating on the frailty of human nature, appealing to Fernand's generosity and his great experience of life.

"Anyone can make a mistake . . . Put yourself in his place . . . It's not easy . . . I'm certain he was acting in good faith . . ."

"Oh, you think so, eh? You really think he was acting in good faith?"

And stretching out his hand to the biscuits, he began devouring them one after another, his face still twisted in anger.

Just before ten, the phone rang. It was Father Beaucage, wanting to know about the search for Charles. Brother Marcel told him that the boy had been found, that he was safe and sound, and that his father had come to collect him; he did not add that the father was sitting right there in his office, waiting for him.

Fernand smiled; he now realized that the camp director was on his side, even though he would never admit it. Brother Albert, who had an ever-ready ear and whose kitchen adjoined the director's office, would be able to testify to the chaplain that Brother Marcel had done everything in his power to avoid a confrontation.

"He'll be here in three-quarters of an hour," Brother Marcel said when he had hung up.

"Thank you very much for your understanding."

"I'm sure I don't know what your talking about. I have done everything in my power to dissuade you. From now on, it's out of my hands."

But the sly curve of his lips told Fernand that, on the contrary, the monk was still taking a great interest in what was about to unfold.

"You'll have to excuse me, I'm afraid," continued Brother Marcel, getting to his feet. "I have to see to poor Father Beaucage's mattress; if it isn't replaced he'll have to sleep in town again tonight."

Left alone, Fernand eyed the biscuit plate for a while. There remained only a few crumbs. Then his eye wandered up to a large, pastel print pinned to the office wall, on which Christ appeared to have recently undergone open-heart surgery. He stood up, paced back and forth for a while, then went out to the car to see how Charles was doing: the boy was sleeping soundly in the back seat, the box on his chest. Fernand returned to the office, sat down in his chair, and also went to sleep.

The sound of the door opening woke him. Father Beaucage was standing in the doorway, looking at him curiously.

"HA!" Fernand thundered, rising. "YOU AT LAST!"

284

Meanwhile, Henri had gone out to the car to join Charles. Charles was awake, and the two boys decided to take a last look at the lake. The beach was deserted, the sand dry and deliciously warm. They took off their shoes and socks and sat in the sun. A few feet away, two wasps were zigzagging around a soft-drink can that had been left by a rock, attracted by the sugar but not daring to enter the opening.

Charles told Henri about his adventure. He had felt nothing but pleasure as he anointed Father Beaucage's bed and the sofa: the priest was "an alcoholic, like my father," he declared in a tone that brooked no appeal. His flight through the rainstorm had been somewhat less pleasant. The cold that had got into him when he had had to lie down in the ditch made his teeth chatter for the rest of the night. But the worst had been the apparition of a huge, black beast (he never knew exactly what it was) that had charged at him from a stand of trees when he'd sat down on a rock to rest. Whatever it was that had come at him, it had sounded like a huge board being smashed in two. He'd jumped to his feet in terror and taken off as fast as though his legs had suddenly become two metres long. Never before had he run so fast!

After running a kilometre or more he'd come to the top of the steep hill that Fernand's car had had so much trouble climbing. He'd felt like he was standing at the edge of a huge gulf that went right down to the centre of the earth. In his terror, still believing the beast to be at his heels, he'd started running down the slope, caught his foot on something, and begun rolling in the mud so fast that he almost lost consciousness. He had no idea what was happening to him. Then his fall ended when he rolled into something soft and wet. He got up, shaken but unharmed except for a pain in his neck and a scraped elbow, and was relieved to find that the beast had abandoned the chase. He could make out the shape of a barn rising on the other side of the road. Through its partly open door he saw some kind of farm machine and, at the back, a big pile of straw. He was so caked with mud from his tumble that he decided, despite the shivers that still wracked his body, to wash himself off under the stream of water that ran off the barn's roof. Then he hung his clothes on the tines of the machine and nestled into the straw. At first the straw made his entire body itch, and he worried about mice, but eventually a sweet warmth crept over him and he slept like a cat in the sun until the farmer – a very nice man, as it turned out – woke him up with a start in the early morning.

Charles told his story, augmenting it with a few embellishments that brought out his nerve, his determination, and his resourcefulness, and Henri listened through to the end, from time to time nodding his head in admiration.

When he finished, they sat in silence, contemplating the lake which was covered in places with sheets of flame from the sun, and which lapped at their feet with a friendly, submissive sound. One of the wasps had become impatient and flown into the can and was now trying desperately to find its way out, throwing itself against the aluminum top like a crazed battering ram and making a noise like an electric razor.

Henri turned to his friend and asked a question. He didn't take a moment to filter his thoughts, and the question leapt from his eyes as much as from his lips, which were bent in a slightly mocking smile.

"Are you still upset?"

Charles stared at him for a second. His face turned pale; he took a short breath that seemed to stick in his windpipe, then suddenly he drove a hard punch into Henri's stomach.

■ ■ ■

"And you are?" asked Father Beaucage with a slight tightening of his features. He stepped two paces forward.

"I am Charles's father," replied Fernand, to simplify matters.

"Ah, good . . . very happy to meet you, sir. Because I wanted to bring you up to date on . . . certain things . . . regarding your son. I've been concerned about him for some time, now. In fact, not to put too fine a point to it, he exerts an unhealthy influence over his companions."

"Don't give me that! I know what's been going on here! I've been told the whole story! And, if you'll pardon my saying so, it's my opinion that so far as this matter is concerned you have behaved like a crow with his ass stuck in the molasses."

"Which is to say?"

"Which is to say! Oh, so you're going to throw a 'Which is to say' at me, are you? Do you think you impress me with your high-falutin' words? Do you? Well, I assure you, sir, you impress me about as much as a fly! Which is to

286

say," he repeated, to give his confidence a boost, the priest's cold demeanour having begun to have its effect, "not at all! Good gracious, man! What were you thinking? It's as if you leave all your brains on the pillow when you get up in the morning. You set everyone against one poor child because he made a joke about wieners? I've never heard anything so ridiculous in all my life! Nor so despicable! I'm just speaking my mind," he thought he had better add, so as to give himself time to calm down.

Father Beaucage had closed the door behind him and, leaning against the edge of his desk with his arms crossed, was listening to Fernand with a faint smile of superiority on his face. Which only served to inflame Fernand's anger even further.

"You are treating the boy's behaviour rather lightly, my dear sir," he finally murmured.

"I'm treating it the way it deserves to be treated. A little boy tells a naughty joke! So what! You'd have to have a twisted mind yourself if something like that's enough to get you so worked up!"

"I've quite a few years of ministering behind me, my friend. Easily enough to allow me to say that evil can sometimes come disguised as innocence in young souls. It's my duty to protect them."

"Let's be frank here," Fernand exclaimed. "I'm a simple man. So what are you saying? That my boy is a pervert? Is that it? Rotten to the core, as you so nicely put it?"

"I never said that."

And a small spasm ran across the priest's left jawbone.

"Well then, it must have been someone who looks like you. Anyway, forget that. There are more important issues here. Like this one: which one of us knows this child better. And that's me, not you."

"I don't doubt it."

"And I know that he is not a pervert!"

"Who said he was?"

"According to you he exerts a bad influence on his companions. It's the same thing. You think I don't understand what you're saying? Those fine words of yours mean something!"

Fernand's face turned an even darker shade of purple. The priest looked down and heaved a deep sigh, either of boredom or commiseration, it was difficult to tell.

"You know, my dear sir, sometimes we think we know a person very well – and we really only know part of him. Habit dulls the senses. We fail to see what we look at every day."

"What's that, some kind of religious mumbo-jumbo? Is that the sort of twisted thinking they teach you in the seminary?"

"No. It's simply the fruit of my observations."

"Well, fine. Keep your rotten fruit to yourself! I don't want any of it! Gives me the trots. You don't know the first thing about that boy, not the first thing! When you talk about him, you're talking in a void, and it sounds hollow! You don't know, for example, that he's not my son!"

"Oh?" said the priest, suddenly showing interest.

"No, sir, he is not! My wife and I took him in because his own father nearly killed him. There, that sets you back a bit, doesn't it? There's something you didn't learn in that seminary of yours, what can I say. And we have never regretted our decision for a second. Not that it's always been easy – have you ever met a kid who was always easy? – but when you look at the big picture" – and here Fernand stretched his huge arms out to each side – "he's been very, very good. He's intelligent, obedient, affectionate, and a good worker. Could you say as much for yourself?"

The chaplain said nothing to this, but contented himself with closing his eyes before such an affront.

"So much so," Fernand continued, carried away by his enthusiasm, "that I intend to adopt him!"

"That speaks to your credit, sir."

"Thank you very much!" he sputtered. "But I must set you straight about a few things before you bury me with your ministering and your good intentions. Have you seen what state the boy is in? I'd be ashamed if I were you! The things I've been hearing! I hear you discouraged him from reading . . . now there's genius for you! Education, my dear chaplain, is the key to the future, it's the goal of society, the gateway to progress . . . In fact, you might say education is everything these days! Very soon a man won't be able to get into an elevator or order a bag of nails without an education. You've probably got more education than me, my wife and all my neighbours put together, so why do I have to remind you of how important education is!"

He had to stop to catch his breath. The shuffle of a heavy foot in the next room indicated that Brother Albert had not missed a word of this relentless diatribe.

"Is there anything else you wish to say to me?" Father Beaucage asked coolly, looking at his watch.

"Oh, I could go on for a while yet, but I've got to get to work. Thanks to you I've already lost half a day."

Relieved to have been given this out, Fernand turned towards the door. But Father Beaucage caught his sleeve.

"Just a moment, if you please. I've let you have your say, now you're going to give me thirty seconds to have mine. Your son – since that is what you choose to call him – has no shortage of ability, no one's disputing that. But it is my duty to warn you that he is following a dangerous path. Don't forget, he's almost an adolescent! You haven't seen anything yet! Everything gets complicated, amplified. If you truly love the boy, you must protect him from himself – or rather from the forces of Evil that have already begun to act on him as they act on each one of us, and feed on us, if I may put it that way, for their own purposes. And if I may be permitted one last comment: without the help of God – and His representatives here on Earth, imperfect though they be – you will fail in your task, because Evil is much stronger than the strength of one man."

Fernand took a step towards the priest, his face exhibiting a curious blend of fury and supplication.

"Shut up! I don't want to hear any more of it, do you hear me? You're going to make my head explode! I'll put my fist down your gullet! And most of all, most of all, stay away from children! You'll never understand a thing about them! Go work with old people! All the damage you could do to them has already been done. When I think of what you . . . my son rotten to the core! It's all I can do to keep from smashing your face in, you . . . you pisser of holy water!"

His massive hand with its large, hairy knuckles, white from being contracted into a fist, wavered a few centimetres from the chaplain's face, shaking only slightly, as though its quivering strength had been diverted at the last second into a hasty detente.

Father Beaucage hadn't moved a hair. Only a tiny hardening of his jaw muscles hinted at his fear.

"Calm yourself, sir," he said deliberately. "And leave this place. Before I lodge a complaint with the police."

Fernand stared him full in the face, looking almost dazed, then grabbed the corner of the desk, lifted it into the air, and let it drop noisily back to the floor. A cacophony of pots answered from the kitchen. But Fernand hardly heard the noise; he was already on his way back to the car.

26

The first to react to Charles's footsteps coming up the sidewalk was Boff. The dog dashed into the hallway, barking and squirming and charging against the door so hard he made the windows rattle. Lucie hurried from the kitchen, where she'd been cooking her first meal since coming out of the hospital, but had to stop in her tracks, her hand on the doorframe and her legs suddenly turned to rubber. Charles burst through the front door, dropped his travel bag in the vestibule, and began shouting with happy protest at the assault of his dog who, paws on the boy's shoulders, was licking his face in a fine frenzy. Henri tried to intervene but was submitted to the same treatment. Then came a shout from Fernand. He stamped his foot on the floor and silence reigned.

Charles walked hesitantly up to Lucie. He saw how thin she was, her washed-out pallor, the frailty that emanated from her entire body, even in the way she looked at him.

"Are you feeling any better, Lucie?" he asked.

"Much better, my boy. The worst is over." She stroked his hair as he pressed himself against her.

Henri pushed Charles aside and hugged his mother, asking her to tell them about her stay in the hospital.

"All in good time, my dear. I have to see to supper first. My potatoes are probably sticking to the bottom of the pan by now."

"You're going to go sit quietly in the rocking chair," Fernand ordered, "while the boys set the table and I finish making dinner."

She smiled at him and picked up the morning newspaper, which had been lying on the kitchen table.

"Are you happy?" she said, holding it up to Fernand. "It's done. They just passed Bill 101. Come September, all immigrant children will have to go to French schools, just like us. And businesses have five years to change their signs from English to French."

"Well, well, that calls for a celebration! Henri, off to the bakery with you and get us a Boston Cream Pie, a big one!"

Boff made another assault on Charles and succeeded in knocking him to the floor. The boy ruffled the hair behind his dog's neck, murmuring into its ear and then looking into its eyes, then ran his hand down its back from its head to the end of its tail, overjoyed at being reunited with his old friend, the sole witness to his earlier trials and tribulations. The dog drooled in ecstasy. But Fernand's increasingly loud sighs finally had their effect, and the dog slunk off to the back porch.

The smell of turkey scallopini simmering in mushroom sauce assailed his nostrils; lying with his muzzle resting on his paws he stared at the bottom of the back door, grinding his teeth. But he knew that any attempt on the food would lead to a dead-end, and probably gain him a few cuffs into the bargain.

In the kitchen there was much laughter. The steady clink of knives and forks on plates seemed louder than usual, as is often the case when people get together around a good table after having been separated for a long time. Without going into too much detail, Lucie told them how the doctors had operated on her intestines to cure her diverticulitis. The incredible pain that had kept her awake at night, and which had eventually caused Fernand to rush her into Emergency at the Maisonneuve-Rosemont Hospital, would not return, according to the doctor, as long as she was careful about what she ate. The word *diverticulitis* made a deep impression on Charles and Henri. It made Charles think of a kind of lobster crawling around in Lucie's entrails, cutting out big chunks of her with their pincers. Henri envisioned a spiny snake slithering through his mother's bowels, its tongue flickering in and out with satisfaction at the extraordinary pain it was causing her.

"And what about you, Charles," Lucie said. "I hear you had a few bad moments yourself. Tell us about them."

The child reddened, looked down at his plate, cut up a carrot and slowly brought a piece of it to his mouth. Then, looking up with a smile, he said: "It's over now, and I'm really glad to be back here."

"Ha!" laughed Henri. "He doesn't want to talk about it because he's ashamed of what he did." And he launched into a recitation of his friend's adventures. Charles tried to look bored with it all, resigned to letting Henri be his spokesman, but he interrupted from time to time to clarify a point or make a correction. The affair with the cognac disturbed Lucie very much, although she tried hard not to let it show on her face.

"With real cognac!" exclaimed Céline, horrified and impressed at the same time. "All over his bed and sofa! He must have been furious!"

"He wasn't too happy about it," Charles said with a smile of satisfaction.

Lucie tweaked the end of his nose: "It doesn't do to cross swords with you, eh? Where did you ever get such an idea? Weren't you afraid of being punished?"

Charles's face darkened and he half closed his eyes: "I hated that man, the chaplain," he said.

"Yes, he doesn't seem to have shown good judgment," Lucie agreed. "That was certainly no way to deal with youngsters . . . and over such a trifle!"

"He's a complete imbecile, is what he is!" piped in Fernand, through a mouthful of scallopini. "And I'm not ashamed to say so! His head is so stuffed with bits of old soutaine that he thinks religion is still the same thing it was in the days of my great-grandmother. One of these days he's going to run into someone who'll leave him sweeping his teeth into a dustpan. That someone was almost me this morning, let me tell you!"

Charles laughed, but his heart wasn't in it. Despite his contentment at being back with his family (which was how he thought of the Fafards), and even with Fernand's energetic and comforting support, there was still a deep sadness in him, and it dampened any pleasure he might have derived from this sun-filled day, a day that ought to have felt like a deliverance.

■ ■ ■

As soon as he got up from the table he phoned Blonblon. After two weeks he was looking forward to seeing his friend again, but Monsieur Blondin told him that his son was spending a couple of days with his aunt in Oka.

Henri had already hurried into the living room to watch television, like a starving man rushing to a stack of warm doughnuts. Charles watched for a while, but was soon bored by the movie. Reading didn't settle him down, either. Céline called him into her room to look at the new way she had arranged her doll collection, but there too he found his mind wandering. He left the house and walked down the street, with Boff at his heels. There were children playing with trucks on the sidewalk, making throaty noises in imitation of a truck's engine. Monsieur Victoire's new dog, which looked like a cross between a spaniel and a salami, bounded towards him, hoping to be petted. Boff growled jealously and showed his teeth. A fight ensued. Charles pulled Boff off by his collar, and the two continued down the street at a rapid pace. Charles looked happily from side to side, glad to be back in his own neighbourhood. Soon he was striding down rue Ontario, looking into the shop windows. One of them had a display of magazines, including one that showed a pretty young woman in a bathing suit, presenting a lot of thigh and a come-hither smile that to Charles seemed laden with mysterious promise. It stopped him short. He suddenly felt a delicious disturbance in the crotch of his pants.

"When I grow up," he murmured to the dog, which was standing on its hind legs with its forepaws on the windowsill, apparently deriving as much pleasure from the magazine cover as Charles was, "that's the kind of wife I'm going to have."

The bulge in his pants was becoming more and more visible. Not wanting to attract attention to his condition, he resumed walking along the sidewalk.

As he walked, his sadness returned. It was a vague, amorphous feeling he couldn't quite get hold of, a sadness that seemed to have become a part of himself, as though he were the source of it. On the corner of rue Frontenac he saw the shabby brick building in which the lecherous hairdresser had his apartment. Surely Old Man Saint-Amour hadn't picked Charles at random from all the other kids in the neighbourhood? Father Beaucage must be right: there was something evil inside him. His reaction just now in front of that store window proved it. He would never be able to tell anyone about it. If his father had really been trying to kill him (as he most certainly had), wasn't it because he'd seen all too clearly that evil had taken over his life and that his death wouldn't have been a great loss to anyone? But then, rather than simply shrug it off, as he would easily have done if he were truly a bad person, he was filled with this ineffable sadness, which he couldn't shake off. Was this the way he was going to feel for the rest of his life?

He turned up a small side street, crossed it diagonally, and continued walking with great strides, hands in his pockets, looking back from time to time to make sure Boff was following. Before he realized where he was he found himself in front of his old daycare on rue Lalonde. The blinds were drawn; it looked as though the building were empty, perhaps even unoccupied. Had Catherine closed up for the summer?

He went up to the building and listened. When he was certain there was no one inside, he pushed open the gate to the play area, walked along the side of the building and into the yard. There had been a lot of changes since his day. Now a cedar hedge surrounded the yard, and a splendid red and blue slide had been set up where the old sandbox had been. The sandbox was now under the old cherry tree, right above the spot where the little yellow dog was resting. Charles went over and sat down in it, thrust his hands into the sand, and watched Boff, who had found a white cardboard box that must have contained either pastries or sandwiches. Excited by the lingering odour, Boff was assiduously tearing the box to shreds; a square of waxed paper flew out and was caught in the wind, and a few doughnut crumbs dropped from it, which the dog lapped up carefully.

With his hands still buried in the sand, Charles thought of the little yellow dog. He'd only known it for a few hours, but during that time the evil inside him had not raised its ugly, black head, not even for a second. On the contrary, it was good that had directed his actions. He'd done everything he could to save the poor animal, almost to the point of getting into trouble for it. In fact, looking at it more closely and taking into account his age at the time, he had acted like a hero. He may not have saved the dog's life, but the animal must surely have sensed, as all dogs seemed to, that it had been surrounded by love and compassion. Surely, as a result, its death had been less painful than if they had left it outside to freeze all alone in the snowstorm?

A simple enough thought, but it brought Charles much comfort. He went on watching Boff and letting the sand trickle slowly through his fingers; the dog had torn the box into a thousand pieces, as though trying to conjure up more doughnut crumbs in the debris.

If Charles could show so much sympathy for a small, stray dog he had just met for the first time, it must be because he had simply wanted to be good that day; and there was nothing to stop him from wanting to be good again, as often as he pleased. Wouldn't that show that bloody-minded priest that he wasn't always a bad influence? But here was the question, a serious one: How could he want to be good all the time?

The warm sand continued to run between his fingers. Boff had tired of his game and was lying on the shredded box, looking up at Charles, mouth open, tail thumping against the ground. No answer to his question came to him. The secret to wanting something remained a mystery. A person could be good and kind at certain moments, but how could he be sure he would always want to be that way? How could he tear the evil into tiny bits – as Boff had just done with the doughnut box – if the evil lived inside him, always on the look-out to push him into doing something wicked or dirty?

He was still reflecting on the matter and had managed to become almost as sad and dejected as he'd been when he first came into the yard, when a strangely sweet feeling began to well up inside him, a warm, soothing sensation, one that he had the distinct impression was coming from below, from under the sandbox. The yellow dog had awakened and was speaking to him, just as if he were a little boy himself. "Forget it," the voice was saying. "You'll drive yourself crazy with all these bizarre thoughts. Get out there and enjoy yourself. Your summer vacation is almost over, there'll be plenty of time to fret about good and evil later. I know you're a good person. In my whole life, no one had ever been as good to me as you were. Get all that stuff out of your head. You'll be much better off, believe me!"

"Come on, let's get out of here," Charles said to Boff, getting to his feet. "I've had enough of this place."

He leaned over and patted the sand above the little yellow dog, even blew it a kiss, and then left the yard. A few minutes later he was back on rue Ontario.

"I can't wait for Blonblon to get back from Oka," he said to his dog. "I always feel good when I'm with him."

A Kik Cola sign above a window ringed with multicoloured lights told him the place was a convenience store. He went inside, leaving a disconsolate Boff on the sidewalk, and stood in front of a rack of potato chips. After much deliberation he chose a bag of salt-and-vinegar chips and resumed his walk, Boff dancing around him with his mouth wide open. Charles toyed with him by wafting a large chip under the dog's nose, before giving it to him. His sadness lifted a bit. He was about to head back to rue Dufresne when the little yellow dog's words came back to him; turning around, he decided to go to rue Bercy to see Monsieur Michaud.

■ ■ ■

"Aha! A surprise visit!" said the notary, opening the door. "It's good to see you, Charles. What can I do for you today?"

Despite his unfeigned pleasure at seeing Charles again, there was a slight hesitation at being taken from his work, and Charles sensed it; a low murmur of voices coming from the office confirmed this. Charles demurred.

"Is . . . is your wife at home?"

"You want to see Amélie? I think she's taking a nap. But hang on, I'll go see if she's ready to get up."

"No, no! Don't wake her. I'll come back some other time."

"Who is it?" a languid voice called from the end of the hall.

"It's Charles, Amélie. Back from his summer camp. He's come to see you," he added, despite Charles's frantic signals.

There was a long silence, then the voice again, sounding slightly stronger and even showing signs of renewed vigour: "Tell him to wait in the living room. I'll join him in a few minutes."

Michaud leaned over and spoke into Charles's ear: "Fernand has told me what happened at camp. Saints preserve us, you're a holy terror, you are! You're like a hero in some novel!"

Charles smiled a little confusedly. Passing the open door of the notary's office, he had time to see that there were two large men in it, both with brown hair and wearing brown tweed suits. They looked like two enormous bran muffins, and Charles wondered if they were twins. He felt uncomfortable in the dark, solemn furnishings of the living room. He sat on a sofa, sorry that he'd come. The notary had closed his office door, and from the room came sounds of a lively conversation.

"Peanuts?" one of the large men was saying, angrily. "*Peanuts?*"

Charles crossed his legs, uncrossed them, let out a sigh, then got up and went to the window. An old man was waiting at the bus stop. His long, thin body and sallow skin reminded Charles of a banana. His cheeks sagged, his chin stuck out, and his small, black, enigmatic eyes darted back and forth like a squirrel's; his whole expression was haggard and austere: "He's sad, too," Charles said to himself. "The older you get, the sadder you become. But Fernand and Lucie aren't sad, at least not very often. I wonder how they manage it?"

He sat down again and occupied his mind by trying to count the record albums piled on a table between two large speakers at the far end of the room. Suddenly he felt his old facial tic coming back and, furious with it, he placed both hands on either side of his jaw and pressed as hard as he could.

It was at this moment that Amélie came into the room. She was wearing a pale green dressing gown and, on her head, a turban of the same colour.

"Do you have a toothache?" she asked.

"No," Charles replied, turning deep red. "I mean yes . . . a bit."

She smiled and ran her fingers through his hair.

"You're sweet," she said. "Even when you're lying."

Charles was taken aback but was not particularly upset at having been so easily unmasked. Amélie's frankness even put him at ease. The notary's wife sat across from him and stretched out a foot on which dangled a pretty slipper made of long, white fur. It looked a bit like a small cat.

"I have a tic," he finally confessed. "Sometimes when I get nervous my mouth opens and closes without my wanting it to. But it's gone now."

"Lots of people have tics," Amélie said. "They go away eventually, you know. But you have to find the right medicine. Have you had it long?"

"Long enough, yes."

His lips tightened and he looked away, his face as closed as a door. He hadn't the slightest intention of telling her the first time his fish-face had appeared, because it would mean talking about the night his father had tried to kill him.

"Everyone has their problems," she said, diplomatically changing he subject. "For the past few months it's been my kidneys. Sometimes after eating I get such a pain . . . it's like someone stuck a soldering iron in my back . . . I went to see someone about it, and now it's not so bad."

She pressed her feet together and her slippers merged into a single ball of immaculate white fur.

"Why did you want to see me, Charles?"

He looked worried for a moment, then he smiled and looked at her. "I wanted you to take me into the Christmas room again. Last time you said if I ever wanted to come back, I could."

She nodded gravely, straightening a fold in her robe. "Are you sad?"

Charles nodded.

"Do you mind if I ask why?"

"It's new," said Charles. "I've never felt anything like it before. I can't explain it. It's too complicated . . . Anyway, I thought if I came here and saw your Christmas tree and all the nice decorations you put up in your room, and there's the music, too, and the lights . . . I thought it might make me feel a bit better."

Amélie stood up slowly. "Of course it will, Charles" – she went over to him and ruffled his hair again – "but it won't cure you of your sadness, you know. It'll only make it better for a while. But that's better than nothing, isn't it?"

She motioned to him to follow her, and together they left the room. Joy surged through Amélie's soul, chasing away the beginning of a headache that had been gnawing at her temples. After all these years, she had finally found a kindred spirit!

They crossed the kitchen, walked down the narrow hall and stopped at the blue door. "Stay as long as you like, dear," she said softly. "The switch is on the right as you go in. Come and see me when you're done. I'll fix you a snack."

She gave him a smile of complicity and tiptoed furtively down the hall.

■　■　■

Charles opened the door and switched on the light. The room filled with a soft, orange-pink glow. The tree was circled by strings of lights and garlands, and beautiful wooden figurines began winking softly. The music box started tinkling the chords of "Silent Night," and they were soon accompanied by the strains of a children's choir. The air was redolent of pine resin, cinnamon and chocolate. Beside the tree, a life-sized Santa Claus surrounded by wrapped and beribboned gifts smiled at him mischievously, his rosy-red cheeks powdered with snow.

Charles looked in wonder about the room: icicles and garlands everywhere, Christmas scenes hanging from the walls, and strewn here and there were little hills of cotton batting on which reclined bears, dogs, cats, tiny reindeer, and even a raccoon! He sat down in a rocking chair that was covered in a bearskin. Near at hand was a candy dish on a small, gilded table.

He contemplated the Christmas tree, which appeared to be shimmering under the glittering play of coloured light. A sigh of contentment escaped his lips. He lay back in the rocking chair, stunned by the strangeness of it all, his limbs turned to lead; he was astonished and overwhelmed by the many delicious sensations that had invaded him, and he began sucking on a candy with a beatific smile.

Once again he remembered the marvellous Christmas when he was three years old. Alice had come into his room to waken him gently. The apartment

299

was filled with the smell of tourtière. On the radio a choir was singing "O Come All Ye Faithful" and it seemed to him that the apartment was floating in the air among the twinkling stars. His father was waiting for him in the kitchen. He had a beer in front of him, but his eyes were clear and sparkling with good humour. He took Charles in his arms and lifted him high in the air, laughing, then carried him into the living room, where Charles ran to the pile of gifts with squeals of joy. His parents had given him four presents that Christmas, and he would remember each of them for the rest of his life: the firetruck with its revolving, flashing light; a huge, yellow, metal bulldozer, massive and indestructible; a colouring book and a box of wax crayons – and Simon the Bear, whose cheerful, adorable face looked up at him from the crumpled, golden wrapping paper.

He remained motionless in the rocking chair for a long time, remembering and reflecting as Christmas carol after Christmas carol floated in the air, along with the brightly coloured figurines on the Christmas tree, which twinkled so welcomingly in the orange half-light.

An hour later, when he left the Christmas room, his face was relaxed and content. A truth had come to him in the room; he wouldn't have been able to articulate it, because it had come to him in a confused and fragmentary way. He had come to understand that life, despite its reversals and deceptions, also held joys for those who took the trouble to look for them. They were modest joys, to be sure, but sweet, and instead of waiting around for Great Happiness to descend on him, which it probably never would, he must learn to appreciate the small pleasures, which were always close to hand.

He'd also discovered that a person could be both sad and happy at the same time: sad at the very centre of your being, but happy everywhere else. Sometimes the core of sadness that you carried inside you shrank until it was almost imperceptible. And sometimes it could disappear altogether for hours or even days. But in the end it always came back. The important thing was always to make sure it was surrounded by a cushion of joy.

He understood now that his sadness would be with him forever, and that he'd better get used to it being there. There was no other way to go on.

Acting on some curious impulse, Amélie had made him pancakes with maple syrup. He devoured four of them, not worried for a second about ruining his appetite for supper.

27

For the first few days after Charles and Henri had left to go to summer camp, Blonblon had thought he would die of boredom. Deprived of the company of his friends, he soon grew tired of watching insipid television programs. Monsieur Blondin began to find his son's enforced leisure weighing heavily on both of them, and he suggested that he start a small business, repairing broken household objects: toys, toasters, flashlights, porcelain, the sort of things that were broken and not too difficult to repair that people keep around in the vague hope that someday somebody would come along and fix them.

His first field of operation was, of course, his own apartment. Then a friend of Monsieur Blondin came over for a visit and saw his son at work. Struck by the boy's ability and resourcefulness, he brought over an iron that needed fixing, as well as a kitchen garbage pail whose lid no longer came up when he stepped on the pedal, and an old ceramic spoon that had suffered a fatal fall. Blonblon had them fixed in no time. The neighbour mentioned it to the superintendent who, out of curiosity, brought Blonblon an old electric kettle and fourteen fragments of a plate on which there was a coloured photograph of Cardinal Léger, aspergillum in hand, blessing the Berri-de Montigny station on the day the metro opened. Blonblon fixed them all.

Someone suggested he put a notice on the bulletin board in the building's foyer. Through word of mouth and the good graces of the superintendent, news of Blonblon's growing expertise spread rapidly. He rarely gave up on a project. Two or three times a day someone would drop off some hopelessly mangled object or other on its way to the dumpster, and Blonblon almost always managed to save its life.

The days passed quickly, and the top drawer of Blonblon's dresser filled nicely with change and bills. Monsieur Blondin was able to relax and concentrate on his work, which was telemarketing and selling mail-order stamps.

With the return of Charles and Henri, Blonblon's workshop activities slackened and threatened to stop altogether. But Blonblon had grown so fond of the work, which blended so well with the talents as a conciliator for which he was so admired at school, that he kept up his business by working at it for an hour or two each morning, long enough to hang on to a good part of his clientele.

One afternoon, shortly before it was time to go back to school, Charles dropped into Blonblon's workshop. After a lengthy, tortuous preamble, which had him in a sweat and almost brought on an attack of the fish-face, he finally managed to blurt out his revelation.

Blonblon listened attentively to the twisting thread of Charles's words, stammered out in a hushed voice, then gave a horrified gasp.

"That's not true . . . You're kidding me, right?"

Charles shook his head. "No. It's as true as your father sits in a wheelchair."

Charles had decided to share with someone the secret of his terrible mis-adventure with Monsieur Saint-Amour, in the hope that doing so would diminish the black weight that pressed so heavily on his chest. And he knew that the someone had to be Blonblon.

"He got you drunk, the old pervert?"

"He gave me something really strong to drink, and really sweet, and it pretty much knocked me out. I'd already had a beer before that," he added bravely.

And he recounted the story of his meeting Sylvie Langlois and her awful friend in the restaurant.

"Poor Charles," murmured Blonblon, as though his friend had just given up the ghost and he was launching into a speech at his funeral. "You must have suffered so much . . . Why didn't you tell me about this before?"

He put a comforting hand on Charles's shoulder.

"That guy in the restaurant," he went on. "He wasn't much better, giving you a beer like that."

Charles looked down. "I didn't have to take it."

"Maybe not. But there's no way you could have known what would happen."

Blonblon turned back to his work table, on which lay fragments of a vase that had already been prepared with glue and were awaiting reassembly. He picked up two pieces and fit them precisely together.

"Blonblon," said Charles, his voice shaking with anxiety, "don't tell anyone about this, okay? Especially not Henri. Promise?"

"You didn't even have to ask," his friend replied calmly.

"No one in the whole world but you knows about it. No one."

Blonblon took one of the shards of the vase and made a tiny cut in his forearm. He squeezed his skin and a large drop of blood fell on the table: he pressed his thumb onto the drop.

"I swear on my own blood. Is that good enough?"

"Good enough," said Charles, with a faint smile.

Blonblon applied a small piece of paper towel to his cut and wiped the table off with a cloth, then, after thinking for a moment, said, "We have to report him to the police, Charles. He needs to be punished. You can't be the only kid he's lured into his apartment, and you certainly won't be the last! I've never liked the look of the old pig, and now I know why."

He went back to working on the vase.

Charles kept his eye on his friend's forearm. Despite the piece of paper, the blood was still flowing lightly, although Blonblon appeared to be unaware of it. He knew that although Blonblon was pretending to be absorbed in fixing the vase, it was just to make Charles feel more at ease, and to show him that, disgusting as his story had been, it didn't make any difference to the high opinion in which he was held. And for this Charles was extremely grateful.

"I don't want to report him," Charles said after a while.

He explained that if they told the police and the police arrested Monsieur Saint-Amour, he would be brought before a judge. There would be a trial, and Charles would have to appear as a witness. Then everyone would know that when he met Monsieur Saint-Amour he was already drunk. And he didn't want anyone to know that.

"Okay, then we have to do something else," said Blonblon. "I don't know what we could do, though," he added.

The vase was standing on the table in one piece. Blonblon turned it around with a slight frown of dissatisfaction; one of the cracks was still more visible than he would have liked. It was like a crack in his reputation.

"I'll let the glue set for a while, and then I'll go over the crack with a wax crayon. That should hide it."

"I know what we can do," Charles said, as though he hadn't heard his friend's words.

Blonblon looked at him.

"I'm going to get my revenge. I've been thinking about it for a long time. But I need your help. If I don't get even with him, I'll always have this on my conscience."

The familiar sound of rolling in the hallway told them that Blonblon's father had finished his nap. They decided to continue their conversation outside.

■ ■ ■

Two days later, at about seven o'clock in the evening, while Monsieur Saint-Amour was walking down rue Ontario, fanning himself with a folded newspaper – the evening air was so cool after the blistering hot afternoon – he saw Charles and Blonblon leaning against the window of Chez Robert; both boys were smiling broadly at him.

This was the third time in two days he'd run into them, and their behaviour had not been without interest. At first he'd thought they were mocking him, and a huge shiver had trickled down his spine and into his soft, fat thighs. The second time, doubt had crept into his mind. They sounded so friendly, the way they said, "Good evening, Monsieur Saint-Amour," and they had even waved to him.

This time there could be no doubt: the two boys were making a point of greeting him. Could it be that the little blond one, the one he had always thought of as mean and vicious, had somehow seduced the other, and now both of them were making advances to him?

If so, he would have to be extremely careful. He would have to exercise the same caution that, so far during his twenty-eight years as an adventurer, had kept him from suffering any of the usual consequences associated with his penchant for little boys. The sacrifices he had had to make, he thought, in order to appear as though he were conforming to the stupid moral code invented by hypocrites who would not hesitate for a moment to take their own pleasures where they found them, so long as no one was looking.

So again he contented himself with passing the two boys, nodding casually to them and continuing on his way as though nothing unusual were in the air.

But once he was home, he began to be haunted by delicious images. He planted himself before the television, but no matter how hard he tried to concentrate on Andréanne Lafond's interview with cabinet minister Camille Laurin, it was as though the program were being broadcast in Chinese. How pleasant it would be to have two young boys here at the same time! Nothing like that had happened to him in such a long, long time!

He clicked off the television, turned off all the lights and went over to look out the window. Then he left the apartment and walked down the street, keeping his eyes peeled. But he was too late. The little dears were probably long in their beds, curled up like kittens. He decided to follow their example. After a good night's rest he got up early, feeling refreshed and full of energy, with a clear head and eager to see what the day held in store. Such a morning always boded well, he thought, for a day full of pleasant surprises. He decided to have breakfast at Chez Robert and read the newspapers.

Rosalie was her usual considerate self. She gave him an extra-large portion of her homemade strawberry jam, which he ate on toast dripping with warm butter, and washed down with three cups of freshly brewed coffee. When he left the restaurant he felt strong enough to knock down Montreal and build it up again in a single day. The cloudless sky was such a clear blue that it made him wish he could turn into a bird and fly off and never come back. The sun was already beginning to make itself felt, but was still well within the bounds of politeness. He bought himself three pairs of boxer shorts at Woolworth's, stopped at the grocery store for his twice-weekly brick of butterscotch ice cream, took it back to his apartment, then decided to go for a little stroll in Stewart Park; he had sometimes seen Charles and his friends playing there on the teeter-totters or chasing one another around the public washrooms; but the only people there today were two mothers with their babies and an old rubbie snoring on the grass, as though lulled to sleep by the incessant hum of the Macdonald's Tobacco plant just down the street. He walked back towards rue Ontario, slightly surprised at not having seen the boys again. All this coming and going had made him thirsty, so he went back into Woolworth's and ordered a large glass of iced tea at the lunch counter.

"How's it going this morning, Monsieur Saint-Amour?" asked Berthe the waitress, a nice girl, if a bit thick, with whom he chatted from time to time.

"Not too bad," he replied, "if you don't count all the problems."

She stopped and gave him an admiring look: "Ah, if only everyone was intelligent like you, Monsieur Saint-Amour, life would be a lot easier . . ."

He left the dimestore and headed towards Chez Robert. A car passed so close to the curb that he felt its wind, and a piece of crumpled paper swept along and became entangled in his feet. For some obscure reason it merely added to his good spirits.

There was no one standing in front of the restaurant, and a quick glance through the window told him that neither of the boys was inside, either. He was used to these periods of waiting, when desire raced inside his ribcage like a demented squirrel, making the days seem endless. But what could he do but wait? To do anything to hasten matters was far too dangerous. There were times when he'd permitted himself a furtive shake of the branch to dislodge a fruit that seemed almost ripe for the plucking, but oh, the anxiety it had cost him! "I'll go home and wash the dishes, straighten up the apartment," he decided. "That'll help pass the time. Then I'll come back after dinner."

Two big black men were walking down the sidewalk carrying a case of beer between them, their faces lit up with delight. As they passed, one of them said to him: "Hot day, ain't it, gramps?" and patted him on the shoulder. The familiarity made him recoil. What did they think he was, senile? He went on walking, then suddenly smiled. When you thought about it, being taken for a senile old man could be an advantage. No one paid any attention to senile old men, which allowed them to do more or less what they pleased.

When he arrived at his apartment building, something in the air – a certain fluttering in the street lamp? the distant sound of a locomotive? the slight squeak coming from his left shoe? – told him that he was in for an agreeable adventure. With one foot on the sidewalk and the other on the cement step that led up to his porch, he was just slipping his key into the lock when his eye was drawn into the alley that ran along the side of the building. There he saw the two boys, the blond one and, coming out behind him, Charles, both smiling impishly.

"Hello, Monsieur Saint-Amour," they both said in unison.

They stopped a few feet from where he was standing.

"Well, well, you two again?" he said, his heart leaping and pounding in his chest. "Goodness gracious me," he added. "Anyone would think you were following me."

Charles and his companion exchanged glances, then Charles said with a nervous edge: "We're not following you, but it's always nice to run into you."

"Especially now," added Blonblon.

"Oh?" said the hairdresser, struggling to keep his voice from trembling. "And why is that?"

"We could discuss it down there," said Blonblon, indicating the alley.

The old man scrutinized their faces. The boys smiled and held his gaze without batting an eye. There was something deliberate about their attitude, some tension that awakened the old caution in him. Everything seemed too easy. But all the same it had not escaped his notice that for several years now changes had taken place in society that never ceased to amaze him. Was it the influence of television? The arrival of all those airplanes full of immigrants? The declining influence of the clergy, who no longer seemed able to attract any but the elderly into their churches? So many divorces, and people living together in sin. Who knew? People let themselves go more, didn't seem to be so worried about appearances. It amazed him, and made him sorry he was no longer a young man.

He put his key in his pocket and stepped down onto the sidewalk. "Fine, let's go," he said. "But I don't have a lot of time. We'll have to make it quick."

He walked the few steps into the alley and stopped by a fence of large, grey planks whose lower edges were eaten ragged by rot. Behind the fence rose a tall, brick building with blank windows, an old factory turned into a warehouse. Across from it were the backs of a row of tenements. No one was at their windows, or out on their balconies. They could talk in private.

"So, what's this about?" he said. "What can I do for you, my friends?" He was trying to strike a breezy tone, but the quiver in his voice made him sound pathetic.

Again the boys exchanged a look, then broke into nervous laughter. Of the two, the blond one seemed surer of himself. He joined his hands behind his back and promenaded back and forth staring boldly at the old man.

"You know what we want," he said.

And he gave his companion a light punch of complicity.

"We've got some wieners to sell you," said Charles, his cheeks reddening as he uttered the forbidden phrase.

Monsieur Saint-Amour hid the trembling in his hands by thrusting them deep into his pockets. Praise the Lord and pass the ammunition! The table was set for the feast, all he had to do was sit down and dig in. No supply problems. No pretence about what was really going on. Nothing to fork out but a little cash. It had been a long time since he'd run across two such resourceful children. It was refreshing! But the sudden change in Charles's attitude still surprised him. "It must be the other one who's leading him on," he told himself. "Everything is so simple with children."

"How much?" he asked, his voice heavy and hollow, like the hoot of an owl.

"Fifty bucks," said Charles.

"Ha!" cried the old man derisively.

"There's two," Blonblon pointed out. "That's why it's more expensive."

"I don't have that kind of money on me, boys. I wish I did, but I don't."

"Oh well, then, see you later," said Charles, turning away and motioning his friend to follow.

"Hold on, not so fast," cried Saint-Amour, alarmed.

The discussion continued. It went on for a long time without an agreement. A passing delivery truck interrupted them twice, obliging the old hairdresser to alter his demeanour to make their conversation look more innocent. Charles and Blonblon remained obstinate; the old man's face glistened with covetous sweat at the sight of two such graceful, young, male bodies, a sight that made him shiver to the ends of his fingers and plunged his mind into uncontrollable turmoil; he was almost quaking at the knees. Knowing they would win in the end, the two children refused to lower their price, watching with a cruel wisdom as the old man fell apart before their eyes.

Finally, Saint-Amour uttered a cry like a sob and gave in: "I have to go to the bank," he gasped. "Wait for me here."

"Oh, we can't do it today," Charles replied. "We'll come back tomorrow."

"Previous commitment, you know," added Blonblon in a tone that suggested their business was flourishing.

The old hairdresser's jaw dropped with disappointment; he felt as though someone had yanked him from the table just as he was about to plunge his fork into a big, juicy steak that had been sizzling under his nose.

"You're toying with me," he said sadly.

"No, we're not," Charles assured him. "I'll call you at ten o'clock tomorrow morning to tell you where to meet us. You can bring the money then."

"It'll have to be in my apartment," insisted Saint-Amour. "It's the best place."

"We're not keen on going into people's houses. Too risky."

"Don't worry, we won't cheat you," Blonblon said, leading him on. He swallowed, blushed delicately, then said: "We'll do whatever you want."

The old man smiled and his face lit up. Looking around nervously, he stepped forward and furtively stroked Blonblon's buttocks, then ran his hand lightly down Charles's back. Charles could not keep from recoiling ever so slightly.

"Still not broken in, eh?" said Saint-Amour, surprised. "You have done this before, haven't you?"

"I don't like to do it where people can see," said Charles almost under his breath.

"Okay, we'll call you tomorrow, Monsieur Saint-Amour!" Blonblon called as he pulled his friend away.

They were about to turn the corner when the old man called after them.

"Hey!" he shouted. "You're not going to trick me, are you?" And he shook his finger at them, all his misgivings having returned.

■ ■ ■

At six o'clock, unable to settle his thoughts sufficiently to prepare himself a meal, Saint-Amour decided to go out to a restaurant. Not Chez Robert, though, not in the state he was in, which he wouldn't be able to hide from Rosalie's perceptive gaze. He decided on a Greek restaurant a few blocks east of his apartment.

It was a dismal meal. They sat him next to a glass-fronted rotisserie, across from a man in his forties whose features were not just unrefined, but practically unformed, and who ate his food with gluttonous speed, his fingers glistening with grease. He pushed food onto his fork with his thumb, uttering little grunts of satisfaction. When his meal was finished he wiped his chin with his paper napkin, crumpled it up into a ball, and tossed it on his plate.

Saint-Amour looked away in disgust.

He was just cutting into a sort of moussaka when the rotisserie over his head shuddered violently and ten lit up, greasy chickens inside began rotating with funereal slowness. He stared at one of them; it was already beginning to drip. "That's me," he thought to himself. "That chicken is me."

309

His night was even worse. Hot and sticky, a night of sick insomnia, shapeless and eternal, each heavy second weighing on him like an anvil. A sudden shout, the growl of a passing bus, or the roar of a car sent horrible tremors coursing through his body. He tossed and turned in bed, his eyelids stinging, his member stiff and painful, his temples swollen, all his thoughts revolving around the next day's meeting, his distrust more active than ever, even though he knew he would go.

A thin, grey, dusty light slid into the room through the crack under the blind. He welcomed it joyfully and leapt from his bed. Minutes later he was walking down the street, his legs stiff with fatigue, his lungs heaving in the pure morning air. The two boys would still be sleeping. He imagined them stretched out on their beds in poses of abandonment, with nothing on but their shorts and that almost imperceptible smile children have when engulfed in peaceful sleep. He ached for them desperately. And yet at the same time he detested them. He hated himself as well, and the life of a sewer rat that his shameful passion had forced on him for the past thirty years.

By nine-twenty he was sitting beside his telephone, waiting for Charles to call. He stared at the instrument, glued to his chair, not daring to make the slightest movement for fear it might prevent the ringing that would sound to him like the call of a sweet, multicoloured bird. He'd left the back door partly open to let in a bit of fresh air, and a ray of sunshine streaked through the gaping fanlight straight into his left eye. When he closed it, a bright red curtain appeared, streaked with black and grey stripes. To pass the time he imagined himself standing inside his eyeball, before the huge, red curtain, staring at its many folds, trying to decipher the message hidden in the stripes. Suddenly they began to swim and intermingle, and Charles's face appeared, also red, his eyes closed, his mouth half open in a grimace. He shook his head, opened his eyes fearfully, and at that moment the telephone rang.

It wasn't Charles's voice, but Blonblon's. The meeting was to take place in an old shed. The boy described the place; it was at the end of an alley not far from Saint-Amour's apartment, beside a large, vacant lot filled with derelict cars.

"We'll expect you in half an hour. Do you have the money?"

"I have it, yes."

"There's a password."

"A password?"

"You have to say it loud, after knocking three times. If you don't, we won't open the door."

"All right."

"The word is *wiener*. You have to say *wiener*. Not hard to remember, eh?" And he hung up.

Minutes later, Saint-Amour was standing in the alley looking towards the shed. He was puffing, and his calves were running with sweat. The building, made of sheet metal with a flat roof, was quite large; it stood slightly to one side of the vacant lot, and appeared to have been abandoned. The area around it also seemed deserted, which he found reassuring. If something went wrong, it would be easy to sneak away undetected. He walked up and stopped before the battered metal door. A few blocks away he heard a jackhammer piercing the air with its incessant chattering. After a careful inspection of the alley, he knocked three times on the door. He thought he heard a slight stirring within. "What's that?" he wondered in alarm. He pressed his ear to the sheet metal. Small crackling sounds were running through the building's metal skin, which was sensitive to the slightest breath of wind. The ferocious attacks of the jack-hammer muffled everything in a thick paste. He shrugged, telling himself his nerves were playing tricks on him, knocked again three times, and, putting his hands to his mouth like a megaphone, called out loudly:

"Wiener!"

The door opened partway and a hand appeared in the crack.

"The money." It was Charles's voice.

Saint-Amour raised his eyebrows and backed away a step.

"The money comes later," he said.

"No. The money first or you don't get in."

The hand remained in place, imperious, fingers spread. A blob of grease glistened on the pink, fresh palm. The old man hesitated, suspecting a trap, but he was afraid of losing his prize now that he was so close.

"The money always comes after," he said stubbornly.

"Not with us. Don't worry. I won't close the door on you. You can come in as soon as you pay. Put your foot in the opening if you don't believe me," the boy added.

Still he hesitated, more suspicious than ever in the light of these bizarre, complicated precautions. But the first time with a new child often got off to a bad start, with mistrust and nervousness on both sides. Once the ice was broken, things fell into place.

"I'll pay you when I get inside," he said by way of compromise.

The hand was withdrawn and a brief consultation could be heard coming from within.

"All right. But get your money out now."

He took four ten-dollar bills from his wallet and rolled them into a tube (the fifth would only be added when everything had gone to his complete satisfaction). Then, after once again looking up and down the alley, he slid through the half-opened door and closed it behind him. For a few seconds everything was dark, and it felt like the shed was spinning about him.

"The money," Charles demanded, a bit breathlessly.

Saint-Amour groped about in the dark, touched a shoulder, and handed over the bills.

"Where's your friend? We need some light in here so we can see each other."

"I'm right here," replied Blonblon. "Come closer, I'll turn a light on."

The old hairdresser took two steps, his hands held out in front of him. Someone pushed him violently from behind. He let out a cry and fell into a sort of pit.

"Now!" Charles shouted.

He heard something heavy being slid across the floor and tried to struggle to his feet. He'd lost his glasses in the fall, and with his knees feeling half dislocated, swearing and trying to climb out of the pit, he suddenly found himself buried under an avalanche of soft, slimy objects that smelled faintly spicy. Flashlights played over him amid shouts, laughter, and taunts.

"Wieners for the old pig! Wieners for the old pig!" sang a group of small boys, who danced around the pit before his spinning, stupefied gaze. The fiercest among them was Henri, who shone the light directly into his eyes, blinding him, and then hit him two or three times on the head with the flashlight.

The next instant, the old man was alone. For a few seconds the sound of retreating footsteps pounded outside, punctuated from time to time by the distant shudder of the jackhammer. Saint-Amour remained motionless in the pit that had been carefully prepared for him, petrified with rage and terror, standing like a giant, wrinkled wiener himself, half buried in a pile of fresh frankfurters whose slightly sickening odour now filled the shed and which a man appearing from nowhere would shortly come to collect, wash off, and place back on his counter for resale.

■ ▨ ■

He stayed in bed for three days, unable to eat a thing. The smell of wieners clung to his skin and made him want to throw up. Once or twice he stretched out his hand to a bottle of Seven-Up on his bedside table and took a minuscule sip, eyes bulging, mouth askew, then issued a defeated sigh. The slightest sound made him sit up in bed in terror. The telephone rang once or twice. Each time he thought he would die. Summoning all his strength he managed to get up and take it off the hook. At night, through the partition separating his bedroom from the next apartment, he heard two youths erupting in great bursts of laughter. They were laughing at him, he was sure of it; if by some means he were to venture outside his building, the entire neighbourhood, the whole city, would turn and point their fingers at him, and keep them pointed until the police arrived.

Days passed. Then one night a truck pulled up in front of his door; he filled it with everything he had collected over the years, clambered inside the cab like a frog, and was never seen again.

28

That afternoon Roberto stood on the sidewalk in front of his restaurant staring up at his sign, rubbing his nose, and making faces for a good five minutes.

CHEZ ROBERT
CUISINE CANADIAN. CANADIAN FOOD
SPÉCIAUX DU JOUR. DAILY SPECIALS
METS POUR EMPORTER. TAKE-OUT MEALS
LICENCE COMPLÈTE. FULLY LICENSED

It was a good sign, metal, lit by two powerful spotlights. It had been through a good many seasons, been covered by God knew how many tons of pigeon and sparrow droppings, and had always given Roberto and Rosalie enough visibility to guarantee them a respectable living. But over the past two or three years he'd noticed that the sign's colours were beginning to lose their sharpness, with little pinpricks of rust showing through in a few places, and someone with a suspicious mind might possibly deduce from it that the bank account of the restaurant's owners was not as healthy as it might have been.

Roberto was looking at it with such rapt attention that an old rubbie in a Panama hat stopped beside him and began examining the sign himself. Then a young woman in lime-green shorts, apparently unconcerned about showing off her cellulite, also stopped to look. Then a delivery man in a red hardhat stopped on his way back to his truck with an armload of empty boxes and stood with his own nose pointed up into the air.

"Is there a problem?" the rubbie asked politely.

"No, sor," said Roberto, with a big smile. "I never have problems."

Whistling, he went back into the restaurant.

"Lili," he called out in his high tenor voice, "we're going to get a new sign."

Rosalie was wiping off the cash register with a chamois cloth. She looked up and frowned. "We are?" she said. "What for?"

"Because it's time, that's what for!"

The restaurant was completely empty, which allowed the couple to discuss the matter in private.

"That sign's in perfect shape. It'll last another three years at least, maybe more."

"Don't matter, Lili, the government's making us change it anyway: we can't have an English sign up any more, as you well know. I read about it inna paper. They passed a law last month. Now everythin's gotta be in French."

"Yeah, but not for five years. I read the papers, too, you know."

"It's all rusted out, come and look."

"I've looked. What are you talking about, rusted out? There's nothing wrong with that sign."

"Whaddaya mean nothin' wrong widdit? People're gonna take us for a coupla cheapsteaks on accounta that sign. The paint's stripped in at least a dozen places!"

"And what about your wallet, you want it stripped, too? Do you know how much a new sign would cost?"

"No, I don't, and neither do you. But we gotta change it to French, what else can we do? Minister Laurin explained it all the other night on TV, whatsa matter, you don't remember? We get what, maybe three English customers a month comin' into this place?"

"You think I'm an idiot or something. I know what you're up to."

"Oh you do, eh? What am I up to?"

"You want to change the name of the restaurant. You want Roberto up there, instead of Robert."

Roberto turned red in the face. He took three long strides to the cash and leaned his hands flat on the counter.

"That's not true! The restaurant's registered Chez Robert and it's gonna stay Chez Robert! You got rocks in your head!"

The discussion continued, becoming more and more lively. Rosalie let it be known that she thought her partner had come under the perfidious

315

influence of the Separatists. Roberto replied that she was an old stick-in-the-mud; if she kept on dragging her heels like that, he predicted, she'd find herself eating everyone else's dust. Rosalie returned that if he didn't give so much money to his daughter things might be different and they might be able to think about a new sign; but since he completely lost his head every time he laid eyes on her, they couldn't, and that was that. Roberto swore that he hadn't given her a penny for at least six months and he had no intention of giving her any more in the near future, now that his no-good son-in-law had finally found a job. Then he dropped a bombshell so big it took Rosalie completely by surprise.

"Listen, Lili, since a new sign has to be all in French, we can make the letters really big. That'll be more publicity for us, right?"

Defeated, Rosalie took refuge in a series of acidic grumblings, then decided to straighten things out under the counter, thus putting an end to their tête-à-tête.

Satisfied, Roberto poured himself a cup of coffee, and since there were still no customers in the restaurant, he sat down at a table with a piece of paper and a pencil and began redesigning the sign. After ten minutes of scribbling, he heaved a deep sigh, got up, paced up and down between the tables, and then went to the telephone. Several minutes later, Charles showed up carrying a dictionary and with such a serious expression on his face that Rosalie forgot her bad mood and nearly laughed out loud. Man and boy went straight to work, but Roberto soon had to go back to the kitchen. The official wording of the new sign wasn't finalized until the middle of the afternoon, at which time Charles tactfully pointed out to the cook that "cuisine familial" had an "*e*" at the end of it, and that, after diligent research that required several telephone calls, he had ascertained that "fully licensed" might be a source of profound mystery to certain tourists, and should be replaced with "wine, beer, and spirits."

"Thanks, Charlie," said the cook, handing him a five-dollar bill. "No, no, no! Go on, take it. See, it pays to get an education, atta boy!"

■ ■ ■

A period of peace and quiet now began in Charles's life. It was as though he had paid his dues and been granted his rightful share of happiness. His wounds healed slowly, and although they didn't disappear altogether, they no longer made him suffer. Lucie and Fernand, who had for a long time considered Charles their own son in spirit, now wanted to make him their son in fact. To do that, however, required either the consent of his natural father or the removal of Wilfrid's parental rights. The carpenter was still sending his meagre pittance from up north. Fernand asked Lucie, who had "been taught to write by the nuns," if she would compose a "diplomatic" letter to convince Wilfrid of the numerous benefits that a stable life would bring to Charles. They worked on the letter together for three nights, their discussions sometimes rising to tumultuous heights, before handing the text over to the notary, who said it was an excellent letter but needed a touch-up here and there, and then reworded it from top to bottom. Finally the letter, along with its burden of hopes and fears, was sent off to James Bay.

Nothing was heard from Thibodeau for several weeks. Then one afternoon, while Fernand was busy arranging for the very lucrative sale of twenty-seven brass doorknobs and locks, the carpenter phoned the store. After a long preamble involving a detailed comparison of the weather in James Bay and Montreal, Thibodeau finally declared that their letter "gave me quite a shock, there, eh?" considering that Charles was "my only kid," but that what they suggested "could turn out to be good for the boy in the long run," and he had "given their proposal a lot of thought." In any case, he said, he was planning to move back to Montreal in a year or two, maybe sooner, and maybe they could discuss the matter then, "face to face like"; in the meantime, he thanked Fernand and Lucie for taking such good care of his son, and assured them that he "wouldn't forget their kindness."

"I didn't like his tone," grumbled Fernand that night when he told Lucie about their conversation. "I've never heard him speak like that before. It's like he's gone into one of those religious sects that suck out your brains as well as your wallet. Or maybe he's just a hypocrite. He's trying to sell his son for as much as he can get out of us."

"Or worse, Fernand: he's thinking of taking the boy back."

"I'd like to see him try! It'll be over my dead body, and I'll have the law on my side, too!"

Purged of all rancour by his two acts of vengeance over the summer, and covered in glory by news of Monsieur Saint-Amour's flight – which caused a sensation in the neighbourhood and explained to many people the old man's queer behaviour – Charles knew nothing of the negotiations between

317

his adoptive parents and his father. He was happy just growing up and leading the life of a young boy, eating enough for four, devouring books by the dozen, throwing himself into the Machiavellian intrigues of the schoolyard, where his reputation as a tough devil-may-care was supplanting that of Henri, and getting the best marks of his entire school career. With a few other friends he founded a newspaper, *The Five B* (his homeroom number), of which he was the publisher, editor, and proofreader. With ideas as original as its typography, the bi-monthly publication garnered praise from the parish priest as well as from the head of the local school board. Charles didn't let his success go to his head, however, and always reacted to such elegies with a calm modesty, saying he and his team still had a long way to go before they could take on the city's two major newspapers, *La Presse* and *Le Devoir*.

In a shrewd editorial about the fighting that often went on at school, he wrote these lines:

The big problem is that those who are weak are often mistaken for cowards. In my view, however, courage is not to be found in muscles, but in the head. It takes as much courage, maybe even more, to tell someone what you think of them when you know they're not going to like it, than it does to punch out a kid who is getting on your nerves, especially when that kid is smaller than you.

For his eleventh birthday, Parfait Michaud gave him an unabridged edition of *The Three Musketeers*; Charles read it in five days, to the detriment of his sleep and of an English assignment, which somehow was incomprehensible gibberish when it was handed in (to the stupefaction of his teacher, Madame Ouimet).

Blonblon was still his best friend and confidant – Henri had to content himself with being entrusted with only second-rank secrets – and only he knew the full extent of the fear and aversion Charles felt for his father, as well as of the first timid, astonishing, almost shameful flutterings of emotion he had been feeling towards Céline for quite some time.

She had celebrated her ninth birthday at the end of August and for some inexplicable reason Charles suddenly began to see that she was no longer a little girl; something other than the somewhat disinterested tenderness he'd felt for her until that moment came waltzing into his awareness. The warm, tender looks she sometimes gave him, slightly puckering her lips as though to prevent the tip of her tongue from appearing between them; the special way she had of smiling as she rubbed his arm; the silly, nervous laugh he always gave when she said something funny; all that seemed to have built a small nest in his brain, where her image shimmered softly in a delicate, shadowy light.

One evening he went into the bathroom without thinking and surprised her; she was standing naked, her bum pink and chubby, examining her breasts in the full-length mirror. He laughed at her and left, closing the door behind him, but for quite a few minutes he felt his heart racing in his chest.

There were other incidents, each one seemingly insignificant but added up giving him the sense that his life, or at least the version of it he thought he knew, was on the verge of being transformed into something totally new and of which he had only the most confused idea, as though he had advanced so far along a darkened corridor and suddenly come up against a closed door. He could sense that on the other side of the door was an immense room, and a thin line of light at his feet told him something was shining brightly on the other side, something that made his whole body quiver.

One of these incidents made a deep impression on him.

■　■　■

One night at about eleven o'clock, while he was surreptitiously reading a book in bed with his flashlight, he heard moans coming from Fernand and Lucie's bedroom, across the corridor. He recognized Lucie's voice; she sounded as though she were in great pain, but at the same time something him told him she was not suffering at all, far from it. He listened, partly out of anxiety but also with keen interest, with the confused awareness that Lucie was not merely a mother but was something else as well, something people outside the family called a woman – with all the restrictions, attractions, and mystery that went with the term. He felt as though he were being cheated, or having something torn away that had for a long time been a vital part of him. The moaning continued, joined now by squeaks from the bed, sharp gasps and truncated words mumbled in rapid succession (he now recognized Fernand's voice). Then once again there was silence.

He turned off his flashlight, put his book on the floor, and curled up into a ball with his hands between his legs, holding his rigid, pulsating penis as tightly as he could manage. All the dirty stories he had ever heard, all the risqué jokes murmured to him with suppressed giggling or told boldly in front of everyone, ran through his head; only now they took on a clarity and a reality that was totally new to him. Staring wide-eyed off into the darkness he smiled broadly at all his friends at Saint-Anselme Elementary.

■ ■ ■

Eight months went by. It was the beginning of the summer of 1978. Charles was sitting in a chair facing Parfait Michaud's desk, wondering why the notary had asked him to drop by.

"Charles, old chum," Michaud began slowly, folding his long fingers together and leaning his elbows on the desk. Then he stopped and gave a small smile: "Sorry about the alliteration, but it is nonetheless true that you are a dear friend. You know that, of course. Anyway, Charles, old chum, you have just completed your fifth year at school and completed it in grand style, I must say. You performed brilliantly in the school play last Tuesday. You are a handsome young man, well muscled, your mind is ever expanding and exploring..."

He stopped again and frowned slightly, becoming emotional.

"... and I consider it one of the luckiest days of my life when you came to me for advice, when was it, two years ago now?"

"Thank you, Monsieur Michaud," Charles said, smiling. "It's very nice of you to say that."

"I say it because I mean it!" replied the notary with perhaps more force than he had intended. He pushed the candy dish towards Charles. "Please help yourself. They're called Mocca Delights. Have you started drinking coffee yet, Charles?"

"Lucie doesn't want me to. She says I'm enough of a bundle of nerves already."

Charles slowly unwrapped the cellophane from the candy and slipped it into his mouth, letting it roll around in the saliva for a while before speaking, forcing his voice to sound casual. "So what is it you wanted to speak to me about, Monsieur Michaud?"

"It was Fernand who asked me to see you."

"I know. He told me earlier."

"It's about your father."

Charles abruptly stopped sucking on the candy. His face went pale.

"What does he want?"

"Fernand wanted me to talk to you first because he thinks, however misguidedly, that my training as a notary will allow me to explain things more clearly and dispassionately than he could. Don't worry, Charles," he added when he saw Charles fidgeting in his chair, "I didn't call you in here to give you bad news. Everything will work out just as you want it to. Fernand and Lucie love you very much and consider you as their own child. You know that as well as I do, in fact better than I do."

"What does my father want?" Charles repeated in a subdued voice.

Michaud decided to take a candy himself, to ease the tension in the room. Like Charles, he let it melt in his mouth, while trying to assume an unconcerned air.

"Your father and Fernand have been in negotiation for some time now," he said finally. "Are you aware of that?"

Charles shook his head.

"It's about your adoption. Fernand and Lucie want to adopt you. But your father is dragging his feet."

"He's not my father any more."

"I understand what you're saying. But in the eyes of the law, he is still your father. That is what Fernand and Lucie want to change. In order to do that, we have to obtain the written consent of . . . Monsieur Thibodeau. Or else we have to convince a judge to revoke his paternal rights. Do you follow me?"

"Why won't he sign the paper?"

"Well, we're not sure. He hasn't exactly refused to sign, but he hesitates, he dawdles, he asks for more time to think about it, then more time, then more time again."

Michaud gave a sudden start, as though the candy had just caught in his throat.

"Two days ago," he continued, "he told Fernand that he was returning to Montreal at the end of the summer."

Charles jumped to his feet and, in a strangled voice, cried out angrily: "I will not live with him! Never! I'll run away first! I'll hide somewhere where no one will ever find me!"

Boff, confined to the vestibule because of Amélie's allergies, felt the need to support his young master by barking frantically.

"What in the world is going on?" Amélie could be heard asking as she marched down the hall.

"Nothing, nothing at all, my dear. Charles and I are discussing business, that's all."

Amélie's head appeared in the half-opened doorway, her ever-present turban above her dripping wet hair.

"It looks like pretty serious business to me," she said sternly after giving her husband, and then Charles, a long look.

"Sometimes business does get serious, as you well know. If it didn't, no one would need lawyers. Go dry your hair, my love, before you catch cold. And you, Charles, go out and calm down your dog before he shatters the windowpanes."

"If he tries to bamboozle you, come and see me," said Amélie, winking at Charles before disappearing down the hall.

Charles came back very soon. One word from him had been enough to calm Boff down, and the dog now lay sheepishly curled up into a ball, its nose between its paws.

"What is it you're trying to tell me?" he asked, his hands on his hips. "That I have to go back to live with my father?"

"No, not at all. There's never been a question of that. That would be irresponsible on our part after . . . what happened. Sit still and listen to me calmly, Charles, please. You're old enough that I can speak frankly to you. Some of the things your father said made Fernand suspect that he wanted to . . . hmmm . . . how can I put this? – sell his permission. Do you understand? It's as though he wanted to . . . well . . . in a way . . . get as much for you as he possibly could. This is only a hypothesis, mind you," he corrected himself, seeing the change in Charles's face, "one hypothesis among many others. It's always hard to figure out what someone else is thinking, isn't it? Another hypothesis, which has also been suggested by some of your father's remarks, is that he's become involved in some sort of religious sect that has managed to turn his mind into a complete muddle, as some sects know very well how to do. They may have convinced him that he must climb some sort of ladder to holiness (that's the kind of expression they use), and that in order to do so he must take you back to live with him, as God has ordained. Do you follow all this? But I repeat, these are only suppositions, nothing more . . . It could be one of these, or it could be something completely different. We won't really know what's going on in his head until we talk to him in person. All we know now is that the whole thing is a bit complicated. Either we have to grease the man's palm in order to get him to sign the paper, or else we have to go to trial to have him declared incompetent as a father. Either way it's going to cost money. But one thing that you can do right now, because we probably won't be able to prevent it from happening, is for you to go into court and tell a judge about the kind of treatment he subjected you to, and also about that . . . famous night . . . Sylvie will have to appear as well, of course, since she's our only witness. You will both be questioned, and your testimonies will be compared, and after that . . . I know it won't be very pleasant for you, but we will all be at your side. At any rate, Charles, that is why I asked you to come here, and what Fernand and Lucie couldn't bring themselves to say to you, even though as far as I'm concerned they're as capable of saying it as I am."

Charles's face had darkened and he was staring at the tips of his shoes in silence. The candy he was sucking had suddenly lost its flavour and was sticking to the roof of his mouth. If he could, he'd have spat it out on the rug. Suddenly, under the startled gaze of the notary, he pursed his lips tightly and pressed his cheeks between his hands. The fish-face was trying to reappear. He jumped up from his chair and ran towards the door. A few seconds later he was fleeing madly down the street, with Boff at his heels.

■ ■ ■

When he got home he went straight to his room and sat down on the bed for several moments, waiting; his fish-face had gone, no doubt to wreak its havoc somewhere else. Feeling better, he leaned his chin on his hands and, under the anxious gaze of the dog, which was lying in the middle of the room, tried to think. It wasn't easy. All kinds of thoughts tumbled painfully into one another in his head. First there was all that money he'd have to come up with in order to escape from his father (this brought back his father's face from that horrid night, with its haggard, blood-shot eyes and menacing, twitching, foam-flecked mouth). In his bank account there were only three hundred and fifty-two dollars. A lot for an eleven-year-old, but not nearly enough to settle a problem of this magnitude. Who would pay the bill?

Something Fernand had said one night during dinner came to mind. It had been a few weeks back, and at the time he hadn't paid much attention. Fernand had been complaining about a decline in sales since the beginning of the year. The brief spurt of business brought in by the Olympic Games in 1976 was long over, he'd said, unemployment was going up everywhere you looked, customers were so reluctant to spend money you practically had to pay them to buy anything. And as if that weren't enough, there was that goldarned RONA store that had just opened on rue Ontario, almost at his doorstep, making things even worse. Throughout the meal, Lucie had gently reprimanded him for his pessimism: Fafard & Sons was celebrating its sixtieth anniversary, the store had weathered worse storms than this, and Fernand was a much better businessman than his father had been. He had turned a small, local hardware store into a thriving modern business. Everyone came to him for advice. Maybe they weren't buying as much, but that was just the economic climate. Sooner or later his reputation, his good business sense, and his ingenuity would bring customers back into the store; all he had to do was be patient.

Fernand had been moved and flattered. He'd reached across the table for his wife's hand, nearly dragging his sleeve in the butter, and given her a tender smile. But it had been the smile of a sad, tired man.

And it was this man, Charles now asked himself indignantly, who was going to pay to make him his son? The man who had already seen to his every need for the past two years? No, that mustn't happen! He had to find the money himself. It was a question of honour. But how was he to do it?

It was at this moment that Lucie, worried that he was being so quiet, tapped on the door to his room.

"May I come in?"

Charles took a few seconds to compose himself, then called out, "Come in!" a bit too loudly to sound natural.

"So," she said, standing in the doorway looking slightly embarrassed, "you've been to see Monsieur Michaud?"

The boy nodded.

Céline's small face appeared in the doorway, looking curious and a bit worried. She leaned her head against her mother's plump waist, and opened her mouth partway with a question playing on her lips. Lucie bent down towards her: "Go play outside, sweetheart, do you mind? I have to speak to Charles."

"Come and get me when you're done, Charles," she called as she skipped off down the hall.

But after watching a grosbeak grooming itself on a fencepost for a few minutes, she slipped back into the kitchen and stood as still as a statue, with one hand cupped at her ear.

Lucie looked down the hallway, waited a moment, then went into Charles's room.

"Did Monsieur Michaud . . . did he explain things to you?"

Charles nodded again. His cheeks turned red, his eyes narrowed, and the tendons in his throat stood out sharply.

"He told me my father was coming back to Montreal and that you'll have to spend a lot of money for me not to have to go live with him. He said my father's looking for a way to make money off me – either that or he's gone crazy because of religion or something like that. If you can't get him to agree to let me stay here, he said I'd have to go see a judge and hire lawyers and do all kinds of complicated things that cost a lot of money."

He leapt up from his bed and ran to Lucie, throwing his arms around her waist and pressing his face into her chest. She began smoothing his hair.

"There, there, my little Charlie," she said softly, her eyes filling with tears. "Don't you worry about a thing, everything is going to turn out just fine. You'll see."

"I don't want you to have to spend a lot of money for me," Charles sobbed, taking in great gulps of air. "You can't afford it any more."

At these words she took him by the shoulders and, holding him away from her, looked deep into his eyes.

"Where did you get that idea from? Eh?"

"Fernand said so himself."

He told her what Fernand had said at dinner.

She began to laugh. But the laugh sounded a bit forced.

"My poor child, if we went around taking seriously everything Fernand says when he's tired there wouldn't be a tear left in our bodies! He's told me we're bankrupt at least ten times since we've been married. One bad night's sleep, two or three setbacks, and it's the end of the world. He forgets all about it the next day." To herself she added: Whatever possessed me to send him to Michaud's, I'd have done a better job myself. "Listen to me, Charles. I forbid you, do you hear me, I absolutely forbid you to worry yourself over questions of money. Thanks be to God we've always had enough to get by, and unless we both become as dumb as posts, we'll stay that way. All I wanted Parfait Michaud to do was explain all those legal questions that were too complicated for us, that's all."

Charles gave a somewhat sardonic smile.

"They seemed to be too complicated for him, too."

"Well, I was wrong and I'm sorry. He's just a notary public, after all, not a real lawyer. Sometimes we expect too much from educated people. They still have five toes on their feet like everyone else, and one head on their shoulders – if they'd only use it!"

She looked at him again, holding his gaze.

"Are you feeling better now?"

He nodded, both to please her and because he was tired of the discussion.

She smiled at him and turned to leave. Then she turned back: "There's one thing I want to say before I go, Charles. One thing I've learned in my life, and you'll learn it, too, as you grow up, is that money is always the least of our problems."

And having delivered herself of this philosophical observation, she pinched his nose and left the room.

■ ■ ■

Charles did manage to calm himself. The prospect of his father's return gradually became less and less of a threat and seemed just one of a number of possibilities, none of which concerned him directly. The evening after his meeting with the notary he had a long talk in the living room with Fernand. The hardware-store owner began the whole discussion by saying he had a bone to pick with Parfait Michaud; the notary "got the whole thing bass-ackwards," and ended up upsetting Charles for no good reason, because all this business about adopting him would work itself out "like a fart from a work-horse." As for Fafard & Sons' supposed financial difficulties, he told Charles not to give it another thought.

"There are always ups and downs in business, my boy. That's the name of the game. We've been going through a bad patch, but there's light at the end of the tunnel just as sure as the Queen of England sits on her throne twice a day like the rest of us. I've seen worse, and I'll see it again. What you've got to remember first and foremost and above all else is that we love you like you were our own son, and we will never, and I mean never, do you hear me? never let you leave this place. Unless of course you tell us yourself that you *want* to leave. Can you please get that into your coconut once and for all?"

"I'll try," Charles said, smiling brightly with a prickling feeling in his throat.

A few moments later, Céline called Charles into her room and, after swearing him to secrecy, told him she'd overheard what Lucie had said to him that afternoon.

"You're too nice to ever leave here, Charles," she said, taking him by the hand. "Mama is crazy about you, Papa too, and me, I love you very much. So don't be sad. Smile like you always do, Charles. Smile all the time."

All these marks of affection made Charles feel a little drunk, a bit like he was floating on air. He had never felt so wanted. To have had such a terrible man for a father now seemed to him to have been a piece of good luck, since it had allowed him to find this marvellous new family. The matter of his adoption, however, with all the costs it was likely to entail, still hung like a shadow over his summer vacation. Despite what anyone said, Charles felt more and more unhappy about adding to the worries of Fernand and his family. He thought about offering them his own savings, but he didn't, because he was sure they would refuse them. One night in July when he and Henri were on their way home from swimming, Henri noticed that Charles was very quiet, guessed the reason and tried to cheer him up, in his own rough fashion.

"Charles, I know what you're stewing about. Forget it. Even if it does cost my father a lot to hang on to you, you can always pay him back when you get older. Right?"

"When I'm older, he'll be older, too. What good would my money be to him then?"

"No, no, that's where you're wrong, Charles. Money's always good, no matter when it comes. My Uncle Ernest is eighty-two and he still plays the stock market. There's nothing he likes better than making money, believe me. All grown-ups are like that."

"I'll never be like that," replied Charles fervently. "And your father isn't, either. What your father likes is his work, talking with customers and helping them out."

Henri shrugged his shoulders, decided that the conversation was becoming too serious, and changed the subject.

Charles ended up confiding his worries to Blonblon, who, instead of trying to convince him that he was spinning his wheels uselessly, suggested he become a partner in Blonblon's appliance-repair business. That way he could add to his bank account. Charles joyfully accepted the offer. But the warm summer weather had noticeably slowed down operations in Blonblon's small business; in fact, he hadn't had any work in some time. This had put a strain on his customer relations. In order to improve his image as a businessman, he decided to launch a publicity campaign that would have more or less instant results. The two boys came up with the idea of distributing a circular in the neighbourhood praising their unparalleled talents as restorers of hopelessly irreparable objects. This they would follow up by knocking on the doors of former clients to renew the customers' acquaintance with their services and to reinforce the effect of the circular.

While they were waiting for business to pick up, it occurred to Charles that he could go back to work for Roberto and Rosalie, who welcomed him back much more warmly than did their current delivery boy, a sallow, seventeen-year-old beanpole with onion breath who was constantly sneaking bottles of pop and took a suspiciously long time making deliveries to two or three of the restaurant's older customers.

Charles turned up at Chez Robert every day at five o'clock (the beanpole handled the afternoon deliveries) after having spent a good part of his day in Blonblon's workshop. Since the latter's apartment was small, Charles obtained Fernand's permission to set up their shop in the Fafards' garage, to the great delight of Boff, who made it a habit to take his afternoon siesta at the feet of his young master.

After spending several days as an admiring assistant to his friend, Charles left the more delicate jobs, such as repairs to china and porcelain, to Blonblon, and specialized in small electrical appliances – toasters, hairdryers, fans, heaters, kettles, and the like. At first there were a few short-circuits, the odd irreparable screw-up, and even the beginnings of a small electrical fire, but after a week or so, with occasional advice from Fernand, handyman extraordinaire, Charles began to make remarkable progress.

It wasn't long before Henri was feeling a bit miffed at not being part of their team. One day when he was leaning against the garage door, hands in his pockets, making little mocking comments about their famous aptitude as "junk repairmen" who "specialized in women's work," Charles calmly suggested to him if he had nothing better to do than screw around, bitching and moaning, would he mind doing it somewhere else and leave them to get on with their work in peace? Blonblon, however, always eager to restore harmony, asked Henri if he'd like to come in and join them. They'd be able to take on more jobs that way, he reasoned, and everyone's profit would increase. After some hesitation, Henri accepted the invitation, but quickly grew bored with the exacting nature of the work, which required the patience of an ant, and went back to playing baseball and watching television.

By mid-August, Charles had five hundred and sixty-three dollars in the bank. One day, Lucie, surprised to see him saving with such zeal, asked him what he intended to do with so much money.

"It's for the future," Charles replied seriously with an air of mystery, looking away.

Although he had only the vaguest notion of how much it would cost to hire a lawyer, he knew that his meagre savings would cover only a small fraction of the fee. On the other hand, if it was a question of buying his father off, how much would Fernand have to give him?

Two or three times he risked asking Fernand how business was going. The third time, Fernand became annoyed and told him to take a hike. Charles thought about selling his books. He picked one up, then another, opened it, closed it again, subject to terribly conflicting emotions. In the end he decided he couldn't part with any of them. Some nights he tossed miserably in bed, unable to sleep. He would have loved to curl up with Simon, but a mocking remark from Henri at the beginning of summer had made him relegate his adored bear to a shelf in the closet so that he wouldn't be called a "big baby," or even a "fifi."

Occasionally all these questions became tangled together and produced a kind of explosion in his head. When that happened he would suddenly quit making deliveries and drop his repair work. Feverishly, almost out of control, he would drag Henri and Blonblon outside to play Cowboys and Indians, or Cops and Robbers, or lead them on dangerous missions of exploration and interplanetary voyages, filling the neighbourhood with the sounds of their stampeding feet, their shouting and bloodcurdling howls, intermingled with Boff's incessant yapping.

29

On September 5, 1978, Charles started his last year at Saint-Anselme Elementary. He vividly recalled the long-ago day when he had entered the school for the first time, a small boy darting timid but envious glances at the older kids in the sixth grade who teased and taunted the newcomers with their air of having travelled to the four corners of the Earth and back.

He was walking along rue Bercy with Blonblon and young Lamouche, busy as usual telling a dirty joke, when he looked across the street and saw what looked like a Milou terrier that seemed to be in a hurry to get nowhere in particular. It was the first time Charles had seen the dog in the neighbourhood. He called it and, as was always the case, the dog stopped dead in its tracks, looked over at Charles, began wagging its tail, and crossed the street to join him. Charles's friends went on without him, long accustomed to the magnetic effect he always seemed to have on dogs.

He knelt down on the sidewalk and began petting the animal. The terrier sneezed and wagged its tail in a transport of joy, from time to time running its tongue along Charles's hand.

"Hello, Charles," came a familiar voice. "Have you had a good summer?"

"Oh, hello, Mademoiselle Laramée," Charles replied happily as he saw the teacher walking towards him. She was limping slightly, Charles noticed for the first time. "Yes, I had a very good summer, thank you. And you?"

She looked away, as though to evade the question. Charles stood up and held out his hand. Instead, she leaned over and kissed him on the cheek. He was always pleased to see his former teacher. She had been good to him, despite her somewhat brusque manner. But his pleasure had always been balanced, unfortunately, by his fear of being thought a teacher's pet.

"You've grown so much since June," she said quietly, looking at him dreamily. "You'll be as tall as me pretty soon. Your last year at Saint-Anselme . . . already."

"Yes," Charles replied proudly.

"Mine too, probably. Can you believe it?"

She told him that she had developed osteoarthritis in her hips and knees, and would probably have to take early retirement because of it.

Although the terrier was somewhat put off by the woman's presence, it nonetheless followed Charles as they walked towards school, on the expectation of more petting. The three of them crossed rue Rouen.

"And there's no cure for that?" Charles asked, saddened by the news and realizing for the first time that he was talking to an *old person*.

"Doctors!" the teacher grumbled. "They don't know a thing!"

Pupils were now running past them. One of them gave Charles a shove as he went by, and Charles smiled and leaned down to pet the dog.

"Aren't you afraid you'll be bored staying home all day, Mademoiselle?"

"Not at all. I'm going to take some courses at the University of Montreal, and I'll be doing the books for my younger sister's business. She owns a fashion boutique on Saint-Hubert. Charles, there's something I want to tell you," she added, stopping.

Her face took on an intense, severe look that soon gave way to an expression of maternal solicitude.

Seeing it wasn't going to get much more attention from its new friend, the dog gave Charles a quick lick of the hand and crossed the street.

"I've heard you're going to have Madame Prud'homme for a homeroom teacher."

Charles couldn't keep his disappointment from showing.

"I know, I know, she's not an easy person to get along with. I must admit she's not much liked in the school (and you don't have to go around telling everyone what I said). But listen to me, Charles. Keep that little clown inside you in check when you're in her class. Pay attention to her lessons, keep your cool even when she doesn't, and everything will go fine. It's very important that you do well in sixth grade before going into secondary school. You've done extremely well so far against some pretty hefty odds, and it would be a shame to waste it all now. Okay, off you go; your friends are calling you."

■ ■ ■

Fall came and Wilfrid Thibodeau still hadn't shown any sign of life. His small cheques continued to arrive at the Fafards' house each month, as though merely to remind everyone of the bond that united him and his son. Fernand didn't dare write back to get him to clarify his intentions, since he knew it would only bring on more worries, and the Lord knew he had enough worries already.

"I know it isn't a very Catholic thing to say," he confided to his wife one evening, "but it wouldn't bother me very much if he fell off a scaffold one day and broke his neck. That would certainly solve our problem, don't you agree? That man's been a blasted nuisance all his life. The only way he'll ever be of any use is when he's six feet under."

"Don't you dare let the children hear you say that," Lucie warned him, looking nervously about to make sure there was no one within earshot.

Fernand laughed: "Come on, Lucie, get with it: they feel the same way, for crying out loud!"

■ ■ ■

The eleventh of October was Charles's twelfth birthday. Lucie baked him a magnificent vanilla cake in the form of a dog; Fernand gave him a new flashlight with a fluorescent bulb ("for reading with at night," he said, with a knowing smile), and Céline gave him one of her *Tintin* books. There was no present from his father, which pleased Fernand and his wife. After supper, Amélie and Parfait Michaud came over for dessert, and they gave him an almond-green envelope containing a birthday card with dogs on it (naturally) and a ten-dollar bill.

"You can use it to buy books," declared the notary, shaking Charles gravely by the hand.

"Thank you, I will," Charles said, smiling broadly.

But the next day he deposited eight dollars into his account at the Credit Union, keeping only two for himself. On Saturday, he took the metro to rue Saint-Denis, where the notary had said there were several used bookstores. He returned home with four excellent novels purchased for thirty-five cents each, amazed at the thought of all the money he could save; from now on he would be able to satisfy his passion for books and still be able to put money aside for Fernand.

■ ■ ■

His relationship with his teacher didn't get off to a good start. Madame Prud'homme was forty-nine, with florid cheeks, thighs that started down at her calves, and a mouth that seemed too small for her teeth. The pupils called her the Shark; she knew it, and she did her best to live up to her nickname.

For Charles, there was no escaping her wrath. His reputation for being a brilliant but troublesome student had evidently reached her ears. On the first day of school, no sooner had Charles taken the seat that had been assigned to him than she came over. Bent over him with her arms spread and her hands leaning on either side of his desk, she stared at him silently for a moment or two, then spoke in a voice that was somehow both rasping and sharp. It reminded Charles of the sound of a hairdryer.

"Now you listen to me, Charles Thibodeau. I'm warning you right now so there won't be any misunderstanding between us. Just because you manage to get good marks doesn't mean you have the right to disturb my class. The other teachers in this school can do what they like, but in here I'm the one who calls the shots. Do you understand me?"

Charles looked up at her, his mouth open, his face turning red, torn between fear and the desire to burst out laughing.

"Do you understand me?" she repeated more forcefully.

"Yes, Madame," he finally said, gracefully lowering his eyes as he had seen someone do the previous week in a French film on television.

He made his mind up on the spot to try to stay on the good side of Madame Prud'homme. But it soon became clear that this would not be easy. He realized that the best way to manage it was to turn himself into an automaton, to blindly follow her instructions, which were legion, to the letter. These included: no unnecessary gestures, no looking from side to side, no shuffling of feet on the floor; coughing was to be kept to a minimum, and any pupil so unwise as to use the drinking fountain before class had better hope he or she had a strong sphincter muscle, since Madame Prud'homme had little sympathy for anyone who couldn't control their bladder.

Like his classmates, Charles had to get used to the torrent of rebukes that made up the better part of his teacher's educational curriculum. He was clipped on the head a few times, had his ear pinched (once almost hard enough to draw blood), and repeatedly had to endure such discouraging remarks as, "Deep down, he isn't that much better than any of the others."

One Saturday in December, however, the situation changed once and for all. It was during an abominable snowstorm that transformed the streets of Montreal into white corridors along which one staggered and slid, breath cut short by sudden gusts of snow. That morning around nine o'clock, Lucie was making crème anglaise and noticed that she was out of sugar, so she asked Charles to go to the grocery store to buy some.

Charles sighed and got into his coat and boots, pushed open the door and found himself in a tempest; snow instantly blew down his neck and a second later was transformed into icy water. He quickly zipped his parka up to the top and made his descent into the maelstrom.

The grocery store was a good ten-minute walk from the house, but there was a convenience store that was closer, on rue Fullum. Charles decided it was worth the few extra cents for the sugar in order to spend as little time as possible outside, and turned down rue Coupal, heading west. He could barely force his feet through the thick snow that was piling up faster and faster. A good part of it was being blown up into the air by sudden gusts of wind, creating a kind of wild carnival that had been paralyzing the city all night. From time to time his heels would meet a thin sheet of ice, exposed by the wind like treacherous, white skin, and he'd nearly go down. Half suffocated, he would utter a curse, stretch his arms out from his sides to keep his balance, and move forward inch by inch.

Halfway to the store, he stopped in his tracks in amazement. A small boy was standing in front of him, blocking the sidewalk, his head stuck in a huge blue toque with a white pompom, his eyes squinting and his mouth gaping open. Enveloped in swirls of whistling, whirling snow, he was squinting intently at something in the street.

Charles turned and looked in the same direction and uttered a cry of alarm. There was a human form lying on the street, half covered by snow.

"Hey!" he shouted at the boy, "what are you doing? Come and give me a hand! We've got to get whoever it is off the street! A car could come by any minute!"

"I just saw him," the child explained, heading out into the street. His feet slid out from under him and he fell on his back.

A half-empty grocery bag hid the face of the prone figure, but they could tell it was a woman. The two boys each took a leg and began to drag her towards the sidewalk. It was hard work, since their feet could get no purchase on the slippery pavement. Finally, after much herculean effort, they succeeded in dragging her off the street.

"Is she dead?" Charles wondered aloud.

They were both gripped by fear, and the smaller boy backed away, holding his hands over his mouth and nearly falling over again. Charles leaned over the woman and removed the grocery bag – and saw that it was Madame Prud'homme! Her eyes were closed, her cheeks had turned blue, and her small mouth was wide open, making her enormous teeth look like a row of prisoners trying to escape from their cramped quarters.

Charles ran to the nearest door and began pounding on it with his fists. A few minutes later the teacher was lying on a bed, her coat removed, being subjected to a series of slaps, rubs, loud shouts in the ear, and other improvised treatments while they waited for the ambulance to make its way through the snow-clogged streets. After fifteen minutes she opened her eyes, gave a long groan and managed to utter a few words. An hour later she was taken to Notre-Dame Hospital, where she stayed for a week, her mind in a fog. No long-term cerebral damage, the doctors assured her.

From then on, Madame Prud'homme treated Charles as her saviour. Her venomous, reptilian nature didn't exactly evaporate, but some of the edge was taken off it, and a kind of understanding existed between them. It was a cold, almost calculated understanding, and it gave neither of them much pleasure, but at least it saved Charles from bearing the brunt of the daily harassments the rest of the class continued to endure.

■ ■ ■

Towards the end of June the school administration held a small party for Mademoiselle Laramée, who was retiring after thirty-two years of loyal, energetic service. There were cakes and sparkling wine in the staff room. After three bottles of Faisca, the illustrious corps of teachers began to resemble a hen party. Mademoiselle Laramée brought her colleagues to tears with a story of one of her uncles who came home late one night without knowing that that afternoon his wife had sent the furniture out to be reupholstered; he went into the dark living room with a glass of scotch in his hand with the idea of sitting quietly for a moment before going up to bed, sat down where one of the vanished chairs had been, and ended up spending the night sleeping against a radiator. In the morning he had fourteen stitches and a slight loss of memory.

When she left the school a while later, she was slightly tipsy. She wondered if perhaps she shouldn't delay her retirement for a while; after all, the pain in her knees and hip hadn't bothered her for the past hour. She was making her way along the sidewalk a little shakily, trying to remember what it was she had meant to pick up for supper on her way home, when she saw Charles walking ahead of her with two of his friends. She waved and called to him in a curiously crooning voice.

"Yes, Mademoiselle?" Charles said, walking back to meet her.

"My poor child," she said, her eyes moistening, "in two days we won't be seeing each other any more. I'm leaving school for ever after this week."

"I know, Mademoiselle. I was going to come to see you to say goodbye after class."

She remained silent for a few seconds, sideswiped by such a show of kindness.

"Ah, Charles, Charles," she finally said, her voice trembling. "Of all the pupils I've had in my thirty-two years, you're the one I've liked the best."

She stroked the back of his neck. Charles smiled, slightly embarrassed by the bizarre change in the behaviour of his former teacher, as well as by the looks he imagined he was getting from his two friends; he could feel their eyes boring into his back. Then suddenly, defying all schoolboy protocol, he took her hand.

"My beautiful boy," she blubbered, "my beautiful, lovely boy." Two tears rolled down her cheeks.

But then her practical sense and indomitable energy reasserted themselves. Tossing her head and shaking her shoulders she began fumbling for something in her purse.

"Listen, Charles," she said, taking out a pen, "tell me honestly. Would you like to see me again from time to time – not too often, of course, two or three times a year, if you want? We can exchange news, you can tell me what you've been up to – that is, only what you want to tell me about. Would you like that? Tell me the truth, now."

"Yes, Mademoiselle," Charles replied, surprised but sincere.

"Good. Then I'll write my address and phone number on this scrap of paper. Don't lose it. Whenever you feel like it, and only when you feel like it, you know, come and see me. Call first, though, because I might not always be home."

She handed him the paper, touched him on the cheek, and limped off, her eyes fixed proudly straight ahead.

■ ■ ■

Charles finished Grade Six first in his class in French, but with more middling results in most of his other subjects. This was partly because so much of his energy and attention was going into his extracurricular activities (to use the jargon of the time), and partly because his raging thirst for reading often made him give short shrift to his studies. Despite all their efforts, Lucie and Fernand were unable to convince him to limit his work in the appliance repair shop to weekends. He was becoming amazingly adept at fixing things. However, they did manage to get Rosalie and Roberto to agree not to let him work as a delivery boy during the week.

30

The night gathered slowly. A warm, moist wind tore at the clouds in the turbulent sky, and between them the moon appeared fitfully against a backdrop of mauve turning to black. A vagrant gull glided above the city, riding the wind, its feet still greasy from a day spent at the dump. Its impassive eye scanned the rooftops and streets as they darkened imperceptibly with the movement of the sky. In most houses people were sleeping. In some, however, they were still up, talking or eating or making love or watching television, with weary rings around their eyes. Bitter voices were raised in certain quarters. Piles of bills were being added up and then added up again. Plans were being made and unmade and then remade in different guises. Through it all blew the warm, humid wind, swept aloft as though on a strangely drunken spree, a spring-like binge despite the fact that fall was approaching, continuing its attack on the fleeing clouds.

Charles was asleep in his bedroom, his body jerking fitfully from time to time. His eyes were squeezed tightly shut, his hands grasped at objects that were always just out of reach, and fragmentary phrases escaped from his lips. Simon had secretly crept back under his covers, but could offer little comfort from the nightmare in which Charles was once again locked. Every now and then Boff, awakened by an errant knee, would open one eye, cast a quizzical look at his master and heave a deep sigh before going back to sleep.

Twice Lucie had got up to listen at Charles's door, had almost gone into his room, and then had returned to her bed, where she and Fernand continued their whispered conversation.

Charles had been having nightmares for the past several weeks, ever since a scorching Saturday night towards the end of the summer. It had started with a small triumph at Chez Robert. At five o'clock, just after he'd arrived to begin his deliveries, he was enjoying listening to a parrot that Monsieur Victoire had bought that afternoon from a man of shady credentials in a fleamarket in Prévost, where he had gone in his cab with a customer.

"Of course it's a stolen parrot," the taxi-driver was saying, looking admiringly at the bird perched on his shoulder. "The son of a bitch didn't even know its name! But like I said to myself, it wouldn't be any less stolen if I didn't buy it, would it? What's done is done, so we might as well make the best of it. Besides, at the price he was asking, it was more like a gift. What d'you think, Charles? I did the right thing buying it, eh?"

"I don't know," Charles replied, his entire attention riveted on the bird. Its feathers were magnificent, all green and red. It jerked its head continuously and rolled its lidless eyes.

"ARMAND!" it suddenly cried in a furious, raucous voice. "I'M GONNA KICK YOUR ASS GOOD AN' PROPER!"

For the fifth time the restaurant filled with roars of laughter.

"I don't know where it came from," Rosalie remarked, "but I don't think it was Westmount!"

A small, wrinkled man with a grey beard put his hands on his hips and said with fierce conviction: "No, it comes from someplace where people say what they think! An' if you ask me, that's a darned good place to come from!"

"THE VANQUISHED SHALL BE BEATEN!" the parrot continued, trying to lower its voice.

"What a dumb bird!" Charles scoffed. "Of course the vanquished are beaten. That's what vanquished means!"

"Listen, kid," said the man with the grey beard sententiously, "some things seem stupid when you first hear 'em, and then when you think about 'em they ain't so stupid after all. You just gotta think about 'em."

Charles gave the man a bored look and decided to ignore him. It was the first time anyone had seen him in the restaurant.

"ARMAND!" the parrot repeated, "I'M GONNA KICK YOUR ASS GOOD AN' PROPER!"

And grabbing a tuft of Monsieur Victoire's hair in its beak (which made the taxi-driver grimace), it swung from his right shoulder to his left.

"I hope you don't intend to come in here every day with that thing," Rosalie said half-jokingly. "You'll give the place a bad name."

Since there were no deliveries to be made, Charles thought he would go home and bring Céline and Henri back to look at the foul-mouthed bird. He was at the front of the restaurant when a violent curse issued from the kitchen. A dozen faces turned towards the kitchen door, and Rosalie, dropping an order of Spanish omelette and fries in front of a customer, ran off to see what had happened.

"The fan just quit on us!" Roberto bellowed in his resonant, tenor voice, pointing to the range hood. "I knew she was gonna break down . . . she nearly give out four times already today . . . And now she's gone for good! Aye-yi-yi, where'm I gonna get a repair guy on a Saturday night! You know how hot it's gonna be in here an hour from now?"

"But there's an emergency number," Rosalie said. "I'll call it right away."

"Don't waste your time, Lili. Giovanni never comes on Saturdays. He goes down to Venise-en-Québec . . ."

"Can I help?" Charles asked modestly, coming into the kitchen. "I know a bit about electric motors."

"Thank you, Charlie, thank you," answered Roberto, patting him on the head, "but there's nothin' you can do here."

Liette came in with three orders for the kitchen, and Roberto went back to work. Charles left without a word, and five minutes later came back with a small tool box and his flashlight. Roberto told him to keep away from the hood.

"Roberto," said Monsieur Victoire, who was standing in the doorway, "give the boy a chance, why don't you! What've you got to lose? He's pretty handy with things. The other day he fixed a telephone for me in ten minutes flat. I was gonna throw the darn thing out the window, and now it works like new!"

"And he fixed my hairdryer," added Liette, putting in her two-cents' worth. "The plastic casing was all melted and the cord was hanging half off. Now you can hardly tell there was anything wrong with it!"

"But this is an *industrial* fan," Roberto objected, holding his hand out towards the hood. "It ain't child's play! And anyways, he might burn himself in the grease in the deep-fryer."

"Roberto," said the taxi-driver, picking up the large cutting board the chef used to roll out his pizza dough, "have a bit of faith in the little fella, will you? He just might solve your problem."

341

And he set the cutting board on top of the deep-fryer, tested it for solidity, and motioned Charles to climb on.

"Ten minutes! That's all!" declared the chef, holding one index finger up and using the other to wipe sweat from his eye.

He opened a small wall cupboard to reveal an electrical panel, and unscrewed a fuse. Meanwhile, Charles took a stool, climbed up onto the stove and kneeled on the cutting board.

"Ugh, it's filthy in there!" he couldn't help remarking when he saw the thick layer of grease that covered every surface.

"What'd you expect?" Roberto said hotly. "You're the one who wanted to stick your nose in it, so quit gripin'."

Charles heaved a sigh. The heat and the smell of fried food was suffocating. He almost wished he hadn't offered to help. He turned on his flashlight and with a grimace of distaste began exploring the inner workings of the range hood with his fingertips.

"Well?" asked Roberto, impatiently.

"Give him time!" admonished Monsieur Victoire in his best circus-master's voice. "When you can't wait to make love, you still have to get your pants off, don't you?"

Feeling sheepish, Charles was just about to admit defeat when he suddenly thought he'd found the source of the problem. It was simple! The screw attaching the power cable to the electric motor seemed to have worked itself loose, probably from the motor's vibration, and the connection was broken. Three turns of his screwdriver and the fan would no doubt work like a charm.

He nodded to the taxi-driver, his eyes blurred with sweat, his mouth feeling pasty, and his ears burning, and asked for his toolbox. Two minutes later the range hood was humming and Roberto was ecstatic. He hugged Charles as though the boy had just saved the restaurant from certain ruin. A small group of admirers gathered around.

"Rosalie!" called Roberto. "Make this guy a sundae like you never made a sundae in your life! Use the pink bowl from up on the high shelf, the one for a four-scoop banana split!"

Charles was radiant. He had just sat down at the counter, ready to attack a sundae made with vanilla ice-cream smothered in chocolate and caramel sauce, dotted with four maraschino cherries, four wafers, and sprinkled with sliced almonds and grated cocoa beans, when he had to leave to make a delivery.

"Hurry back, kiddo," said Rosalie with a warm smile. "I'll keep your sundae cold in the refrigerator."

■ ■ ■

He ran full-speed to Frontenac Towers, even at the risk of visiting indescribable havoc on the club sandwich that was inside the cardboard box. Ten minutes later he was on his way back, breathless and with a good tip in his pocket and a craving for ice-cream such as he had never known before.

He started to cross the small square outside the Frontenac metro station. That evening it was busy. A half-dozen street kids were skateboarding around it, shouting and making a racket with their endless collisions; a little farther on, two Jehovah's Witnesses, surrounded by a handful of skeptical listeners, were making heroic efforts to convert an old pensioner in a panama hat and a pale blue Fortel suit who hadn't had a conversation that wasn't about money, gin, or women for thirty years. Charles had just passed them when a dark figure fell into step a little to his left. In his hurry to get back, Charles paid no attention to the figure, except to feel a vague presentiment of menace.

"Charles!" called a voice that was all too familiar. "C'mere, I wanna talk to you."

The boy stopped dead in his tracks and saw his father sidling up to him, a broad smile on his face and his hand held out.

"Hi, there, sonny. My God, you're all grown up! I hardly recognized you! How's it goin'?"

"Not bad," Charles replied woodenly.

Thibodeau kept on smiling, his small, inquisitive eyes behind their puffy, red lids looking the boy up and down, his head nodding slightly as though he had finally arrived at a conclusion that had long been eluding him. He seemed smaller and more sickly looking than Charles remembered, his face dark and dried out, his cheekbones protruding, his lips thin and pale, his hair dull and streaked with grey. He looked as though he'd suffered years of gruelling, inhuman work, or had endured an endless series of trials that had drained his body of much of its vitality. But a sort of dark energy surged within him, tormenting his meagre body; Charles could see it showing itself in several unpredictable ways, tremendous shudders followed by long, sinuous movements that seemed intended to induce nothing but surprise, trouble, and consternation.

"Well, I gotta say," he went on, "you're not a bad-looking kid! You'll be turning girls' heads pretty soon, if you ain't already. You interested in girls yet?"

Charles shook his head.

"At your age I was all over 'em. Hey, you don't look all that glad to see me," the carpenter added spitefully.

Charles looked down, not knowing what to say. He wanted to be in the restaurant, sitting at the counter with his sundae, even though with the horrible contractions now going on in his stomach he knew he wouldn't be able to swallow a mouthful of it. But at the moment the restaurant was two blocks away, and might was well have been at the other end of the universe.

"*Hey!*" shouted Thibodeau, in a strange sort of whistling whine. "Look at me when I'm talkin' to you! That's better. When someone's talkin' to you, kid, you look at 'em. It's only polite. What's eatin' you, anyways? Cat got your tongue?"

"I don't feel well," Charles lied.

The carpenter lit a cigarette, took a deep drag, and said: "Who am I?"

Taken aback, Charles shrugged his shoulders.

"Who am I to you?"

"My father," Charles whispered after a moment.

"Eggs-actly! Couldn't'a put it better myself! I'm your old man. I've always been your old man, and I'll always be your old man. You follow me?"

Charles nodded.

"An' stop openin' and closin' your yap like that, makes you look like a fish or somethin'. Gets on my nerves."

Humiliated and furious, Charles clenched his teeth with all his strength and took several deep breaths. To his great relief the spasms slowly decreased in intensity.

Maybe by now Rosalie would be worried by his absence and come out onto the street to look for him, and call him to come back right away. Maybe Fernand would be out buying a newspaper and would see him with this detestable man, and would come up to them with his solid, decisive step, stop in front of Wilfrid and give him such a shove with his arm that he would go spinning right down to the bottom of the metro. But nothing like that happened. No one came to his rescue. He was still there, paralyzed before this man who filled him with such terror.

"And the best proof that I'm your old man, like I said," Thibodeau went on, "is that I never stopped payin' your support, even if there were plenty of times when I had to scrape the barrel to get it. I was always good for it. Because you're my kid, y'unnerstand what I'm sayin', and a father's gotta see to it that his kid's bein' taken care of, at least to the best of his ability. Come on. We're gonna go somewhere quiet so's we can talk better."

"B-but . . . I'm working at the restaurant," Charles stammered.

"You can work some other time. Come on."

And he took Charles by the arm.

"Where are we going?" Charles asked, his voice shaking.

Thibodeau replied by pointing his chin down the street to some undefined destination ahead of them. They crossed one corner, then another, heading east. The carpenter had let go of the boy's arm and was walking in silence, casting his gaze all around him, obviously looking for something. Finally he turned up a side street and began walking more quickly, looking down from time to time at his son, who was having more and more difficulty hiding his misgivings. Charles was certain he was being kidnapped. He would never see the Fafards again, or any of his friends, not even Boff. His stomach contracted violently. What would happen to him? Suddenly the scene with the paring knife flashed through his mind. He raised his head and looked up at his father, waiting for a chance to run away, but Thibodeau never took his suspicious eyes off him, and in any case the boy's stifling fear had almost robbed him of the power to walk, let alone run.

They came to a huge church, a stone edifice in the Neogothic style, flanked on its left by a parking lot with a row of tall trees along one side. The church's entranceway was dark and empty, which seemed to please the carpenter. He turned into it and sat down on one of the stone steps, motioning Charles to do the same.

"This is as good place as any to have our little talk. Because we got a lot to talk about, you and me."

He told Charles that he had been back in Montreal for two weeks and was looking for work in construction. Despite the huge wages to be made up north, he said, he'd grown tired of the life up there and was glad to be back

345

in the city. Fernand's proposal of adoption had given him a lot to think about, and he was still thinking about it. As a matter of fact, he was feeling less and less inclined to go along with it. On the contrary, he was thinking of taking Charles back. (At these words, Charles bit the inside of his cheek so hard his mouth filled with the taste of blood.) Why? Because he had begun to see things differently. Working up at James Bay all those months had given him a chance to look inside himself in a way he'd never been able to do before. His mind had been so confused after the night of their little disagreement! Because that's all it was, when you came right down to it, a little quarrel between them, despite whatever was said about it at the time. He'd run into Sylvie a couple of days ago and had talked it over with her, and she'd ended up agreeing that the whole thing had been greatly exaggerated, probably because everyone was so on edge. Even Charles had to admit that the whole story was nothing but imagination gone wild. For proof? He'd got out of the house without a scratch, hadn't he? A judge – if the matter ever came before a judge – would have to come to the same conclusion.

Charles listened to him, thunderstruck. What world was his father living in? What was he up to? The boy's fear had gradually diminished. He realized that Wilfrid was not going to take him by force that night. He had other plans, although it was impossible to guess what they were. Maybe Wilfrid himself didn't know what they were.

"Okay, let's go," said the carpenter, standing up. "It's getting late and you have to go home. They'll be worried about you. I got a lot off my chest tonight. Next time it'll be your turn. Good night, my boy."

And once again he held out his hand, a faint, sly smile playing on his lips.

"There won't be a next time," Charles muttered to himself as he moved off down the sidewalk, teeth clenched, tears of rage running down his face. "There'll never be a next time. Never, never, never!"

When he arrived at the Fafards' the whole household was in an uproar. Alarmed by his failure to return, Rosalie had telephoned the house to speak to him. Lucie had become even more alarmed, and had called Blonblon, then the parents of some of his other friends. When no one knew where he was, she had asked her son and husband to go out and look for him. Forty-five minutes later they'd come back empty-handed. Céline was crying her heart out in the living room. Boff was running from room to room, his head down, emitting short, distressed barks, as though he understood the seriousness of the situation. The click-click of his claws on the hardwood floors had been getting on everyone's nerves.

When Lucie saw the expression on Charles's face, she ran up and took him in her arms. Fernand listened to his story in silence, his face dark with anger, as Charles recited what had happened in a feverish high-pitched voice. Céline and Henri sat at the end of the room their father had indicated, listening, holding their breath, and exchanging worried looks.

"Don't you worry about a thing, my boy," Fernand said when Charles was finished. "I'll take care of this."

He put on his jacket, left the house, and headed straight to Parfait Michaud's house. Passersby on rue Ontario turned to look at him in astonishment, a massive man with a furious expression cutting a swath like a sword through the happy, animated, Saturday-night crowd.

■ ■ ■

The notary was sitting with his wife in their living room, his shirt collar open and a mug of beer in his hand. Despite the overbearing heat he had turned off the fan, which had been giving them at least the illusion of fresh air, because its roaring had drowned out the notes of the cello in the Beethoven quartet they were listening to. When the doorbell rang, he made a face but got up, lifted the turntable arm from the record, and went to open the door.

"Ah, Fernand, how are you?" he said, making an effort to be cordial. "Come in and have a beer."

Fernand made a horizontal motion with his hand, rejecting the notary's offer.

"I'm here on business."

"Business? On Saturday night?" said the notary in surprise. "In this heat? Have a heart, my friend. Couldn't it wait until Monday?"

"It's about Charles. His father just accosted him. There's trouble brewing again."

"What's that you say?" cried Amélie, appearing in the hallway, a Chinese fan in her hand (which made Fernand's eyes widen). "My poor little Charles, is he still having trouble with that impossible man?"

347

"Yes, Madame! He wants the boy back, nothing else will satisfy the bastard. Pardon me. But he's going to find out who he's dealing with, you can take that to the bank!"

And he turned to the notary.

"I'll need your help, though. Not a minute to lose!"

The two men went into Michaud's office. The notary carefully closed the door and put his finger to his lips.

"Not too loud, if you don't mind," he said. "My wife has been very excitable lately. I can't let her become too worked up. Tell me what happened. Just a minute, though," he said, holding up his hand. He left the room and came back with two mugs of beer.

"Please allow me to insist, my dear Fernand. It's too hot!"

Fernand gave in. His quick-march to the notary's office had made him thirsty; he took the mug and drained it in two gulps, then launched into his story. The notary listened attentively, moving sheets of paper about on his desk as though these slight changes in position would influence the course of events.

"Hmm," he said with a worried look when his visitor had finished, "it seems the situation has become more complicated. We only had one witness to the affair with the knife, and that was this Sylvie. Now it seems that Thibodeau has neutralized her, either by intimidating her or else by buying her off, hard to say which."

"What about me? And my wife? And you, even? What are we? Chopped liver?"

The notary nodded with a dismissive expression.

"Our testimonies depend entirely on that of Charles, my friend. *We saw nothing with our own eyes.* I'm not saying Charles will have no credibility with a judge, but . . ."

"With a judge?" Fernand said, taken aback.

"Of course, with a judge. Let's be realistic here, Fernand. You and I both know that this kind of thing has to be settled in court. Where else would we settle it? At the beauty parlour?"

"With a judge means with a lawyer," Fernand said quietly, thinking about the expenses the affair was going to entail.

"I'll act as your counsel, of course. That'll save you a bit. But there's something that bothers me about your story," he went on, reaching out for his beer, "something we need to discuss."

348

He sipped his beer for a moment, looking off into space, while Fernand squirmed in his seat, looking unhappy and becoming increasingly embarrassed by the demands of his bladder.

"What bothers me . . ."

". . . is that the bastard didn't take Charles with him tonight."

"Exactly, Fernand, you've hit the nail on the head. It could mean one of two things: either he actually wants to take Charles back, in which case he could easily have done just that, since he still retains parental authority over the boy, or else he intends to –"

"– sell him to us for as much as he can get, and to hell with everyone else."

"I might have put it a bit more delicately," replied the notary, smiling, and a bit disconcerted by his companion's ferocity, "but that more or less sums up what I was going to say."

The two men talked for a few more minutes before deciding to let Thibodeau make the next move. In order to prepare for any eventuality, the notary undertook to obtain the necessary documents and procedural manuals for adoption, and to find out what steps were needed to make a representation for the withdrawal of Thibodeau's parental authority. Meanwhile, they would have to keep a close eye on Charles to make sure there was no opportunity for a kidnapping; he would have to be forbidden to leave the Fafards' house unless accompanied by an adult.

During their discussion, Amélie's ear had been glued to the door. Now she hurried to the bathroom, completely shaken by what she had overheard. She quickly swallowed four capsules of valerian in the hope of warding off the night of insomnia she could already see looming on the horizon.

31

E ight days went by. Wilfrid Thibodeau showed no signs of life. To be on the safe side, Charles had been forbidden to go back to work at Chez Robert. The precaution wasn't necessary: terrified at the thought of having to go back to living with his father, Charles was content to hide out at home. He didn't even show any interest in working with Blonblon. He spent most of his day watching television.

When it was time to go back to school, Charles and Henri began their first term at Jean-Baptiste-Meilleur Secondary School, on rue Fullum, which was quite close to the Fafard house. It was one of those brick buildings trimmed in granite in the Beaux-Arts style, from the turn of the century; despite its age, it had maintained a solemn, imposing, almost haughty dignity that contrasted sharply with the colourful, energetic students that coursed through its dark-panelled hallways. Before its main entrance, which was flanked by four massive granite columns, was a painted cement statue of Christ, arms held out, a thoughtful frown on His face, as though He were apologizing to the students in advance for the trouble that awaited them in their lives. The pedestal was piously engraved:

Sacred Heart of Jesus
Bless our Students
DONATED BY ALUMNI
1901–1951

The establishment was run by a small man with iron-grey hair, a former priest who had been transformed by the Quiet Revolution only as far as a kind of half lay brother; he had a reputation for not tolerating boisterous or lazy students.

Along with the many unfamiliar faces in the school were several of Charles's former comrades from Saint-Anselme Elementary. There were a few new routines he had to learn. Rather than having a single homeroom teacher upon whom rested the sole responsibility for the entire school curriculum, here the teaching was shared by a half-dozen specialists. What was more, for the first time in his life (except for his gym teacher at Saint-Anselme), Charles was being taught by men. But what was worrisome was that he seemed to be completely out of step with these new developments in his life as though he was unaware that things had changed, or at least as though the changes were having no effect upon him. His friends no longer recognized him. What could have happened to turn him into a ball of putty that only wanted to curl up in a corner with a sullen expression on his face? He made Henri swear to say nothing of the problems he was having. Blonblon tried to wheedle it out of him, but after being rebuffed several times he advised Charles to take some vitamins.

Since Thibodeau's reappearance, Lucie had been accompanying Charles to and from school, until the situation settled down. These daily escorts drew some attention, and then teasing, from the other students. One morning after Lucie had left him in front of the school, a large, dark-haired, big-boned kid from the second form, whose claim to fame was his ability to contort his body into impossible shapes and to stuff his cheeks with balls of paper like a hamster storing food for the winter, pranced up to Charles in a loose-limbed manner, his forearms raised and his wrists limp, and said in a high, squeaky voice:

"Mama's little boy-child too scared to go anywhere on his own?"

Before Charles could react, Henri, who was standing next to him, gave the idiot such a punch in the stomach that the latter decided to sit down by the Sacred Heart statue for a moment to reflect on the nature of his conduct.

"If you can't say anything nice," Henri called by way of a parting shot, "then don't say anything at all."

But word spread quickly that Charles was in grave danger. That made him the focus of attention. His friends from Saint-Anselme let it be known that he lived with an adopted family, that his father drank like a fish and probably worked for the mob, and that he himself could be a holy terror when his

351

dander was up, easily capable of putting anyone in their place without any help from Henri.

He was able to prove this three days later, when he was on his way to French class. Richard Daviault, an overweight but not necessarily malicious boy who liked his soups as thick as he was, was imprudent enough to trot out the "Mama's little boy-child" line in the stairwell leading up to the second floor. Charles responded with such a fusillade of violence that the fat boy went over backwards down the stairs and might have broken his neck had he not rolled into the French teacher, who was coming up behind him.

Jean-René Dupras was in his mid-twenties and in the first flush of his new career. He had been keeping an eye on Charles since the first day of school, struck by his intelligence as well as by the sadness in the boy's eyes.

"I didn't know I was on your hit list," he said calmly, after blocking the other student's descent down the stairs. The latter scampered off without hanging around to see the outcome.

"I'm sorry, sir, I didn't see you coming up," Charles replied, turning scarlet.

He hung his head and waited for the order to report to the principal's office, which would have been an unfortunate start to his time at Jean-Baptiste-Meilleur. By this time the whole stairwell was deserted.

"It didn't look like it was going to go much farther," said the teacher. "At least not this time."

Charles continued to stare at the steps in silence.

"Is there something wrong?" the teacher asked.

The child shook his head, still looking down.

"You don't want to be teased again after class, do you?"

"Don't worry, sir, everything will work out okay," Charles replied in a constricted voice, on the verge of tears. Then, realizing he was not going to be given a detention, he managed a faint smile and climbed the stairs to class.

At four o'clock, when school was over, Dupras hesitated then decided to call the Fafards to try to find out what was going on with Charles. His call upset Lucie. The idea that a total stranger, completely unaware of what Charles was going through, could pick up on his distress, put her in such a state that she gave the teacher the whole tumultuous story of their protégé. It took her more than half an hour.

"Is there anything I can do to help, Madame?" Dupras finally asked, overwhelmed by the deluge of confidences.

"Gracious God in heaven, Monsieur Dupras, how should I know? You have so many other children to look after . . . There are a few of them worse off than my Charles, from what I've heard after twenty years living in this neighbourhood. If you're a church-goer, you might put in a good word for him the next time you're speaking to God. I hardly have time to go myself these days, what with everything I have to do. But even knowing you're keeping an eye on him is a comfort to me, sir. I thank you for that with all my heart."

She hung up the phone and, seized by an excess of piety as rare as it was sudden, left the house and made her way to church in order to bring Heaven up to date on Charles's situation. But her fervour was thwarted, unfortunately, when she found the doors of the church locked. She'd forgotten that for several years now there had been so much theft and vandalism in God's house that the church authorities had been forced to limit the faithful's access to it, which in turn had rendered it even more useless and ineffective. She considered sitting for a moment on the steps of the entrance to send a mental prayer to the Lord on High, but the noise from the street made it impossible for her to concentrate.

"Good Heavens," she complained as she made her way home, "even God is keeping office hours these days. The whole world is becoming more and more business-like . . ."

She hurried home, for supper time was drawing near and she knew from experience that there was no greater adversary than an empty stomach.

Still mentally concocting her menu, she pushed open the small metal gate that opened onto the minuscule patch of lawn in front of their house, raised her head and saw Wilfrid Thibodeau sitting on the porch steps, with an amused, even mocking, look on his face. He was wearing a suit and tie, although his trousers were slightly worn and the toes of his shoes were scuffed from use. But his body was straight, his shoulders squared, and his entire attitude suggested the sober, confident family man who had come to assert his rights.

"Hello, Madame Fafard," he said loudly, if a bit shrilly. "How are you this fine day? I've come to collect my son."

"He's not home from school yet," she muttered breathlessly.

The front of her house wavered faintly before her eyes, and her legs felt as though they had suddenly turned to marshmallow. She had to lean back on the fence to prevent herself from fainting.

Within less than an hour some critical decisions had been made in the Fafard household. Fernand had rushed home, where he found his wife and the notary, to whom Lucie had also made a frantic call, sitting in the living room with Wilfrid Thibodeau, trying their best to worm some information out of him. Thibodeau seemed to be taking a malicious pleasure in withholding it.

Fernand's arrival changed the dynamic of the conversation.

"Hello, there, Wilf!" the hardware-store owner said. The sight of the hated man seemed to have filled him with a sudden dark energy. "It's been quite a while, eh? We've been expecting you! Come back to your old stomping grounds, eh? Can't remember the last time I saw you in a suit! What, are you getting married again or something? What's new with you, anyway?"

"I've got somethin' lined up," Thibodeau replied calmly. "Somethin' I think's gonna pay very well."

Then he repeated what he had said earlier, in the same firm, detached voice: "And so I've come to pick up my son."

The notary looked up at Fernand, who was still standing in the doorway with his massive arms folded across his chest like a shield. Michaud coughed twice, trying to signal to Fernand to go gently, that things had come to a very delicate pass. Lucie managed to maintain a courageous smile, despite the fact that she was trembling.

"Yeah, well," said Fernand, sighing so hard the carpenter could smell his breath, "that's something we could talk about till the cows come home. You want a beer?"

"I don't drink any more," Thibodeau replied, smiling nastily.

"Good for you!" Fernand blurted out with a nervous laugh.

"I think I'll have one, if you don't mind," said the notary timidly. "I don't know why, but my throat's been as dry as an old board all afternoon."

Lucie got up, left the room and returned shortly with two glasses of beer crowned with enormous heads of foam.

"So you want your son back," Fernand said, sitting down heavily on a chair across from Thibodeau. "Do you mind my asking what made you change your mind? I thought you'd, er, decided against it."

"He's my son," the carpenter replied, his expression unreadable.

The notary joined his hands together and coughed again, then spoke with the obsequiousness of a funeral director trying to sell an expensive coffin.

"Yes, of course he is. That's a fact. No doubt about that. An incontestable fact. Once you're a father, you're pretty much a father for life. Both nature and the law agree on that point. But aren't you afraid there'll be certain, er, difficulties down the road? Please allow me to remind you that it wasn't that long ago . . ."

Thibodeau's face hardened and his thin, dry lips took on an evil twist. "That's nothing but lies from a kid who was half asleep at the time!" he snarled. "There's nobody can prove that I tried to hurt him. Nobody at all, d'you get me?"

"Lies? From a kid who was half awake?" Fernand repeated, trying to obey his wife's signal by keeping the threatening tones from his voice. "But at the time, Wilfrid, you believed it yourself, didn't you? When I went over to your place the next morning with the notary, you weren't exactly behaving like a man whose conscience was without stain, as the priests put it. You even signed . . ."

"You intimidated me," cut in the carpenter. "It was the two of you against me. Piece of cake, especially when one of you is educated. Yeah, yeah, I'm always intimidated by educated people. My head goes belly up. I've always been like that."

He raised his hand to the inside pocket of his suit jacket and took out a pack of cigarettes. When he had taken a deep drag, he went on:

"Anyway, I didn't do nothing I should be sorry for, believe me." He was staring at a cloud of smoke, as though that were what he was talking to. "And no one here can stop me from leaving with my son."

"But he's very happy here. Really, he is," Lucie murmured, her voice quivering. "Ask him. He'll tell you."

The carpenter studied her red, tension-filled face and his eyes crinkled with satisfaction.

Silence ensued. Michaud took a sip of beer and a small meringue of foam stuck to the end of his nose. Fernand made a furtive gesture to get him to wipe it off.

"I saw Sylvie last week," the carpenter went on. "We talked the whole thing over, top to bottom. She agrees it happened just like I said."

"Now you listen to me, my friend!" shouted Fernand, leaping to his feet, his voice thundering in the house. "I'm going to –"

But before he could say what he was going to do, Parfait Michaud was also on his feet and, forgetting both his education and his mild temperament, clapped his hand firmly over Fernand's mouth and ordered him with his eyes to sit back down and keep quiet. Stunned, Fernand let himself fall back onto his chair like a sack of potatoes.

"You see, Monsieur Thibodeau," the notary said as though nothing untoward had taken place, his voice assuming that smooth preciousness that had gained him the admiration of some and the secret disdain of others, "the whole thing would be much simpler if we could come to some kind of amiable accord. As you must have guessed by now, since you are obviously a man of intelligence, Monsieur and Madame Fafard, as well as myself, intend to contest your right to take Charles back into your custody. The thing will obviously have to go to court. And you don't get into court without having a thick wallet, as you can well imagine. No, it's going to cost us a pretty penny. But it's also going to cost you a fair amount, because you're going to have to be represented by a lawyer; and when you add court costs, not to mention all the worry, the time lost from work and all the rest of it . . ."

Leaning to one side, he picked up his leather briefcase.

"On the other hand, if you sign this Letter of Consent, everything can be settled quick as a wink, no worrying, no headaches for any of us, and you will have regularized a particularly confused situation. This would mean a lot to Charles, I can assure you."

Thibodeau sat immobile, his arm raised, observing the smoking tip of his cigarette, deeply engrossed, it seemed, in a profound reverie that tugged gently at the corners of his mouth.

"It is, however, my duty to explain to you precisely," added the notary after a moment's pause, "that by signing this document you definitely lose all parental authority over Charles."

"Do you have an ashtray?" Thibodeau asked Fernand in a detached, almost relaxed tone of voice.

With almost servile haste, Fernand stepped over to a side table, took a handful of business cards out of a huge, cut-glass ashtray, and brought it to the carpenter.

Thibodeau carefully tapped the end of his cigarette with his index finger, took a drag, pursed his lips, and blew a thin jet of smoke into the room. His expression was one of disdain, even spite. Then he turned to the notary with a sickly sweet smile on his lips.

"And if I refuse to sign . . .?" he said.

"Then we'll get the whole, boring machinery rolling, Monsieur Thibodeau. We'll petition the director of Youth Services, who will present a judge with a request for adoption, and if you contest that there will be a trial, the consequences of which I have already outlined."

Again there was a long silence. Lucie was holding her head so far forward she thought she would faint.

Thibodeau went on smoking, taking short, nervous puffs, his face almost disappearing behind a bank of white smoke. Fernand watched him humbly, submissively, almost pleadingly; huge sweat stains appeared under his arms and the tips of his oversize black shoes tapped nervously on the carpet.

"Uh-huh," Thibodeau finally said. "Yup. A real poser, ain't it, this whole business? Don't know what to say . . ."

An expression of utter dismay suddenly appeared on the man's face, as though the horror of his present situation and all the past evils of his life that had led up to it had just struck him. It lasted only a moment. Then his mouth hardened and a cold brutality filled his eyes. When he addressed Fernand his manner was as hard and cold as ice.

"If you want me to sign that letter of yours, it'll cost you five thousand dollars. Cash. Or else I take Charles with me. And once I get my hands on him, you'll never get him away from me again, I can promise you that."

■ ■ ■

It was seven o'clock at night. Charles was sitting on the asphalt with his back against the garden shed, gazing up at the sky. Darkness was approaching swiftly, like a fine powder suspended in space, swallowing the light. The other side of the street could be seen between the basswood tree by the fence and the rear wall of the house, at the foot of which a narrow sidewalk ran across a stretch of grass. The house where Charles had once lived with his parents was also visible. Its peak was adorned with a brilliant sheen by the setting sun, giving the otherwise unimposing building a golden lustre.

Céline and Henri had just left the yard, having sat with Charles for some time. They felt he needed to be alone for a while to think about what had happened during the day. He didn't seem to have grasped its significance. A few vigilant stars twinkled in the flat, charcoal-grey sky now that the light was almost gone. Charles looked up, feeling a curious bond with them despite the incomprehensible distance that separated their world from his. He recalled a remark by a character in a novel he'd read a long time ago. Every man, the character said, must find his own star if he wants to make his way in the world. There is no secret way to finding it. You just have to be lucky.

Charles began counting the stars above the basswood tree. There were five, or four, if you didn't count the one that had just disappeared behind a cloud. Maybe one of those remaining was his own star? Could he simply choose his own star? No, it was no doubt the star that chose us. Charles stared at the stars hopefully, willing luck to come to his aid, and decided on the brightest one, the one right at the top of the tree. It would be a good day for finding my own star, he thought. A day when something solid had been established. He felt calm, at peace with himself, settled into a sense of satisfaction he hadn't felt for a long time.

He'd arrived home with Henri about five-thirty, just in time to catch the tail end of a very important scene. His father was in the living room with Fernand, Lucie, and Parfait Michaud, surrounded by so much smoke it made his eyes sting. His father had been signing a document that would allow him to remain living with the Fafards for as long as he wanted.

"Ah, Charles, my boy!" Fernand had cried with an odd catch in his voice. "You've got here just in time!"

And he'd explained briefly what had just taken place. Then he took Charles in his arms. Lucie ran towards him, crying in huge gulps, and after hugging him for a long time she'd hurried off to the bathroom to "fix her face," since she said she was no longer "presentable." The notary's eyes were blinking rapidly and his face appeared strained, as though he had just worked a twelve-hour shift. He'd punched Charles on the upper arm with a grin, and Thibodeau punched his other arm, although his smile seemed strangely forced, showing that he was feeling awkward and wanted to leave. He'd moved off towards the door, where he turned to his son for the last time and said, "Good luck!" dryly, as though he were giving an order. Then, curiously, he'd winked at Charles. Charles would never forget that wink. He'd never seen anything so pathetic in his life. The next instant he was moving off down the street, in the company of Fernand.

Over supper Charles had learned that the two men had been hurrying off to the Credit Union on Saint-Eusèbe, where the manager was waiting to meet with them on urgent business.

It was almost dark. The basswood had become a dark, shapeless mass. It appeared to have taken over the entire yard, but from its heavy, menacing shadow came a soft, delicate sound that seemed to be whispering to Charles that life wouldn't always be as difficult as it seemed now.

Suddenly he was enveloped by the smell of french fries and grilled meat, carried on a breeze that raised goosebumps on his skin. Somewhere in the neighbourhood a baby was crying its lungs out, as though demanding the entire universe to be born in. The sound reminded him of little Madeleine. He'd had to hide in the bathroom with his hands covering his ears to escape that sound. He thought of everything he'd been through since those terrible days. How often he'd felt like that desperate, raging baby. But somehow a tiny glow floating in his chest, a kind of smile like that of Alice's Cheshire cat, had refused to go out despite all the unhappiness raining down on it, and had allowed him to rise above his trials – and finally overcome them.

Left to his own devices he definitely wouldn't have made it. He let the faces of all the people who had helped him run pell-mell through his mind: first of all Alice, sweet Alice whom he still missed terribly and to whom he still felt close at the most unexpected moments; then Lucie and Fernand, Rosalie and Roberto, Boff, the notary Monsieur Michaud and his odd wife Amélie, Mademoiselle Laramée (he mustn't forget her!), Simon the Bear, Brother Albert, Blonblon, Henri, Céline, and even Sylvie, who'd been cold and distant but on his side in her own way. That was a lot of people, a kind of team who backed him up in his fight against some formidable enemies. Of course he owed their support to Luck, but also, he had to admit, to that weird kind of smile inside him that refused to go out, and had won him so many friends. From now on everything would be all right. He could go back to work for Rosalie and Roberto and make a lot of money, which he would one day hand over to Fernand and Lucie to thank them for their help. He'd be able to work with Blonblon again. He'd slacked off these last few days, but now his eagerness to get back to work fixing things was stronger than he'd ever felt before.

Little thrills of happiness ran through his body and he began kicking his heels against the ground. He was so happy he wanted to sing out loud. He would have liked to stay outside for a while longer, sitting alone in the darkness, but there, in the kitchen window, he saw the blind move for the second time, which meant that inside they were getting worried about him. It was late, after all, and he hadn't even started his homework.

Suddenly there was a scraping sound and the back door opened.

"Charles?" It was Lucie's voice, sing-song but with a hint of worry. "What are you doing out there? Talking to the moon?"

Before he could reply there was a flurry of feet crossing the yard and Boff was on him like a locomotive, his tongue quick and slobbery, his paws pummelling Charles's shoulder.

END OF VOLUME ONE